2/27

THE SIGN OF

VALANCOURT CLASSICS

THE SIGN OF THE SPIDER

An Episode

BY

BERTRAM MITFORD

AUTHOR OF RENSHAW FANNING'S QUEST, THE WEIRD OF DEADLY HOLLOW,
THE KING'S ASSEGAI, THE WHITE SHIELD, THE INDUNA'S WIFE, ETC., ETC.

Edited with an introduction and notes by
Gerald Monsman

Kansas City:
VALANCOURT BOOKS
2008

The Sign of the Spider by Bertram Mitford
First published in 1896 by Methuen
First Valancourt Books edition 2008

Introduction and notes © 2008 by Gerald Monsman
This edition © 2008 by Valancourt Books

Library of Congress Cataloging-in-Publication Data

Mitford, Bertram, 1855-1914.
The sign of the spider : an episode / by Bertram Mitford ;
edited with an introduction and notes by Gerald Monsman. – 1st
Valancourt Books ed.
p. cm. – (Valancourt classics)
ISBN 1-934555-46-0 (alk. paper)
1. South Africa–History–1836-1909–Fiction. 2. Johannesburg
(South Africa)–Fiction. I. Monsman, Gerald Cornelius. II. Title.
PR5021.M8S54 2008
823'.6–dc22

2008009599

Composition by James D. Jenkins
Published by Valancourt Books
Kansas City, Missouri
http://www.valancourtbooks.com

CONTENTS

INTRODUCTION

JOSEPH CONRAD once observed that "Fiction is history, human history, or it is nothing. But it is also more than that; it stands on firmer ground, being based on the reality of forms and the observation of social phenomena, whereas history is based on documents, and the reading of print and handwriting—on second-hand impression. Thus fiction is nearer truth. But let that pass. A historian may be an artist too, and a novelist is a historian, the preserver, the keeper, the expounder, of human experience."[1] A simple point and logically irrefutable, but its truth demands a progressive updating of our notions of canonical inclusion. After a long period in which Bertram Mitford's novels were only found on the shelves of a few academic libraries, he is again becoming available in new scholarly editions.[2] Certainly there was nothing second-hand in Mitford's South African experiences of which he wrote—he spoke Zulu, served with the frontier mounted police, labored on farms, owned a newspaper, and as a military historian placed battlefield archaeology in the context of native oral testimony. Originally a successful writer of popular fiction, Mitford's work has become even more significant now than in its heyday. At its broadest, Mitford's fiction portrays with authentic local color the sudden changes wrought by the British empire upon traditional, indigenous ways of life in South Africa.

With a small step of the historical imagination, the mature reader discovers in Mitford's "period adventures" whole dimensions beyond the escapist pleasure of "what next" to which he probably owed his first popularity. Even back then the artificial distinction between high-brow social realism and popular adventure fiction might have suggested negative assessments of his work. For a time also from the 1920s onwards, Mitford's upper class values clashed with a growing distrust of foreign influences and with a populist resentment at the unequal distribution of wealth—even the aristocratic heritage of Edgar Rice Burroughs's Tarzan is erased from populist celluloid adaptations. But currently Mitford can be appreciated in the hindsight of the intervening years, allowing his novels to be read as more allusive and prescient than when they were first published. A fresh critical re-evaluation focusing on the range of Mitford's contributions to the high romance of Africa—on his narrative voice, his sophisticated, complex characterization and use of irony, and particularly on his socio-imperial vision—would show the importance of this author "more often named than read, and more often read than profitably studied."[3]

Possibly the most popularly successful of Mitford's novels is *The Sign of the Spider* (1896), which combines native conflict with such late nineteenth-century concerns as the discovery and rush to exploit Africa's mineral resources; slavery and cannibalism; social Darwinism; a new anthropological interest in myths; the vogue of psychic phenomena then under scientific scrutiny; and—most exotically—the "cryptozoological" horror of the vampire Spider. This last was an important milestone in the elaboration of high Victorian dark fantasy of which *Beowulf*'s Grendel was perhaps the distant precursor. In the novel's climactic struggle, the protagonist is confronted with a hairy bear-sized arachnid fed with living men, a giant *vagina dentata* that he stabs and bludgeons into submission— his phallic club a human leg bone with a massive band of gold at the extremity that in a putative deathblow he hurls into the spider's eye. What gives imaginative force and artistic structure to *The Sign of the Spider* is its brilliant fusion of the classic quest for wealth and love with the exotically dangerous yet inviting "dark continent," its darkness metaphoric of the association of the feminine with the moistened earth and its secret recesses: "This wonderful land—the dim, mysterious recesses of its interior—what possibilities did it not hold?" In this respect, although Mitford's novel in large part certainly reflected colonial life as it actually was in nineteenth-century South Africa, its presentation of ethnic rituals and beliefs in tribal societies is an intentional parable of the internal economic and class tensions at the metropolitan centers of empire. The Bagcatya cannibals, "The People of the Spider" (Zulu: *Ba*, they, of + *gcatya*, "Venomous spider, which is often seen running nimbly about the road"[4]), are a dystopian parallel to colonial and European society, the new cannibalism of industrial capitalism.

The novel's protagonist, Laurence Stanninghame of "sixteen

heraldic quarterings,"⁵ disgruntled with loss of wealth and prestige, and living in genteel poverty in overcrowded London housing, leaves wife and children for Johannesburg to make his fortune or die. Mitford presents the contradictions and unrest of Victorianism owing to growing urbanization and the global expansion of the British empire, particularly a capitalist world of multiplying markets where person to person social relations are reducible to material self-interest and even people, not only as African slaves, are defined by a cash value. Stanninghame in pursuit of the "oof-bird" of wealth and its economic freedom (note that as a gentle-man he never for a moment entertains the possibility of manual labor) is not unlike many historical and fictional colonial figures with brave but flawed ambitions. The time is 1890,⁶ approximately four years after the first discovery of gold at Johannesburg. Aboard the *Persian* on his voyage to Africa, Stanninghame's routine of daily domestic strife is replaced by relaxing private moments in a tropical climate of sun and stars (even the ship's Oriental name suggests a legacy of mystery, adventure, passion) and Laurence, in spite of himself, falls in love with Lilith Ormskirk, a beautiful young woman of superior intellect. Seemingly irrevocably ruined by stock speculation after he arrives, Stanninghame is about to shoot himself when a vision of Lilith appears to him. At this crisis he resolves to join a slave-trading party into the far interior, raising for the reader the complex moral issue of how to sympathize with an anti-hero of this ilk. Mitford incidentally manages to convey a great deal of ethnographic data in his descriptions of slavery and cannibalism, harking back to his sources for *The King's Assegai* (1894). Among the high romances of Africa, Mitford's is possibly the most historically graphic account of slaving, although H. Rider Haggard's account in *People of the Mist* (1894) runs a close second.⁷

Mitford exempts hunters of treasure, if they betray no trust, from his readers' opprobrium; also the economically desperate are tolerantly evaluated, not only if they follow a gentleman's code (a chivalrous, honorable moral vision, such as the titular hero of *Renshaw Fanning's Quest*, 1894) but apparently even if, like Stanninghame, they are driven to shockingly primitive immo-rality by the economic barricades of "home," what Mitford in *Averno* (1913) calls the drab, unhealthy life of "stuccodom." The dark continent is the site for acts that elsewhere are cloaked in a heavily sublimated adherence to the façade of civilized respectability. Stanninghame's journey becomes an expedition into the unknown, battling the horrors of a psychic and physical darkness, either to triumph over them or to be consumed by them. For an untraceable but profitable interval he tears off the social and religious masks of conformity to indulge the less respectable but ever-present animal-like rapacity of human desire, confronting in this way the apocalyptic manifestation of his own bestiality. Together with his companions Hazon and Holmes, he carries to the extreme the exploitative aspect of imperialism—if gold speculators are vile but socially respectable, then Stanninghame will be viler than all and, for the nonce, bourgeois respectability be damned.

Johannesburg is the corrupt Jerusalem of Isaiah, as Hazon's name suggests. The opening words of Isaiah 1:1, the prophet's "vision" or "revelation" (Hebrew: *hazon*) is of Judah and Jerusalem as religiously empty, self-indulgent, and under judgment of God. Thus too in *The Sign of the Spider*, whatever the truth of Isaiah's vision, for Stanninghame the corresponding hypocritical morality of the empire is a historically constructed form of hegemony, a system of duty and honor neither natural nor beneficial: "Duty? Hang duty! He had made a most ruinous muddle of his whole life through reverencing that fetish word. Honour? There was no breach of honour where there was no deception, no pretence. Consideration for others? Who on earth ever dreamt of considering him—when to do so would cost them anything, that is? Unselfishness? Everybody was selfish—every*thing* even. What had he ever gained by striving to improve upon the universal law? Nothing. Nothing good. Everything bad—bad and deteriorating—morally and physically." Mitford even gives Stanninghame and Hazon a grotesque morality familiar enough: not only does the readers' repulsion to cannibalism allow Stanninghame's slaving to seem less criminal by contrast—better to be a slave than a cannibal's dinner—but perhaps Stanninghame is simply a reverse evangelist, sending the natives to civilization rather than coming as a civilizing missionary to them.[8] Early in the nineteenth century when British slavery was criminalized, anti-slavery writers such as Robert Burns sentimentalized the noble native in his idyllic African landscape in "The Slave's Lament" to counter any suggestion that transportation to a fairer clime was feasible.

Mitford owes more than a little to the new values of evolutionary ethics, and to its debates concerning species selection and social Darwinist assumptions. He embeds a quotation from Alfred Lord Tennyson's *Maud*, about "a world of plunder and prey." Unlike Wordsworth, Tennyson the scientific modernist saw no divine spirit of love in nature; for him evolutionary survival meant a ravening nature:

> For nature is one with rapine, a harm no preacher can heal;
> The Mayfly is torn by the swallow, the sparrow speared by the
>   shrike,
> And the whole little wood where I sit is a world of plunder and
>   prey.[9]

Although the speaker in *Maud* is palpably an imperfect moralist, "a morbid poetic soul" confined to a madhouse, his bitterness prepares the way, even while it casts doubt upon his sanity, for a social philosophy of "the struggle for existence" and "the survival of the fittest." In *Sign of the Spider* the meaning and morality of an idea or a proposition seems to lie in its observable practical consequences. But there is a whole basketful of "ifs," "buts" and "maybes" between the permissible and the immoral in terrestrial affairs. Animals may be rational, but consider them within a nature "red in tooth and claw" (Tennyson again): for the prey, being eaten is a disaster; for the predator, without food for self or brood, eating the prey is commonsense. On the human level compare the enemy who would seize for himself and his clan one's possessions (and destroy one's life if practical)—an obligatory duty for him, wrongful to oneself.

Indeed, perhaps Mitford's world of "preyer or preyed upon" is consistent with the ideas of Friedrich Nietzsche. Nietzsche posited a will to power beyond good and evil, denying absolute criteria in morals and presenting a master-slave world-view:

> Life itself is *essentially* appropriation, injury, overpowering of
> what is alien and weaker; suppression, hardness, imposition of
> one's own forms, incorporation and at least, at its mildest, exploi-

tation ... "Exploitation" does not belong to a corrupt or imperfect
and primitive society: it belongs to the *essence* of what lives, as a
basic organic function; it is a consequence of the will to power,
which is after all the will of life. If this should be an innovation
as a theory—as a reality it is the *primordial fact* of all history:
people ought to be honest with themselves at least that far.[10]

In Nietzsche's slave morality, the stronger individual's asser-
tive creativity is rivaled by the weaker's notions of conformity
to duty, authority, and rules of emotional expression; and those
who brush aside such societal limits are impugned and vilified.
In this sense the slaving expedition of Stanninghame is a *reductio*
of Nietzschean philosophy—a literalistic application of its principles. However, although Nietzsche had little use for any altruistic
morality, Stanninghame keeps his word, believes one good turn
deserves another, intercedes for Lutali's life, and out of loyalty
and friendship substitutes himself for Holmes. These are chival-
ric virtues, and Mitford's caste-like social views—very much akin
to those of H. Rider Haggard—are ultimately not in competition
with the scientific morality of Darwin or such English utilitarian
philosophers as Bentham, Mill, and Spencer. Between cannibals
and Anglican bishops there may be a culturally common moral
substrate; and attempts at ethical consensus may not have mutu-
ally incompatible features supported by majorities and minorities.
In this, Mitford follows the utilitarian belief that altruism was a
biological phenomenon opposed to the unmitigated self-assertion
of the physical universe: "But the influence of the cosmic process
on the evolution of society is the greater the more rudimentary
its civilization. Social progress means a checking of the cosmic
process at each step and the substitution for it of another, which
may be called ethically the best."[11]

Mitford's description of white slaving and black cannibalism
might be impeached as being based on sources that validate or
reinforce racist and colonial notions of European superiority.
Stanninghame, like Robinson Crusoe, confronts an unfamiliar
culture and is disgusted with its cannibalism. But unlike Crusoe, he
has little moral problem holding the cannibals entirely responsible
for their practices. In those days few, if any, missionaries, traders,
hunters, scientific explorers, soldiers, or settler-colonizers believed

that what was heinous in their society might not be in another. Two years previously in writing *The King's Assegai* Mitford had drawn on the first-person description of physical and oral evidence for past and recent cannibalism in South Africa by his second cousin, J. H. Bowker, to whom he dedicated that novel.[12] Mitford's colonial biases, however, were corrected or qualified by oral traditions of the natives themselves, evidence strongly rooted in historical places and events. Henry Callaway, in the 1860s, observed that "It is probable that the native accounts of cannibals are, for the most part, the traditional record of incursions of foreign slave-hunters."[13] But in response to more recent positions that severely minimize the extent of African cannibalism by blaming the disappearance of inhabitants on European slave-hunting, one could point out that the old Zulu name for South Africa is *Ningizimu*, meaning literally "the place of many cannibals." Conceivably, Mitford was indebted to highly figurative accounts presented in native poetry and song, the referential content of such thematic and imagistic patterns explained to him by the performers or intended auditors. Other of Mitford's multiple sources are not directly traceable, but coincidentally in the same year that *The Sign of the Spider* was published, the Swiss priest Émile Jacottet published his transcriptions of the Basuto tales of Kholumolumo, an ogre-cannibal.[14] F. D. Ellenberger later quoted a Christianized cannibal: "I am Kholumolumo, the horrible beast of our ancient fable, who swallowed all mankind, and the beasts of the field."[15] The Zulus have a similar devouring figure, Usilosimapundu, emblem of the earth and its "eating up" of man, as well as other tales and traditions encoding cannibalistic scenes.[16] As frightening personifications, Usilosimapundu and Kholumolumo are similar to the devouring Spider of the Ba-gcatya (perhaps more than affinities, less than influences). The figurative leap from a literal cannibalism to capitalistic consumption is an easy step for Mitford who only needed to adapt the satiric trope of Jonathan Swift's "Modest Proposal" relating to the English landlords of Ireland: "who, as they have already devoured most of the parents, seem to have the best title to the children." From the anthropophagoi, the "man-eating savages" of the geographer Claudius Ptolemy in the second-century A.D., to the voracious mining consortiums and stock markets of Jo'burg in the nineteenth century, the once-literal horror of cannibalism becomes a rhetorical trope for industrial victimization, especially a metaphor of the earth that swallows its miners.

So much is made on-board ship of Lilith's name as Adam's first wife, the reader would be obtuse indeed not to suspect a deeper connection to her mythic namesake. (Her family name of Ormskirk is Old Norse, derived from *Ormr*, a Viking name which means serpent or dragon, and *kirkja*, church; certainly this figure of a serpent's church supports her given name in the novel's plot). It is almost certain that Mitford would have known D. G. Rossetti's sonnet "Lilith" either upon its first appearance as paired with his painting "Lady Lilith" (1867-68) or, more likely, later from "The House of Life" (1870) when Rossetti retitled this sonnet "Body's Beauty" to contrast with its contrary, "Soul's Beauty" (see Appendix). In these paired sonnets, he attempts the ideal unification of spirit and flesh. Much has been made of "Lady Lilith's" self-contained indifference to the male gaze. By looking in her mirror only at herself does she reject her Victorian role as wife, the submissive and sexualized other? Rossetti's icon may be less a feminist rejection of the Victorian female's putative need of a man than an embodiment of her narcissistic capacity for self-seduction. His painting-*cum*-poem recasts the pre-Biblical Lilith, an aggressive and outright evil demon, as a "*Modern Lilith* combing out her abundant golden hair and gazing on herself in the glass with that self-absorption by whose strange fascination such natures draw others within their own circle."[17] She is taken from a mythical past into a realistic nineteenth century, as males who watch her imperturbable self-absorption become spell-bound:

> Of Adam's first wife, Lilith, it is told
>   (The witch he loved before the gift of Eve,)
>   That, ere the snake's, her sweet tongue could deceive,
> And her enchanted hair was the first gold.
> And still she sits, young while the earth is old,
>   And, subtly of herself contemplative,
>   Draws men to watch the bright web she can weave,
> Till heart and body and life are in its hold.

Lilith, temptress of mankind, and Eve, temptress of Adam, are akin: both are beautiful, seductive, and deadly. Goethe earlier in *Faust* (1808-32) had used this medieval legend of Lilith as Adam's first wife. Lilith is the new romantic "femme fatale" of ensnaring sexuality:

> Faust: Who's that there?
> Mephistopheles: Take a good look. *Lilith.*
> Faust: Lilith? Who is that?
> Mephistopheles: 'Tis the first wife of the first man. Adam's first wife, Lilith. Beware, beware of her bright hair . . . Many a young man she beguileth, smiles winningly on youthful faces. But woe to him whom she embraces!

On the back of his picture of "Lady Lilith," Rossetti inscribed Shelley's translation from Goethe's *Walpurgis-Nacht* in *Faust*:

> Hold then thy heart against her shining hair,
> If, by thy fate, she spread it once for thee,
> For, when she nets a young man in that snare
> So twines she him he never may be free.

After Mephistopheles gives this warning, he nevertheless encourages Faust to dance with "the Pretty Witch."[18]

Only great saints or necromancers can bind or exorcize spirits and devils, and Lilith's Ormskirk's "unholy spells" are those of a modern enchantress. From Goethe, Rossetti took his idea of Lilith's "strangling" golden hair that ensnares and chokes the emotional life of the young Adam. Like a spider she "Draws men to watch the bright web she can weave." Indeed, one orb-web spider is called *Araneus circe*—and like Circe with her pigs, Lilith Ormskirk is surrounded by her admirers, her "poodles." Lilith's "enchanted hair" belongs as a doppelgänger to the two worlds of death and beauty. Lilith Ormskirk's sinister side as the spider's web expresses nature's cruelty, killing those who see, approach, or woo her. But also the modern Lilith, in the spirit of John Keats' "Lamia" or his "La Belle Dame," is less the murderously jealous or selfish temptress than one whose beauty unintentionally, though ineluctably, destroys. Icon of the temptress though she may be, she too has become the victim of her own power, her own helpless humanity caught in the common grip of a mortal love.

Mitford could not have read Freud on "The Uncanny" or *Dreams in Folklore,* but psychoanalysis has attested that the spider, like the serpent, is an over-determined or highly condensed symbol expressing the core fantasies and conflicts from various developmental levels. Spiders emblematize feelings of repulsion and anxiety, of being "caught in the web" of desires, emotions and personal feelings of dependence and need. The spider-woman is the *femme fatale* that lures men to their doom with cunning and trickery, appearing in the dreams of men disgusted or guilty about sexuality for whom the lure of a web-entrapping woman represents the threat of sexual engulfment.[19] When an intensely ambivalent person battles against a break with reality, the spider often emerges as a symbol of the feared and deeply repressed aspects both of the self's potentially psychotic core and of the parasitic woman who subtly debilitates and drains her prey. Disgust with such hideous practices embodies fears of the loss of spiritual direction, of de-evolution and of the species in social decline.[20] Often psychoanalytic interpretation suggests that to define the feminine as innately predatory merely conceals a misogynistic aberration. On the other hand, a mythic interpretation stresses that the dangerous woman is like the primordial earth in its changes, prolific and procreative yet also wild and deadly. This allegorical interpretation entails two sides to love: the demonic and the angelic, both representative of phases in the energies of nature, the earth-mother's cycle of life, death, rebirth.

The spider, presented here in the novel as a grotesque, monstrous chimera, a Chthonian eater of men's raw flesh that looms like a massy *vagina dentata,* is a trope of the "sarcophagus" (*sarco,* flesh + *phages,* eating) or grave, that old and œcumenical cannibal, who gapes and consumes all living things. The egregious superstition of the People of the Spider is identical with nineteenth-century British respectability—both cultures have strangling webs of spiders that must be escaped to gain freedom to live and love; but the spider does not allow his web to be broken easily. In this the Bagcatya cannibals are an ironic parallel to Victorian society—both demand obedience; both feed people to a devouring maw, consumerism or the vampire spider. Here spiders represent codes that controvert the enjoyment of life—of speech, opinions, behavior, customs, institutions, and laws controlled by fetishists or amoral cadres intertwined by favoritism, bribery, and connivance—those tyrannies that many Romantic and Victorian poets, particularly P. B. Shelley and A. C. Swinburne, militated against. The man-eat-man morality of the slavers is morally not unlike the South African settlers' exploitation of the natives. Colonial society concocts a mask of respectability, but demands an involuntary behavioral servitude akin to the literal enslavement of Stanninghame's cannibals. Stanninghame, a lawless huntsman transforming himself in his fierce desire for wealth, has sold his soul to the devil. He becomes in his hunt for humans the apocalyptic manifestation of his own dark possibilities, El Afà, the poisonous serpent, even as Hazon, Stanninghame's partner, bore the sobriquet of El Khanac, the strangler.

The Ba-gcatya maiden, Lindela, rescuing Laurence from the spider's lair, becomes a perfected reincarnation of Lilith Ormskirk. Although initially merely an expedient way of avoiding his death-by-spider, she not only assumes the role of his savior but conducts him safely through the nether regions of passion towards a perfection more than mortal, a heroic love glimpsed above daily life, a neo-Platonic "Beauty" enthroned. He had lacked this imaginatively perfect love when "at the twelfth hour" Lilith and he each had played upon the other's algolagnia of pleasure-pain; but now he attains his ideal. During Stanninghame's and Lindela's near-idyll, they enjoy the fruits of freedom, a perfection of physical and spiritual love that cannot last in a world of getting and spending. Disentangled from the conventions of civilized femininity, Lindela had represented for him "the Eternal Feminine that draws us ever onward"—*das Ewig Weibliche* that in the figure of Gretchen had redeemed Goethe's Faust.[21] Numerous times Mitford observes that Lindela defied convention as she knew it—her clan, its laws, its priests, even its protocol of emotional feelings: "We girls of the Ba-gcatya do not love—not like this." But Stanninghame cannot convey Lindela back to civilization, not just because she is a "savage" African, nor merely because he already is married, but because neither her love nor his could fit the bourgeois and proletarian paradigms of contemporary society. Just as his entrapment in an unsatisfactory marriage and a degrading poverty seemingly had impeded his love for such as Lilith Ormskirk, so now Lindela's love is checked not long before Stanninghame crosses the frontier back into civilization. Stanninghame's descent into hell and ascent with this African "Beatrice" into the possibilities (or impossibilities) of the future is thwarted by his second spider encounter. In the first Stanninghame had wounded the hideous creature, but not as fatally as supposed; now he cannot save Lindela and vents his fury by pounding her deadly nemesis to death. This fatal spider bite expresses indirectly the constructedness of social values, the poison against which even their elite individualism, their disdain, boldness, and profound indifference to the self-delusions and materialism of society will be no antidote.

Unsullied by the inhibitions of modern capitalistic culture, Lindela was an emblem of love without entrapment in relationships organized in terms of conformity to cultural, religious, or racial codes. Such love Lilith Ormskirk could not provide— Stanninghame had berated her for waiting too long to declare her affection for him at the twelfth hour (although in this veiling of feelings he too is guilty). We may suppose Lilith and Laurence to be childishly and ruinously proper; however, in Victorian society (and one might add in anthropophagite or any native culture also) who can express what, and when, and where, was and is a closely controlled matter of precept and proscription. Thus Lilith accedes to an illusory "duty" of self-sacrifice by betraying her first love and marrying her boorish cousin George. This "life-time of the awful pain of loss" already surrounds her as she entrusts to Stanninghame her monogram, its decorative floral "O" (or less likely interwoven initials "L" and "O"), like the "sign of the spider," indicating the presence of her protective love by spiritual affinity. A "sign" is an external mark carrying a meaning, derived etymologically from its incised, cut letters; and the spider amulet traditionally had been a charm inscribed or cut with a magic incantation worn to protect against evil. Like the sign of the cross which invokes divine protection or blessing, so Lilith Ormskirk's monogram severs the strangling net with the pledge of an ideal liberty. After Stanninghame seemingly has won his freedom from the webs of thraldom—both from the economic entrapments of civilized society and the literal prison of the spider's cave—he returns to civilization only to encounter a forlornly enslaved Lilith, victim of her own beauty. His love for Lilith thus is swallowed by what he left England to evade—the snare of a humdrum and deadening existence—a sacrifice of passion to family obligation. Not so inconsistently, in the light of her capitulation and society's censure of unfaithful wives, the lovelorn Stanninghame accepts her unhappy marriage—"for your own sake"—as final, despite its misplaced motive of self-denial.

Stanninghame—"selfish cynic," as Mitford describes him, and supporter of the gender double standard—is nevertheless a believable, sympathetic character—perhaps too much so (one recalls, possibly, John Milton's not-always-successful editorializing against a rebellious Satan in *Paradise Lost*). Yet the reader still struggles to disconnect the corrupt maxim that "the end justifies the means" from Stanninghame's finish. As has been noted, the reader's repulsion to cannibalism (not to mention also the Zulu Ba-gcatya) allows Stanninghame's slaving by contrast to seem less criminal; and, moreover, certainly some of his new-found affluence is owing to the diamonds he unoffendingly picked up in the spider's lair, the result of his original altruistic rescue of Holmes. He is admirable to such a degree that the abstract legalities of slaving are seen as less important than the parade of troubles he finally overcomes. Still, why does Mitford invite the reader to endorse Stanninghame's goal of wealth if his actions perpetuate and reward racist and imperial practices? Mitford remarks, in what perhaps is "a" moral of Stanninghame's tale: "He fell to thinking on what strange experience had been his—of the consistent and unswerving irony of life as he had known it. Every conventionality violated, every rule of morality, each set aside, had brought him nothing but good—had brought nothing but good to him and his." Yet—and here is "the" specific moral posture of the author—for Stanninghame, rusticated from the circle of sociality, Lindela is dead; Lilith, her "charm" locked away never to be worn again, has vanished into an unhappy marriage; and his tenure on the newly-rented estate is provisional—not because he could not buy it but because he is clueless about his future, has no home in the ulti-

mate sense. Rich after four years, he is now also decisively alien-
ated from the primordial energies of love. Nor does the journey
into the heart of his own darkness prompt a penitential retelling
and recognition of good and evil, like S. T. Coleridge's ancient
mariner to the wedding guest or (just three years in the offing) like
Conrad's Marlow on the yacht. Rather, his wealth, even without
his recognizing it, has absorbed him back into the spider's web
of conventional mores. Stanninghame is very much like Mitford's
character Maurice Sellon at the end of *Renshaw Fanning's Quest.*
In that novel Sellon appropriates the great diamond "eye" of the
Bushmen with its wealth but loses the future happiness that will
be Fanning's.

Stanninghame's story ends with his child Fay's new-found
idyll of leisure and play misting over his memories of violence and
passion. Now vastly more wealthy and with the last perils of his
criminality blotted out by Holmes' marriage, he ends where his
wife always wanted him to be—in a world where basic attach-
ments between people assume the form of a relationship between
things, in which material self-interest, not such intensities as his
African loves, defines the ties that bind. Stanninghame has sacrificed his manhood to this domesticity, as truly emasculated as
when he lived in stuccodom. H. Rider Haggard's landed and gen-
trified hero, Allan Quatermain, had observed: "no man who has for
forty years lived the life I have, can with impunity go coop himself
in this prim English country, with its trim hedgerows and cultivated fields, its stiff formal manners, and its well-dressed crowds.
He begins to long—ah, how he longs!—for the keen breath of
the desert air; he dreams of the sight of Zulu impis breaking on
their foes like surf upon the rocks, and his heart rises up in rebel-
lion against the strict limits of the civilized life."[22] Stanninghame's
world is now the drawing-room culture and its emerging mass
consumerism of accumulated possessions. Of course, from the
first Stanninghame had been complicitous with this system, inas-
much as the new money at Johannesburg and those who put economic gain above other values remained his exclusive focus; he
even tried to shun love's "spell." Curiously, the novel's final pages
omit all mention of the nagging wife to which Stanninghame has
been fated to return, almost as if she has evaporated from his life,

which indeed figuratively she has—or, rather, she together with him and their children have been swallowed by the hollow maw of opulence. If the primordial energies flow anew, it will only be in the next generation, perhaps with his daughter Fay, who may become the next Lilith or Lindela. But don't bet on it.

GERALD MONSMAN
Tucson

February 11, 2008

GERALD MONSMAN is Professor of English and former head of the English Department at the University of Arizona, where he specializes in nineteenth-century British and Anglo-African literature. He has published books with Hopkins, Duke, Yale, and in the area of South African literature has written *Olive Schreiner's Fiction: Landscape and Power* (Rutgers, 1991), has edited H. Rider Haggard's *King Solomon's Mines* (Broadview, 2002), and most recently has authored *H. Rider Haggard on the Imperial Frontier: The Political and Literary Contexts of his African Romances* (ELT, 2006). He has also edited three other novels by Bertram Mitford, *The Weird of Deadly Hollow*, *The King's Assegai*, and *Renshaw Fanning's Quest*, for Valancourt Books.

NOTES

1 Joseph Conrad, "Henry James—An Appreciation—1905," *Notes on Life and Letters* (London: Dent, 1921), 20-21.

2 Several of his novels are now in print under the Valancourt Books imprimis. Valancourt describes itself as "an independent small press based in Kansas City . . . founded in 2005 with the intention of making rare eighteenth- and nineteenth-century texts widely available using modern publishing technology" (2007-08 Catalogue).

3 T. S. Eliot, "The Metaphysical Poets" (1921), *Selected Essays: New Edition* (New York: Harcourt, Brace, 1960), 241.

4 J. W. Colenso, *Zulu-English Dictionary* (Pietermaritzburg: Davis, 1861), 141.

5 "A *seize quartiers* man . . . could prove his sixteen heraldic quarterings, which is the open sesame to every chapter, community, and court in Europe. It . . . implies that the individual belongs to the old nobility, entitled to bear arms for five generations on both sides of the house." "Rome and the Romans," *The New York Times*, February 19, 1905, Sunday Section: Second Magazine Section, p. X-8.

6 Dated by internal references to railway construction, population figures, and the recent Republican revolution in Brazil.

7 Mitford's first novel, *The Fire Trumpet* (1889), also contained a chapter on slaving. Slaving as a theme in empire romance runs from well before R. M. Ballantyne's *The Gorilla Hunters* (1861) all the way to the end of the nineteenth century in Conrad's "Heart of Darkness" (1899).

8 "Whatever evils the slave trade may be attended with . . . it is mercy . . . to poor wretches, who . . . would otherwise suffer from the butcher's knife." Archibald Dalzel, Introduction, *The History of Dahomy* (London: T. Spilsbury, 1793), xxiv-xxv.

9 Tennyson, *Maud* I, 123-125.

10 F. W. Nietzsche, *Beyond Good and Evil* (1886), Section 259.

11 See T.H. Huxley, "The Struggle for Existence in Human Society" (1888) and "Evolution and Ethics" (1893), *Collected Essays* (London: Macmillan, 1893) 9: 81, 88.

12 James Henry Bowker; Dr. Bleek; John Beddoe, "The Cave Cannibals of South Africa," *Anthropological Review*, 7:25 (April 1869), 121-128.

13 Callaway, *Izinganekwane, Nensumansumane, Nezindaba Zabantu* [*Nursery Tales, Traditions, and Histories of the Zulus*, 1868] (Natal: John Blair; London: Trübner, 1866), 155-164; I cite here the serial version that originally belonged to the missionary, F. D. Ellenberger. See Appendix.

14 Émile Jacottet, "*Mœurs, coutumes et superstitions des Ba-souto,*" *Bulletin de la Société de Géographie de Neuchâtel*, 9 (1896-97), 107-151; Samson Mbizo Guma, *The Form, Content and Technique of Traditional Literature in Southern Sotho* (Pretoria: Van Schaik, 1967), 194-201.

15 D. Fred Ellenberger and J. MacGregor, *History of the Basuto, Ancient and Modern* (London: Caxton Publishers, 1912), 226.

16 Callaway, 159.

17 *The Collected Works of Dante Gabriel Rossetti*, ed. with preface and notes by W. M. Rossetti (London: Ellis and Elvey, 1887) II: 850.

18 *Faust* I: 4206-4211, 4216-4223.

19 In one bizarre adaptation the female spider cannibalizes the male immediately after copulation for the extra energy required to bear her young. In another spider case, the male is paralyzed by an injection from the female and his body supplies the food for the young when they are first born.

20 This decline into cannibalism was most forcefully presented a year previous to Mitford's novel in H. G. Wells's *The Time Machine* (1895).

21 Goethe, *Faust*, final couplet.

22 H. Rider Haggard, Introduction, *Allan Quatermain* (London: Longmans, Green, 1887), 4.

A Note on the Text

The Valancourt Books edition follows the 1896 first edition of *The Sign of the Spider*, published at London by Methuen. In 1897, an American edition appeared, published by Dodd, Mead and Co. of New York, with some minor changes of spelling and punctuation. The book ran into at least seven British editions, being reprinted by Methuen as late as 1913.

The Sign of the Spider

"After all, the more noteworthy epochs in the lives of individuals, are they not even as those in the lives of nations—a chain of events and strange coincidences working for good or for ill to those concerned, but oftener for ill?"—*The Gun-runner.*

THE SIGN OF THE SPIDER

◆

CHAPTER I

"SWEET HOME!"

SHE was talking *at* him.

This was a thing she frequently did, and she had two ways of doing it. One was to talk at him through a third party when they two were not alone together; the other to convey moralisings and innuendo for his edification when they were—as in the present case.

Just now she was extolling the superabundant virtues of somebody else's husband, with a tone and meaning which were intended to convey to Laurence Stanninghame that she wished to heaven one-twentieth part of them was vested in hers.

He was accustomed to being thus talked at. He ought to be, seeing he had known about thirteen years of it, on and off. But he did not like it any the better from force of habit. We doubt if anybody ever does. However, he had long ceased to take any notice, in the way of retort, no matter how acrid the tone, how biting the innuendo. Now, pushing back his chair from the break-fast-table, he got up, and, turning to the mantelpiece, proceeded to fill a pipe. His spouse, exasperated by his silence, continued to talk at—his back.

The sickly rays of the autumn sun struggled feebly through the murk of the suburban atmosphere, creeping half-ashamedly over the well-worn carpet, then up to the dingy wall-paper, whose dinginess had this redeeming point, that it toned down what otherwise would have been staring, crude, hideous. The furniture was bat-

3

tered and worn, and there was an atmosphere of dustiness, thick-laid, grimy, which seemed inseparable from the place. In the street, a piano-organ, engineered by a brace of sham Italians, was rapping out the latest music-hall abomination. Laurence Stanninghame turned again to his wife, who was still seated at the table.

"Continue," he said. "It is a great art knowing when to make the most of one's opportunities, which, for present purposes, may be taken to mean that you had better let off all the steam you can, for you have only two days more to do it in—only two whole days."

"Going away again?" (staccato).

Laurence nodded, and emitted a cloud or two of smoke.

There rumbled forth a cannonade of words, which did not precisely express approval. Then, staccato—

"Where are you going to this time?"

"Johannesburg."

"What? But it's nonsense."

"It's fact."

"Well—of course you can't go."

"Who says so?"

"Of course you can't go, and leave us here all alone," she replied, speaking quickly. "Why, it's too preposterous! I've been treated shamefully enough all these years, but this puts the crowning straw on to it," she went on, beginning to mix her metaphor, as angry people—and especially angry women—will. "Of course you can't go."

To one statement, as made above, he was at no pains to reply. He had heard it so often that it had long since passed into the category of "not new, not true, and doesn't signify." To the other he answered—

"I've an idea that the term 'of course' makes the other way; I *can* go, and I am going—in fact, I have already booked my passage by the *Persian*, sailing from Southampton the day after to-morrow. Look! will that convince you?" holding out the passage ticket.

Then there was a scene—an awful racket. It was infamous. She would not put up with such treatment. It amounted to desertion, and so forth. Yes, it was a "scene," indeed. But force of habit had utterly dulled its effectiveness as a weapon. Indeed, the only effect it might have been calculated to produce in the mind of the offending party, had he not already secured his berth, would be that of moving him to sally forth and carry out that operation on the spot.

"Look here!" he said, when failure of breath and vocabulary had perforce effected a lull. "I've had about enough of this awful life, and so I'm going to try if I can't do something to set things right again before it's too late. Now, the Johannesburg 'boom' is the thing to do it, if anything will. It's kill or cure."

"And what if it's kill?"

"What if it's kill? Then, one may as well take it fighting. Better, anyway, than scattering one's brains on that hearth-rug some morning, in the small hours, out of sheer disgust with the dead hopelessness of life. That's what it is coming to as things now are."

"All very well. But, in that case, what is to become of me—of us?"

A very hard look came into the man's face at the question.

"In that case—draw on the other side of the house. There's plenty there," he answered shortly, re-lighting his pipe, which had gone out in mid-blast.

The reply seemed to fan up her wrath anew, and she started in to talk to him again. Under which circumstances, perhaps it was just as well that a couple of heavy bangs overhead and a series of appalling yells, betokening a nursery catastrophe, should cut short her eloquence, and start her off, panic-stricken, to investigate.

Left alone, still standing with his back to the mantelpiece, Laurence Stanninghame put forth a hand. It shook—was, in fact, all of a tremble.

"Look at that!" he said to himself. "The squalid racket of this rough-and-tumble life is playing the devil with my nerves. I believe I couldn't drink a wineglassful of grog at this moment without spilling half of it on the floor. I'll try, anyhow."

He unlocked a chiffonier, produced a whisky bottle, and, having poured some into a wineglass, not filling it, tossed off the "nip."

"That's better," he said. Then mechanically he moved to the window and stood looking out, though in reality seeing nothing. He was thinking—thinking hard. The course he had decided to adopt was the right thing—as to that he had no sort of doubt. He had no regular income, and such remnant of capital as he still possessed was dwindling alarmingly. Men had made fortunes at places like Johannesburg, starting with almost literally the traditional half-crown, why should not he? Not that he expected to make a fortune; a sufficiency, a fair competence would satisfy him. The thought of no longer being obliged to hold an inquest on every sixpence; of bidding farewell for ever to this life of pinching and screwing; of dwelling decently instead of pigging it in a cramped and jerry-built semi-detached; of enjoying once more some of life's brightnesses—sport, for instance, of which he was passionately fond; of the means to wander, when disposed, through earth's fairest places—these reflections would have fired his soul as he stood there, but that the flame of hopefulness had long since died within him and gone out. Now they only evoked bitterness by their tantalising allurement.

Other men had made their pile, why should not he? Rainsford, for instance, who had been, if possible, more down on his luck than himself—Rainsford had gone out to the new gold-town while it was yet very new and had made a good thing of it. Two or three other acquaintances of his had gone there and had made very much more than a good thing of it. Why should not he?

Laurence Stanninghame was just touching middle age. As he stood at the window, the murky September sun seemed to bring out the lines and wrinkles of his clear-cut face, which was distinctly the face of a man who has not made a good thing of life, and who can never for a moment lose sight of that fact. There were lines above the eyes, clear blue and somewhat sunken eyes, which denoted the habit of the brows to contract on very slight provocation, and far oftener than was good for their owner's peace of mind, and the bronze underlying the clear skin told of a former life in the open—possibly under a warmer sun than that now playing upon it. As to its features, it was a strong face, but there was a certain indefinable something about it when off its guard, which would have told a close physiognomist of the possession of latent instincts, unknown to their possessor, instincts which, if stifled, choked, were not dead, and which, if ever their depths were stirred, would yield forth strange and dangerous possibilities.

He was of fine constitution, active and wiry; but the cramped

life and squalid worry of a year-in year-out, semi-detached, suburban existence had, as he told himself, played the mischief with
his nerves, and now to this was added the ghastly vista of impending actual beggary. Whatever he did and wherever he went this
thought would not be quenched. It was ever with him, gnawing
like an aching tooth. Lying awake at night it would glare at him
with spectral eyes in the darkness. Then, unless he could force
himself by all manner of strange and artificial means, such as
repeating a favourite verse, and so forth, to throw it off, good-
bye to sleep—result, nerves yet further shaken, a succession of
brooding days, and system thrown off its balance by domestic fric-
tion and strife. Many a man has sought a remedy for far less ill in
the bottle, whether of grog or laudanum; but this one's character was in its strength proof against the first, while, for the latter,
that might come, but only as a very last extremity. Meanwhile
oft-times he wondered how that blank, hopeless feeling of having
completely done with life could be his, seeing that he was still in
his prime. Formerly eager, sanguine, warm-hearted, glowing with
good impulses; now indifferent, sceptical, with a heart of stone
and the chronic sneer of a cynic.

He was one of those men who seem born never to succeed.
With everything in his favour apparently, Laurence Stanninghame
never did succeed. Everything he touched seemed to go wrong.
If he speculated, whether it was a half-crown bet or a thousand-
pound investment, smash went the concern. He was of an inven-
tive turn and had patented—of course at considerable expendi-
ture—a thing or two; but by some crafty twist of the law's subtle
rascalities, others had managed to reap the benefit. He had tried his
hand at writing, but press and publisher alike shied at him. He was
too bitter, too bold, too sweeping, too thorough. So he threw that,
as he had thrown other things, in sheer disgust and hopelessness.

Now he was going to cast in the net for a final effort, and
already his spirits began to revive at the thought. Any faint spark
of lingering sentiment, if any there were, was quenched in the
thought. The turn of the wheel might bring good luck, but it was
impossible it could strand him in worse case. For the sentimental
side of it—separation, long absence—well, the droop of the cynical
corners of the mouth became more emphasised at the recollection

of that faded old figment, "home, sweet home," and glowing aspirations after the so-called holy and pure joys of the family circle;
whereas the reality? A sort of Punch and Judy show[1] at best. No,
there was no sentimental side to this undertaking.

Yet Laurence Stanninghame's partner in life was by no means
a bad sort of a woman. She had plenty of redeeming qualities,
in that she was good-hearted at bottom and well-meaning, and
withal a most devoted mother. But she had a tongue and a temper,
together with an exceedingly injudicious, not to say foolish, twist
of mind; and this combination, other good points notwithstanding,
the quality which should avail to redeem has hitherto remained
undiscoverable in any live human being. Furthermore, she owned
a will. When two wills come into contact the weakest goes under,
and that soon. Then there may be peace. In this case neither went
under, because, presumably, evenly balanced. Result—warfare,
incessant, chronic.

Having finished his pipe, Laurence Stanninghame got out a hat
and an umbrella, and set to work to brush the former and furl
the latter prior to going out. The hat was not of that uniform and
glossy smoothness which one could see into to shave, and the
umbrella was weather-beaten of aspect. The morning coat, though
well cut, was shiny at the seams. Yet, in spite of the wear and tear
of his outer gear, with so unmistakably thoroughbred a look was
their wearer stamped, that it seemed he might have worn anything. Many a man would have looked and felt shabby in this long
service get-up; this one never gave it a thought, or, if he did, it was
only to wonder whether he should ever again, after this time, put
on that venerable "stove-pipe," and if so, what sort of experiences
would have been his—*interim*.

Now there was a patter of feet in the passage. The door-handle
turned softly, and a little girl came in. She was a sweetly pretty
child, with that rare combination of dark-lashed brown eyes and
golden hair. Here, if anywhere, was Laurence Stanninghame's
soft place. His other progeny was represented by two sturdy
boys, combative of instinct and firm of tread, and whose gambols,
whether pacific or bellicose, were apt to shake the rattletrap old
semi-detached and the paternal nerves in about equal proportions;
constituting, furthermore, a standing bone of parental contention.

This little one, however, having turned ten, was of a companionable age; and to the male understanding the baby stage does not, as a rule, commend itself.

She was full of the racket which had just taken place overhead; but to this Laurence hardly listened. There was always a racket overhead, a fight or a fall or a bumping. One more or less hardly mattered. He was thinking of his own weakness. Would she feel parting with him? Children as a rule were easily consoled. A new and gaudy toy would make them forget anything. And appositely to this thought, the little one's mind was also full of a marvellous engine she had seen the last time she had been taken into London—one which wound up with a key and ran a great distance without stopping.

Being alone—for by this time he had come to regard all display of affection before others as a weakness—Laurence drew the child to him and kissed her tenderly.

"And supposing that engine were some day to come puffing in, Fay; to-morrow or the day after?" he said.

The little one's eyes danced. The toy was an expensive one, quite out of reach for her, she knew. If only it were not! And now her delighted look and her reply made him smile with a strange mixture of sadness and cynicism. And as approaching footsteps heralded further invasion, he put the child from him hurriedly, and went out. Hailing a tramcar he made his way up to town to carry out the remainder of his sudden, though not very extensive, preparations.

Now on the following evening arrived a package of toys, of a splendour hitherto unparalleled within that dingy suburban semi-detached, and there was a great banging of gorgeous drums and a tootling of glittering trumpets, and little Fay was round-eyed with delight in the acquisition of the wondrous locomotive, ultimately declining to go to sleep save with one tiny fist shut tight round the chimney thereof. That would counteract any passing effect that might be inspired by a vacant chair, thought Laurence Stanninghame, amid the roar of the mail train speeding through the raw haze of the early morning. Sentiment? Feelings? What had he to do with such? They were luxuries, and as such only for those who could afford to indulge in them. He could not.

CHAPTER II

"ADAM'S FIRST WIFE"

THE R.M.S. *Persian* was cleaving her southward way through the smooth translucence of the tropical sea.

It was the middle of the morning. Her passengers, scattered around her quarter-deck in the coolness of the sheltering awning, were amusing themselves after their kind; some gregarious and chatting in groups, others singly, or in pairs, reading. The men were mostly in flannels and blazers, and deck-shoes; the women affected light array of a cool nature; and all looked as though it were too much trouble to move or even to speak, though here and there an individual more enterprising than his or her fellows would make a spasmodic attempt at a constitutional; said attempt usually resolving itself into five-and-a-half feeble turns up and down the clear part of the deck, to culminate in abrupt collapse. For it is warm in the tropical seas.

"What a lazy Johnnie you are, Stanninghame! Now, what the deuce are you thinking about all this time, I wonder?"

He addressed, who had been gazing out upon the sea and sky-line, plunged in dreamy thought, did not even turn his head.

"Get into this chair, Holmes, if you want to talk," he said. "A fellow can't wring his own neck and emit articulate sound at the same time. What?"

The other, who had come up behind, laughed, and dropped into the empty deck-chair beside Laurence. He was the latter's cabin chum, and the two had become rather friendly.

"Nothing to do and plenty of time to do it in," he went on, stretching himself and yawning. "I'm jolly sick of this voyage already."

"And we're scarcely half through with it? It's a fact, Holmes, but I'm not sick of it a bit."

"Eh?" and the other stared. "That's odd, Stanninghame. You, I should have thought, if anyone, would be just dog-gone tired of it by now. Why, you never even cut into any of the fun that's going—such as it is."

"You may well put that in, Holmes. As, for instance—listen!"

For the whanging of the piano in the saloon beneath had attained to an even greater pitch of discord than was normally the case. To it was added the excruciating rasp of a fiddle.

"Heavens! Are they immolating a stowaway cat down there?" murmured Laurence, with a little shudder. "It would have been more humane to have put the misguided brute to a painless end."

Holmes spluttered.

"It reminds me," he said, "of one voyage I made by this line. Some of the passengers got up what they called an 'Amusement Committee.'"

"A fearful and wonderful monster?"

"Just so. Its mission was to worry the soul out of each and all of us, in search of some nefarious gift. Oh, and we mustered plenty, from the 'cello to the 'bones.' Well, what is going on down there now is sheer delight in comparison. Imagine the present perfor-mance heaped up—only relieved by caterwauls of about equal quality—and that from 6 a.m. until 'lights out.'"

"I don't want to imagine it, thank you, Holmes; so spare what little of that faculty I still retain. But, say now, when was this event-ful voyage?"

"In the summer of '84."

"Precisely. I remember now. It was in the newspapers at the time that in more than one ship's log were entered strange reports of gruesome and wholly indefinable noises heard at night in certain latitudes. Some of the crews mutinied, and there was an instance on record of more than one hand, bursting with super-stition, going mad and jumping overboard. So, you see, Holmes, your 'Amusement Committee' doubly deserved hanging."

The delicious readiness of this "lie" so fetched Holmes that he opened his head and emitted a howl of laughter. He made such a row, in fact, that neither of them heard the convulsive half-repressed splutter which burst forth somewhere behind them.

"Well, you were going to explain how it is you haven't got sick of the voyage yet," said Holmes, when his roar had subsided.

"Was I? I didn't say so. What a chap you are for returning to worry a point, Holmes. However, I don't mind telling you. The fact is, I enjoy this voyage because it is so thoroughly and delightfully restful. You are not only allowed to do nothing, but are actually expected to perform that easy and congenial feat. There is nothing to worry you—absolutely nothing—not even a baby in the next cabin."

"I don't mind a little worry now and then," objected the other, in the tone and with the look of one who was ignorant of the real meaning of the word. "It shakes one up a bit, don't you know—relieves the monotony of life."

"Oh, does it? Look here, Holmes; I don't say it in an 'assert-my-superiority' sense, but I believe I'm a little older than you. Now, I've had a trifle too much of the commodity under discussion. In fact, I would take my chances of the monotony in order to dispense with any more of the other thing."

Holmes cast a furtive and curious glance at his companion, but made no immediate reply. He was an average, good-looking, well-built specimen of Young England, and his healthy sun-burnt countenance showed, in its cheery serenity, that, as the other had hinted, he was not speaking from knowledge. At anyrate, it was a marked contrast to the rather lined and prematurely careworn countenance of Laurence Stanninghame, even as his frank jolly laugh was to the half-stifled grin which would lurk around the satirical corners of the latter's mouth when anything amused him.

"What a row those women are making over there!" remarked Laurence; as peal upon peal of feminine laughter went up from one of the groups above referred to.

"That ass Swaynston, I suppose," growled the other. "Don't know what anybody can see funny about the fellow. He makes me sick. By the way, I haven't seen Miss Ormskirk on deck this morning."

"That'll make Swaynston sick, won't it? Isn't he one of her poodles?"

"Eh? Her what?"

"Fetch and carry; stand up on his hind legs and beg. There—good dog! and all that sort of thing, you know. Go to heel, too, when ordered."

Holmes laughed again, this time in rather a shamefaced way,

for he was conscious of having filled the rôle whose subserviency was thus pungently characterised by his cynical companion.

"Oh, dash it all, Stanninghame, don't be such an old bear!" he burst forth. "A fellow can't help doing things for a devilish pretty girl, eh?"

"A good many fellows can't, apparently, for this one. Directly she appears on the scene they go at her like flies at a honey pot. There's the doctor, and the fourth brass-button man—er, I beg his pardon, the fourth 'officer,'—and Swaynston, and yourself, and Heaven knows how many more. And one gets hold of a cushion—which she doesn't want; another a wrap—of which the same holds good; two of you strive to rend a deck-chair limb from limb in your eagerness to dump it down on the very last spot in the ship where she desires to sit, what time you are all scowling at each other as though there was not room for any given two of you in the same world. I don't want to hurt your feelings, Holmes, but, upon my word, it's the most damn ridiculous spectacle on earth."

"I don't see why it should be," was the half-snuffy rejoinder. "There's nothing ridiculous in common civility."

"No, only to see you all treading on each other's heels to do *konza*[1] to a woman who's nearly losing her life trying not to laugh at the crowd of you."

"Hallo! what's this?" sung out Holmes, not sorry for an excuse to change the subject. "Why, you used a Zulu word, Stanninghame, and yet you say you never were in South Africa before."

"Well, and then? I've once or twice known fellows use a Greek word who had never been near the land of Socrates in their lives."

"Still, that's different. Every fellow learns Greek at school, but no fellow learns Zulu. Eh?"

"You can't swear to that. Well, never mind. Perhaps I have been mugging it up as a preliminary to coming out here. Note, however, Holmes, that I used the word advisedly. *Ukukonza* does not mean to show civility, but to do homage, and that of a tolerably abject kind—in fact, to knuckle under."

"All the same, I believe you have been out here before?" went on Holmes, staring at him with a new interest. "Only you're such a mysterious chap that you won't let on."

"Have it so, if you will. Only, aren't you rather drawing a red herring across the trail, Holmes? We were talking about Miss Ormskirk."

"Um—yes, so we were. But, have you talked to her at all, Stanninghame? I believe even you would be fetched if you did."

"H'm—well, I'd better leave it alone then, hadn't I, seeing that I undertook this voyage not for love, but for money? What's her name, by the way?"

Holmes stared. "Her name," he began—"Oh—er—I see; her other name? By Jove! it's an odd one. Lilith."

"An old one too; the oldest she-name on record, bar none."

"What? How does that come in?"

"Tradition hath it that Lilith was Adam's first wife. That makes it the oldest she-name on record, doesn't it?"

"Of course. What a rum chap you are, Stanninghame! Now, I wonder how many fellows could have told one that?"

"Well, I am a 'know-a-little-of-everything,' they tell me," said Laurence, without a shade of self-complacency. "But, I say, what do these two want bothering around? Not another subscription already?"

Two individuals, armed with mysterious pencil and paper, were moving from group to group, with a word to each. The hawk-like profile of the one bespoke his nationality if not his tribe, even as the pug-nosed, squab-faced figure-head of the other spoke to his.

"It's the 'sweep,'" said Holmes, with kindling interest. "They're going to draw it in the smoke-room. Come along and see it. It'll be something to do."

"But I don't want something to do. I want to do nothing, as I told you just now, and—Hallo! By George, he's gone!"

One glance at the retreating Holmes, who was making all sail for the smoke-room, and Laurence tranquilly resumed his former occupation—gazing out over the blue-green surface, to wit. Not long, however, was he to be left to the enjoyment of the same.

"Can I have this chair? Is it anybody's?"

He turned, but did not start at the voice, which was soft and well modulated. The two deck-chairs had been backed against the companion, in whose doorway now stood framed the form of the speaker.

Rather tall, of exquisite proportions, billowing in splendid curves from the perfectly round waist, the form was about as complete an example of female anatomy as humanity could show of whatever race or clime. The head, well set, was carried rather proudly; the cut of the cool, light blouse displaying a pillarlike throat. Hazel eyes, melting, dark fringed; brows strongly marked, enough to show plenty of character, without being heavy; hair abundant, curled in a fringe upon the forehead, and drawn back from the head in sheeny, dark brown waves. Such was the vision which Laurence Stanninghame beheld, as he turned at the sound of the voice. Well, what then? He had seen it before.

"It isn't anybody's chair," he replied, rising.

"Oh, thank you," she said, stepping forth. "No, don't trouble; I can carry it myself," she added.

"Where do you want it taken to?" he said, ignoring her protest, and thinking, with grim amusement, how he was about to fulfil the very rôle he had been satirising his younger friend about, namely, fetch-and-carry for the spoilt beauty of the quarterdeck.

"Oh, thanks. Anywhere that's cool."

"Then you can't do better than leave it where it is," he rejoined, with a quiet smile, setting down the chair again and resuming his own.

Lilith Ormskirk smiled too, but she made no objection, sliding comfortably into the chair, and gazing meditatively at the point of the neat and shapely deck-shoe just peeping forth from beneath her skirt.

"What are they doing over there?" she began. "Drawing the 'sweep,' are they not? How is it you are not there too, Mr. Stanninghame? Even those of the men who won't help us in getting up any fun are always ready enough for anything of that kind. Well, I suppose it gives them something to do."

Something to do! that eternal 'something to do!'

"But that's just what I don't want—not on board this ship, at anyrate," he retorted. "It's a grand opportunity for lazing, an opportunity that can't occur often in life, and I want to make the most of it."

She glanced furtively at his face. It was a face that interested her; had done so since she first beheld it. A very out-of-the-common

face, she had decided; and the careless reserve, the very indifference of its owner's habit of speech, had powerfully added to her
interest. They had met before, had exchanged a few words now
and again, but had never conversed.

"A thing that is a standing puzzle to me," he went on—"would
be rather, if I knew a little less of human nature—is the alacrity
with which people waste their precious time in order to make a
few shillings. It isn't a craving after profit either, for there can't be
much profit about it. Yet Myers there, the Hebraic instinct ever to
the fore, must needs throw away the splendid recuperative opportunities afforded by a sea voyage, must needs spend the whole of
each and every morning getting up that miserable 'sweep.' It must
be the sheer Hebraic instinct of delighting to handle coin—the
ecstasy of contact with it even."

"And the other—the one who helps him? He's not Hebraic?"

"No, he's English. Therefore he must be for ever 'getting up'
something. We pride ourselves upon our solid deliberation, yet
we are about the fussiest and most interfering race on the face of
the globe."

"Then you don't have anything to do with the popular mid-day
delight?"

"Oh yes. I hand them my shilling every morning when they
come round, and pouch tranquilly later on what they see fit to
restore to me as the result of that modest investment."

She laughed, and as she did so Laurence looked her full in the
face. He wanted to find out again what there could be in this girl
that reduced everybody to subjection so utter and complete. Was
it in the swift flash of the fringed eyes, in the sensuous attractiveness of a certain swarthy, golden, mantling shade of colour which
harmonised so well with the bright clearness of the eyes, with the
smooth serenity of the brow? He could not determine. Yet in that
brief fraction of a moment as he looked, he was uneasily conscious
of a certain magnetic thrill communicating itself even to him.

"You are stronger-minded than I am," she said. "I'm afraid I bet
shockingly at times."

"Well, whenever I do I invariably lose, which is a first-rate cura-
tive to any temptation towards that especial form of dissipation."

"Look now, Mr. Stanninghame, I'm going to take you to

task," she went on. "Why won't you ever help us in getting up anything?"

"But I do help you."

"You do? Why, there was that concert the other night. You refused when you were asked to take part in it."

"But I did take part in it—as audience. You must have an audience, you know. It's essential to the performance."

"Don't be provoking, now," she said, with a laugh which belied the rebuke, for this sort of fencing delighted her. "You never take part in our dances."

"Dances? Did you ever happen to notice the top of my head?"

"I don't think so," she replied, with a splutter of mirth, wondering what whimsicality was coming next. "Why?"

"Only that its covering is getting rather thin, as no self-respecting haircutter ever loses the opportunity of reminding me."

"That's nothing. Look at Mr. Dyson, for instance. Now he might say that. Yet he is a most indefatigable dancer."

"Yes, and that ostrich-egg of his bobbing up and down above the gay and giddy rout is one of the most ridiculous sights on earth. Are you urging me to furnish a similar absurdity?"

"But you might do something to help amuse us. In fact, it is only your duty."

"Hallo! Excuse me, Miss Ormskirk, but that's exactly what that fellow Mac—Mac—something—I never can remember his name—the doctor, you know—was trying to drive into me the other night. I told him I didn't come on board this ship for the purpose of amusing my fellow-creatures—not any—but with the object of being transported to Cape Town with all possible despatch."

"Then you leave the ship at Cape Town? Are you, too, going on to Johannesburg?"

"Not being dead, yes."

"Not being dead? Why, what in the world do you mean?"

"Oh, only that Holmes was asking after all his old friends one night in the smoke-room; and all who were not dead had gone to Johannesburg. Others I've heard talking the same way. So I've got into the habit of thinking there are but two states—death and Johannesburg."

"Tell me, Mr. Stanninghame," said Lilith, struggling with a laugh, "are you ever by any chance serious?"

"Oh yes; I'm never anything else."

She hardly felt inclined to laugh now. There was a subtle something in the tone—a something underlying the whimsicality of the words, that seemed to quell her rising mirth. Again she glanced at his face, and felt her interest deepen tenfold.

"We may meet again then," she said, her tone unconsciously softening; "I am going to Johannesburg soon."

Meet again? Why, they had only just met; and—what was it to him? Yet still more was he conscious of a thrill as of latent witchery thrown over him, as he lounged there in the warm luxuriousness of the tropical noontide, with which this beautiful creature at his side, in her careless attitude, all symmetry and grace, seemed so wholly in keeping.

"What a strange name that is of yours," he said, in the abrupt, unthought-out way which was so characteristic of him.

She started slightly at its very abruptness, then smiled.

"Is it?" she said. "Well, your own is not a very common one."

"No, it isn't; which is a bore at times, because people will persist in spelling it wrong. It might have been worse, though. They went in for giving us all more or less cloth-of-gold sort of names, though mine smacks rather of the cloister than of the lists. One of my brothers they dubbed Aylmer. He was in a regiment, and the mess would persist in calling him Jack, for short. He resented it at first—afterwards came to prefer it; said it was more convenient. Well, it was."

"Mine is older than that. The very oldest feminine name on record," she said, with just a spice of quiet mischief. "Lilith was Adam's first wife."

If she thought the other was going to look foolish at hearing his own words thus reproduced in such literal fashion, she never made a greater mistake in her life.

"So tradition hath it," he rejoined, with perfect unconcern. "It's a queer out-of-the-way sort of name—I'm not sure I don't rather like it. There's a creeping suggestion of witchery about it, too, which is on the whole attractive."

He was looking at her straight in the eyes, for they had both risen, the luncheon-bell having rung. She unflinchingly returned the glance, which on both sides was that of two adversaries mentally appraising each other prior to a rapier-bout.

"Then beware such unholy spells," she replied, with a light but enigmatical laugh. And turning, she left him.

Now Holmes, who, bursting with astonishment and trepidation as he beheld how his friend was engaged, came bustling up, with a scared and furtive demeanour.

"By the Lord, old man, we just have put our foot in it," he sputtered. All the time we were sitting here, Miss Ormskirk was just inside the companion. She must have heard every word we said."

"Don't care a hang if she did."

"Man alive, but we were talking about her! About *her*, and she heard it! Don't you understand?"

"Perfectly. Still I don't care a hang. A hang? No, nor the rope, nor the drop, nor the whole jolly gallows do I care. Will that do?"

Holmes gasped. This fellow Stanninghame was a lunatic. Mad, by Jove! Still gasping as he thought of the enormity of the situation, he left without another word, diving below to try and drown his confusion in a whisky and soda, iced.

But the other, still lingering on the now deserted deck, was conscious of a very unwonted sensation. The spell which he had derided so bitterly when beholding others drawn within its toils had begun to weave itself around him. This vague stirring of his mental pulses, what did it mean? Heavens! it was horrible. It brought back old memories, whose tin-pot unreality was never recalled save as subject matter for bitter gibe and mockery. He could not have believed it possible.

"It's the nerves," he told himself. "These years of squalid worry have done it. My nerves are shaken to bits. Well, I must pull them together again. But—oh, the bosh of it! The utter bosh of it!"

CHAPTER III

"BEWARE SUCH UNHOLY SPELLS!"

THE sway of Lilith Ormskirk over the saloon and quarter-deck of the *Persian* was as complete as any one woman's sway ever is. From the grizzled captain—nominally under who charge she was making the voyage—down to the newly-emancipated school-boy going out to seek employment, the male element was, with scarcely an exception, her collective slave. Among the women, naturally, her rule was less complete; those who were furthest from all possibility of rivalling her in attractiveness of person or charm of manner being, of course, the most virulent in their jealousy and the expression thereof. Lilith, however, cared nothing for this, or, if she did, gave no sign. She was never bitter, even towards those whom she knew to be among her worst detractors, never spiteful. She was not faultless, not by any means, but her failings did not lie in the direction of littleness. But she always seemed bright and happy, and full of life—too much so, thought more than one of her perfervid adorers, who would fain have monopolised her.

She was in the mid-twenties—that age when the egotism and rather narrow enthusiasms and prejudices of the girl shade off into the graciousness and *savoir-vivre* of womanhood. She could look back on more than one foolishness, from whose results she had providentially escaped, with an uneasy shudder, followed by a heartfelt thankfulness, and a sense of having not only learnt but profited by experience, which sense enlarged her mind and her sympathies, and imparted to her demeanour a self-possession and serenity beyond her years.

We said the male element, with scarce an exception, was her collective slave. Such an exception was Laurence Stanninghame.

Without being a misogynist, he had no great opinion of women. He owned they might be delightful—frequently were—up to a certain point, and this was the point at which you began to take them seriously. But to treat any one of them as though the sun had ceased to shine because her presence was withdrawn, struck him as sheer insanity. It might be all right for youngsters like Holmes—or Swaynston, the licensed fool of the smoking-room, or Dyson, to whose senile enthusiasm for the mazy rout we have heard allusion made—the latter on the principle of "no fool like an old fool," but not for him—not for a man in the matured vigour of his physical and mental powers. Wherefore, when forced himself to acknowledge the spell which Lilith had begun to weave around him, he unhesitatingly set it down to impaired nerves.

As a direct result, he avoided the cause. It was a cowardly course of action, he told himself. He was afraid of her. If she could throw the magic of her sorcery over him during a brief ten minutes of conversation, what the very deuce would happen if he allowed himself to be drawn into anything approaching the easy-going shipboard intimacy—deck-walking by moonlight, chairs drawn up in a snug corner during the heat of the day, and so forth! Who knew what latent capacities for being made an ass of might not develop themselves within him. He felt really alarmed.

Let it not be supposed that any scruple on the ground of conventionality, obligation, what not, entered into his misgivings. For Laurence Stanninghame had been clean disillusioned all along the line. He hadn't the shred of an illusion left. He had started life with a fair stock-in-trade of good intentions and straight ideas, and, indeed, had acted up to them honestly, and in good faith. But now?—"I've had a h—l of a time!" he would exclaim to himself, during one of those meditative gazes out seaward, for which we heard his younger friend taking him to task. "Yes—just that." And now, only touching middle life, he believed in nothing and nobody. He had become a cold, keen, strong-headed, selfish cynic. If ever his mind reverted to the fresher and more generous impulses or actions of his younger days, it was with a contemptuous self-pity. His view of the morality of life now was just the amount of success, of advantage, of gratification to be got out of it. He thoroughly endorsed the principle of the old roué's advice to his grandson: "Be good, and you *may* be happy—but you'll have d——d little fun," taking care to italicise the word "may." For he had found that the first clause of the saw had brought him neither happiness nor fun.

With his fellow-passengers on board the *Persian* he was neither popular nor the reverse. Among the men, some liked him, others didn't. He was genial enough, and good company in the smoking-room, but wouldn't do anything in the way of promoting the general amusement—and that voyage was a particularly lively one in the matter of getting things up. The fair section of the saloon was puzzled, and could not make up its mind whether to dislike him or not. For the first, he consistently, though not ostentatiously, avoided it, instead of laying himself out to make himself agree-able—though indications were not wanting that he could so make himself if he chose. For the second, the fact that he remained an unknown quantity was in his favour, if only that the unfamiliarity of reserve—mystery—never fails to appeal strongly to the minds of women and savages.

It was not so difficult for him to avoid Lilith Ormskirk, if only that until that morning he had hardly exchanged a hundred words with her at a time, wherefore the upshot of his resolve was notice-able neither by its object nor by the passengers at large. Holmes indeed, who, having recovered from his consternation, had been secretly watching his friend, was anticipating the fun of seeing the latter fall headlong into the pit, whose brink he had so boldly skirted, so openly derided. But he was disappointed. Laurence, if he referred to Lilith again, did so in the same casual, indifferent way as before, nor did he ever terminate any of his dreamy and seaward-gazing meditations in order to open converse with her, even with such inducement as solitary propinquity on more than one occasion.

"By Jove! the fellow is a cross between an icicle and a stone," quoth Holmes to himself, in mingled wonder and disgust.

It was night—warm, sensuous, tropical night. There was dancing in the saloon, and the glare from the skylight and the banging of the piano and chatter of voices gave forth strange con-trast to the awesome stillness of the great liquid plain, the dewy richness of the air, the stars hanging in golden clusters from a black vault, the fiery eye of some larger planet rolling and flashing among them as the revolving beacon of a lighthouse. Here the muffled throb of the propeller, and the rushing hiss of water as the prow of the great steamer sheared through the placid surface, furrowing up on either side a long line of phosphorescent wave. Such a contrast he who stood alone in the darkness, leaning over the taffrail, could appreciate nicely.

There were quick, light footsteps. Somebody else was walking the deck. Well, whoever it was, he himself was screened by the stem of one of the ship's boats swung in and resting on chocks. They would not see him, which was all right, for he was in a queer mood and not inclined to talk. After a turn or two, the footsteps paused, then something brushed his elbow in the darkness, as suddenly starting away, while a half-frightened voice exclaimed—

"Oh, I beg your pardon. I couldn't see anything in the dark, just coming up out of the light of the saloon, too. Why, it's Mr. Stanninghame."

To one who had been out of doors even a few minutes it was not very dark, for the stars were shining with vivid brilliancy. It needed not the sense of sight, that of hearing was enough. Nay, more, a subtle sixth sense, whatever it might be, had warned Laurence Stanninghame of the identity of the intruder.

"No case of mistaken identity here," he said. "But how is it you are all by yourself?"

"Oh, I got tired of all the whirl and chatter. I craved for some fresh air, and so I stole away," said Lilith. "Why, how heavy the dew is here in these tropical seas," she added, withdrawing her arm from the taffrail upon which she had begun to lean.

The man, watching her furtively, said nothing for a moment. That same chord within him thrilled to her voice, her propinquity. Doubtless his nerves, high strung with recent worry, were playing the fool with him. He was conscious of a kind of envenomed resentment, almost aversion; yet his chief misgiving at that moment, which he recognised with added wrath, was lest she should leave him as quickly as she had come.

"All by yourself as usual!" she went on, flashing at him a bright smile. "Thinking, I suppose?"

"I don't know that I was. I believe I was trying to realise the immensity and silence of the midnight ocean, as far as that tin-pot racket down there would allow one to realise anything. Then it occurred to me how long it would take for the intense solitude to drive a man mad if he were cast away alone in it."

"Not long, I should think," answered Lilith, gazing seriously out over the smooth oily sea. "The horror of it would soon do that for me."

"And yet why should it have such an effect at all?" he went on. "The grandeur of the situation ought to counterpoise any such weakness. Given enough to support life without undue stinting, with a certainty of rescue at the end, and, I think, a fortnight as castaway in these waveless seas would be an uncommonly interesting experience."

"What? A fortnight? A whole fortnight in ghastly solitude! Silence only broken by the splash or snort of heaven knows what horrible sea monster! Any consideration of peril apart, I am sure that one night of it would turn me into a raving, gibbering lunatic."

"Perhaps. People are differently built. For my part, discounting the 'sea monster,' I am certain I should enjoy the experience. For one thing, there would be no post."

"But no more there is here on board," she said, struggling with the laugh which the dry irrelevancy had brought to her lips.

"No—but there's—Swaynston."

This time the laugh came rippling outright, and through it came the sound of footsteps.

"Oh, here you are, Miss Ormskirk. I've been looking for you everywhere. This is our dance."

Lilith, catching the satirical twinkle in the other's eyes in the starlight, did not know which way to turn to control an overmastering impulse to laugh uninterruptedly for about five minutes, the cruel part of it being that the interrupter was Swaynston himself.

The latter, a pursy individual, was holding out an arm somewhat in the attitude of a seal's flapper. But Lilith did not take it.

"Do be very good-natured and excuse me," she said. "I don't want to dance any more to-night. The noise and heat have made my head ache."

"Really, really? I'll find you a chair then, in some quiet corner," fussed Swaynston. But Lilith seemed not enthusiastic over that allurement, and finally, with some difficulty, she got rid of him; he grinning "from the teeth outwards," but consumed with fury nevertheless.

So that was why she had stolen away from them all, to slip up and talk in a quiet corner with that fellow Stanninghame, who was probably some absconding swindler, with a couple of detectives and a warrant waiting for him in Table Bay? Thus Swaynston.

Nor would it have tended to allay his irritation could he have heard the object of it after his departure.

"So you think he is worse than the post?" she said, with a laugh in her eyes. "Yet he is one of the most devoted of my—poodles."

The demure malice of her tone no more disconcerted the other than that had her former endeavour to show him she had over-heard his remarks by quoting his own words.

"Oh yes," was the unconcerned reply. "He sits up on his hind legs a little better than any of them."

For a few moments she said nothing, seeming to have become infected with her companion's dreamy meditativeness. Then—

"And are you not tired of the voyage yet? You were saying the other day that its monotony was enjoyable."

"I say so still. Look!" he broke off, pointing to the sea.

A commotion was going on beneath its surface. Their grisly shapes, vivid in the disturbed phosphorescence, drawing a wake of flame behind them, rushed two great sharks. Hither and thither they darted, every detail of their ugly forms discernible in the framing of the phosphorescent blaze, even the set glare of the cruel eye; and, no less nimble in swift doubling flashes, several smaller fish were trying to evade the laws of Nature—the absorption of the weakest, to wit. There was something indescribably horrible in the fiery rush of the sea-demons beneath the oily blackness of the tropical waters.

"How awful! how truly awful!" murmured Lilith, with a strong shudder of repulsion, yet gazing, as one fascinated, at the weird sight.

"Yet it is the perfection of an object lesson, one that comes in just in time to point the moral to my answer," he said. "If those fish, now in process of being eaten, were caught and kept in an aquarium tank, it might be more monotonous for them than furnishing fun and food to the first comer in the shape of bigger fish. Possibly they might yearn for the excitement of being harried, though I doubt it. That sort of philosophy is reserved for us humans. If we

knock our heads against a brick wall we howl; if we haven't got a
brick wall to knock them against we howl louder."

And the moral is—?"

"'*Dona nobis pacem.*'"[1]

"I see," she said at last, for it took her a little while thoroughly
to grasp the application, partly distracted as her thinking powers
were in trying to find a deeper meaning than the one intended.
"Yet peace is a thing that no one can enjoy in this world. How
should they when the law of life is struggle—struggle and strife?"

"Precisely. That, however, is due to the faultiness of human
nature. The philosophy of the matter is the same. Its soundness
remains untouched."

"Yet you are not consistent. You were implying just now
that, failing a brick wall to knock our heads against, we started in
search of one. Now does not that apply to those who go out into
the world—to the other end of the world—instead of remaining
peacefully at home?" she added, a sly sort of "I-have-you-there"
inflection in her tone.

"Pardon me. My consistency is all right. Begging a question
will not shatter it."

"Begging a question?"

"Of course. For present purposes the said begging is comprised
in the word 'peacefully.' See?"

"Ah!"

Again she was silent. The other watching the flash of the starlight on the meditative upturned eyes, the clearly marked brows,
the firm setting of the lips, was more conscious than ever of the
latent witchery in the sweet serene face. He would not flee from
its spells now, he decided. He would meet them boldly, and throw
them off, coil for coil, however subtly, however dexterously they
were wound about him. Meanwhile, two things had not escaped
him. She had yielded the point gracefully and convinced, instead
of launching out into a voluble farrago of irrelevant rubbish, as
ninety-nine women out of a hundred would have done in order to
have "the last word." That argued sense, judgment, tact. Further,
she had avoided that vulgar commonplace, instinctive to the crude
and unthinking mind, of whatever sex, of importing a personal
application into an abstract discussion. This, too, argued tact and

mental refinement, both qualities of rarer distribution among her sex than is commonly supposed—qualities, however, which Laurence Stanninghame was peculiarly able to appreciate.

Then she talked about other things, and he let her talk, just throwing in a word here and there to stimulate the expansion of her ideas. And they were good ideas, too, he decided, listening keenly, and balancing her every point, whether he agreed with it or not. He was interested, more vividly interested than he would fain admit! This girl, with the enthralling face and noble beauty of form, had a mind as well. All the slavish adoration she received had not robbed her of that. It was an experience to him, as they lounged there on the taffrail together in the gold-spangled velvet hush of the tropical night. How delightfully companionable she could be, he thought; so responsive, so discriminating and unargumentative. Argumentativeness in women was a detestable vice, in his opinion, for it meant everything but what the word itself etymologically did.[2] Craftily he drew her out, cunningly he touched up every fallacy or crudeness in her ideas, in such wise that she unconsciously adopted his amendments, under the impression that they were all her own.

"But—I have been boring you all this time," she broke off at last. "Confess now, you who are nothing if not candid. I have been boring your life out?"

"Then, on your own showing, I am nothing, for I am not candid," he answered. "On the contrary, it is an unadvisable virtue, and one calculated to corner you without loophole. And you certainly have not been boring me."

He thought, sardonically, what anyone of those whom he had caustically defined as her "poodles" would give for an hour or so of similar boredom, if it involved Lilith all to himself. Some of this must have been reflected in his eyes, for Lilith broke in quickly—

"No, you are not candid. I accept the amendment. I can see the sarcasm in your face."

"But not on that account," he rejoined tranquilly, and at the same time dropping his hand on to hers as it rested on the taffrail. The act—an instinctive one—was a dumb protest against the movement she had made to withdraw. And as such Lilith read it; more potent in its impulsiveness than any words could have been.

"Listen!" he went on. "I suppose there is a sort of imp of scepticism sitting ever upon one shoulder, and that is what you saw. Something in my thoughts suggested a droll contrast, that was all. So far from boring me, you have afforded me an intensely agreeable surprise."

"Now you are sneering again. I will not talk any more."

He recognised in her tone a quick sensitiveness—not temper. Accordingly his own took on an unconscious softness, a phenomenally unwonted softness.

"Don't be foolish, child.³ You know I was doing nothing of the sort. Go on with what you were saying at once."

"What was I saying? Oh, I remember. That idea that board-ship life shows people in their real character. Do you believe in it?"

"Only in the case of those who have no real character to show. Wherein is a paradox. Those who have got any—well, don't show it, either on board ship or on shore."

"I believe you are right. Now, my own character, do you think it shows out more readable on board than it would on shore?"

"Do you think you have me so transparently as that? What was I saying just now on that head?"

"I see. Really, though, I had no ulterior motive. I asked the question in perfect good faith. Tell me—if anyone can, you can. Tell me. Shall I make a success—a good thing of life? I often wonder."

She threw up her head with a quick movement, and the wide, serious eyes, fixed full upon his, seemed to flash in the starlight. He met the glance with one as earnest and unswerving as her own.

"You rate my powers of vaticination too high," he said slowly. "And—you are groping after an ideal."

"Perhaps. Tell me, though, what you think, character-reader as you are. Shall I make a success of life?"

"I should think the chances were pretty evenly balanced either way, inclining, if anything, to the reverse."

"Thanks. I shall remember that."

"But you are not obliged to believe it."

"No. Still I shall remember it. And now I must go below; it is nearly time for putting out the saloon lights. Good-night. I have enjoyed our talk so much."

She had extended her hand, and as he took it, the sympathetic—was it magnetic?—pressure was mutual, almost lingering.

"Good-night," he said. "The enjoyment has not been all on one side."

Left alone, he returned to his solitary musings—tried to, rather, for there was no "return" about the matter, because now they took an entirely new line. His late companion would intrude upon them—nay, monopolised them. She had appealed power-fully to his senses, to his mind, how long would it be before she did so to his heart? He had avoided her—he alone—up till then, and yet now, after this first conversation, he was convinced that of all gathered there he alone knew the real Lilith Ormskirk as distinct from the superficial one known to the residue.

And to his mind recurred her former warning, laughingly uttered: "Beware such unholy spells!" With a strange intoxicating recollection did that warning recur, together with the conscious-ness that more than ever was it needed now. But as against this was the protecting strength of a triple chain armour. Life was only rendered interesting by such interest in character studies as this. Oh yes; that was the solution—that, and nothing more.

This was by no means the last talk they had—they two alone together. But it seemed to Laurence Stanninghame that a warning note had been sounded, and one of no uncertain nature. His tone became more acrid, his sarcasm more biting, more envenomed. One day Lilith said—

"Why do you dislike me so?"

He started at the question, thrown momentarily off his guard.

"I don't dislike you," he answered shortly.

"Then why have you such a very poor opinion of me? You never lose an opportunity of letting me see that you have. What have I done? What have I said that you should think so poorly of me?"

There was no spice of temper, of resentment, in the tone. It was soft, and rather pleading. The serious eyes were sweet and wistful. As his own met their steady gaze, it seemed that a current of magnetic thought flashed from mind to mind.

"I hold no such opinion," he said, after a few moments of silence. "Perhaps I dread those 'unholy spells,' thou sorceress. Ah!

there goes the second dinner-bell. Run away now, and make your-self more beautiful than ever—if possible."

A bright laugh flashed in the hazel eyes, and the white teeth showed in a smile.

"I'll try—since *you* wish it," she said, over her shoulder, as she turned away.

CHAPTER IV

THE LAND OF PROMISE

THE throb of the propeller has almost ceased; faint, too, is the vibration of the slowed-down engines. The *Persian* is gliding with well-nigh imperceptible motion through the smooth waters of Table Bay.

It is a perfect morning, cloudless in its dazzling splendour. In front, the huge Table Mountain rears its massive wall, dwarfing the mud-town lying at its base and the bristling masts of shipping, its great line mirrored in the sheeny surface. Away in the distance, the purple cones of the Hottentots Holland Mountains loom thirst-ily through a glimmer of summer haze. A fair scene indeed after three weeks of endless sea and sky.

"And what are your first impressions of my native land?"

Laurence turned.

"I was thinking less of the said land than of myself," he answered. "I was thinking what potentialities would lie between my first impressions of it and my last."

Just a suspicion of gravity came over Lilith Ormskirk's face at the remark.

"And are you glad the voyage is at an end, now that it is?" she went on.

"You know I am not. It was such a rest."

"Which I was everlastingly disturbing."

"By wreathing those unholy spells. Lilith, thou sorceress, how long will it be before those talks of ours are forgotten? A week, perhaps?"

"They will never be forgotten," she answered, her eyes dreamy and serious. "But now, I must go below and finish doing up my things. We shall be in dock directly."

A great crowd is collected on the quay as the steamer warps up, above which rise sunshades coloured and coquettish, pith helmets and sweeping pugarees, and more orthodox white "stove-pipes." Then in the background, yellow-skinned Malays in gaudy Oriental attire, parchment-faced Hottentots, Mozambique blacks, and lighter-hued Kaffirs from the Eastern frontier. The docks are piled with luggage, for the privilege of carrying which and its multifold owners Malay cab-drivers are uttering shrill and competing yells. On board, people are bidding each other good-bye, or greeting those who have come to meet them; and flitting among such groups, a mingled expression of alertness and anxiety on his countenance, is here and there a steward, bent upon rounding up a possibly elusive "tip," or refreshing an inconveniently short memory.

Near the gangway Lilith Ormskirk was holding quite a farewell court. Her "poodles," as Laurence had satirically defined them, were crowding around—Swaynston at their head—for a farewell pat. The last, in the shape of Holmes and another, had taken their sorrowful departure, and now a quick, furtive look seemed to cross the smiling serenity of her face, a shade of wistfulness, of disappointment. Thus one in the hurrying throng at the other side of the deck read it.

"What a tail-wagging!" almost immediately spake a voice at her side.

She turned. Decidedly the expression was one of brightening.

"I thought you had gone—had forgotten to say good-bye," she said.

"I was waiting until the poodles had finally cleared. Now, however, I have come to utter that not always hateful word."

"Not in this instance?"

"Yes, distinctly. I have just heard there is to be a special train made up—we are in too late for the regular mail-train, you know. So I shall leave for Kimberley in about two or three hours' time."

Lilith looked disappointed.

"I thought you would have stayed here at least a few days," she said. And then the friends who had met her on board returned, and Laurence found himself introduced to three pretty girls—fair-haired, blue-eyed, well-dressed—eke¹ to a man—tall, brown-faced, loosely hung, apparently about thirty years of age—none of whose names he could quite succeed in catching, save that the latter was apostrophised as "George." Then, after a commonplace or two, good-byes were uttered and they separated—Lilith and her party to catch the train for Mowbray, her late fellow-passenger to arrange for his own much longer journey.

Having the compartment to themselves, one of the blue-eyed girls opened fire thus—

"Lilith, who is he?"

"Who?"

"He."

"Bless the child," laughed Lilith, "there were about half a hundred he's."

"No, there was only one. Who is he? What is he?"

"I don't know," replied Lilith, affecting ignorance no longer.

"You don't know? After three weeks on board ship together? Three whole weeks of ship life, and you have the face to tell me you don't know anything about him. After the way in which you said goodbye to each other, too? Oh, I saw."

"Well, I don't know."

"Or care?"

"Chaff away, if it's any fun to you," answered Lilith, quite serenely, as the trio rippled into peals of laughter. "I liked the man, liked to talk to him on board—you are welcome to that admission—but all I know is that he is going to Johannesburg. We may never see each other again."

"These English Johnnies who come out here, and whom one knows nothing about, are now and again slippery fish," gruffly spoke the brown-faced one. "Watch it, Lilith."

"I thought this one looked as if he might be interesting," said another of the blue-eyed girls. "Pity he wasn't staying a day or two. We might have got him out to the house and seen what he was made of."

"Watch it," repeated George sententiously. "Watch it, Lilith."

Meanwhile, the object of this discussion—and warning— having resignedly "passed" the Customs at the dock gates, was spinning townwards in one of the innumerable hansoms. Sizing up the South African metropolis, it gave him the idea of a mud city, just dumped down wet and left to dry in the sun. Its general aspect suggested the vagaries of some sportive Titan, who, from the summit of the lofty rock wall behind it, had amused himself, out of office hours, by chucking down chunks of clay of all sorts and sizes, trying how near he could "lob" them into the position of streets and squares.

At that time the railway line ended at Kimberley—the distance thence to Johannesburg, close upon three hundred miles, had to be done by stage. It occurred to Laurence that, having a couple of hours to spare, he had better look up the coach-agent and secure a seat by wire.

The agent was not in his office. Laurence Stanninghame, however, who knew the ways of similar countries, albeit a new arrival in this, inquired for that functionary's favourite bar. The reply was prompt and accurate withal. In a few minutes, seated on stools facing each other, he and the object of his search were transacting business.

The latter did not seem entirely satisfactory. The agent could not say when the earliest chance might occur by regular coach. He might have to wait at Kimberley—well, it might be for days, or it might be for ever. On the other hand, he might not even have to wait at all. He could not tell. Even the people at the other end could not say for certain. Laurence began to lose patience.

"See here," he said, somewhat testily. "I haven't been long in your country, but that's about the only reply I've been able to meet with to any question yet. Tell me, as a matter of curiosity. Is there any one thing you are ever certain of out here? Just one."

The agent looked at him with faint amazement.

"There is one," he said; "just one."

"Well—and that?"

"Death. That's always a dead cert. Let's liquor. Put a name to it, skipper."

The special train consisted of a mail van and a first-class carriage. There being only three or four other travellers, each had a compartment to himself, an arrangement which met with

Laurence Stanninghame's unfeigned approval. He did not want to talk—especially in a clattering, dusty railway carriage. At intervals the passengers foregathered for meals at some wayside buffet or accommodation house—meals whose quality was in inverse ratio to the exuberance of the prices charged therefor—then each would return to his own box and smoke and read and sleep away the little matter of seven hundred miles.

On they sped for hours and hours—on through sleepy Dutch villages, whose gardens and cultivation made an oasis on the surrounding flats—on, winding in slow ascent through the gloomy grandeur of the Hex River Poort, with its iron-bound heights rearing in mighty masses from the level valley bottom. Then it grew dark, and, the dim oil lamp being inadequate for reading purposes, Laurence went to sleep.

"Afar in the desert I love to ride,"

sang Pringle, the South African bard.[2]

"Pringle was a liar, or a lunatic," quoth Laurence Stanninghame, to whom the passage was familiar, on opening his eyes next morning and looking around. For the train was speeding—when not slowing—through the identical desert of which Pringle sang; that heartbreaking, dead-level, waterless, treeless belt known as the Karroo. Not a human habitation in sight, for hours at a stretch—the same low table-topped mountains rising hours ahead, and which never seem to get any closer; looking, moreover, in the distant, mirage-effects like vast slabs poised in mid-air and resting on nothing. At long intervals a group of foul and tumble-down Hottentot huts, with their squalid inhabitants—lean curs and ape-like men—their *raison d'être*, in the shape of a flock of prematurely aged and disappointed-looking goats, trying all they are worth to extract sustenance from the red shaly earth and its sparse growth of coarse, bush-like herbage. Looking out on this horrible desert, the eye and the mind alike grow weary, and the latter starts speculating in a shuddering sort of way as to how the deuce anything human can find it in its heart to exist in such a place. Yet though an awful desert in time of drought it is not always so.

But, gazing forth upon the surrounding waste, Laurence

was able to read into it a certain charm—the charm of freedom, of boundlessness, so vividly standing out in contrast to his own cramped, narrow, shut-in life. All the changed conditions—the wildness, the solitude, the flaming and unclouded sun—were as a new awakening to life. The current of a certain joy of living, long since sluggish, congealed, now coursed swiftly and without hindrance through his being.

Now through all those hours of tedious travelling—in the flaming glow of day, or in the still, cool watches of the night, he had with him a recollection—Lilith Ormskirk's face haunted him. Those eyes seemed to follow him—sweet, serious; or again mirthful, flashing from out their dark fringe of lashes, but ever entrancing, ever inviting. Her whole personality, in fact, seemed to pervade his mind, warring for sole possession, to the exclusion of all other thought, all other consideration. Into the conflict his own mind entered with zest. It was a psychological struggle which appealed to him, and that thoroughly. She should not, by her witchery, take entire possession. Yet the recollection of her was so potent that at length he ceased to strive against it. He gave way—abandoned himself, contentedly, voluptuously, to its sway—even aiding it in the pictures it conjured up. Now he saw her, as he had first passed her, day after day on board ship, with indifference, with faintly ironical curiosity; again, as when they had first begun to talk together; and yet again, when he had found himself resorting to all manner of cowardly mental expedients to persuade himself that he did not revel in her dangerously winning attractiveness, and sweet, sympathetic converse. In the monotonous three-four time beat of the wheels he could conjure up her voice—even the colonial trick of clipping the final "r" in words ending with that letter—as to which he had often rallied her, while secretly liking it—for this, like a touch of the brogue, can be winsome enough when uttered by pretty lips. Now all these reflections could not but be profitless, possibly dangerous, yet they had this advantage—they helped to kill time, and that during a thirty-odd-hour journey across the Karroo—well it *is* an advantage!

On through the long, hot day, and still that memory was with him. The solitude, the stillness, the mile after mile over the desolate and barren waste, the novelty of the scene, the monotonous rattle of the wheels—all went to perpetuate it. Then the sun drew down to the horizon, and the departing glow, striking upon the red soil, painted the latter the colour of blood, making up an extraordinarily vivid study in red and blue. Overhead a cloudless sky, the horizon all aflame, and the whole earth, far as the eye could reach, steeped in the richest purple red. Laurence fell fast asleep.

He dreamed they were steaming into Charing Cross Station. Lilith was waiting to meet him. He swore, in his dream, because they had halted on the railway bridge too long to take the tickets. Then he awoke. They were steaming slowly into a terminus, amid the familiar flashing of lamps and the rumbling of porters' trucks. But it was not Charing Cross, it was Kimberley.

Not long did it take him to collect his scanty baggage and fling it into a "cab," otherwise an open, two-seated Cape cart. Hardly had he taken his seat than the driver uttered a war-whoop, and, with a jerk that nearly sent its passenger somersaulting into the road, the concern started off as hard as its eight legs and two wheels could carry it.

The night was dark, the streets guiltless of lighting. As the trap zigzagged furiously from one side of the way to the other, now poised on one wheel, now leaping bodily into the air as it charged through a deep hole or rut, it was a comfort to the said passenger to reflect that the road being feet deep in sand one was bound to fall soft anyhow. Yet, candidly, he rather enjoyed it. After thirty-three hours in a South African "Flying Watkin"[3] even this spurious excitement was welcome.

They shaved corners, always on one wheel, sometimes even scraping the corners of houses, and causing those pedestrians in their line of flight to skip like young unicorns. Then, recovering, the startled wayfarers would hurl their choicest blessings after the cab. To these, the madcap driver would reply with a shrill and fiendish yell, belabouring his frantic cattle with a view to attempting fresh feats. They succeeded. It only wanted a bullock-waggon coming down the street to afford them the opportunity. The bullock-waggon came. Then a dead, dull scrunch—an awful shock—and the cab was at a standstill. The waggon people opened their safety-valves and let off a fearful blast of profanity; the cab-driver replied in suitable and feeling terms, then backed clear of the wreck and whipped on.

Vastly amused by this lively experience, Laurence still ventured to expostulate, mildly, and as a matter of form. But he got no more change out of his present Jehu than Horace Greeley did out of Hank Monk.[4] The reply, accompanied by a jovial guffaw, was—

"All right, mister. You sit tight, and I'll fetch you through. Which hotel did you say?"

Laurence refreshed his memory—and swaying, jerking, pounding into ruts and holes, the chariot drew up like a hurricane blast before quite an imposing-looking building at the corner of the Market Square. Having paid off the lunatic of the whip and stood him a drink, Laurence engaged a room, and wondered what the deuce he should do with himself if delayed here any time. For the glimpse he had obtained of the place seemed not inviting. The same crowded bars, the same roaring racket, the same dust—yea, even the same thirst. He had seen it all before in other parts of the world.

He was destined to wonder still more, and wearily, what he should do with himself; for nearly a week went by before he could secure a seat in the coach. A great depression came upon him, begotten of the heat and the drowsiness and the dust, as day after day seemed to bring with it no emancipation from the wind-swept, tin-built town, dumped down on its surrounding flat and sad-looking desert waste. Yet nothing akin to home-sickness was there in his depression. He wanted to get onward, not to return. He was bored and in the blues. Yet, as he looked back, the feeling which predominated was that of freedom—of having a certain measure of life and its prospects before him. Stay, though. His thoughts would, at times, travel backward, and that in spite of himself, and they would land him with a lingering, though unacknowledged, regretfulness, on the deck of the *Persian*. Well, that was only an episode. It had passed away out of his life, and it was as well that it had.

But—had it?

At last, to our wayfarer's unspeakable joy, deliverance came. It had been Laurence's lot to travel in far worse conveyances than the regular coaches which at that time performed the journey between Kimberley and Johannesburg, a distance of close upon three hundred miles; consequently, although not among the fortunate ones who had secured a corner seat, he managed to make himself as comfortable as any traveller in comparatively outlandish regions has a right to expect. His fellow-passengers consisted, for the most part, of mechanics of the better sort and a loquacious Jew—not at all a bad sort of fellow—in conversation with whom he would now and then beguile the weariness of the route. And it was weary. The flat sameness of the treeless plains, as mile after mile brought no change; the same stony kopjes; the same deserted and tumble-down mining structures; the same God-forsaken-looking Dutch homesteads, whose owners had apparently taken on the *triste* hopelessness of their surroundings; the same miserable wayside inns, where leathery goat-flesh and bones and rice, painted yellow, were dispensed under the title of breakfast and dinner, what time the coach halted to change horses, and even then only served up when the driver was frantically vociferating, "All aboard!" Thus they journeyed day and night, allowing, perhaps, three hours, or four at the outside, for sleep—on a bed. But the latter proved an institution of dubious beneficence, because of its far from dubious animation; the said "animation" scorning blithely and imperviously accumulations of insect powder, reaching back into the dim past, left there and added to by a countless procession of tortured travellers. Howbeit, of these and like discomforts are such journeyings productive, wherefore they are scarcely to be reckoned as worthy of note.

CHAPTER V

KING SCRIP[1]

"HALLO, Stanninghame! And so, here you are?"

"Here I am, Rainsford, as you say. And from what I have heard in process of getting here, I'm afraid I have got here a day too late."

The other laughed, as they shook hands. He was a man of Laurence's own age, straight and active, and his bronzed face wore that alert eager look which was noticeable upon the faces of most of the fortune-seekers, for of such was the bulk of the inhabitants of Johannesburg at that time.

"You never can tell," he rejoined. "Things are a bit slack now, because of this infernal drought; but a good sousing rain, or a few smart thunder showers, would fill all the dams and set the batteries working again harder than ever. It's the rainy time of year, too."

It was the morning after Laurence's arrival in Johannesburg, and, while sallying forth to find Rainsford, the two had met on Commissioner Street. The brand-new gold-town looked anything but what it was. It did not look new. In spite of the general unfinishedness of the streets and sidewalks, the latter largely conspicuous by their absence; in spite of the predominance of scaffolding poles and half-reared structures of red brick; in spite of the countless tenements of corrugated iron, and the tall chimneys of mining works which came in here, where steeples would have arisen in an ordinary town; in spite of all this there was a battered and weatherbeaten aspect about the place which made it look centuries old. Great pillars of dust towered skywards, then dispersing, whirled in mighty wreaths over the shining iron roofs, to fall hissing back into the red, powdery streets whence they had arisen, choking with pungent particles the throats, eyes and ears of the eager, busy, speculative, acquisitive crowd, who had flocked hither like wasps to a jar of beer and honey. And to many, indeed, it was destined to prove just such a trap.

"Well, what do you advise, Rainsford?" said Laurence, after some more talk about the Rand[2] and its prospects.

"Wait a day or two. You don't want to buy in a falling market. There are several good companies to put into, but things haven't touched bottom yet. When they do and just begin to rise, then buy in. Meanwhile lie low."

"You speak like a book, Rainsford," said one of two men who joined them at that moment. "There's a capital company now whose shares are on the rise again. Couldn't do better than take two or three hundred of them. What do you say?"

"Name?"

"Bai-praatfonteins."

"I'll watch it!" said Rainsford, with an emphatic and negative shake of the head.

"I say, you don't want a couple of building stands? They'll treble their value in as many weeks. Going cheap as dirt now."

"Not taking any, Rankin," was the uncompromising reply, for Rainsford knew something about those building stands.

"You're making a mistake. Bless my soul, if only I had the money to spare, I'd take them at double myself. I'm only agent in the matter, though. I can't do any business at all with you fellows this morning."

All this was said in the most genial and good-humoured a tone imaginable. The speaker was a spare, straight, neatly-dressed individual of middle age. His face was of a dark bronze hue, and lit up by a pair of keen black eyes, and his beard was prematurely grey, almost white. The expression of keenness on a deal was not characteristic of him alone. Everyone wore it in those days.

"That was a great old shot you did on me, Rainsford, with those Verneuk Draais," cut in the other man, in a jolly, hail-the-maintop sort of voice. He was a tall, fair-haired, athletic fellow, whose condition looked as hard as nails. "*Ja*, it just was."

"Well, I'll buy them back if you like, Wheeler."

"How much?"

"Sixteen and a half."

A roar of good-humoured derision went up from the other.

"Sixteen and a half? And I took them over from you at twenty-eight. Sixteen and a half?"

"Well, are you taking?" said Rainsford.

"Dead off," returned the other.

"What do you say, you fellows?" cut in the first who had spoken. "A little 'smile' of something before lunch won't do us any harm. Eh? what do you say?"

"*Ja*, that's so. Come along," sung out the tall man, spinning round upon one heel and heading for the Exchange bar.

"There's nothing like an Angostura[3] to give one an appetite," said the dark man to Laurence as they walked along. "It gives tone to the system. Angostura—with a little drop of gin in it."

"With a little drop of gin in it?" repeated Wheeler, with a derisive roar. "That's where the tone to the system comes in—eh, Rankin?"

"Only just out from home, are you?" said the latter to Laurence as, having named their respective "poisons," the original four, with two or three others who had joined them *en route*, stood absorbing the same. "Heavens! did you ever hear such a row in your life?" he went on, as through the open door connecting with the Exchange came the frantic bawling of brokers, competing wildly for Blazesfonteins, and Verneuk Laagtes, and Hellpoorts, and Vulture's Vleis, and Madeiras, and Marshes, and up and down the whole gamut. And there in the crowd lining the bar, and in the crowd outside the Exchange, and in the crowd upon Market Square, where the auctioneers stood, well-nigh elbow to elbow, bellowing from their tubs, and where you might bid for anything from a building stand or a pair of horses to a concertina or a pair of stays—everywhere the talk was the same, and it was of scrip. King Scrip ruled the roost.

Just then, however, the subjects of King Scrip were undergoing rather an anxious time, for the drought was becoming serious. Dams being empty, batteries could not work; result, scrip drawing within alarming distance of touching its own value—paper, to wit. And as the dams became more empty, those with an "n" appended became more and more full—yea, exceeding full-bodied, and both loud and deep. In the churches they were praying for rain,—praying hard,—for rain meant money; and in the bars they were "cussing" for lack of it,—"cussing" hard,—on the same principle. Then the rain came, and in the churches they sang "Te Deum"[4]; and in the bars they drove a humming trade in champagne, where "John Walker"[5] had been good enough before. Up went scrip, and Laurence Stanninghame, having judiciously invested his little all, cleared about three hundred pounds in as many days. Things began to look rosy.

By this time, too, Laurence got sick of hanging around the Exchange and talking scrip. He had no turn that way, wherefore now he was glad enough to leave his affairs in the hands of Rainsford, who, being an inhabitant of Johannesburg, was, of course, a broker; and, having picked up a very decent No. 12 bore on one of the open-air sales aforesaid, laid himself out to see what sport was obtainable in the surrounding country. This was not much, but it involved many a hard and long tramp; and the Transvaal atmosphere is brisk and exhilarating, with the result that eye and brain grew clearer, and his condition became as hard as nails. And as there is nothing like a thoroughly healthy condition of body, combined with an equally healthy mental state—in this instance the elation produced by an intensely longed-for measure of success—Laurence began to realise a certain pleasure in living, a sensation to which he had been a stranger for many a long year, and which, assuredly, he had never expected to experience again.

For the market still continued to hum, and, by dint of judicious investments and quick turnings over, Laurence had more than doubled the original amount he had put in. At this rate the moderate wealth to which he aspired would soon be his.

And now, with the ball of success apparently at his feet, so unsatisfying, so ironical are the conditions of life, that he was conscious of a something to damp the anticipatory delights of that success. Those long, solitary tramps over the veldt after scant coveys of partridge, or the stealthy stalk of wild duck at some vlei, were very conducive to introspection. That wealth which he imagined within his grasp did not now look so all-in-all sufficing, and yet he had deemed it the end and all-in-all of life. Even with his past experience,—the depressing, deteriorating effects, mental and physical, of years of poverty in its most squalid and depressing form, "shabby-genteel" poverty,—he realised that even the possession of wealth might leave something to be desired. In fact, he became conscious of an unsatisfied longing, by no means vague, but very real, which came to him at his time of life with a sort of dismayed surprise. He would give up these solitary wanderings in search of sport. The sport was of a poor description, and the intervals between were too long. He had too much time to think. He would knock around the town a little for a change, and talk to fellows.

One morning he was walking down the street with Rainsford and Wheeler,—the latter, who was an upcountry hunter, busy, in pursuit of the prevailing spirit, in trying to trade him sundry pairs of big game horns, and other trophies,—when he heard his name called in a very well-remembered voice. Turning, he beheld Holmes.

"Stanninghame, old chap, I am glad to run against you again!" cried the latter, advancing upon him with outstretched hand.

"I begin to believe you are," answered Laurence genially, with a comical glance at the other's beaming countenance. "Why, you actually have a look that way. When did you get here?"

"By last night's coach. And, I say,"—trying to look wondrously mysterious and knowing,—"who do you think travelled up by it too?"

"I can't even venture the feeblest guess."

"Can't you?" chuckled Holmes. "What about Miss Ormskirk, eh? How's that?"

"So? Now I remember, she did say something about a possibility of coming up here before long," replied Laurence equably, while conscious that the announcement had convulsed his inner being with a strange, sweet thrill. For it came so aptly upon his meditations of late. The one unsatisfied longing—her presence. And now even that was to be fulfilled.

"You don't seem to take it over-enthusiastically, Stanninghame," went on Holmes. "And you and she were rather thick towards the end of the voyage," he added mischievously.

"Did you ever know me enthuse about anything, Holmes? But it's about lunch time; let's go and get some, and you can tell me what you have been doing since we landed from the old *Persian*, and what the deuce has brought you up here."

This was all very friendly and plausible; but before they had been seated many minutes at lunch, in a conveniently adjacent restaurant, Holmes was discoursing singularly little upon his doings spread over the weeks which had elapsed since he had landed, but most volubly upon his recent coach journey, congested within a space of three days—to which topic he was tactfully moved by his audience of one, and also by his own inclination, as will hereinafter appear.

"Was Miss Ormskirk travelling alone, did you say, Holmes?" queried Laurence, in initiation of his deft scheme for 'drawing' the other.

"Not much. There was a big, parchment-faced Johnny with her. He scowled at me like sin when we were introduced—was inclined to be beastly rude in fact, until he saw that I—er—that I—talked most to the other. Then he got quite affable."

"To the other? What other? Out with it, Holmes," said Laurence, with a half smile at his friend's thinly veiled embarrassment.

"Oh, there was another girl in the crowd—Miss Falkner—

deuced pretty girl, too. The sulky chappie was her brother."

"Whose brother? Miss Ormskirk's?" said Laurence innocently.

"No; the blue-eyed one's. At least they both called him George."

"Yes. I remember they came on board the *Persian*. You had landed already, I think. From your description I recognise them. So they are up here? Where are they staying?"

"At that outlying place where the coach first begins to get among houses. I can't remember the name. There's a biggish pub, you know, and a lot of houses."

"Booysens?"[6]

"That was it; Booysens. They asked me to go and see them. You'd better come along too, Stanninghame. I say, d'you think it'd be too soon if we went to-morrow, eh? Sort of excuse to ask if they'd recovered from the journey—eh?"

"Was George so very exhausted, then?"

"Oh, hang your chaff, Stanninghame! What do you think? You're an older chap than I am, and know more about these things. Would it be too soon if we went to-morrow?"

"Be comforted, Holmes. As far as it rests with me, you shall behold your forget-me-not-eyed charmer to-morrow—if she's at home."

The conversation worked round to the inevitable topic, King Scrip. Holmes was fired with eagerness when in his unenthusiastic way the other began to tell of such successes as he had already scored. For he, too, had come up there to take advantage of the boom. He was eager to rush out there and then to buy shares. Nothing would satisfy him but that Laurence must take him round and introduce him to Rainsford on the spot.

But on the way to that worthy's office something happened. Turning into Commissioner Street, they ran right into a party of four. Result—exclamations of astonishment, of recognition, greetings from both sides.

Three of the quartette we have already made the acquaintance of. The fourth, Mrs. Falkner, a good-looking middle-aged lady, was the aunt of the other three, and with her they were staying.

"I've heard of you, Mr. Stanninghame," said this one, when introductions had been effected. "I hope you have made a success

of Johannesburg, so far. Everybody turns up here. I can hardly
come up to the Camp—we used to call it that in the old days—I
was among the first up here, you know, and it's difficult to get
into the way of calling it the town,—I can hardly come up here,
I was saying, without meeting some one or other I had known
elsewhere."

"Yes, it's an astonishing place, Mrs. Falkner," answered
Laurence. "Only bare veldt but a very few years ago, now a population of forty thousand—mostly brokers."

She laughed, and Lilith cut in—

"I thought you were going to adopt the Carlylean definition[7] of
the people of England, Mr. Stanninghame."

"Oh, that'll come in time. I only trust I may not hold on too
long so as to fall under its lash."

"Let us hope none of us will," said Mrs. Falkner. "Oh dear, we
are all dreadfully reckless, I fear. We are nothing but gamblers up
here. Have you caught the contagion too, Mr. Stanninghame?"

"I'm afraid so," he answered, thinking how, even among the
softer sex here, King Scrip bore the principal sway.

He was thinking of something else at the same time. Lilith was
looking even more sweet, more bewitchingly attractive than when
last he had seen her. There was a warm seductive glow of health
in her dark brilliant beauty, a winsomeness in her simple, tasteful
attire—the cool easy-fitting blouse and skirt in a soft harmony of
cream colour and light grey, and the plain, wide-brimmed straw
hat of the "sailor" kind—which made, to his eyes, an irresistibly
entrancing picture.

She, no less than himself, was comparing notes—as two people
will who have been apart for a space, and have thought much of
each other in the interim. He, too, was improved in appearance.
The fine climate, the open-air life, had lent a deeper bronze to his
face and a clearness to his eyes—even as an emancipation from
sordid cares, together with a present modicum of success and a
prospect of further in the future, had imparted a certain stamp
of serenity to his expression which was not there before. "Air,
freedom, life's healthier side are good—success is good—all good
things are good—behold their result," was Lilith's inner verdict as
the summing up of this inspection.

Now George Falkner's efforts at cordiality were about as effective as the demeanour of a crusty mastiff encountering another of his kind well within sweep of his owner's lash. His jealous soul had noted the glance exchanged between his cousin and Laurence Stanninghame—the responsive glance which for a brief second would not be disguised; the great and deep-reaching gladness, which shone in both pairs of eyes as a result of this meeting. He stood gloomy and grim, while the two were talking together, and then rather brusquely—and to the disgust of Holmes, who was discoursing eagerly with pretty Mabel Falkner—he reminded his aunt that they were due to call at So-and-So's, and were far behind their time.

"Ah yes, I was forgetting. Well, good-bye, Mr. Stanninghame. I hope you will come and see us. It is nothing of a walk out to Booysens, and besides, there are several omnibuses in the course of the day. Mind you come too, Mr. Holmes. Good-bye."

And the four resumed their way, and so did our two.

"Jolly, genial old party that Mrs. Falkner," pronounced Holmes, half turning, slily, to sneak a last glance after the blue-eyed and receding Mabel.

"Spare my susceptibilities, Holmes, even in your exuberance. That 'old party,' as you so unfeelingly define her, cannot own to more than two or three years' seniority over my respectable self—four at the outside," said Laurence maliciously.

"Oh, go along with you, old chap," retorted Holmes, yet conscious of feeling just a trifle foolish. "But, I say," eagerly, "can we still go and look them up so soon as to-morrow, eh?"

"Don't let that misgiving interfere with your beauty sleep, Holmes," was the reply, dashed with a touch of good-humoured impatience. "People are not so beastly ceremonious over here."

"I've brought you another sheep to shear, Rainsford," said Laurence, as they entered the broker's office. "Don't clip him any closer than you did me, though he's dying to set up as a millionaire on the spot."

And then, having effected this introduction, he left the pair to do business or not, as the case might be, and strolled back to his own quarters.

What was this marvellous metamorphosis which had come upon him, flooding his life with golden waves of sweetness and of light? Now that he had beheld Lilith once more, he realised what entire hold she had taken of his thoughts since they two had parted on the deck of the *Persian*. It was a certainty there was no getting away from—but a certainty now which he was not in the least desirous of getting away from. He had beheld her once more. Their meeting had been of the briefest, their interchange of remarks of the most commonplace, everyday nature. Yet he had beheld her, had listened to the sound of her voice, had looked into her eyes. And the glance of those sweet eyes had been responsive; and his ear could detect a subtle note in the tones of her voice. Sweet Lilith! the spells she had begun to wreathe around him, so unconsciously to herself, so unconsciously to him, when first they talked together, were drawn, woven, more thoroughly now. And in his strange, new revivification—the return of strength and health and spirits—he rejoiced that it was so, and laughed, and defied circumstances, and Fate and the Future.

CHAPTER VI

"PIRATE" HAZON

If the population of Johannesburg devoted its days to doing *konza* to King Scrip, it devoted its nights to amusing itself. There was an enterprising theatrical company and a lively circus. There was a menagerie, where an exceedingly fine young woman was wont nightly to place her head within a lion's mouth for the delectation, and to the enthusiastic admiration, of Judæa and all the region round about.[1] There were smoking-concerts galore—more or less good of their kind; and, failing sporadic forms of pastime, there were numerous bars—and barmaids. All of which counted for something in the relaxation of the forty thousand inhabitants of Johannesburg—mostly brokers. We are forgetting. There were other phases of nocturnal excitement, more or less of a stimulating nature—frequent rows, to wit, culminating in a nasty rough-and-tumble, and now and then a startling and barbarous murder.

Now, to Laurence Stanninghame not any of the above forms of diversion held out the slightest possible attractiveness. The theatrical show struck him as third-rate, and, as for circuses and menageries, he supposed they had been good fun when he was a child. He did not care twopence about the pleasures of the bar unless he wanted a drink, and for barmaids and their allurements less than nothing. So having already, with Rainsford or Wheeler, and seven other spirits more wicked than themselves, gone the round three or four times, just to see what there was to be seen, and found that not much, he had subsided into a good bit of a stay-at-home. A pipe, a newspaper or book, and bed, would be his evening programme—normally, that is—for now and then he would stroll out to Booysens. But of that more anon.

The hotel at which he had taken up his quarters was rather a quiet one, and frequented by quiet people. One set of rooms, among which was his, opened upon a *stoep*,[2] which fronted a yard, which opened upon the street. Here of an evening he would drag a chair out upon the *stoep* and smoke and read, or occasionally chat with some fellow-sojourner in the house.

One evening he was seated thus alone. Holmes, who had taken up his quarters at the same hotel, was out, as usual. We say as usual, because Holmes seldom stayed in at night. Holmes was young, and for him the "attractions" we have striven to enumerate above, and others which we have not, were attractions. He liked to go the round. He liked to see all there was to be seen. Well, he saw it.

One evening Laurence, seated thus alone, became aware that another man was dragging a chair out upon the *stoep*, intending, like himself, to take the air. Looking up, he saw that it was the man to whom nobody ever seemed to talk, beyond exchanging the time of day, and that in the most curt and perfunctory fashion. He had noticed, further, that this individual seemed no more anxious to converse with other people than they were to converse with him. He himself had never got beyond this stage with him, although on easy and friendly terms with the other people staying in the house.

Yet the man had awakened in him a strange interest, a curiosity that was almost acute; but beyond the fact that his name was Hazon, and the darkly-veiled hints on the part of those who alluded to the subject, that he was a ruffian of the deepest dye,

Laurence could learn nothing about him. He noted, however, that if the man seemed disliked, he seemed about equally feared.

This Hazon was, in truth, somewhat of a remarkable individual. He was of powerful build, standing about five feet nine. He had a strong, good-looking face, the lower part hidden in a dark beard, and his eyes were black, piercing, and rather deep set. The bronze hue of his complexion, and of the sinewy hands, seemed to tell of a life of hardness and adventure; and the square jaw and straight, piercing glance was that of a man who, when roused, would prove a resolute, relentless, and most dangerous enemy. In repose the face wore a placidity which was almost that of melancholy.

In trying to estimate his years, Laurence owned himself puzzled again and again. He might be about his own age or he might be a great deal older, that is, anything from forty to sixty. But whatever his age, whatever his past, the man was always the same—dark, self-possessed, coldly reticent, inscrutable, somewhat of an awe-inspiring personality.

The nature of his business, too, was no more open than was his past history. He had been some months in his present quarters, yet was not known to be doing anything in scrip to any appreciable extent. The boom, the one engrossing idea in the minds of all alike, seemed to hold no fascination for Hazon. To him it was a matter of absolutely no importance. What the deuce, then, was he there for? His impenetrable reserve, his out-of-the-common and striking personality, his rather sinister expression, had earned for him a nick-name. He was known all over the Rand as "Pirate" Hazon, or more commonly "The Pirate," because, declared the Rand, he looked like one, and at anyrate ought to be hanged for one, to make sure.

Nobody, however, cared to use the epithet within his hearing. People were afraid of him. One day in the street a tough, swaggering bully, fearless in the consciousness of his powers as a first-class boxer, lurched up against him, deliberately, and with offensive intent. Those who witnessed the act stood by for the phase of excitement dearest of all to their hearts, a row. There was that in Hazon's look which told they were not to be disappointed.

"English manners?" he queried, in cutting, contemptuous tone.

"I'll teach you some," rejoined the fellow promptly. And

without more ado he dashed out a terrific lefthander, which the other just escaped receiving full in the eye but not entirely as to the cheekbone.

Hazon did not hit back, but what followed amazed even the bystanders. It was like the spring of an animal—of a leopard or a bull-dog—combining the lightning swiftness of the one with the grim, fell ferocity of purpose of the other. The powerful rowdy was lying on his back in the red dust, swinging flail-like blows into empty air, and upon him, in leopard-like crouch, pressing him to the earth, the man whom he had so wantonly attacked. And his throat was compressed in those brown, lean, muscular fingers, as in a claw of steel. It was horrible. His eyes were starting from his head; his face grew blue, then black; his swollen tongue protruded hideously. His struggles were terrific, yet, powerful of frame as he was, he seemed like a child in the grasp of a panther.

A shout of dismay, of warning, broke from the spectators, some of whom sprang forward to separate the pair. But there was something so awful in the expression of Hazon's countenance, in the glare of the coal-black eyes, in the drawn-in brows and livid horror of fiendish wrath, that even they stopped short. It was, as they said afterwards, as though they had looked into the blasting countenance of a devil.

"Leave go!" they cried. "For God's sake, leave go! You're killing the man. He'll be dead in a second longer."

Hazon relaxed his grasp, and stood upright. Beyond a slight heaving of the chest attendant upon his exertion, he seemed as cool and collected as though nothing had happened.

"I believe you're right," he said, turning away. "Well, he isn't that yet."

The attention of the onlookers was concentrated on the prostrate bully, to restore whom a doctor was promptly sent for from the most likely bar, for it was mid-day. But all were constrained to allow that the fellow had only got what he deserved, which consensus of opinion may or may not have been due to the fact that he was, if anything, a trifle more unpopular than Hazon himself.

Now among those who had witnessed this scene from first to last was Laurence Stanninghame. Not among those who would have interfered—oh no—for did he not hold it a primary tenet never on any pretext, to interfere in what did not concern him? nor did this principle in those days involve any effort to keep, all impulse to violate it being long since dead. Moreover, if the last held good of the badly damaged bully, society at large could not but be the gainer, since it was clear that he was a fit representative of a class which is utterly destitute of any redeeming point which should go to justify its unspeakably vicious, useless, and rather dangerous existence.

This incident, while enhancing the respect in which Hazon was held, in no sense tended to lessen his unpopularity, and indeed at that time nobody had a good word to say for him. Either they said nothing, and looked the more, or they said a word that was not good—oh no, not good.

Now in spite of all such ill repute, possibly by reason of it, his temperament being what it was, Laurence felt drawn towards this mysterious personage, for he was pre-eminently one given to forming his own judgment instead of accepting it ready made from Dick, Tom, and Harry. If Hazon was vindictive, why, so was he; if unscrupulous, so could he be if driven to it. He resolved to find an opportunity of cultivating the man, and if he could not find one he would make it. Now he saw such an opportunity.

"What do you think of this rumour that the revolution in Brazil is going to knock out our share market?" he said, suddenly looking up from the paper he was reading.

"It may do that," answered Hazon. "This year's boom has been a mere sick attempt at one. Wouldn't take much to knock out what little there is of it."

Laurence felt a cold qualm. There had been an ominous drop the last day or two. Still Rainsford and one or two others had recommended him to hold on. This man spoke so quietly, yet withal so prophetically. What if he, in his inscrutable way, were more than ordinarily in the know?

"Queer place this," pursued Hazon, the other having uttered a dubious affirmative. "Taking it all round, it and its crowd, it's not far from the queerest place I've ever seen in my life, and I've seen some queer places and some queerish crowds."

"I expect you have. By the way, I suppose you've done a good deal of up-country hunting?"

"A goodish deal. Are you fond of the gun? I notice you go out pretty often, but there's nothing to shoot around here."

"I just am fond of it," replied Laurence. "If things turn out all right I shall cut in with some fellow for an up-country trip if I can. Big game this time."

The other smiled darkly, enigmatically.

"Yes. That's real—real," he said. "Try some of this," handing his tobacco bag, as Laurence began to scratch out his empty pipe, "unless, that is, you haven't got over the new-comer's prejudice against the best tobacco in the world, the name whereof is Transvaal."

"Thanks. No, I have no prejudice against it. On the contrary, as to its merits I am disposed to agree with you."

Throughout this conversation Laurence, who had a keen ear for that sort of thing, could not help noticing the other's voice. It was a pleasing voice, a cultured voice, and refined withal, nor could his fastidious ear detect the faintest trace of provincialism or vulgarity about it. The intonation was perfect. There is nothing so quick to betray to the sensitive ear any strain of plebeian descent as the voice, and of this no one was more thoroughly aware than Laurence Stanninghame. This man, he decided, was of good birth.

The ice broken they talked on, in the apparently careless, but in reality guarded way which had become second nature to both of them. More than one strange and very shady anecdote was Hazon able to narrate concerning the place and its inhabitants and especially concerning certain among the latter who ranked high for morality, commercially or otherwise. There were actions done in their midst every day, he declared, which, for barefaced and unscrupulous rascality, would put to the blush other actions for which the law would hang a man without mercy, all other men applauding. But with this difference, that whereas the former demanded a creeping and crawling cowardliness to ensure success, the latter involved iron nerve and the well-nigh daily shaking hands with death—death, too, in many an appalling and ghastly form. All of which was "dark" talking so far as Laurence was concerned, though the day was to come when its meaning should stand forth as clear as a printed page.

Even now, however, he was not absolutely mystified—far from it, indeed; for he himself was a hard thinker, owning an ever-vivid and busy brain. He could put half a dozen meanings to any one or other of his companion's utterances, and among them probably the right one. And, as they talked on, he became alive to something almost magnetic—a sort of subtle, compelling force about Hazon. Was it his voice or manner or general aspect, or a combination of all three? He could not tell. He could only realise that it existed.

For some days after this conversation the two men did not come together, though they would nod the time of day to each other as before, and Laurence, who had other considerations upon his hands—monetary and agreeable—did not give the matter a thought. At last he noticed that Hazon's place at the table was vacant—remembering, too, that it had been so for a day or two. Had he left?

To his inquiries on that head he obtained scant and uncordial response. Hazon was ill, some believed, while others charitably opined that he was "on the booze." Whatever it was no one cared, and strongly recommended Laurence to do likewise.

The latter, we have shown, was peculiarly unsusceptible to public opinion, which, if it influenced him at all, did so in the very opposite direction to that which was intended. Accordingly, he now made up his mind to ascertain the truth for himself—to which end he found himself speedily knocking at the door of Hazon's room, the while marvelling at his own unwonted perturbation lest his overture should be regarded as an intrusion.

"Heard you were ill," he said shortly, having entered in obedience to the responsive "Come in." "Rough luck being ill in a place like this, or indeed in any place, for that matter. Thought I'd see if there's anything I could do for you?"

"Very good of you, Stanninghame. Sit down there on that box—it's lower than the chair, and therefore more comfortable. Yes, I feel a bit knocked out. A touch of the old up-country shivers, or something of the kind. It's a thing you never entirely pull round from, once you've had it. I'll be all right, though, in a day or two."

The speaker was lying on his bed, clad in his trousers and

shirt. The latter, open from the throat, revealed part of a great livid scar, running diagonally across the swarthy chest, and representing what must have been a terrific slash. Two other scars also showed on the muscular fore-arm, halfway between elbow and wrist. What was it to Laurence whether this person or that person lived or died? Why, nothing. Yet there was something so pathetic, so helpless, in the aspect of the man, lying there day after day, patient, solitary, uncomplaining—shunned and avoided by those around—that appealed powerfully to his feelings. Heavens! was he turning softhearted at his time of life, that he should feel so unaccountably stirred by the bare act of coming to visit this ailing and unbefriended stranger?

In truth, there was nothing awe-inspiring about the latter now. His piercing, black eyes seemed large and soft; the expression of his dark face was one of weariful helplessness, yet of schooled patience. A queer thought flashed through Laurence's brain. Was it in Hazon's power to produce whatever effect he chose upon the minds of others? Had he chosen, for some inscrutable purpose, to render himself shunned and feared? Was he now, on like principle, adopting the surest means to win over to him this one man who had sought him out on his lonely sick-bed? And if so, to what end? It was more than a passing thought, nor from that moment onward could Laurence ever get it entirely out of his mind.

"Fill your pipe, Stanninghame," said Hazon, breaking into this train of thought, which, all unconsciously, had entailed a long gap of silence. "I don't in the least mind smoke, although I can't blow off a cloud myself just now—at least I have no inclination that way," he added, reaching for a bottle of white powder which stood upon a box by the bedside, and mixing himself a modicum of quinine.[3]

"Had a doctor of any sort, Hazon?"

"What good would that do—except to the doctor? I know what's the matter with me, and I know exactly what to do for it. I don't want to pay another fellow a couple of guineas or so to tell me. Not but what doctors have their uses—in wounds and surgery, for instance. But I'm curiously like an animal. When I get anything the matter with me—which I don't often—I like to creep away and lie low. I like to take it alone."

"Well, I'm built rather that way myself, Hazon. I won't apologise for intruding, because you know as well as I do that no such consideration enters into the matter. Still, I want you to know that if there's anything I can do for you, you have only to say so."

"Thanks. You're not quite like—other people, Stanninghame. Life is no great thing, is it, that everybody should stir up such a mighty fuss about clearing out of it?"

"No, it's no great thing," assented Laurence darkly. "Yet it might be made so."

"How that?"

"With wealth. With wealth you can do anything—command anything—buy anything. They say that wealth won't purchase life, but very often it will."

"You're about three parts right. It will, for instance, enable a man to lead the life he needs in order to preserve his physical and mental vigour at its highest. Even from the moralist's point of view it is all round desirable, for nothing is so morally deteriorating as a life of narrow and cramped pinching, when all one's best years are spent in hungering and longing for what one will never again attain."

"You speak like a book, Hazon," said Laurence, not wondering that the other should have sized up his own case so exhaustively—not wondering, because he was an observer of human nature and a character-reader himself. Then, bitterly, "Yet that pumpkin-pated entity, the ponderous moralist, would contend that the lack of all that made life worth living was good as a stimulus to urge to exertion, and all the hollow old clap-trap."

"Quite so. But how many attain to the reward—the end of the said exertion? Not one in a hundred. And then, in nine cases out of ten, how does that one do it? By fraud and thieving and over-reaching and sycophancy—in short, by running through the whole gamut of the scale of rascality—rascality of the meaner kind, mark you. Then when this winner in the battle of life comes out top, the world crowns him with fat and fulsome eulogy, and falls down and worships his cheque-book, crying, 'Behold a self-made man; go thou and do likewise!'"

"You've not merely hit the right nail on the head, Hazon, but you've driven it right home," said Laurence decisively, recognising that here was a man after his own heart.

Two or three days went by before Hazon felt able or inclined to leave his bed, and a good part of each was spent by Laurence sitting in the sick man's room and talking. And it may have been that the lonely man felt cheered by the companionship and the friendliness that proffered it, what time all others held aloof; or that the two were akin in ideas, or both; but henceforward a sort of intimacy struck up between them, and it was noticed that Hazon no longer went about invariably alone. Then people began to look somewhat queerly at Laurence.

"You and 'the Pirate' have become quite thick together, Stanninghame," said Rainsford one day, meeting him alone.

"Well, why not?" answered Laurence, rather shortly, resenting the inquisitorial nature of the question. Then, point blank, "See here, Rainsford. Why are you all so down on the man? What has he done, anyway?"

"You needn't get your shirt out, old chap," was the answer, made quite good-humouredly. "Look here, now—we are alone together—so just between ourselves. Do you notice how all of these up-country going fellows shunt him—Wheeler, for instance? and Garway, who is at your hotel, never speaks to him. And Garway, you'll admit, is as good a fellow as ever lived."

"Yes, I'll own up to that. What then?"

"Only this, that they know a good deal that we don't."

"Well, what do they know—or say they know?"

"Look here, Stanninghame," said Rainsford, rather mysteriously. "Has Hazon ever told you any of his up-country experiences?"

"A few—yes."

"Did he ever suggest you should take a trip with him?"

"We have even discussed that possibility."

"Ah——!" Then Rainsford gave a long whistle, and his voice became impressive as he resumed. "Watch it, Stanninghame. From time to time other men have gone up country with Hazon, but—*not one of them has ever returned.*"

"Oh, that's what you're all down on him about, is it?"

The other nodded; then, with a "so-long," he cut across the street and disappeared into an office where he had business.

CHAPTER VII

"THE WHOLE SOUL PRISONER . . ."

No more foolish passion was ever implanted in the human breast than that of jealousy—unless it were that of which it is the direct outcome—nor is there any which the average human is less potent to resist. The victim of either, or both, is, for the time being, outside reason.

Now the first-mentioned form of disease is, to the philosophical mind, of all others the most essentially foolish—indeed, we can hardly call to mind any other so thoroughly calculated to turn the average well-constructed man or woman into an exuberantly incurable idiot. For what does it amount to when we come to pan it out? If there exist grounds for the misgiving, why then it is going begging—grovelling for something which the other party has not got to give; if groundless, is it not a fulfilling of the homely old saw relating to cutting off one's nose to spite one's face? (we disclaim any intent to pun).[1] In either case it is such a full and whole-souled giving of himself, or herself, away on the part of the patient; while on that of its object—is he, or she, worth it?

Now, from a very acute form of this insanity George Falkner was a chronic sufferer. He had cherished a secret weakness for Lilith, almost when she was yet in short frocks, but since her return from England, from the moment he had once more set eyes upon her on the deck of the *Persian*, he had tumbled madly, uncontrollably, headlong in love. Did a member of the opposite sex so much as exchange commonplaces with her, George Falkner's personality would contrive to loom, grim and dark, and almost threatening, in the background; while such male animal who should enjoy the pleasure of say an hour of Lilith's society *à deux*, even with no more flirtatious or ultimate intent than the same period spent in the society of his grandmother, would inspire in George a fell murderousness, which was nothing short of a reversion to first principles. As for Lilith herself, she was fond of him, very, in a sisterly, cousinly way—and what way, indeed, could be more fatal to that by which he desired to travel? Nor did it mend matters any that their mutual relatives were the reverse of favourable to his aspirations, on the ground of the near relationship existing between the parties. So, poor George, seeing no light, became morose and quarrelsome, and wholly and violently unreasonable—in short, a bore. All of which was a pity, because, this weakness apart, he was, on the whole, rather a good fellow.

He had come to the Rand, like everybody else, to wait for the "boom"—which "boom," like the chariots of Israel,[2] though totally unlike the children of the same, tarried long in coming; indeed, by that time there were not wanting those who feared that it might not come at all. He had pleaded with his aunt to invite Lilith at the same time, artfully putting it that the opportunity of his escort was too good to be missed; and Mrs. Falkner, with whom he was a prime favourite, although she did not approve his aspirations, weakly agreed. And so here they were beneath the same roof, with the addition of his second sister, the blue-eyed Mabel, whose acquaintance we have already made.

The latter, in her soft, fair-haired, pink and roses style, was a very pretty girl. She, for her part, could count "coup" to a creditable extent, and among the latest scalps which she had hung to her dainty twenty-inch girdle was that of our friend Holmes.

This—idiot, we were going to say, looked back upon that deadly monotonous, starved, dusty, flea-bitten coach-ride of three days and two nights as a species of Elysium, and in the result was perennially importuning Laurence to take a stroll down to Booysens, "just for a constitutional, you know." And the latter would laugh, and good-naturedly acquiesce. It was a cheap way of setting up a character for amiability, he would say to himself satirically; for as yet Holmes hardly suspected he was almost as powerfully drawn thither as Holmes was himself—more powerfully, perhaps—only, with the advantage of years and experience and cooler brain, he had himself more in hand.

"Instead of making a prize gooseberry of me, Holmes, as a very appropriate item against the 'silly' season," he said one day, "you had much better go over by yourself. You are getting into Falkner's black books. He hates me like poison, you know."

"But that's just why I want you along, Stanninghame. While

he's trying to stand you off in the other quarter, I'm in it, don't you see?" replied the other, with whole-hearted ingenuousness.

Holmes had stated no more than the truth. Of all the "rivals," real or imaginary, whom the jealous George hated and, feared, *quâ* rival, none could touch Laurence Stanninghame. For by this time it had become patent to his watchful eyes that among the swarms of visitors of the male, and therefore to him, obnoxious sex, at whose coming Lilith's glance would brighten, and with whom she would converse with a kind of affectionate confidentiality when others were present, and, apparently, even more so when others were not, that objectionable personage was the said Laurence Stanninghame.

This being the case, it followed that George Falkner, looking out on the *stoep* one fine afternoon, and descrying the approach of his bugbear, stifled a bad cuss-word or two, and then exploded aloud in more approved and passworthy fashion.

"There's that bounder coming here again."

"'Bounder' being Dutch for somebody you detest—eh, George?" said Lilith sweetly.

"Confound it! That everlasting trying to be sharp is one of the most deadly things a man has to put up with. It's catching—eh, Lilith?" was the sneering retort.

"But who is it?" said Mrs. Falkner, who was shortsighted, or affected to be.

"Oh, the great god, Stanninghame, of course, and his pup, Holmes."

Now the ill-conditioned George had stirred up a hornet's nest, for his sister took up the parable.

"Well, there are lessons to be learned even from 'pups,'" said Mabel scathingly. "They are not *always* growling, at anyrate."

"Oh, you're on the would-be smart lay, too? Didn't I say it was catching?" he jeered.

"Yes, and you say a great many things that are supremely foolish," retorted Mabel, turning up her tip-tilted nose a little more, in fine scorn.

"Well, I'm off to the Camp," said George, with a sort of snarl, reaching for a hat. "Clearly, I'm not wanted here."

"You're not, if you're going to do nothing but make yourself fiendishly disagreeable," rejoined his sister, pertly pitiless. In reality she was very fond of him, and he of her, but he had trampled on a tender place. For she liked Holmes.

George banged on his hat, strode angrily to the door, and—got no farther. He did not see why he should leave the field clear to all comers, even if he were out of the running himself; a line of irreso-luteness which affords an excellent exemplification of the remarks wherewith we have opened this chapter.

By all but George, who was excusably undemonstrative, the two new arrivals were greeted with customary cordiality.

"Why, Mr. Stanninghame, it seems quite a long time since we saw you last," said Mrs. Falkner, as they were all seated out on the *stoep*. "What have you been doing with yourself?"

"The usual thing—studying the share market, and—talking about it."

"And is the outlook still as bad as it was?"

"Worse. However, we must hope it'll go better."

"I hear that you and that queer man, Mr. Hazon, have become such friends, Mr. Stanninghame."

This was the sort of remark with which Laurence had scant patience, the more so that it met him at every turn. What concern was it of the Rand collectively who he chose to be friendly with, that every third person he met should rap out such kind of comment?

"Oh, we get along all right, Mrs. Falkner," he answered. "But then I have a special faculty for hitting it off with unpopu-lar persons—possibly a kind of fellow-feeling. Besides, accept-ing ready-made judgments concerning other people does not commend itself to my mind on any score of logic or sound sense. It is just a trifle less insane than taking up other people's quarrels, but only just."

"I daresay you're right; only it is difficult for most of us to be so consistently, so faultlessly logical. No doubt most of the things they say about him are not true."

"But what are most of the things they say, Mrs. Falkner? Now I, for my part, never can get anybody to say anything. They will hint unutterables and look unutterables, but when it comes to *saying*— no, thank you, they are not taking any."

"But he is such a very mysterious personage. Not a soul here knows anything about him—about his affairs, I mean—and who he is."

"Perhaps that enhances his attractiveness in my eyes, Mrs. Falkner. There is prestige in the unknown."

"Not of a good kind, as a rule," she replied, and then stopped short, for a dry malicious cough on the part of George brought home to her the consciousness that she was putting her foot in it pretty effectively. For the same held good of the man to whom she was talking. About Laurence Stanninghame and his affairs not a soul there knew anything.

Not a soul? Yes one, peradventure. For between himself and Lilith the interchange of ideas had been plenteous and frequent, and the subtle, sympathetic vein existing between them had deepened and grown apace. About himself and his affairs he had *told* her nothing, yet it is probable that he could tell her but little on this head that would be news in any sense of the word. Lilith's aunt, however, who was a good-hearted soul, without a grain of malice in her composition, felt supremely uncomfortable and quite savage with George, who was now grinning, sourly and significantly.

None of this byplay was lost upon Laurence, but he showed no consciousness. He knew that George Falkner detested him—detested him cordially, yet he in no wise reciprocated this dislike. He did not blame George. Probably he would have felt the same way himself, had he been in George's place and at George's age; for the latter had the advantage of him on the side of youth by at least ten years. He was inclined to like him, and at anyrate was sorry for him, perhaps with a dash of pity that came near contempt. Poor George did give himself away so, and it was so foolish—so supremely foolish. Yet not for a moment did it occur to Laurence to efface himself in this connection. Duty? Hang duty! He had made a most ruinous muddle of his whole life through reverencing that fetish word. Honour? There was no breach of honour where there was no deception, no pretence. Consideration for others? Who on earth ever dreamt of considering him—when to do so would cost them anything, that is? Unselfishness? Everybody was selfish—every*thing* even. What had he ever gained by striving to improve upon the universal law? Nothing. Nothing good. Everything bad—bad and deteriorating—morally and physically.

And now, should he put the goblet from his lips? Not he. This strong, new wine of life had rejuvenated him. Its rich, sweet fumes, so far from clouding his brain, had cleared it. It had enwrapped his heart in a glow as of re-enkindled fire, and caused the stagnated blood to course once more through his veins, warm and strong and free. His very step had gained an elasticity, a firmness, to which it had long been strange. And yet with all this, his judgment had remained undimmed, keen, clear, subject to no illusions. The logic of the situation was rather pitiless, perchance cruel. He was under no sort of illusion on that score. Well, let it be. Here again came in the universal law of life, the battle to the strong. There was no weakness left in him.

"For my part, I like Hazon," cut in Holmes decisively. "He only wants knowing. And because he doesn't let himself go for the benefit of every bounder on the Rand, they talk about him as if he'd committed no end of murders. It's my belief that half the fellows who abuse him are ten thousand times worse than him," he added, with the robust partisanship of hearty youth.

Further discussion of Hazon and his derelictions, real or imaginary, was cut short by the arrival of more visitors, mostly of the sterner sex; for Mrs. Falkner liked her acquaintance to drop in informally—a predilection her acquaintance, if young and especially of the harder sex aforesaid, for obvious reasons, delighted just at present to humour. George, however, in no wise shared his aunt's expansiveness in this direction, if only that it meant that Lilith was promptly surrounded by an adoring phalanx, even as on the deck of the *Persian*.

Now it was voted cool enough for lawn tennis—for which distraction, indeed, some of the droppers-in were suitably attired— and there was keen competition for Lilith as a partner; and Holmes, being first in the field, resolutely bore off Mabel Falkner as his auxiliary. And George, realising that he was "out of it" for some time to come; perhaps too, taking vague comfort in the thought that there is safety in numbers, actually did proceed to carry out his threat, and betook himself townwards.

Laurence remained seated on the *stoep*, talking to Mrs. Falkner and one of the visitors; but all the while, though never absent-minded or answering at random, his eyes were following, with a soothing and restful sense of enjoyment, every movement of Lilith's form—a very embodiment of grace and supple ease, he pronounced it. The movement of the game suited her as it suited but few. She never seemed to grow hot, or flurried, or dishevelled, as so many of the fair are wont to do while engaged in that popular pastime. Every movement was one of unstudied, unconscious grace. In point of hard fact, she played indifferently; but she did so in a manner that was infinitely good to look at.

"Don't you play at this, Mr. Stanninghame?" said the other visitor, "or have you got a soul above such frivolities?"

"That doesn't exactly express it," he answered. "The truth is, I don't derive sufficient enjoyment from skipping about on one or both legs at the end of a racket, making frantic attempts to stop a ball which the other side is making equally frantic and fruitless efforts to drive at me through a net. As a dispassionate observer, the essence of the game seems to me to consist in sending the ball against the net as hard and as frequently as practicable."

At this the visitor spluttered, and, being of the softer sex, declared that he must be a most dreadful cynic; and Lilith, who was near enough to hear his remarks, turned her head, with a rippling flash of mirth in her eyes, and said "Thank you!" which diversion indeed caused her to perform the very feat he had just been so whimsically describing.

Presently, growing tired of talking, he withdrew from the others. It happened that there was a book in the drawing-room which had caught his attention during a former visit; and now he sought it, and, taking it up from the table, stood there alone in the cool, shaded room turning from page to page, absorbed in comparing passages of its contents. Then a light step, a rustle of skirts, a lilt of song—which broke off short as he raised his eyes. Lilith was passing through, her tennis racket still in her hand. Slightly flushed with her recent exercise, she looked radiantly sweet, in her dark, brilliant beauty.

"Oh, I didn't know anyone was here; least of all, you," she said. "You startled me."

"Sorceress, remove those unholy spells; for thou art indeed good to look upon this day."

She flashed a smile at him, throwing back her head with that slight, quick movement which constituted in her a very subtle and potent charm.

"Flatterer! Do you think so? Well, I am glad."

She dropped her hand down upon his, as it rested on the table, with a swift, light, caressing pressure, and her eyes softened entrancingly as they looked up into his. Then she was gone.

He stood there, cool, immovable, self-possessed, outwardly to all appearance still intent upon the book which he held. But in reality he saw it not. All his mental faculties were called into play to endeavour in imagination to retain that soft, light pressure upon his hand. His resources of memory were concentrated upon the picture of her as she stood there a moment since—lovely, smiling, enchanting—and then the sombre brain-wave, reminding of the hopelessness, the mockery of life's inexorable circumstance, would roll in upon his mind; and his heart would seem tightened, crushed, strangled with a pain that was actually physical—of such acuteness indeed, that, had that organ been weak, he would be in danger of falling dead on the spot. And this was a part of the penalty he had to pay for his well-nigh superhuman self-control.

He loved her—this man who loved nothing and nobody living, not even himself. He loved her—this man whose life was all behind him, and whose heart was of stone, and whose speech was acrid as the most corrosive element known to chemistry. But a few "passes" of sweet sorceress Lilith's magical wand and the stone heart had split to fragments, pouring forth, giving release to, a warm well-spring. A well-spring? A very torrent, deep, fierce, strong, but not irresistible—as yet. Still there were moments when, to keep it penned within its limits was agony—agony untold, superhuman, well-nigh unendurable.

He loved her—he who was bound by legal ties until death. With all the strong concentrative might of his otherwise hard nature, he loved her. The dead dismal failure of the past, the sombre vistas of the future, were as nothing compared with such moments as this. Yet none suspected, so marvellously did he hold himself in hand. Even the most jealous of those who saw them frequently together—George Falkner, for instance, and others—were blind and unsuspecting. But—what of Lilith herself?

CHAPTER VIII

FOR GOOD OR FOR ILL?

THE share market at Johannesburg was rapidly going to the deuce.

Some there were who ardently wished that Johannesburg itself had gone thither, before they had heard of its unlucky and delusive existence, and among this daily increasing number might now be reckoned Laurence Stanninghame. He, infected with the gambler's fever of speculation, had not thought it worth while to "hedge." It was to be all or nothing. And now, as things turned out, it was nothing. The old story—a fictitious market, bolstered up by fictitious and inflated prices; a sudden "slump," and then—everybody with one mind eager to dispose of scrip, barely worth the paper of which it consisted—in fact, unsaleable. King Scrip had landed his devoted subjects in a pretty hole.

"You're not the only one, Stanninghame—no, not by a long, long chalk," said Rainsford ruefully, as they were talking matters over one day. "I'm hard hit myself, and I could point you out men here who were worth tens of thousands a month ago, and couldn't muster a hard hundred cash at this moment if their lives depended on it. Worse, too, men whose overdraft is nearly as big as their capital was the same time back."

"I suppose so. Yet most fellows of that kind are adepts at the fine old business quality of besting their neighbours, one in which I am totally lacking, possibly owing to want of practice. They can go smash and come up smiling, and in a little while be worth more than ever. They know how to do it, you see, and I don't. Smash for me means smash, and that of a signally grievous kind."

Rainsford looked at him curiously.

"Oh, bother it, Stanninghame, you're no worse off than the rest of us. We've got to lie low and hang on for a bit, and watch our chances."

"Possibly you are right, Rainsford. No doubt you are. Still every donkey knows where his own saddle galls him."

"Rather, old chap," replied the other, whose hat covered the total of his liability. "The only thing to do is to hold on tight, have a drink, and trust in Providence. We'll go and have the drink."

They adjourned to a convenient bar. It was about noon, and the place was fairly full. Here they found Holmes in the middle of a crowd, also Rankin and Wheeler. The consumption of "John Walker" was proceeding at a brisk rate.

"Hallo, Stanninghame, how are you?" cried Rankin.

"Haven't seen you for a long time. I think another 'smile' wouldn't hurt us, eh? What do you say? I'm doing bitters. Nothing like Angostura—with a little drop of gin in it. Gives tone to the system. What's yours?"

Laurence named his, and the genial Rankin having shouted for it and other "rounds," proceeded to unfold some wondrous scheme by which he was infallibly bound to retrieve all their fortunes at least cent. per cent.[1] It was only a matter of a little capital. Anyone who had the foresight to entrust him with a few hundreds might consider his fortune made. But, somehow,—nobody could be found to hand over those few hundreds. In point of fact, nobody had got them.

"Here, Rainsford," sung out somebody, "we are tossing for another 'all round.' Won't your friend cut in?"

Laurence did cut in, and then Holmes, who, being of genial disposition, and very hard hit too in the scrip line, began uproariously to suggest a further "drown care."

"Excuse me, eh, Holmes?" said Laurence. "It's getting too thick, and I don't think this is a sort of care that'll bear drowning. I'm off. So long, everybody."

"Hold on, Stanninghame," sung out Rankin, who was the most hospitable soul alive. "Come round to the house and dine with us. I'm just going along. We'd better do another bitters though, first. What do you say?"

But Laurence declined both hospitalities. A very dark mood was upon him—one which rendered the idea of the society of his fellows distasteful to the last degree. So he left the carousing crowd, and betook himself to his quarters.

Now the method of drowning care as thus practised commended itself to him on no principle of practical efficacy. He had care enough to drown, Heaven knew! but against any temptation to fly to the bottle in order to swamp it he was proof. His very cynicism, selfish, egotistical as it might be in its hard and sweeping ruthlessness, was a safeguard to him in this connection. That he, Laurence Stanninghame, to whom the vast bulk of mankind represented a commingling of rogue and fool in about equal proportion, should ever come to render himself unsteady on his feet, and hardly responsible for the words which came from his brain, presented a picture so unutterably degraded and loathsome, that his mind recoiled from the barest contemplation of it.

Yes, he had care enough, in all conscience, that day as he walked back to his quarters; for unless the market took a turn for the better, so sudden as to be almost miraculous, the time when he would any longer have a roof over his head might be counted by weeks. And now every mail brought him grumbling, querulous letters asking for money when there was none to send—bitter and contentious letters, full of complaint and the raking up of old sores and soul-wearying lamentation; gibing reproaches, too, to him who had beggared himself that these might live. It would have been burden enough had it mattered greatly to him whether any one in the world lived or not; but here the burden was tenfold by reason of its utter lack of appreciation, of common gratitude, of consideration for the shoulders which, sorely weighed-down and chafed, yet still supported it.

But if the refuge which is the resort of the weak held out no temptation to him, there was another refuge of which the exact opposite held good. In weird and gloomy form all the recollections and failures of his past life would rise up and confront him. What an unutterable hash he had made of it and its opportunities! It did not do to run straight—the world was not good enough for it; so he had found. That for the past. For the future—what? Nothing. For some there was no future, and he was one of these. He saw no light.

Lying on his bed, in the heat of the early afternoon, he realised all this for the hundredth time. The temptation to end it all was strong upon him. Stronger and stronger it grew, as though shadowy demon-shapes were hovering in the shaded, half-darkened room. It grew until it was well-nigh overmastering. His eyes began to wander meaningly towards a locked drawer, and he half rose.

Against this temptation his hardened cynicism was no safeguard at all; rather did it tend to foster it, and that by reason of a corrosive disgust with life and the conditions thereof which it engendered within him. Then, in his half dreamy state, a sweet and softening influence seemed to steal in upon his soul. He thought he would like to see Lilith Ormskirk once more. Was it foolishness, weakness? Not a bit. Rather was it hard, matter-of-fact, logical philosophy. He had made an unparalleled hash of life. If he were going to leave it now it was sound logic to do so with, as it were, a sweet taste upon his mental palate.

Was it an omen for good, an earnest of a turn in the wheel of ill-luck? On reaching Booysens he was so fortunate as to find Lilith not only at home but alone. Her face lighted up at the sight of him.

"How sweet of you to toil out here this hot afternoon," she said, as he took within his the two hands she had instinctively held out to him. For a moment he looked at her without replying, contrasting the grim motive which had brought him hither with this perfect embodiment of youth and health and beauty, with all of life, all of the future yet before—all of life with its possibilities. She was in radiant spirits, and the hazel eyes shone entrancingly, and the slight flush under the dark warmth of the satin skin, caused by the unaffected pleasure inspired by his arrival, rendered even his strong head a trifle unsteady, as though with a rich, sweet, overpowering intoxication.

"Well, the reward is great," he answered, still retaining her hands in a lingering pressure. "Are you all alone, child?"

"Yes," she said, that pleased flush mantling again, the diminutive sounding strangely sweet to her ears as coming from him.

"But you—we—may not be much longer. People might drop in at any moment, and I want to be alone with you this afternoon. I am spoiling for one of our long talks, so put on a hat and come for a stroll across the veldt. Or is it too hot?"

"You know it is not," she answered. "Now, I won't be a minute."

She was as good as her word, for she reappeared almost immediately with a hat and sunshade, and they set forth, striking out over the bare open veldt which extended around and behind the Booysens' estate. The heat was great, greater than most women would have cared to face, but the blue cloudlessness of the sky, the sheeny glow of the sun upon the free open country was so much delight to Lilith Ormskirk. In her love for all that was bright and glowing she was a true daughter of the South.

"Oh, Laurence, how good it is to live," she exclaimed, as they stepped out at a brisk pace in the glorious openness of the warm air. "Do you know, I feel at times so bright and well and happy, in the very joy and thankfulness of being alive, that it almost brings tears. Do you understand the feeling? Tell me."

"I think so."

"But did you ever feel that way yourself?"

"Perhaps. In fact, I must have, because I understand so thoroughly what you mean. But it must have been a very, very long time ago."

His tone was that of one gravely amused, indulgently caressing. Heavens! he was thinking. The contrast here was quite delicious. In fact, it was unique. If only Lilith could have seen into his thoughts at that moment, if only she had had the faintest inkling as to their nature an hour or so back.—Still something in his look or in his tone sobered her.

"Ah, Laurence, forgive me," she cried. "How unfeeling I am, throwing my light-heartedness at you in this way, when things are going so badly with you."

"Unfeeling? Why, child, I love to see you rejoicing in the bright happiness of your youth and glowing spirits. I would not have you otherwise for all the world."

"No, I ought not to feel that way just now, when you—when so many all around us—are passing through such a dreadfully anxious and critical time. Tell me, Laurence, are things brightening for you even a little?"

"Not even a little. The case is all the other way. But don't you think about it, child. Be happy while you can and as long as you can. It is the worst possible philosophy to afflict yourself over the woes of other people."

Now the tears did indeed well to Lilith's eyes, but assuredly this time they were not tears of joy and thankfulness. One or two even fell.

"Don't sneer, Laurence. You must keep the satire and cynicism for all the world, if you will, but keep the inner side of your nature for me," she said, and in the sweet, pleading ring in her voice there was no lack of feeling now. "You have had about ten times more than your share of all the dark and bitter side of life. You will not refuse my sympathy—my deepest, most heartfelt sympathy—will you, dear? Ah, would that it were only of any use at all!"

"Your sympathy? Why, I value and prize it more than anything else in the world—in fact it is the only thing in the world I do value. 'Of any use at all?' It is of some use—of incalculable use, perhaps."

A smile lit up the clouded sadness of her face.

"If I only thought that," she said. "Still, it is more than sweet to hear you say so. Tell me, Laurence, what was the strange sympathetic magnetism that existed between us from the very first—yes, long before we talked together? I was conscious of it, if you were not—a sympathy that makes it easy for me to follow you, when you talk so darkly that nobody else could."

"Oh, there is such a sympathy, then?"

"Of course there is, and you know it."

"Perhaps. Tell me, Lilith, do you still cherish certain fusty and antiquated superstitions which make that good results and beneficial can never come out of abstract wrong? Abstract wrong being for present purposes a mere conventionality."

She looked at him for a moment. The interchange of that steady silent glance was sufficient.

"No, I do not," she said.

"I thought not. Well, that being so, you can perhaps realise of what 'use,' as you put it, that sweetest gift of your deepest, most heartfelt sympathy may be to its object, and in its results wholly beneficial. Do you follow?"

"Why, of course. And is it really in my power to brighten life for you ever so little? Ah, that would be happiness indeed."

"Continue to think so, then, for it is in your power to do just that, and you are doing it at this moment. And, child, when you feel that sense of boundless elation with the joy of living, add this to the happiness you are feeling, not to lessen but to enhance it."

"I will do that, Laurence," she said. "And if the consciousness that you have what you say—is of use to you, let it be to strengthen you. Clear-headed, strong as you are, dear, there must come hours of terrible gloom, even to you. Well, when such come on, think of our talk to-day and strive to throw them off because of it—because of the strengthening influences of it."

Thus she spoke, bravely. But beneath her outwardly sweet serenity a hard battle was being waged. She was fighting with her innermost self; striving hard to retain her self-control. She would not even raise her eyes to his lest she should lose it, lest she should betray herself. And all the while the chords of her innermost being thrilled and quivered with an indescribable tenderness, taking words within her mind: "My Laurence, my love, my ideal, what would I not do to brighten life for you—you for whom life is all too hard! I would draw down that life-weary head till it rested on my heart; I would wind my arms round your neck and whisper into your tired ear words of comfort, and of soothing and of love. Ah, how I would love you, care for you, shield your ear from ever being hurt by a discordant word! And I would draw your heart within mine to rest there, and would feel life all too blissfully, ineffably sweet to live."

His voice broke in upon her meditations, causing her a very perceptible start, so rapt were they.

"What is the subject of your very deep thought, my Lilith? Are you wreathing some strange and hitherto unsuspected spell, sorceress?"

The tone, playful, half sad, nearly upset her self-control then and there. Was it with design that, after the first keen penetrating gaze, he half averted his glance?

"I am afraid I am poor company," she said, rather lamely. "I must have been silent quite a long time. I was thinking—thinking out some knotty problem which would draw down your superior lordship's indulgent pity," with a flash of all her former bright spirits.

"And its nature?"

"If you will promise not to sneer I'll tell you. You will? Well, then, I was thinking whether I would have that gold-yellow dress done up with mauve sleeves or black, for Wednesday week."

Whether he believed her or not it was impossible to determine from the demeanour wherewith this statement was received. She was inclined to think he did, which spoke volumes for his tactfulness; and is it not of the very essence of that far too uncommon virtue to impress your interlocutor with the conviction that you believe exactly as he—or she—wants you to? In point of fact, there was something heroically pathetic in the way in which each mind strove to—veil from the other its inner workings, while every day showed more and more the impossibility of keeping up the figment.

Yet, for all this, there were times when the possession, the certainty of Lilith's—"sympathy" she had called it—would fail to cheer, to strengthen. Darker and darker grew the days, more hopeless the prospect, and soon Laurence Stanninghame found himself not merely face to face with poverty, but on the actual verge of destitution. Grim, fell spectres haunted his waking hours no less than his dreams. Did he return from a few hours of hard exercise with a fine appetite, that healthy possession served but to remind him how soon he would be without the means of gratifying it. He pictured himself utterly destitute, and through his sleeping visions would loom hideous spectres of want, and degradation. Day or night, waking or sleeping, it was ever the same; the horror of the position was ever before him and would not be laid. His mind was a hell to him; his heart of lead; his hard, clear brain deadly, self-pitiless in its purpose. Obviously, there was no further room in the world for such as he.

CHAPTER IX

HIS GUARDIAN ANGEL

"I'D sell my immortal soul, twenty times over, for a few thousands of the damnation stuff; but as that article isn't negotiable, why, better make an end of the whole bother."

Thus Laurence to himself, though unconsciously aloud. His room was an end one on the *stoep*, and the door was open. The time was the middle of the morning, and he sat thinking.

His thoughts were black and bitter—as how indeed should

they be otherwise? He had come to this place to make one final effort to retrieve his fortunes. That effort had failed. He had put what little remained to him into various companies—awaiting the boom—and no boom had ensued. On the contrary, things had never looked more dead than at this moment, never since the Rand had been opened up. The bulk of the scrip owned by him was now barely saleable at any price; for the residue he might have obtained a quarter of the price he had paid for it. He was ruined.

He was not alone in this—not by a very large number. But what sort of consolation was that? He had received letters too by the last mail. Money! money! That was their burden. He tossed them aside half read. What mattered anything? The accursed luck which had followed him throughout life had stuck to him most consistently—would do so until the end. The end? Ha, had not "the end" come? What more was left? More squalor, more deterioration—gradually dragging him down, down. Heaven knew what he might come to, what final degradation might not be his. The end? Yes, better let it be the end—now, here—while in the full possession of his faculties, in the full possession of the dignity of his self-respect. The dead blank hopelessness of life! Better end it—now, here.

He rose and went to the open door. All was quiet. The occupants of the other rooms were away, drowning their cares in liquor saloons, or feverishly hanging around 'Change to grasp at any possible straw. He was about to close the door. No. It had better remain as it was. The thing would look more accidental that way.

He returned into the room, and, unlocking his portmanteau, took out a six-shooter. It was loaded in every chamber, for in those days such a companion was not far from a necessity in the great restless gold-town. He sat down at the table, and, placing the weapon in front of him, passed his fingers up and down the blue shiny metal in a strange, half-meditative way. Then, grasping the butt, he placed the muzzle against his forehead.

The hard metal imprinted a cold ring just between the eyes. He did not flinch at the grisly contact. His hand was as firm as a rock. He must depress the muzzle just a trifle—it would make more certain. He began to press the trigger, ever so faintly, then a little more firmly, strangely wondering how much more imperceptible a degree of pressure would be required to produce the roaring shattering shock which should whirl him into the dark night of Death.

Well, but—afterwards? Who knew? If it were as they taught, even then it could be no augmentation of the hopelessness of this life. Perhaps they might make a devil of him, he thought, with grim satisfaction, as a black wave of hatred towards humanity at large surged through his brain. In that eventuality his rôle of tormentor as well as tormented would be a congenial one.

The dark night of death! What would it matter about money then, and all the sordid and pitiful wretchednesses entailed by the want of it? A leap in the dark! It held all the excitement of an unknown adventure to the man who sat there, pressing the muzzle of the deadly weapon hard against his forehead. The additional pressure of so much as a hair's weight upon that trigger now!

Could it be that the man's guardian angel was with him still, that a saving presence really hovered about him in the prosaic noonday? A strange chord seemed to thrill and vibrate within his brain, bringing before his vision the face of Lilith Ormskirk. There it was, as he had beheld it but a few days since; but now the sweet eyes were troubled, as though clouded with pain and bitter disappointment.

"You, whom I thought so strong, are weak after all! You, to whom I loved to listen as the very ideal of a well-balanced mind and judgment, are about to do what will stamp your memory for ever as that of one who was insane! Have I been no more to you than that—I who thought to have brightened and strengthened your life all that within me lay? It cannot be! You shall not do it."

He could not. The voice thrilled to his hearing, as plainly, as articulately as it had ever done when she had stood before him. He laid down the weapon, and passed his hand in a dazed sort of manner over his brows. Laurence Stanninghame was saved!

He stared around, somewhat unsteadily, as though more than half expecting to behold her there in the room. What did it all mean? At anyrate she had saved him. Was it for good or for ill? Then the full irony of the position struck upon his satirical soul. His mind went back over his acquaintance with Lilith. What if his disillusioning had been a little less complete? What if he had fled the rich attractiveness of her presence, had shunned her with heroic scrupulousness, acting from some fiddle-faddle notion of so-called "honour"? Just this. He, Laurence Stanninghame, would at that moment be lying a lifeless thing, with brains scattered all over the room—a memory, a standing monument of common-place weakness. But she had saved him from this—had saved him as surely and completely as though she had struck the weapon from his hand. Was it—for good or for ill?

He fell thinking again. Had he indeed played his last card, or did one more solitary trump yet lurk up his sleeve unknown to himself? No, it could not be; and his thoughts grew dark again. Yet he was safe now—safe from himself. Lilith had done it—her influence, her love!

He thought long and thought hard, but still hopelessly. And again, unconsciously, he broke out into soliloquy.

"Yes, I'd sell my soul to the devil himself!"

"Maybe the old man would be dead off the deal. Likely he reckons you a dead cert. already, Stanninghame."

Laurence did not start at the voice, which was that of Hazon, whose shadow darkened the door. The up-country man at that moment especially noticed that he did not.

"Daresay you're right, Hazon," was the reply. "That's it, come in," which the other had already done. "Talking out loud, was I? It's a damn bad habit, and grows on one."

"It does. Say, though, what game were you up to with that plaything?" glancing meaningly at the six-shooter lying on the table.

"This? Oh, I thought likely it wanted cleaning."

"So?" and the corners of Hazon's saturnine mouth drooped in ever so faint a grin as his keen eyes fixed themselves for a moment full upon the other's face. Laurence had forgotten the tell-tale imprint left in the centre of his forehead by the muzzle. "So? See here, Stanninghame, don't be at the trouble to invent any more sick old lies, but put the thing away. It might go off. Don't mind me; I've been through the same stage myself."

"Have you? How did it feel, eh?" said Laurence, with a sort of weary imperturbability, filling his pipe and pushing the pouch across the table to his friend.

"Bad. Ah, that's right! Instead of fooling about 'cleaning' guns at such times fill your pipe. That's the right lay, depend upon it."

Laurence made no reply, but, lighting up, puffed away in silence. His thoughts were wandering from Hazon.

"Broke, eh?" queried the latter sententiously.

"Stony."

"So? Ah, I knew it'd come; I knew it'd come."

This remark, redolent as it was of that sort of cheap prophecy which consists of being wise after the event, Laurence did not deem worthy of answer.

"And I was waiting for it to come," pursued Hazon. "Say, now, why not make a trip up country with me?"

"That sounds likely, doesn't it? Didn't I just tell you I was stony broke?"

"You did. The very reason why I made my proposal."

"Don't see it. If I were to sell out every rag of my scrip now, I couldn't raise enough to pay my shot towards the outfit. And I couldn't even render service in kind, for I've had no experience of waggons and all that sort of thing. So where does it come in?"

"It does come in. You can render service in kind—darned much so. I don't want you to pay any shot toward the outfit. See here, Stanninghame, if you go up country with me now, you'll come back a fairly rich man, or——"

"Or—what?"

"—You'll never come back at all."

In spite of his normal imperturbability, Laurence was conscious of a quickening of the pulses. The suggestion of adventure—of an adventure on a magnificent scale, and with magnificent results if successful, as conveyed in the other's reply, caused the blood to surge hotly through his frame. He had been strangely drawn towards this dark, reticent, solitary individual, beneath whose quiet demeanour lurked such a suggestion of force and power, who shunned the friendship of all even as all shunned his, who had been moderately intimate even with none but himself. This wonderful land—the dim, mysterious recesses of its interior— what possibilities did it not hold? And in groping into such possibilities this, above all others, was the comrade he would have chosen to have at his side. Not that he had forgotten the words of dark warning spoken by Rainsford and others. But at such he laughed.

"Are you taking it on any?" queried Hazon, after a pause of silence on the part of both.

"I am. I don't mind telling you, Hazon, that life, so far as I am concerned, was no great thing before."

"I guessed as much," assented the other, with a nod of the head.

"Quite. Now, I'm broke, stony broke, and it's more than ever a case of stealing away to hang oneself in a well. I tell you squarely, I'd walk into the jaws of the devil himself to effect the capture of the oof-bird."

"Yes? How are your nerves, Stanninghame?"

"Hard—hard as nails now. That's not to say they have been always."

"Quite so. Ever seen a man's head cut off?"

"Two."

"So? Where was that?" said Hazon, ever so faintly surprised at receiving an affirmative reply.

"In Paris. A press friend of mine had to go and see two fellows guillotined, and managed to work me in with him. We were as close to the machine, too, as it was possible to get."

"Did it make you feel sick at all?"

"Not any. The other Johnny took it pretty badly, though. I had to fill him up with cocktails before he could eat any breakfast."

"That's a very good test. I never expected you to say you had stood it. Well, you may see a little more in that line before we come through. Can't make omelettes without breaking eggs though, as the French say. Well now, Stanninghame, I've had my eye on you ever since you came up here. I'm pretty good at reading people, and I read you. That's the man for me, I said to myself. He's come to the end of his tether. He's just at that stage of life when it's kill or cure, and he means kill or cure."

"Well, we had talked enough together to let you into that much, eh, Hazon?" said Laurence with a laugh which was not altogether free from a dash of scepticism.

"We have. Still, I'm not gassing when I tell you I knew all about it before. How? you want to ask. Because I've been through it all myself. I thought, 'That chap is throwing his last card; if he loses, he's my man.' And you have lost."

"But what's the object of the trip, Hazon? Gold?"

"No."

"Stones?"[1]

"Not stones."

"Ivory, then?"

"That's it; ivory," and a gleam of saturnine mirth shot across the other's dark features.

"You have to go a good way up for that now, don't you, Hazon?"

"Yes, a good way up. And it's contraband."

"The devil it is!"

Hazon nodded. Then he went to the door and looked out.

"Leave it open. It's better so. We can hear anyone coming," he said, returning. "And now, Stanninghame, listen carefully, and we'll talk out the scheme. If you're on, well and good; if you're dead off it, why, I told you I had read you, and you're not the man to let drop by word or hint to a living soul any of what has passed between us."

"Quite right, Hazon. You never formed a safer judgment in your life."

Then, for upwards of an hour, the pair talked together; and when the luncheon bell rang, and Laurence Stanninghame took his seat at the table along with the rest, to talk scrip in the scathingly despondent way in which the darling topic was conversationally dealt with in these days, he was conscious that he had turned the corner of a curious psychological crisis in his life.

In the afternoon he took his way down to Booysens. Would he find Lilith in? It was almost too much good luck to hope to find her alone. As he walked, he was filled with a strange elation. The dull pain of a very near parting was largely counteracted by the manner of it. Such a parting had been before his mind for long; but then he would have gone forth broken down, ruined, more utterly without hope in life than ever. Now it was different. He was going forth upon an adventure fraught with all manner of stirring potentialities—one from which he would return wealthy, or, as his friend and thenceforth comrade had said, one from which he would not return at all.

Had his luck already begun to turn, he thought? As he mounted the *stoep* Lilith herself came forth to meet him. It struck him that the omen was a good one.

"Why, you are becoming quite a stranger," she said. But the note of gladness underlying the reproach did not escape him, nor a certain lighting up of her face as they clasped hands, with the subtle lingering pressure now never absent from that outwardly formal method of greeting.

"Am I?" he answered, thinking how soon, how very soon, he would become one in reality. "But you were going out?" For she had on her hat and gloves, and carried a sunshade.

"I was. You are only just in time—only just. But I won't now that you have come."

"On the contrary, I want you to. I want you to come out with me, and at once, before an irruption of bores renders that manœuvre impracticable. Will you?"

"Of course I will. Which way shall we go? Up to the town?"

"Not much. Right in the opposite direction, and as far away from it as possible. Are you alone?"

"Not quite alone. Aunt is having her afternoon sleep; but May and George went to the town this morning. They intended to have lunch at the Stevensons, and then go on to the cricket ground. There's a match or something on to-day. George was cross because I wouldn't go too; but I had a touch of headache, and went to sleep instead. And oh, Laurence, I had such a horrid dream. It was about you."

"Oh, was it?" The words rapped themselves out quickly, nervously, more so than she had ever heard him talk before. But the awful and ghastly crisis of the morning was recalled by her words. "About me? Tell it to me."

"I can't. It was all rather vague, and yet so real. I dreamed that you were in the face of some strange, some horrible danger, against which I was powerless to warn you. I struggled to, even prayed. Then I was able. I warned you, and the danger seemed to pass. And oh, Laurence, I woke up crying."

"Your dream was a true one, my Lilith. No, I will not tell you how or in what way. And will you always be empowered to warn me—to save me, my sweet guardian angel? I shall need it often enough during the next—er—in the time that is coming."

His face had taken on an unwonted expression, and his tones were suspiciously husky. Lilith looked wonderingly at him, and her own expression was grave and earnest. The sweet eyes became dewy with unshed tears.

"You know I will, if I may," she answered, stealing a hand into his for a sympathetic pressure, as they walked side by side.

They had been walking at a good pace over the open, treeless veldt, and the roofs of Booysens were now quite dwarfed behind them.

"But, tell me," she continued. "Are things any better? Oh, it is dreadful that you should have come all this way only to be more completely ruined than before—dreadful! I am always thinking about it. Yet I am of a hopeful disposition, as I told you. I never despair. Things will take a turn. They must."

"They have taken a turn, Lilith, but not in the direction you mean. I am going away."

She started. She knew that those words must one day be spoken. Now that they had been, they hurt.

"Back to England?"

The words came out breathlessly, and with a sort of gasp.

"No, not there. I am going up country, into the interior."

"Oh!"

There was relief in the ejaculation. For the moment she lost sight of all that was involved by such a destination. They would still be in the same land. That was something—or seemed so.

Now all the latent instincts, never half drawn forth, surged like molten volcano fires through Laurence Stanninghame's soul. The dead and stony nature, slain within him, revivified, burst forth into warm, pulsating, struggling, rebellious life. This striving of heart against heart, this desperate effort still to patch up the rents in the flimsy veil, moved him infinitely. The veldt on the Witwatersrand is as open and devoid of cover as a billiard-table. The two were visible for miles. But for this he knew not what he might have done—rather he knew full well what he certainly would have done.

They took refuge in practical topics; they talked of the up-country trip.

"You are very friendly with that Mr. Hazon, are you not, Laurence? Nobody else is, and there are strange stories, not told, but hinted about him. He is a man I should be almost afraid of, and yet half admire. He strikes me as one who would be a terrible and relentless enemy, but as true as steel, true to self-sacrificing point, to a friend."

"That's exactly my opinion. Now, Hazon and I suit each other down to the ground. I have an especial faculty, remember, for getting on with unpopular individuals."

Thus they talked, and at length time forced them to turn their steps homeward. And as the sun rays began to slant golden upon the surrounding veldt, it seemed to Laurence that even that *triste* wilderness took on a glow that was more than of earth. How that afternoon, that walk, would dwell within his memory, stamped there indelibly! He thought how the day had opened, of that gnawing mental struggle culminating in—what? But for this girl at his side he would now be—what? She had saved him, she alone— her confidence in him, her high opinion of him, and—her love. Yes, her love. He looked upon her as she walked beside him, entrancing beyond words in her rich, warm beauty, a perfect dream of grace and symmetry. Even the hot sunlight seemed to linger, as with a kiss, upon the dark brilliant loveliness of her eyes, on the soft curve of her lips.

"You are cruel, sorceress," he broke forth. "You have made yourself look especially enchanting because soon I shall see you no more. You are looking perfect."

She flashed a bright smile upon him, but it seemed to fade into a shadow, as of pain.

"Am I? Well, Laurence, one knows instinctively when one is looking one's best. It would be affectation to pretend otherwise. And I love to make myself look bright and sweet and attractive for you. And now—oh dear, we are nearly home again. Come in with me now and stay the evening. We shall not be alone together again, I fear—this evening, I mean. But you will be going away so soon now, and I must see as much of you as I can."

He needed no persuasion. And as Lilith had said, they were

not alone together again. But even the jealous George, who came back from the town more cantankerous than ever on learning of this addition, found balm in Gilead. That brute Stanninghame was going away up country soon, he put it. Heaven send a convenient shot of malaria or a providential assegai prod to keep him there for ever!

CHAPTER X

PREPARATION

THE days went by and Hazon's preparations were nearly completed, and it became patent to the Rand at large that "The Pirate" intended to relieve that delusive locality of his unwelcome presence; for a couple of waggons appeared on the scene, bearing his name, and in charge of a mysterious native of vast proportions and forbidding physiognomy, who seemed not to be indigenous to those parts, nor, indeed, to hail from anywhere around. And Hazon, in his quiet, thorough way, was very busy in fitting out these waggons, loading them with articles suitable for up-country trade, eke with munitions of sport, and, if need be, war. Wherein he was ably assisted by Laurence Stanninghame.

On learning that the latter was a party to the undertaking, whatever it was, the Rand shrugged its shoulders, and whispered; and the burden of its whispering consisted mainly of the ancient innuendo relating to those who had heretofore accompanied Hazon anywhere. This one—would he not travel the same dark road as others had done, whatever that road might be? But that was his own look-out, and he had been warned. And the two men would hold long and earnest confabs together; but those which were the most earnest were held in the course of long rides away into the veldt. Then they would dismount at some sequestered spot, where, secure from all interruption, weather-beaten maps and plans and darkly written memos., also cyphers, would be produced and long and carefully discussed. Of this, however, the Rand knew nothing; yet from such Laurence would return feeling a trifle graver, for even he had to accustom himself to such a road to wealth as was here held out. But his case was desperate. He was utterly ruined, and to the same extent reckless. It was sink or swim, and not his was the mind to elect to go under when the jettison of a last lingering scruple or two would keep him afloat. As for potential—nay, certain—risk, that did not enter into his calculations.

Now, while these preparations were in progress, Holmes was going about with a very gloomy countenance; more than hinting, indeed, at a desire to take part in the trip. Finally, he put it plainly to Laurence himself.

"Take my advice and watch it," the latter decisively replied. Then remembering that the ostensible object of the undertaking was sport and native trade, he went on, "You see, Holmes, it's going to be a hard business. Not just three or four months up in the bush-veldt and so forth, but—well, Heaven only knows where the thing will end, let alone how."

"I don't care about that. Why, it's just the very thing that'll suit me down to the ground. I say, Stanninghame, I know you don't mind, but Hazon? I've always stood up for Hazon, and we seem to get on all right? Do put it to Hazon. I could pay my shot, of course."

There was a despondency of manner and tone that was extremely foreign to the mercurial Holmes, and this, together with certain signs he had read of late, caused Laurence to look up with a queer half smile.

"Why are you so anxious to clear from here, Holmes? Rather sudden, isn't it?"

"Oh, I'm dead off waiting for a 'boom' that never comes. It's dashed sickening, don't you know."

"It is. And what else is dashed sickening? That isn't all."

The other stared for a moment, then, as though he were bringing it out with an effort, he burst forth "Oh, well, hang it all, Stanninghame, I don't see why I shouldn't tell you. The fact is I've—I've got the chuck."

Laurence laughed inwardly. He understood.

"Why, I thought you were bringing it on all right," he said.

"So did I; but when I put it to her, she was dead off," said Holmes, disconsolately savage.

"Sure?"

"Cert."

"Well, give her another show. Some women—girls especially—like that sort of application twice over. They think it enhances their value in some inexplicable way," said Laurence, with a touch of characteristic satire. "I don't, but that's a matter of opinion. And—I don't want to hurt your feelings Holmes, but is this one worth it?"

"I don't know," answered the other savagely, driving his heel into the ground. "It's that beast Barstow. What the deuce she can see in him, bangs me."

"Yes, unless it is that you hold a quantity of unsaleable scrip and he doesn't," rejoined Laurence, who had been secretly amused in watching the progress of pretty Mabel Falkner's latest preference. "But in any case I think you'd better not touch it, or you'll find yourself on the one horn or other of this dilemma: if she is coming the 'playing off' trick, why, that is despicable, and in fact not good enough; if she means business, why, you can't go begging to her for what she has given to the other Johnny without any begging at all. See?"

"Oh yes, I see," was the rueful rejoinder. "By the Lord, Stanninghame, I used to think you a deuced snarling, cynical beggar at first, but now, 'pon my soul, I believe you're right."

"Do you? Well, then, you don't want to go away up country and get bowled out with fever or struck by a nigger, and all that sort of thing, because one girl don't care a cent for you."

"Perhaps not. Still, I hate this place now. I'm sick of it. By the way, Stanninghame, you're the sort a fellow can tell anything to; you don't start a lot of cheap blatant chaff as some chappies do when you want them to talk sound sense."

There was a great deal underlying the remark, also the tone. Though lacking the elements which go to make up the "popular" man, Laurence possessed the faculty of winning the devoted attachment of individuals, and that to an extent of which he himself little dreamed. Not the least important item which went to make up that attribute lay in the fact that he was a most indulgent listener, whom nothing astonished, and who could look at all sides of any given question with the tact and toleration of a man who thinks. This faculty he seldom exercised, and then almost unconsciously.

To the other's remark he made no immediate reply. Taking into consideration age and temperament, he had no belief that Holmes' rejection and disappointment had left any deep wound. Still, it had come at an unfortunate time—a time when the sufferer, in common with most of them, had been hard hit in a more material way. He had a genuine liking for the sunny-natured, open-hearted youth; a liking begotten, it might be, of the ingenuously unconscious manner in which the latter looked up to him; in fact, made a sort of elder brother of him. Holmes was no stronger-headed than most youngsters of his temperament and circumstances, and Laurence did not want to see him—soured and dejected by disappointment all round—throw himself in with the reckless, indiscriminate bar-frequenter, of whom there were not lacking woful examples in those days, though, poor fellows, much from the same motive, to drown care; and into this current would Holmes in all probability be swept if left by himself in Johannesburg. Was there no method of taking him with them for a month or two's shoot in the bush-veldt, and sending him back by some returning expedition before the serious part of the undertaking was entered upon? He decided to sound Hazon upon the matter, yet of this resolve he said nothing now to Holmes. The latter broke the silence.

"By Jove, Stanninghame, I envy you," he said. "You are such a hard-headed chap. Why, I don't believe you care a little d—— for any mortal thing in the world. Yes, I envy you."

"You needn't, if it means hankering after the process by which that blissful state is attained. But you are wrong. I care most infernally about one thing."

"And what's that? What is it, old chap? You needn't be afraid I'll let on!" said Holmes eagerly, anticipating it might be something similar in the way of a confidence to that which his own exuberant heart had not been able to refrain from making.

"Why, that I was stewed idiot enough to go on investing in this infernal scrip instead of clearing out just when I had made the modest profit of four hundred per cent."

"Oh!" said the other, in disappointed surprise, adding, "But you don't show it. You take it smiling, Stanninghame. You don't turn a hair."

"H'm!"

With the ejaculation, Laurence was thinking of a certain room, shaded from the glare of the sunlight without, and of a very grim

moment indeed. He was looking, too, at the hearty, bright-man-
nered youngster who had already begun to forget his recent disappointment in the prospect of adventure and novelty. He himself
had been nearly as lighthearted, just as ready to mirth and laughter
at that age. Yet now? Would it be the same with this one? Who
could say?

The suggestion that Holmes should accompany the expedition was not received with enthusiasm by Hazon, neither did it
meet with immediate and decisive repudiation. Characteristically,
Hazon proceeded to argue out the matter pro and con.

"He doesn't know the real nature of our business, Stanninghame?
no, of course not. Thinks it's only a shooting trip?—good. Well,
the question is, are we dead certain of finding opportunities for
sending him back; for we can't turn him loose on the veldt and say
good-bye?"

"There are several places where we might drop him," said
Laurence, consulting a map and mentioning a few.

"Quite so. Well, here's another consideration. He's a youngster, and probably has scores of relations more or less interested
in him. We don't want to draw down inquiries and investigations
into our movements and affairs."

"That won't count seriously, Hazon."

"Think not? Um! Well then, what if we were to take him
along—run him into the whole shoot with us?"

"Phew! That's a horse whose colour I've never scrutinised.
And the point?"

"Might help us in more ways than one; in case of difficulties afterwards, I mean. The idea seems to knock you out some,
Stanninghame?"

There was something in it. Laurence, reckless, unscrupulous as
he was, could not but hesitate. In striving to save his young friend
from one form of ruin, was it written that he should plunge him
into another more irretrievable, more sweeping, more lifelong?

"I am thinking he might give us trouble," he replied deliberately. "What if he sickened of the whole business, and kicked just
when we wanted to pull together the most? No, no, Hazon. If we
take him at all, we must send him back as I say. It's all very well for

us two, but it doesn't seem quite the thing to run a fresh-hearted youngster, with all his life before him, and bursting with hopes and ideals, into a grim business of this kind. But taking him, or leaving him, rests with you entirely."

"Leave it that way, then. I'll think it over and see if it pans out any," said Hazon, leisurely lighting a fresh pipe. "But, Stanninghame, what's this?" he added, with a sudden, keen glance out of his piercing eyes. "You are letting yourself go with regard to this matter—showing feeling. That won't do, you know. You've got to have no sample of that sort of goods about you, no more than can be put into a block of granite. Aren't you in training yet?"

"Well, I think so; or, at anyrate, shall be long before it is wanted seriously."

No more was said on the subject then.

As the preparations progressed, and the time for the start drew near, it seemed to Laurence Stanninghame that more and more was the old life a mere dream, a dream of the past. Sometimes in his sleep he would be back in it, would see the dinginess of the ramshackle semi-detached, would hear the vulgar sounds of the vulgar suburban street; and he would turn uneasily in his dreams, with a depressing consciousness of dust and discord, and a blank wall as of the hopelessness of life drawn across his path. Feeling? Pooh! Who would miss him out of the traditional "charm" of the family circle? A new toy, costing an extra shilling or so, would quite knock out all and any recollection of himself. There were times when in his dreams he had even returned to the domestic ark, and in the result a day of welcome and comparative peace, then discord and jangling strife as before, and the ever weighing-down, depressing, crushing consciousness of squalid penury for the rest of his natural life. From such visions he had awakened, awakened with a start of exultant gratulation, to find the glow of the African sun streaming into the room; every nerve tingling with a consciousness of strength and braced-up vigour; his mind rejoicing to look forward into the boundless possibilities held out by the adventure in which he was involved; that other ghastly horror, which had haunted him for so long, now put far away. Risk, excitement, peril, daring, to be rewarded by wealth, after long years of unnatural stagnation. The prospect opened out a vista as of boundless delight.

Yet was this dashed—dashed by an impending parting. The certainty of this would ever obtrude, and quench his exultation. Sweet Lilith! how she had subtly intertwined herself within his life! Well, he was strong; he could surely keep himself in hand. It should be a part of his training. Still, though the certainty of impending separation would quench his exultation, on awakening to the light of each new day which brought that parting nearer, yet there was another certainty, that at least a portion of every such day should be spent with her.

But even he, with all his strength, with all his foresight, little realised what the actual moment of that parting should mean.

CHAPTER XI

"AT THE TWELFTH HOUR"

HE was there to say good-bye.

As he sat waiting, the soft subdued hush of the shaded room, in its cool fragrance, struck upon his senses as with an influence of depression, of sadness, of loss. He had come to bid farewell. Farewell! Now the moment had arrived he, somehow, felt it.

Would she never come in? His nerves seemed all on edge, and ever upon the glowing midday heat, the jarring thump of the Crown Reef battery[1] beat its monotonous time. Then the door opened softly, and Lilith entered.

Never had she seemed to look more sweet, more inviting. The rich, dark beauty, always more enthralling, more captivating, when warmed by the constant kiss of its native southern sun; the starry eyes, wide with earnestness; the sad, sweet expression of the wistful lips; the glorious splendour of the perfect form, in its cool, creamy white draperies—Laurence Stanninghame, gazing upon her, realised with a dull, dead ache at the heart, that all his self-boasted strength was but the veriest weakness. And now he had come to say farewell.

"I can hardly realise that we shall not see each other again,"

Lilith said, after a transparently feeble attempt or two on the part of both of them to talk on indifferent subjects. "When do you expect to return? How long will you be away?"

"'It may be for years, and it may be for ever,'" quoted Laurence, a bitter ring in his tone. "Probably the latter."

"You must not say that. Remember what I told you, more than once before. I am always hopeful—I never despair, even when things look blackest—either for myself or for other people. Though, I daresay, you are laughing to yourself now at the idea of things being anything but bright to me. Well, then, I predict you will come back with what you want. You will return rich, and all will look up then for you."

She spoke lightly, smilingly. He, listening, gazing at her, felt bitter. He had been mistaken. Well, he had found out his mistake, only just in time—only just. But even he, with all his observant perceptiveness, had failed to penetrate Lilith's magnificent self-command.

"Let us hope your prediction will prove a true one," he said, falling in with her supposed mood. "The one thing to make life worth living is wealth. I will stick at nothing to obtain it—nothing! Without it, life is a hell; with it—well, life is at one's feet. There is nothing one cannot do with it—nothing!"

His eyes glowed with a sombre light. There was a world of repressed passion in his tone, the resentful snarl, as he thought of the past squalor and bitterness of life, mingling with the savage determination and unscrupulous recklessness of the born adventurer.

"There is one thing you cannot obtain for it," she said. "That is—love."

"But it can bring you all that will cause you to feel no longing for that deceptive illusion. You can forget that such a thing exists—can forget it in the renewed exuberance of vitality which is sheer enjoyment of living. Well, wish me luck. 'Good-bye' is a dreadful word, but it has to be said."

He had risen and stood blindly, half-bewilderedly. The shaded room, the sensuous fragrance of her presence, every graceful movement, the fascination of the wide, earnest eyes, all was more than beginning to intoxicate him, to shatter his chain-armour of bitterness and self-control. He, the strong, the invulnerable, the man in whom all heart, all feeling was dead—what sorcery was this? He was bewitched, entranced, enthralled. His strength was as water. Yet not.

They stood facing each other, glance fused into glance. At that moment heart seemed opened to heart—to be gazing therein.

"Good-bye," he said. "Don't quite forget me, Lilith dear. Think a little now and then of the times we have had together." Then their lips met in a long kiss. And she said—nothing. Perhaps she could not. The flood-gate of an awful torrent of pent-up, bravely-controlled grief may be opened in the utterance of that word "good-bye."

Laurence Stanninghame seemed to walk blindly, staggering in the strong sunlight. Was it the midday heat, or the strong glare? The ever-monotonous beat of the Crown Reef stamps seemed to hammer within his brain, which seethed and swirled with the recollection of that last long kiss. He would not look back. Impervious to the furnace-like heat, he stepped out over the veldt at a pace which, by the time he reached the corner of the Wemmer property, caused him to look up wonderingly, that he should already be entering the town.

"Oh, there you are, Stanninghame," sung out a voice, whose owner nearly cannoned into him. Laurence looked up.

"Here I am, as you say, Holmes," he answered, quite coolly and unconcernedly. "But where are you bound for, and what's the excitement, anyway?"

"Why, I thought I'd see if I could meet you. Hazon said you had gone down to Booysens this morning. What do you think? I've got round him, and I'm going with you."

Laurence stared, then looked grave.

"Going with us, eh? I say, youngster, have you made your will?"

"Haven't got anything to leave. But, Stanninghame, I'm awfully obliged to you, old fellow. It's all through you I've got round the old man."

"Have you any sort of idea what our programme is?"

"None. And I don't care."

Laurence whistled.

"See here, Holmes," he said. "This thing has got to be looked into. In fact, it can't go on."

"Yes it can, and it shall. Don't be a beast, now, Stanninghame. I'd go anywhere with you two fellows, and I'm dead off this waiting for a boom that never comes. I shall be as stony-broke as the rest of them if I hold on any longer. So I'm going to realise at a loss, and go with you. Come along, now, to Phillips' bar and we'll split a bottle of cham. to the undertaking."

"You don't need to buzz to that extent, Holmes. I hate 'gooseberry.' 'John Walker' is good enough for me."

They reached Phillips', and found that historic bar far from empty; and young Holmes, who was full of exhilaration over the prospects of his trip, was insisting that many should drink success thereto. Laurence, silent amid the racket of voices, was curiously watching him. This joyous-hearted youngster, would he ever come to look back upon life as a thing that had far better have never been lived? And he smiled queerly to himself as he thought what would be the effect upon Holmes of the experiences he would bring back with him from that trip to which he was looking forward so joyously, so hopefully—if he returned from it at all, that was—if, indeed, any of them did. But throughout the racket—the strife of tongues, the boisterous guffaw over some cheap "wheeze"—the recollection of the shaded room—of that last good-bye in the cloudless noontide—pressed like a living weight upon his heart. Never would it be obliterated—never.

Throughout the afternoon Laurence busied himself greatly over the final preparations. He did not even feel tempted to ride over to Booysens, on some pretext. Lilith would not be alone. There was always a host of people there of an afternoon—callers, lawn-tennis players, and so forth. The ineffably sweet sadness of that last parting must be the recollection he was to carry forth with him.

It was evening. The waggons had been started just before sundown, and now their owners were riding out of the town to overtake them. Young Holmes, suffering under an exuberance of exhilaration begotten of multifold good-byes effected to a spirituous accompaniment, was not so firm in his saddle as he might have been; but on the hardened heads of the other two the effect of such farewells had been *nil*. They were just getting clear of the town when they became aware of a panting, puffing native striving to overtake them.

"Why, it's John," said Hazon, recognising one of the coloured waiters at their hotel.

The boy ran straight up to Laurence, and held out an envelope.

"For you, Baas," he said. "The Baas forgot to give it you. Dank you, Baas!" catching, with a grin, something that was flung to him.

It was a delicate-looking envelope, and sealed. What new surprise was this? as he took in the puzzling yet characteristic handwriting of the address.

"I *must* see you once more," he read. "I cannot let you go, like this, Laurence darling. Come to me for one more good-bye. I shall be alone this evening. Come to me, love of my heart.   L."

"Pho! Of course it was not! It was too ridiculous. It was not as if all Heaven had opened before his eyes. Of course not!" he told himself.

But——it was.

"By the way, Hazon," he said indifferently, "I find there is still a matter I have to attend to. So you must go on without me. I expect I'll overtake you to-morrow not long after sunrise—or not much later. So long."

The dark, impassive face of the up-country man underwent no change. He had understood the whole change of plan, but it was no concern of his. So he merely said "*Ja*. So-long," and continued his way.

Laurence did not go back to the hotel. The last thing he desired was that his return should be noticed and commented upon. He sought out Rainsford, who, having stable-room, willingly consented to put up his steed, and, being a discreet fellow, was not likely to indulge in undue tongue-wagging. Then he took his way down to Booysens.

As he stepped forth through the gloom—for by this time it was quite dark—the words of that missive seemed burned into his brain in characters of fire and of gold. What words they were, too! He had read her glance aright, then? It was only that intrepidity of self-command which he had failed to allow for. And he? Why had he been so strong that morning? Seldom indeed did a second opportunity occur. But now? When he should return up the hill he was now descending, what a memory would be his to carry forth with him into the solitude and peril and privation of his enterprise. Yet to what end? Even if he were successful in amassing wealth untold, yet they two must be as far apart as ever. Well, that need not follow, he told himself. With wealth one can do anything—anything; without it nothing, was at this time the primary article of Laurence Stanninghame's creed; and at the thought his step grew more elastic, and all unconsciously his head threw itself back in a gesture of anticipatory triumph.

The house was all quiet as he approached. At the sound of his step on the *stoep*—almost before he had time to knock—the door was opened—was opened by Lilith herself—then closed behind him.

She said no word; she only looked up at him. The subdued light of the half-darkened hall softened as with an almost unearthly beauty the upturned face, and forth from it her eyes shone, glowed with the lustre of a radiant tenderness, too vast, too overwhelming for her lips to utter.

And he? He, too, said no word. Those lips of hers, sweet, inviting, were pressed to his; that peerless form was wrapped in his embrace, sinking therein with a soft sigh of contentment. What room was there for mere words? as again and again he kissed the lips—eyes—hair—then the lips again. This was only the beginning of a farewell visit—a sad, whirling, heart-break of farewell—yet as the blood surged boiling through Laurence Stanninghame's veins, and heart, pressed against heart, seemed swelled to bursting point, he thought that life, even such as it had been, was worth living if it could contain such a moment as this. Equally, too, did he realise that, in life or in death, the triumph-joy of this moment should illumine his memory, dark though it might be, for ever and ever.

"What did you think of me when you got my note, dear one?" she whispered at last. "And I have been in a perfect agony ever since, for fear it should be too late. But I could not let you go as I did this morning. I felt such an irresistible craving to see you again, Laurence, my darling—to hear your voice. I felt we could not part as we did—each trying to deceive the other, each knowing, the while, that it was impossible. I wanted more than that for a memory throughout the blank time that is coming."

"Yes, we were both too strong, my Lilith. And why should we have been? What scruple ever stood anybody to the good in this hell-fraud of a state called 'Life?' Not one—not one! Yes, we were too strong, and your self-command deceived even me."

"My self-command? Ah, Laurence, my love, how little you knew. All the time I was battling hard with myself, forcing down an irresistible longing to do this—and this—and this!" And drawing down his head, she kissed him again and again, long, tender kisses, as though her whole soul sought entrance into his.

"But I shall tire you, my dearest, if I keep you standing here like this," she went on. "Come inside now, and our last talk—our last for a long time—shall, at anyrate, be a cosy one."

She drew him within the half open door of an adjoining room. The window curtains were drawn, and a shaded lamp gave forth the same subdued and chastened light as that which burned in the hall. There were flowers in vases and sprays, arranged in every tasteful and delicate manner, and distilling a fragrance subtle and pervading. The sumptuous prettiness of the furniture and ornaments—picture frames encasing mystic and thought-evoking subjects, books disposed here and there, delicate embroidery, the work of her fingers—in short, the hundred and one dainty knick-knacks pleasing to the eye seemed to reflect the bright beautiful personality of Lilith; for, indeed, the arrangement and disposal of them was almost entirely her own.

She made him sit down upon the softest and most comfortable couch; then, as she seated herself beside him, he drew her head down to rest upon his shoulder and wound his arms about her.

"Why did you wait until even the twelfth hour?" he said. "Why did you blind me all this time, my Lilith? Only think what we have lost by it!"

"Ah yes, I have indeed. But tell me, dear one, it is not too late, is it, even though it be the twelfth hour?"

"It came very near being too late. I had already started. Yes, it is indeed the twelfth hour. Too late? I don't know," he went on, in a tone of sombre bitterness. "Think of the blissful times that might have been ours had I but known. I would have taught you the real meaning of the word 'love.' I would have drawn your innermost soul from you—would have drawn it into mine—have twined every thought of your being around mine—had I but known. And I could have done this. You know I could, do you not? Think a moment, then answer."

The head which rested on his shoulder seemed to lean heavier there; the arm which encircled her was pressed tighter by hers to the round, beautiful waist, as though to bring herself closer within his embrace. The answer came, rapturously sweet, but with a thrill of pain—

"I know you could have. There is no need to think, even for a moment. You have done it."

"I have tried to, even against difficulties. Come what may, Lilith, you shall never be free from the spell of this love of ours. All thoughts of other love shall be flat and stale and dead; and now, when I am gone, your whole soul shall ache and throb with a sense of loss—love and pain intertwined—yet not one pang of the latter would you forego, lest it should lessen the rapturous keenness of the former in the minutest degree. This is what you have caused me to suffer by reason of your stony self-command up till this morning. Now you shall suffer it too."

His tones were calm, even, almost stern as those of a judge pronouncing sentence. Lilith, drinking in every word, felt already that every word was true. That sense of love and pain was already in possession of her soul, and would retain possession until all capacity for feeling was dulled and dead.

"You were cruel to draw my very soul out of me as you have done—to force me to love you as I do," she answered—"cruel and pitiless."

"What then? I was but carrying out the programme of life. It is that way. But tell me, would you have preferred that I had not done it—that I had passed by on the other side?"

"Oh, my Laurence, no! No, no—ten thousand times no! The mere recollection of such an hour as this is worth a life-time of the awful pain of loss of which you speak and which is around me already."

"That was my own judgment when I first recognised that a strong mutual 'draw' was bringing us together. I foresaw this moment, and deliberately acquiesced in Fate."

Now the soft waves of her hair swept his face, now the satin smoothness of her cheek lay against his. Lips met lips again and again, and never for a moment did the clasp of that firm embrace relax. The dead blank hopelessness of life and its conditions, then, had still contained this, had culminated in this? As he thus held her to him, as though he would hold her for ever, some dreamy brain-wave seemed to carry Laurence's mind into the dim and somewhat awesome vistas of the future, to bring it face to face with death in varying and appalling forms. What mattered? The recollection of this farewell hour, here in the half-shaded room, with its subtle fragrance of flowers and mysterious light, would be with him then. Such an hour as this would be a crowning triumph to the apex of life. Better that life should end than lengthen out to witness a decline from this apex.

As Lilith had said, he was cruel and pitiless in his love. What then? It was characteristic of him. Had not all experience taught him that the slightest weakness, the slightest compunction, was that faulty link which should snap the chain, be the latter never so massively forged? He remembered how they had held discussion as to whether right might ensue from what was wrong in the abstract. He remembered the cold hard imprint of the revolver muzzle against his forehead, the increasing pressure of his thumb upon the trigger, then the thought of Lilith's love had come in as a hand stretched forth to snatch him from the jaws of death. And it had so snatched him. What were the mere conventional rules of abstract right or wrong beside such an instance of cause and effect? Old wives' fables.

They were standing up, face to face, looking into each other's eyes. The hour was late now. Any moment the household might return. Both desired that the last farewell should take place alone.

Not for the sake of a few more precious moments would they run the risk of being cheated out of that last farewell.

"You sweet, cruel, pitiless torturer," Lilith said, locking her hands in his, as they rose. "You have placed my life under one great lasting shadow, because of the recollection of you. How will it be, think you, when I wake up to-morrow and find you are gone—if I sleep at all, that is? How will it be when, day after day, week after week——Ah, love, love," she broke off, "and yet I cannot say, 'Why did you do it?' for your very cruelty in doing it is sweet—sweet, do you hear, Laurence? Have you ever been loved—tell me, have you, have you?" she went on, drawing his head down with a sort of fierceness and again pressing her burning lips to his.

"At the twelfth hour! at the twelfth hour!" he repeated, in a kind of condemnatory merciless tone, while his clasp tightened around the lovely form, which seemed literally to hang within his arms. "Love of my heart, think what such an hour as this might have been, not once, but again and again, and that undashed with the pain of immediate parting as now. Why did we—why did you—wait until the very twelfth hour? Why?"

"Why, indeed? Darling, darling, don't reproach me. You have drawn my very heart and soul into yours. Think of it ever, day and night, whatever may befall you, O Laurence, my heart's life!"

Now this hard, stony, self-controlled stoic discovered that his granite nature was shaken to its foundation. But, even then, the unutterable sweetness of the thought that he, and he alone, had lived to inspire the anguish of the pleading tones that thrilled to his ear, thrilled with love for him, to enkindle the light that shone from those eyes, melting with love for him; this thought flowed in upon the torrent-wave of his pain, rendering it bliss, yet lashing it up the more fiercely.

There was silence for a few moments. Both stood gazing into each other's eyes; gazing, as it were, into the innermost depths of each other's soul. Then the sound of voices drawing nearer, rising above the clanking hum of the Crown Reef battery, seemed to warn them that if their last farewell was to be made alone the time to make it had come.

"Good-bye, now, love of my heart," he whispered, between

long, burning, clinging kisses. Now that this final parting had come, the dead, dreary, heartsick pain of it seemed to choke all utterance.

She strained him to her, and heart throbbed against heart. Even now she seemed to see his face mistily and far away.

"Oh, it is too bitter!" she gasped, striving to drown her rising sobs. "Laurence, my darling. Oh, my love, my life, my ideal—yes, you were that from the moment I first saw you—good-bye—and goodbye!"

He was gone. It was as though their embrace had literally been wrenched asunder. He was gone. And even as he passed from her vision, from the light into the gloom, so it seemed as though he had borne the light of her life with him, and, as Lilith stood there in the open doorway, gazing forth into the night, the dull measured clank of the battery stamps seemed to beat in cruel, pitiless refrain within her heart

"At the twelfth hour! at the twelfth hour."

CHAPTER XII

"THE DARK PLACES OF THE EARTH"

THE sun is setting above the tropical forest—hot and red and smoky—his fiery ball imparting something of a coppery molten hue to the vast seas of luxuriant verdure, rolling, with scarce a break, on all sides, far as the eye can reach. But beneath, in the dim shade, where the air is choked by rotting undergrowth and tangled vegetation, the now slanting rays are powerless to penetrate, powerless to dispel the steamy miasmic exhalations. Silence, too, is the rule in that semi-gloom, save for here and there the half-frightened chirp of a bird far up among the tree-tops, or the stealthy rustle beneath as some serpent, or huge venomous insect, moves upon its way. For among the decayed wood of fallen tree trunks, and dry lichens and hoary mosses growing therefrom, do such delight to dwell.

Beautiful as this shaded solitude is with its vistas of massive tree-trunk and sombre foliage, the latter here and there relieved

by clusters of scarlet-hued blossoms, there is withal an awesome-
ness about its beauty. Even the surroundings will soon begin to
take on shape, and the boles and tossing boughs, and naked, dead,
and broken fragments starting from the dank soil, assume form,
attitude, countenance, in a hundred divers contortions—gnome-
like, grotesque, diabolical. Strange, too, if the wayfarer threading
the steamy mazes of these unending glades does not soon think to
hear ghostly whisperings in the awed silence of the air, does not
conjure up unseen eyes marking his every step—for the hot moist
depression is such as to weigh alike upon nerve and brain.

And now, through the sombre vistas of this phantom-evoking
solitude, faint and far comes a strange sound—a low, vibrating,
booming hum, above which, now and again, arises a shrill, long-
drawn wail. The effect is indescribably gruesome and eerie—in
fact, terror-striking—even if human, for there is an indefinable
something, in sight and sound and surrounding, calculated to tell,
if telling were needed, that this is indeed one of "the dark places
of the earth."[1]

But if the sinking beams of the orb of light fail to penetrate
this foliage-enshrouded gloom, they slant hot and red upon an
open space, and that which this space contains. Enclosed within
an irregular stockade—mud-plastered, reed-thatched—stand the
huts of a native village.

The noise which penetrated in faint eerie murmur to yon
distant forest shades is here terrific—the booming of drums, the
cavernous bellowing of the native horns, drowning rather than
supporting the shrill yelling chorus of the singers. For a great dance
is proceeding.

Immediately within the principal gate of the stockade is a large
open space, and in this the dancers are performing. In a half circle
in the background sit a number of women and children, aiding
with shrill nasal voices the efforts of the "musicians."

The dancers, to the number of about a hundred, seem to represent the warrior strength of the place. They are wild-looking
savages enough with their cicatrised and tattooed faces, and wool,
red with grease and ochre and plaited into tags, standing out like
horns from their heads, giving them a frightfully demoniacal aspect
as they whirl and leap, brandishing spears and axes, and going

through the pantomime of slaying an enemy. They are of fair physique, though tall and gaunt rather than sturdy of build. And—is
it a mere accident, or in accordance with some custom—not one
there present, whether among the truculent crew executing the
dance or among the women in the background, appears to have
attained old age.

The whole scene is sufficiently repulsive, even terrifying, to
come upon suddenly from the silent heart of the dark, repellent
forest. But there is yet another setting to the picture, which shall
render it complete in every hideous and horrifying detail. For
the principal gate itself is decorated with a complete archway of
human heads.

Heads in every stage of horror and decay—from the white,
bleached skull, grinning dolefully, to the bloated features of that
but lately severed, scowling outward with an awful expression of
terror and agony and hate—an archway of them arranged in some
grim approach to regularity or taste. This dreadful gate is indeed a
fitting entrance to a devil's abode, and now, as the red, fiery rays
of the sinking sun play full upon it, the tortured features seem to
move and pucker as though blasted with the flame of satanic fires.
A crow, withdrawing his beak from the sightless eyeholes of one
of the skulls, soars upward, black and demon-like, uttering a weird,
raucous croak.

But as the sun touches the far-away skyline the dance suddenly
ceases. In wild hubbub the fighting men stream out of the stockade, through the awful archway of heads. They are followed by
women, bearing strange-looking baskets and great knives. All are
in high spirits, chattering and laughing with each other.

The forest on this side grows almost to the gate. Just where its
shade begins the crowd halts, clustering eagerly around two trees
which stand a little apart from the rest. But from one to the other
of these two trees is lashed a stout beam, such as butchers might
use for hoisting the carcass of a slain bullock. And look! below are
oblong slabs of massive wood, and upon them is blood. This is the
cattle-killing place, then, and these warriors are about to slaughter
the material for a feast?

Now there is more chatter and hubbub, and all faces are turned
toward the grim gate—are turned expectantly; for the cattle are

awaited. Then a shout, an exclamation, goes up. The material for the feast is drawing near.

The material for the feast! Heavens! No cattle this, but *human beings*.

Human beings! Bound, trussed, helpless, five human bodies are borne along by the head and heels, and flung down anyhow at the place of slaughter. The eyeballs of the victims are starting from their heads with terror and despair as their glance falls upon the grisly instruments of death. Yet no surprise is there, for they have seen it all before.

Three of the five are old men. These are seized first, and, a thong being made fast to their ankles, they are hauled up to the beam, where, hanging head downwards, they are butchered like calves. And those who are most active in at anyrate preparing them for the slaughter, are their own children—*their own sons*.

These go about their work without one spark of pity, one qualm of ruth. Will not their own turn come in the course of years, should they not be slain in battle or the chase in the interim? Of course. Why then heed such vain sentiment? It is the custom. Old and useless people are not kept among this tribe.

The other two, who are not old but prisoners of war, suffer in like manner; and then all five of the bodies are flung on to the blocks and quartered and disjointed with astonishing celerity. And women bearing the oblong baskets return within the stockade, passing through the hideous gateway, staggering beneath the weight of limbs and trunks of their slaughtered fellow-species. Within the open space great fires now leap and crackle into life, roaring upward upon the still air, reddening as with a demon-glow this hellish scene; and, gathering around, the savages impatiently and with hungry eyes watch the cooking of the disjointed members, and, hardly able to restrain their impatience, snatch their horrible roast from the flames and embers before it is much more than warmed through; and with laugh and shout the cannibal orgie goes on, prolonged far into the night, the bones and refuse being flung to the women in the background.

At last, surfeited with their frightful feast, these demons in human shape drop down and sleep like brute beasts. And the full moon soaring high in the heavens looks down, with a gibing sneer in her cold cruel face, upon this scene of a shocking human shambles; and her light, so far from irradiating this "dark place of the earth," seems but to shed a livid sulphurous glare upon a very antechamber of hell.

The moon floats higher and higher above the tropical forest, flooding the seas of slumbering foliage with silver light. Hour follows upon hour, and in the stockaded village all is silent as with the stillness of death. The ghastly remnants of that fearful feast lie around in the moonbeams—human bones, picked clean, yet expressive in their shape; spectral, as though they would fain reunite, and, vampire-like, return to drain the life-blood of these human wolves who devour their own kind. But the sleep of the latter is calm, peaceful, secure.

Secure? Wait! What are these stealthy forms rising noiselessly among the undergrowth on the outskirts of the clearing? Are they ghosts? Ghosts of those thus barbarously slain and of many others before them? The moonlit sward is alive with flitting shapes, gliding towards the stockade, surrounding it on all sides with a celerity and fixity of purpose which can have but one meaning. And among them is the glint of metal, the shining of rifle barrels and spear blades.

The inhabitants of that village are savages, and thus, for all their flesh-gorged state of heavy slumber, are instinctively on the alert. They wake, and rush forth with wild yells of alarm, of warning. But to many of them it is the last sound they shall utter, for numberless forms are already swarming over the stockade, and now the stillness is rent by the roar of firearms. Dark, ferocious faces grin with exultation as the panic-stricken inhabitants, decimated by that deadly volley, turn wildly in headlong flight for the only side of the stockade apparently left open. But before these arises another mass of assailants, barring their way, then springing upon them spear in hand; and the fiendish war-whistle screeches its strident chorus, as the broad spears shear down through flesh and muscle; and the earth is slippery with blood, ghastly with writhing and disembowelled corpses.

If this nest of man-eaters was hellish before in its bloodstained horror, words fail to describe its aspect now. The savage shouts of the assailants; the despairing screeches of women and children, who have come forth only to find all escape cut off; the gasping groans of the wounded and of the slain; the gaping gashes and staggering forms; and ever around, grim, demon-like countenances, with teeth bared and a perfect hell of blood-fury gleaming from distended eyeballs. All is but another Inferno picture, too common here in the dark places of the earth. It seems that in a very few minutes not a living being in that surprised village will be left alive.

But now voices are raised in remonstrance, in command—loud voices, authoritative voices—ordering a cessation of the massacre, for this is no expedition of vengeance, but a slave-hunting party. In Swahili and Zulu the leaders strive to curb this blood-rage once let loose among their followers. But the savage Wangoni,[2] who are the speakers of the latter tongue and who constitute about half the attacking party, have tasted slaughter, and their ferocity is well-nigh beyond control; indeed, but for the fact of being allowed to massacre a proportion of the inhabitants of each place attacked, they could not be enlisted for such a purpose at all. Still their broad spears flash in the moonlight, and all who are in the way feel them—combatants, shrieking women, paralysed, crouching children; and not until the leader has threatened to turn his rifles upon them will these ferocious auxiliaries be persuaded to desist, and then only sullenly, and growling like a pack of disappointed wolves.

Fully one-half of the male inhabitants have been slain and not a few women and children, and now, as the heavy sulphurous fumes of powder-smoke roll forth on the still, solemn beauty of the night, and the Wangoni, reluctantly quitting the congenial work of plunder and rapine, drive into the open space every living being they can muster, the two leaders step forward, and with critical decision inspect the extent and quality of their capture. Of the latter there are none but able-bodied, for the sufficiently hideous reason already set forth. These are drafted into gangs according to age or sex, and yoked together like oxen, with heavy wooden yokes.

Upon the whole of this wild scene of carnage and massacre the principal leader of the slave-hunters has gazed unmoved. Not a shot has he fired, not deeming it necessary, so complete was the panic wherewith the cannibal village was overwhelmed. Rather have his energies been devoted to restraining the blood-thirst of his ferocious followers, for he looks upon the tragedy with a cold commercial eye. Prisoners represent so many saleable wares. If it is essential that his hell-hounds shall taste a modicum of blood, or their appetite for this species of quarry would be gone, it is his business to see that they destroy no more "property" than can be avoided.

The force is made up of Swahili and negroid Arabs, and a strong contingent of Wangoni—a Zulu-speaking tribe, turbulent, warlike, and to whom such a maraud as this comes as the most congenial occupation in the world.

The last-named savages are still engaged looting the reed huts in search of food, arms, anything portable. If during their quest they happen upon a terrified fugitive hoping for concealment, their delight knows no bounds, for have they not the enjoyment of privily spearing such, away from their leader's eye?

The said leader now gives the word to march, and as the moon-light pales into the first greys of dawn the scene of the massacre becomes plain in all its appalling detail. Corpses ripped and slashed, lying around in every contorted attitude, among broken weapons and strewn about articles of clothing or furniture. Everywhere blood. The ground is slippery with it, the huts are splashed with it, the persons and weapons of the raiders are all horrid with it; and in the midst that band of men and women yoked like cattle, and with the same hopeless, stolid expression now upon their coun-tenances. Yet they are not dejected. Their lives have been spared where others have been slain. But—they are slaves.

"Bid farewell to home, O foul and evil dogs who devour each other," jeer the savage Wangoni, as these are driven forth. "*Whau!* Ye shall keep each other in meat on the way. Ha, ha! For in truth ye are as fat oxen to each other," pointing with their broad spears to the gruesome trees and crossbeam—the scene of the hideous can-nibal slaughter. For the Wangoni, by virtue of their Zulu origin, hold cannibalism in the deepest horror and aversion.

These barbarians now, humming a bass war-song as they march, are in high glee, for there are more villages to raid. And as the whole party moves forth from the glade once more to plunge within the forest gloom, the air is alive with the circling of carrion birds; and the newly-risen sun darts his first arrowy beam upon the scene of horror, lighting up the red gore and the slain corpses, and the ghastly staring heads upon the gateway. Even as his last ray fell upon a tragedy of blood and of cruelty so now does his first, for in very truth this is one of the "dark places of the earth."

CHAPTER XIII

THE MAN-HUNTERS

FOR some three hours the party moves forward through the forest shades. Then a halt is called, and, sentinels having been posted, soon the smoke of bivouac fires ascends, and the clatter of cooking utensils mingles with the hum of many voices.

The place selected is an open glade or clearing, overhung on one side by hoary masses of rock. The slave-hunters, as we have said, are divided into two sections, one consisting of negroid Arabs and Wa-Swahili, believers in the Prophet mostly, and clad in array once gaudy but now soiled and tarnished, some few, however, wearing the white haik and burnous; the other of Wangoni, stalwart, martial savages, believers in nothing and clad in not much more. These form camps apart, for at heart each section despises the other, though for purposes of self-interest temporarily welded. A few, but very few, are Arabs of pure blood.

One of these is now engaged in converse with the leader of the party. He is a tall, dignified, keen-faced man, with eyes as piercing as those of a hawk, and his speech is sparing. But if his words are few his deeds are many, and the name of Lutali—which, however, he makes no secret is not his real name—is known and feared at least as far and as thoroughly as that of the chief of the slavers himself.

For the latter, one glance at him is sufficient to show that if ever man was born to rule with firm but judicious hand such a gang of bloodthirsty freebooters it is this one. The vigour of his powerful frame is apparent with every movement, and the strength and fixity of will expressed in his keen dark face there is no mistaking.

But the black, piercing eyes and bronzed features belong to no Arab, no half-caste. He is a white man, a European.

Stay! To be accurate, there is just a strain of Arab in him; faint, indeed, as of several generations intervening, yet real enough to qualify him for mysterious rites of blood brotherhood with some of the most powerful chiefs from Tanganyika to Khartoum. And throughout the Congo territory, and many an equatorial tribe beyond, this man's name has been known and feared. No leader of slave-hunters can come near him for bold and wide sweeping raids, the terror and unexpectedness of which, together with the complete and ruthless fixity of purpose wherewith the objects of them, however strong, however alert, are struck and promptly subjugated, have gained for him among his followers and allies the sobriquet of El Khanac, "The Strangler." But the reader—together with Johannesburg at large—knows him under another name, and that is "Pirate" Hazon.

"Is it prudent, think you, Lutali?" he is saying. "Consider. These Wajalu are a trifle too near the land of the Ba-gcatya. Indeed, we ourselves are too near it now, and a day's journey or more in the same direction is it not to run our heads into the jaws of the lion?"

"Allah is great, my brother," replies the Arab, with a shrug of the shoulders. "But I would ask, what have we, in our numbers and with arms such as these," gripping significantly his Express rifle,[1] "to fear from those devil-worshippers armed with spears and shields—yea, even the whole nation of them?"

"Yet I have seen an army of the nation of which those 'devil-worshippers' are sprung, armed only with spears and shields, eat up a force three times as large as our own and infinitely better armed, I being one of the few who escaped.[2] And 'The People of the Spider' cannot, from all accounts, be inferior to the stock whence they came."

Lutali shrugs his shoulders again.

"It may be so," he says, "yet there is a large village of these Wajalu which would prove an easy capture and would complete the number we need."

"Then let us chance it," is Hazon's rejoinder.

The Arab makes a murmur of assent and stalks away to his

own people, while Hazon returns to where he has left his white colleague.

"Well, Holmes. According to Lutali, they are bent on risking it," he begins, throwing himself upon a rug and proceeding to fill a pipe.

"Are they? I'm not altogether glad, yet if it tends towards hurrying us out of this butchery line of business I'm not altogether sorry. I think I hate it more and more every day."

"It isn't a bad line of business, Holmes," returns Hazon, completely ignoring the smothered reproachfulness, resentment even, underlying the tone and reply. "Come now, you've made a goodish bit of money the short time you have been at it. Anyhow, I want to know in what other you would have made anything like as much in the time. Not in fooling with those rotten swindling stocks at the Rand, for instance?"

"Maybe not. But we haven't realised yet. In other words, we are not safe out of the wood yet, Hazon, and so it's too soon to hulloa. I don't believe we are going to get off so easily," he adds.

"Are you going to get on your croaking horse again, and threaten us with 'judgments' and 'curses,' and all that sort of thing?" rejoins the other, with a good-humoured laugh. "Why, man, we are philanthropists—real philanthropists. And I never heard of 'judgments' and 'curses' being showered upon such."

"Philanthropists, are we? That's a good idea. But where, by the way, does the philanthropy come in?"

"Why, just here." Then, impressively, "Listen, now, Holmes. Carry your mind back to all the sights you have seen since we came up the Lualaba³ until now. Have you forgotten that round dozen of niggers we happened on, buried in the ground up to their necks, and when we had dug up one fellow we found we had taken a lot of trouble for nothing because he'd got his arms and legs broken? The same held good of all the others, except that some were mutilated as well. You remember how sick it made you coming upon those heads in the half darkness; or those quarters of a human body swinging from branches, to which their owner had been spliced so that, in springing back, the boughs should drag him asunder, as in fact they did? Or the sight of people feeding on the flesh of their own blood relations, and many and many another spectacle no more amusing? Well, then, these barbarities were practised by no wicked slave-raiders, mind, but by the 'quiet, harmless' people upon each other. And they are of every-day occurrence. So that, in capturing these gentle souls, and deporting them—for a price— whither they will perforce be taught better manners, we are acting the part of real philanthropists. Do you catch on?"

"What of those we kill? Those Wangoni brutes are never happy unless killing."

"That is inevitable and is the law of life, which is always hard. And, as Lutali would say—who may fight against his destiny? Not that I mean to say we embarked in this business from motives of philanthropy, friend Holmes; I only cite the argument as one to quiet that singularly inconvenient conscience of yours. We did so, Stanninghame and I, at anyrate, to make money—quickly, and plenty of it; and I'm not sure Stanninghame doesn't need it more than you and I put together."

"By the bye, I wonder what on earth has become of Stanninghame all this time?" said Holmes, apparently glad to quit an unprofitable subject.

"So do I. He ought to have joined us by now. He is just a trifle foolhardy, is Stanninghame, in knocking about so far afield alone," and a shade of anxiety steals over the speaker's face.

Holmes makes no reply, and for a while lies back on his rug, puffing away at his pipe and busy with his thoughts. These are not altogether pleasant. The process which had transformed the fine, open-natured, wholesome-hearted young Englishman into a slave-hunter, the confederate of ruthless cut-throats and desperadoes, had, in truth, been such as to engender the reverse of pleasant thoughts. Yet, that he had come to this was rather the fault of circumstances than the fault of Holmes. He had enjoyed the big-game shooting and the ivory trading of the earlier stage of the trip, the more so from the consciousness that there was profit in both; and when a large caravan of the above and other legitimate merchandise had been run down to the coast, he had steadfastly refused to take the opportunity of parting company with the others. Then when they had pushed farther into the equatorial regions, and, joining with Lutali, had embarked on their present enterprise, all opportunity of withdrawing had gone. The precise point at which he had cast in his lot with this, Holmes could not with certainty define. Yet there were times when he thought he could. He had relieved his conscience with indignant, passionate protest, when first his eyes became fairly opened to the real nature of the enterprise; and then had supervened that terrible bout of malarial fever, his tardy recovery from which he owed entirely to the care and nursing of both Hazon and Stanninghame. But it left him for a long time weakened in mind and will no less than in body, and what could he do but succumb to the inevitable? Yet he had never entered into the sinister undertaking with the whole-heartedness of his two conscienceless confederates, and of this the latter were aware.

However, of his scruples they were tolerant enough. He was brimful of pluck, and seemed to enjoy the situation when they were attacked by overwhelming odds and had to fight hard and fiercely, such as befell more than once. And they would insidiously lay salve to his misgivings by such arguments as we have just heard Hazon adduce, or by reminding him of the fortune they were making, or even of the physical advantage he was deriving from the trip.

The latter, indeed, was a fact. The life in the open, the varying climates, frequent and inevitable hardships and never-absent peril, had made their mark upon Holmes. Once recovered from his attack, he began to put on flesh and muscle, and his eyes were clear and bright with that keen alertness which is the result of peril as a constant companion. In short, as they said, he looked twice the man he had seemed when lounging around the Stock Exchange or the liquor bars of Johannesburg.

Through the hot hours of noontide the raiders lie at their ease. Many are asleep, others conversing in drowsy tones, smoking or chewing tobacco. The Wangoni divide their time about equally between taking snuff and jeering at and teasing the unfortunate captives. These, crouching on the ground, relieved during the halt of their heavy forked yokes, endure it all with the stoicism of the most practical phase of humanity—the savage. No good is to be got out of bewailing their lot, therefore they do not bewail it; moreover, belonging to a savage race, and far from the highest type of the same, they have no thought of the future, and are thus spared the discomfort and anxiety of speculating as to what it may contain for them. Indeed, their chief anxiety at this moment is that of food, of which they would fain have more, and gaze with wistful eyes upon their captors, who are feasting on the remnant of what was until lately their own property. But the latter jeeringly suggest to them the expediency of their devouring each other, since they seem to have a preference for such diet.

Then, as the sun's rays abate somewhat in fierceness, the temporary camp is struck. Bearers take up their loads, fighters look to their arms, the soiled and gaudy finery of the semi-civilised sons of the Prophet contrasting with the shining skins of the naked Wangoni, even as the Winchester and Snider rifles and great sheath-knives and revolvers of the first do with the broad spears and tufted hide-shields of the latter. And with the files of dejected-looking slaves, yoked together in their heavy wooden forks, or chained only, the whole caravan, numbering now some six hundred souls, moves onward.

But in the mind of the principal of the two white leaders, as he traces a cypher[4] on the scene of their recent halt, and in that of the other, who watches him, is present, now with deepening anxiety, the same thought, the same speculation: What has become of the third?

CHAPTER XIV

A DREAM

UNDER the shade of a large tree-fern a man is lying asleep.

Around, the wilderness spreads in rolling undulation, open here for the most part, though dotted with clumps of bush and trees, which seem to have become detached from the dark line of forest. This, on the one hand, stretches away into endless blue; on the other a broad expanse of water—apparently a fine river, actually a chain of lagoons—with reed-fringed banks; and here and there a low spit, where red flamingoes roost lazily on one leg. Beyond this again lies an unbroken line of forest.

The man is arrayed in the simple costume of the wilderness—a calico shirt, and moleskin trousers protected by leather leggings. A broad-brimmed hat lies under his head, to which, indeed, it serves as sole pillow. He is heavily armed. The right hand still grips an Express rifle in mute suggestion of one accustomed to slumber in the midst of peril. A revolver in a holster rests beside him, and in his leathern belt is a strong sheath knife. Now and again he moves in his sleep, and at such times his unarmed hand seems instinctively to seek out something which is concealed from view, possibly something which is suspended round his neck by that light but strong chain. Thus hour after hour rolls over him, as he slumbers on in the burning equatorial heat.

The sleeper turns again uneasily, and as he does so his hand again seeks the steel chain just visible through his open shirt, and, instinctively working down it, closes over that which is secured thereto; then, as though the effect is lulling, once more he is still again, slumbering easily, peacefully.

The sun's rays, slanting now, dart in beneath the scanty shade of the tree-fern, and as they burn upon the dark face, bronzed and hardened by climate and toil, the sleeper's lips are moving, and a peculiarly soft and wistful expression seems to rest upon the firm features. Then his eyes open wide. For a moment he lies, staring up at the green fronds which afford shade no longer, then starts up into a sitting posture. And simultaneous with the movement here and there a faint circular ripple widens on the slimy surface of the lagoon, as each of those dark specks, representing the snout of a basking crocodile, vanishes.

Laurence Stanninghame's outward aspect has undergone some change since last we beheld it, now more than two years ago. The expression of the dark, firm face, burned and bronzed by an equatorial sun, heavily bearded too, has become hard and ruthless, and there is a quick alertness in the penetrating glance of the clear eyes which tells of an ever-present familiarity with peril. Even the movement of sitting up, of suddenly awakening from sleep, yet being wide awake in a moment, contains unconsciously more than a suggestion of this.

A rapid, careful look on all sides. Nothing is stirring in the sultry, penetrating heat; the palmetto thatch of clustering huts away beyond the opposite bank might contain no life for all of it they show. Hardly a bird twittering in the reeds but does so half-heartedly. The man's face softens again, taking on the expression it wore while he slept.

While he slept! Why could he not have slept on for ever, he thought, his whole being athrill with the memory revived by his dreams? For his dreams had been sweet—wildly, entrancingly sweet. Seldom, indeed, were such vouchsafed to him; but when they were their effect would last, would last vividly. He would treasure up their recollection, would go back upon it.

Now, slumbering there in the torrid heat, by the reed-fringed, crocodile-haunted lagoon, his dreams had wafted him into a more than Paradise. Eyes, starry with a radiant love-light, had laughed into his; around his neck the twining of arms, and the soft, caressing touch of soothing hands upon his life-weary head; the whisper of love-tones, deep, burning, tremulous, into his ear. And from this he had awakened, had awakened to the reality—to the weird and depressing surroundings of human life in its most cruel and debased form; to the recollection of scenes of recurring and hideous peril, of pitiless atrocity, which seemed to render the burning, brassy glare even as the glare of hell; and to the consciousness of similar scenes now immediately impending. Yet the remembrance of that sleeping vision shut him in, surrounded him as with a very halo, sweet, fragrant, enthralling, rolling around his soul as a cloud of intoxicating ether.

Upon a temperament such as that of Laurence Stanninghame the life of the past two years was bound to tell. The hot African glow, the adventurous life, with peril continually for a fellow-traveller, a familiarity with weird and shocking deeds, an utter indifference to human suffering and human life, had strangely affected his inner self. Callous to the woes of others, yet high-strung to a degree, his nature at this time presented a stage of complexity which was utterly baffling. That mesmeric property to which Hazon had alluded more than once as one of the effects of travel in the interior was upon him too. It seemed as though he had somehow passed into another world, so dulled was all recollection of his former life, all desire to recall it. Yet one memory remained undimmed.

"Lilith, my soul!" he murmured, his eyes wandering over the

brassy, glaring expanse of water and dried-up reed-bed, as though to annihilate space and distance. "Lilith, my life! It is time I looked once more upon that dear face which rendered my dreams so sweet."

His hand, still clasping something within his breast, was drawn forth, that which hung by the steel chain still enclosed within it. A small, flat, metal box it was, oblong in shape, and shutting so tightly that at first glance it was hard to see where it opened at all. But open it did, for now he is holding what it contains—holding it lovingly, almost reverently, in the palm of his hand. It is a little case; green velvet worked with flowers, and in the centre, spreading fantastically in spidery pattern in dark maroon, is a monogram—Lilith's. And in like manner is this same monogram inlaid upon the lid of the box.

Two tiny portraits it contains when opened—photographic portraits, small, yet clear and delicate as miniatures. Lilith's eyes gaze forth, seeming to shine from the inanimate cardboard as though with the love-light of gladness; Lilith's beautiful form, erect in characteristic attitude, the head slightly thrown back, the sweet lips compressed, just a touch of sadness in their serenity, as though dwelling upon the recollection of that last parting; even the soft curling waves of hair, rippling back from the temples, are lifelike in the clearness of the portrait.

The strong, sweet dream-wave still enclouding his brain, Laurence stands gazing upon these, and his heart is as though enwrapped with a dull tightening pain.

"Sorceress! and does the spell still enthral me here?" he murmurs. "Here, and after all this time? Have you forgotten me? Perhaps. No, that cannot be, and yet—Time! Time dulls everything. Time brings changes. Perhaps even the memory of me is waning, is becoming dulled."

But the softening love-light in the pictured eyes seems to contradict the conjecture. Here, in the hot brassy glare of the far wilderness, in the haunts of bloodshed and wrong, that sweet, pure image seems clothed as with a divinity to his hungry gaze.

"Others can see you in life; others can hear the music of your voice, my beloved; others can look into the light of those eyes, can melt to the radiance of your smile, while I—only the image is mine, the tiny oblong of hard inanimate cardboard," he murmurs, in a tone that is half weariful, half passionate. "And now for the words!"

A slip of folded paper occupies the side of the little tin box. This he extracts and unfolds with a touch that is almost reverent, and, as his eyes wander over the writing, his every faculty of soul and mind and being is concentrated in rapt love upon each word. For not every day will he suffer his eyes to rest upon them, lest too great familiarity with them should dull them with a mechanical nature when seen so often. They are kept for rare occasions, and this, his waking thoughts sweet with the influence of the recent dream, he reckons just such an occasion.

The history of the box, the portraits, the letter, was a strange one. After that last parting, as Laurence was wending his way in the darkness, he became aware that his breast-pocket contained something which was not there before. He drew it forth. It was small, flat, hard, oblong. By the light of successive vestas[1] he proceeded to investigate, and there, in the flickering glow, Lilith's sweet eyes gazed out at him from the cardboard, daintily framed within the work of her fingers, even as here in the burning glare of the equatorial sun; and there too, within the box, lay a folded slip of paper covered with her hand-writing—her last words to him, drawing out, perpetuating the echo of her last spoken ones. With a thrill of love and pain, he had stood there in the darkness until his last vesta had burned out, and then the letter was not half read, but from that moment the box and its contents had rested upon his heart day and night—through scenes of blood and of woe, through every conceivable phase of hardship and starvation and peril—had rested there as a charm, or amulet, which should shield him from harm. And as such, indeed, its donor had intended it.

And now his eyes, wandering over the paper, as though devouring every word, are nearing the end:——

"Does this come as a surprise, my darling—a very sweet surprise?" it ran. "I mean it to be that. Is it for good or for ill this love of ours? you have said. Surely for good. Keep, then, this image of me, my beloved. Never part with it, day or night, and may it ever, by the very strength of my love for you, be as a talisman—a 'charm'—to stand between you and all peril, as you say the mental image of me has already done, how, I cannot see, but it is enough for me that you say so. And the consciousness that I should have been the means of averting evil from you is sweet, unutterably so. May it continue, and strengthen me as it will mysteriously shield you, while we are far apart. My Laurence! my ideal!—yes, you are that; the very moment my eyes first met the firm full gaze of yours I recognised it. I knew what you were, and my heart went out to you."

The blood surged hotly, in a dark flush, beneath Laurence Stanninghame's bronzed face, as he pictured the full force and passion of those parting utterances murmured into his ear instead of confided only to cold inanimate paper; then the demon of cynicism ingrained within him came uppermost with hateful and haunting suggestions——

"She is safe? Yes. But those words were penned more than two years ago. More than two years ago! That is a long time for one in the full glow of her glorious youth. More than two years ago! And in the joy and delight of living, what charm has the memory—the daily fading memory—of the absent for such as she? Think of it, O fool, not yet free from the shackles of the last illusion. Think of circumstances, of surroundings, of temperament,—above all, of such a temperament as hers. Is your mature knowledge of life to go for nothing that you are so easily fooled? Ha, ha!"

Thus laughed the demon voice in mocking gibe. But he—no, he would not listen; he would stifle it. Those words were the outcome of one love—the love of a lifetime, and nothing less.

Suddenly, with multifold splash and a great winnowing of wings, a flight of cranes and egrets arose from the bank some little distance farther down. Dark forms were moving among the reeds. All the instincts of a constant familiarity with peril alert within him, Laurence had, in a moment, replaced the case and its contents. His Express was grasped in readiness as he peered forth eagerly from his place of concealment. He was the crafty, ruthless slaver once more.

Then the expression, stealthy, resolute, which his discovery had evoked, faded, giving way to one of half-interested curiosity, as he saw that the potential enemies—more or less redoubtable assailants—were merely a few small boys, wandering along the reed-fringed bank, jabbering light-heartedly as they strolled.

Suddenly there was a splash, a smothered cry, and a loud burst of shrill laughter. The sooty imps were dancing and capering with glee, gazing at and chaffing one of their number who had fallen from the bank—high and perpendicular there—into the water among the reeds. But almost as suddenly the cachinnations turned to a sharp yell of terror and warning. The reeds swayed in a quivering line of undulation, as though something were moving through them—something swift and mighty and terrible—and so it was. The black boy, who could swim like a fish, had thrown himself clear of the reeds, deeming his chances better in the open water, but after him, its long grisly snout and cruel beady eyes flush with the surface, glided a large crocodile.

Half instinctively the unseen spectator put up his piece, then dropped it again. He might shoot the reptile, but what then? All their plans would be upset—the villages would be alarmed, and his own life greatly jeopardised. Too steep a price by far to pay, to save one wretched little black imp from being devoured by a crocodile, he told himself. The road to wealth did not lie that way; and the cruel sneer that drooped his lips as he lowered his weapon was not good to behold, as he stood up to witness the end of this impromptu hunt, whose quarry was human.

The boys on the bank were shouting and screaming, partly for help, partly in the hope of scaring the hideous saurian. That wily reptile, however; heeded them not one atom. His great jaws opened and closed with a snap—but not on the crunch of human flesh, not on the crackle of human bones. The wretched little native, with incredible dexterity, had swerved and dived, just eluding the hungry jaws by no more than a hair's-breadth. But to what avail?

For the smooth surface of the lagoon was now rippling into long furrow-like waves. Dark objects were gliding through the water with noiseless rapidity, converging on the point where the human quarry had now risen to breathe. More of the dreadful reptiles, with which the lagoons were swarming, had found out there was prey, and were bearing down to obtain their share. From his concealment, Laurence could see it all—the glistening of the hideous snouts, the round woolly head and staring, terror-stricken eyeballs of the miserable little victim. Then, with a wild, piercing, soul-curdling shriek, the latter disappeared, and there arose to the surface a boil of foam, bubbling upon the slimy water in a bright red stain. Below, in the depths, the crocodiles were rending asunder their unexpected prey.

"The moral of that episode," said the concealed spectator to himself, as he turned away, "is that little boys should not play too near the bank. No, there is yet another—the incredibly short space of time in which the refined and civilised being can turn into a stony-hearted demon; and the causes which accomplish such transmogrification are twain—the parting with all his illusions, and the parting with all his cash."

These ruminations were cut short in a manner that was violent, not to say alarming. Two spears whizzed past him with a vicious, angry hiss, one burying itself deep in the stem of the tree-fern just behind him, the other flying into empty space, but grazing his ear by very few inches indeed. Then, in the wild, barking, hoarse-throated yell, bloodcurdling in its note of hate and fury, Laurence Stanninghame realised that he was in a tight place—a very tight place.

CHAPTER XV

AN AWAKENING

TEN or a dozen tall savages were advancing through the somewhat sparse scrub. Yielding to a first impulse of self preservation, Laurence, quick as thought, stepped behind the stem of the tree-fern. Then he peered forth.

His first glance, keen and quick, took in every detail. His assailants were fine warrior-like men, ferocious-looking, in great crested headgear of plumes. Their bodies were adorned with cowhair circlets, but, save for a short kilt of catstails and hide, they were quite unclad. They carried large shields of the Zulu pattern, and a sheaf of gleaming spears—some light, others heavy and strong, with the blade like a cutlass.

Who, what could they be? he wondered. They were too fine

and stately of aspect—with their lofty, commanding brows, and clear, full glance—to belong to any of the tribes around. They were not Wangoni—they wore too striking a look to come of even that fine race. Who could they be?

His conjectures on that head, rapid as they were, ceased abruptly, for a perfect volley of spears came whizzing about him, several burying their heads deep within the stem of the tree-fern. Well indeed for him that he had so rapidly placed even that slight rampart between himself and his enemies.

Deeming parley better than fight, under the circumstances, Laurence began quickly upon them in a mixture of Swahili and Zulu, declaring that he could be no enemy to them or to their race. But a loud mocking laugh drowned his words; and, seeing that the savages had suddenly half crouched behind their shields for a charge, his quick, resourceful brain grasped the situation at once. A puff of smoke, a jet of flame from behind the tree-fern. One of the warriors fell forward on his shield, beating the earth with his great limbs in the throes of death.

They had hardly reckoned upon this. Crouching low, now they glide away among the scrub, keeping well within cover. But that solitary, determined man, flattened there against the tree-fern, draws no hope from this. Their manœuvre is a simple one enough. They are going to enfilade the position. Surrounded on all sides, and by such foes as these, where will he be? for he has no cover.

But in Laurence Stanninghame's stern eyes there is a lurid battle-glow, a very demon light. His enemies will have his life, but they will purchase it at a long price. A dead silence now reigns, and through it he can hear the stealthy rustle made by his foes in their efforts to surround him. Were he in the comparative security of cover, or behind a rampart of any sort, he might hope, by a super-human effort of quick firing, to hold them back. As it is, he dare not move from behind his tree, suspecting an intention to draw him thence.

The sun flames blood-red upon the lagoon and upon a flight of flamingoes winnowing above the mirror-like surface, and, as though the situation were not deadly and desperate enough, the shimmer of light and water has, even in that brief glance, brought a spot in front of his eyes, at the moment when, if ever, his sight should be at its clearest and quickest. The odds against him are indeed terrible. He can hardly hope to come through; yet to his assailants it may well prove the dearest victory they have ever won.

A dark body, creeping among the scrub—just a glimpse and nothing more. His piece is at his shoulder, and the trigger is pressed. He has not missed—of that he is sure. But the echoes of his shot are swallowed up, drowned in a hundred other echoes reverberating upon the dim silence of the scrub.

Echoes? No. The screech and tear of missiles very near to his own head, the smoke, the jets of flame from half a hundred different points—all this is sufficient to show that these are no echoes. His own people have come up. He is rescued, but only just in the nick of time.

"Look out," he shouts in stentorian tones. "Don't fire this way. Hazon—Holmes, I'm here! Keep the fools in hand. They are blazing at *me*."

But the crash of the volley drowns his voice, and the scrub is alive with swarming natives armed with firelocks of every description. Yet, above the volley and the savage shouts, Laurence can hear the hoarse, barking yell, can descry the forms of his late enemies—such as are left of them—as they flee, leaping and bounding, zigzagging with incredible velocity and address, to avoid the hail of bullets which is poured after them.

He can realise something more—something which sends through his whole being a cold shudder of dismay and despair. Not his own people are these otherwise so opportune arrivals. Not his own people, but—the inhabitants of the villages his own people are on their way to raid—fierce and savage cannibals by habit, but with physique which will furnish excellent slaves. He has literally fallen from the frying-pan into the fire.

How he curses his raw folly in making his presence known. But for this he might have slipped away unnoticed during the scrimmage. Now they come crowding up, brandishing their weapons and yelling hideously. Although inferior both in aspect and stature to those they have just defeated, these barbarians are formidable enough; and terror-striking their wildly ferocious mien. Many of them, too, have filed teeth, which imparts to their hideous countenances the most fiend-like appearance.

Is it that in the apparently fearless attitude, the stern, even commanding, glance of this solitary white man, there is something that overawes them? It may be so, for they stop short in their hostile demonstrations and commence a parley. Yet not altogether does Laurence Stanninghame feel relieved, for a sudden thought surges through his brain which causes a shade of paleness to sweep over his firm, bronzed countenance. What if this were but a scheme to get him into their power? What if he were not suffered to die fighting, were to fall into their hands alive? Why, then, his fate was certain—certain and inexpressibly horrible. He would be butchered like a calf—butchered and eaten—by these repulsive wretches. Such would be his end. Now, however, to make the best of the situation!

But little can he make of their tongue. Then he tries them in Swahili. Ah! several of them have a smattering of that. They have come to his aid at a critical moment, he puts it—he is willing therefore to call them friends. Yet it was a pity they had. He had already killed two of his assailants and was prepared to kill them all, one after another. It was only a question of time. After all, if anything, the new arrivals had rather spoiled his sport.

These stared. The tone was one of patronage, of condescension. This white man was but one; he was alone, and in their power, yet he spoke to them as a great chief might speak. Yet, was he but one? Was he alone or were there many others not far off? Perceptibly their own replies took on a respectful air.

The while, Laurence kept every sense on the alert, indeed even to its uttermost tension. Was this parley designed to keep him preoccupied while others stole up treacherously to strike him down from behind? To guard against this idea he stepped boldly forth from the tree-fern and advanced towards the half threatening crowd.

"Where are those we have slain?" he said. "Let us examine them."

"Yonder," answered some in a wondering tone, while others on the outskirts of the crowd scowled and muttered.

Leisurely, and now moving actually among these people, did Laurence fare forth to look upon the bodies of his late assailants. The thoroughly bold and fearless line he had adopted had told, as he was all but sure it would. These wild barbarians, armed to the teeth, had only to stretch forth a hand and spear him, yet somehow they refrained.

The slain warriors were lying as they fell, and even in death Laurence could not but admire their noble proportions, and the set and martial expression of their countenances. Six lay dead, while another, sorely wounded, was promptly beheaded by the new arrivals. These, their savage instincts all afire, set to work to hack the heads off each corpse; then, tying grass ropes around the ankles, the trunks were dragged away to the village.

To the latter now they invited Laurence. To hesitate might be an act of weakness sufficient to cause his slaughter. To acquiesce, on the other hand, was it not an act of unexampled foolhardiness thus to place himself more absolutely within the power of these savage cannibals? His policy of boldness had availed so far, it would not do to break down at the last moment. So he accepted without a shade of hesitation.

"How is your tribe named?" he asked, as they proceeded along.

"Wajalu," replied the man who had done chief spokesman, rather a good-looking native, with almost a Zulu cast of countenance.

"And the head man of yonder village, who is he?"

"I am he. I—Mgara," was the reply, with a satisfied smile.

"And those we have slain, they seemed fine fighters. Of what race were they?"

"Ba-gcatya."

Laurence looked grave, but said nothing. Strange rumours, mysterious and vague, had reached him already—rumours relating to an immensely powerful tribe inhabiting the dark and unexplored country away to the north, whose raids were extending more and more, whose wrath fell alike upon all—upon Arab slave-hunter and the prey sought by the latter—a Zulu-speaking tribe said to have taken its origin in some hardly recorded exodus in the days of Tshaka[1]—Zulu alike in its habits and customs, and in the despotism of its ruler. This nation was known as the Aba-gcatya or Ba-gcatya, "The People of the Spider." Hazon, too, believed in its existence, and Hazon was a first-class authority on such subjects. And now the warriors who had attacked him, and upon whom the tables were so strangely turned, were Zulu in aspect, and bore Zulu shields. The thing began to look serious. What if that handful of warriors was the outpost of a huge *impi*?[2] Would not the vengeance of the latter be fearful and complete?

And, indeed, time was when Laurence Stanninghame's blood would have boiled with rage and disgust at the indignities offered to the remains of these noble-looking warriors. The trunks dragged along by the heels seemed nothing now but a bleeding mass. The heads, too, stuck upon spear points, were borne aloft above the rabble. To them were all sorts of mockeries addressed.

Now, however, it was different. The hardening process had been, if anything, all too complete. A man had his hands full even if occupied solely in taking care of himself—this had become the sum total of his creed.

As they drew near the village, the Wajalu set up the most hideously discordant war-song he had ever heard in his life. They were met in the gate by a crowd of women howling and blowing horns, and otherwise adding to the horrific tumult. These, on beholding the stranger, imagined him a prisoner, and began clamouring for his death, pointing to the bloodstained place of slaughter where such were wont to be immolated.

And then once more, hearing the shout of demoniacal laughter which arose from some of the fighting-men, noting a ferociously sardonic grin upon not a few faces, Laurence felt his former misgivings all return. Accustomed as he was to perilous situations, to horrifying sights, the strain upon his nerves was becoming painfully intense. Fortunate, indeed, for him that those nerves were now hardened to the cold consistency of cast steel by almost daily trial.

"Men of the Wajalu," he began, in a decisive commanding voice, "well is it for all here that I am among you this day as a friend and guest, for, but for that, this village was doomed. You know not who I am, but you shall know in time. Then you will know that but for my presence here to-day the spear and the slave-yoke would have been your portion, that of your village the flames. Now I give you your lives."

The words, hurriedly rendered to those who could not understand by those who could, together with the haughty indifference of his tone, his bearing, his appearance in general, hard and determined, overawed the crowd. No further voice was raised against him. Their advances of hospitality became even profuse.

He was shown to the best hut. But before he entered it he could not avoid seeing the bodies of his late assailants in process of dismemberment as though they had been slaughtered cattle, and, inured as he was to horrible and sickening sights, never had he been conscious of so overpowering a feeling of repulsion as now. The cannibal atrocities of these human beasts, the glowering heads stuck all over the stockade,—the latest addition thereto being those of the slain Ba-gcatya,—the all-pervading influence of death brooding over this demoniacal haunt, even as the ever-present circlings of carrion birds high in mid-air—all this weighed upon his mind until he could have blown out his own brains for sheer horror and loathing.

But upon this dark, enshrouding shadow, piercing, partly dispelling it, came a ray of searching light—sweet, golden, penetrating. The vision of his midday slumbers—Lilith. But a few hours had gone by since that dream, and within them he had fought fiercely for his life; and now, in this hell-haunt, the sweet entrancement of it came back to charm away, as with a hallowed spell, the black horrors that hung over his soul as though on vulture wing.

Presently Mgara entered, followed by people bearing food—cooked goat-flesh and millet and plantains. From the smoking meat Laurence recoiled with a loathing he could hardly repress. It was too suggestive of the foul and fearful feast proceeding outside; and even when the chief, with a furtive half-smile, assured him he might safely partake of it, yet he could not touch it, contenting himself with the other fare, cereal and vegetable.

After some further talk Mgara withdrew, and Laurence, left alone, gave his meditations the rein once more. Never had he loathed the sinister occupation upon which he was embarked as he did now, possibly because the term of the undertaking was nearing its end. "I predict you will come back with what you want," Lilith had said, and her words had been fully verified. He had gained riches—even beyond his wildest dreams, but how he had gained them—trafficking in human flesh and blood, yea, even human life—she should never know. It seemed to him as though he were already returning with that which should place all the world at his feet.

But for once he seemed to forget that he had not yet returned—not yet. And as the drums and yelling of the barbarous orgie outside gradually sank into the silence of night, even that, strange to say, failed to remind him.

CHAPTER XVI

"AN ANGEL UNAWARES"

NOT much sleep did Laurence get that night—such, indeed, as he obtained being of the "with one eye open" order. Simple trust in anybody or anything was not one of his failings, as we think we have shown; wherefore, having carefully scrutinised the plastered walls of his rude quarters, he took the precaution to secure the wicker door from the inside, and lay down with his Express so covering the same that but the very slightest movement of the hand would be needed on his part in order to rake from stem to stern whosoever should be so ill-advised as to essay a stealthy ingress.

Still more would he have applauded his own foresight in taking these precautions could he have known that a large portion of the night was spent by his "entertainers" keenly debating the expediency of treacherously putting him to death. Here, it was urged, was an opportunity such as might never again come their way. Here was one of the leaders of that dreaded band of slave-hunters—one whose very name was a terror and a scourge. Here was this man actually in their hands. It was in their power to slay him without the smallest risk to themselves. Let them not miss such an opportunity of setting up his head above their gates. As for his party, now that its existence was known, they could surprise it, and slaughter every man it contained. They, the Wajalu, were numerous, and had good fire-weapons, and knew how to use them. Why should they not rid the land of this terror? It was in their power to do so.

This sounded all very plausible; many tales do, until their other side is told. And the other side was unfolded by the head man, Mgara, and others, much to this effect: The slave-hunters were

more numerous than many there imagined. They had been rein-
forced by a large body of Wangoni—fierce and formidable fighters.
To surprise and overwhelm such a force would be impossible, and
in the event of failure what would their own fate be? Moreover,
it was certain that the slavers were much better armed than the
Wajalu. Their best policy would be to treat the man well; he had
already given what was as good as an assurance of his protection.
These counsels prevailed.

And soon the wisdom thereof was made manifest, for with
earliest dawn one of their scouts came running in with the news
that the slave-hunters were approaching; that they were in great
numbers, and mostly armed with rifles; that it was too late for
retreat, in that a large detachment had already gained a position
which was practically such as to surround the village.

The effect of this news was to stamp with an expression of
the most terror-stricken despair the countenance of every man
who heard it. But Mgara, remembering the words of their white
"guest," hurried to the hut where the latter was sleeping.

Yet as the head man approached the door with a quick deferential word of greeting, Laurence Stanninghame was wide awake.
The talk outside, the rapid note of fear underlying the tone had not
escaped him, and even though he understood not a word of their
talk among themselves he knew what these people wanted of him.
And the situation looked serious, for he felt far less confident of his
ability to redeem his half-implied pledge than when, moved by the
first instincts of self-preservation, he had given the same.

Well, and what then? The extinction of this horde of cannibal
barbarians was a mere trifle, a drop in the bucket, when looked
at beside other dark and ruthless deeds which he had witnessed,
and even actually aided in. But hard, pitiless, utterly impervious
to human suffering as he had become, there was one point in
Laurence Stanninghame's character—a weak point, he regarded
it—which he had never succeeded in eradicating. He could not
forget or ignore a good turn. These people, monstrous, repulsive
as they were in his sight, had saved his life—twice indeed—the
first time unconsciously from the Ba-gcatya, the second time from
themselves. They might have slain him barbarously at almost any
moment—he was but one among a number; yet they had not, but

instead had treated him hospitably and well. He was resolved, at any risk, to save them.

Mgara, entering, lost no time in making known his errand.

"O stranger guest, whom we have treated as a friend," he began, in Swahili, "save us from the slave-yoke, and the guns and spears of your people, for they are upon us already." And rapidly he narrated the tidings brought in by the scouts.

"I will do what I can, Mgara," answered Laurence. "Listen. All your people must retire within the huts; not one must be seen. Further, two of your men must bear a token from me to El Khanac, my brother-chief, who leads yonder host, and that at once. Now, call those two men."

Swift of resource, Laurence picked up a flat piece of wood and, scraping it smooth with his knife, wrote upon it in pencil:—

"*I owe these people my life. Keep ours in hand until we meet.*"

"These are the messengers, Mgara?" he went on, as the head man returned accompanied by two men. "Are they reliable, and, above all, fearless?"

"They are both, Sidi,'" answered the chief, now very deferential. "One is my son, the other my brother's son."

"Good. Let them now get a piece of white flaxen cloth, and bind it and this token to a staff. Then let them seek out El Khanac yonder."

In a moment this was done, and, bearing the impromptu white flag and the writing on the board, the two young men started off into the scrub.

"Retire now into your houses, Mgara, you and all your people. I alone will stand within the gate, and maybe it will be well with you."

The Wajalu, who had been hanging on every word, now hastened to obey; nevertheless there was terror and dejection in every face. And their thoughts were much the same as those of their would-be deliverer. Had he the power to make good his word?

The hot morning hours dragged slowly by, and still no sign of attack. The village was as a deserted place, in its brooding death-like silence, the latter so still, so complete as to render distinctly audible the sweep of the wings of carrion birds circling aloft. The severed heads grinned hideously from the stockade, and the unearthly molten stillness of the silent noon was such as to get upon the nerves of the ordinary watcher. But he who now stood there had no nerves—not in a matter of this kind. His experiences had been such as to kill and crush them out of all being.

Ha! What was this? The crows and vultures, which, emboldened by the deathly silence, had been circling nearer and nearer to the tree-tops, suddenly and with one accord shot upward, now seeming mere specks in the blue ether. Then the silence was broken in appalling fashion. Rending the air in a terrific note of savagery and blood-thirst, there burst forth the harsh, hissing war-yell of the Wangoni.

It came from the forest edge on the farther side of the village. Laurence realised, with vexation and concern, that his merciful plan would be extremely difficult to carry out. That these ferocious auxiliaries should be allowed to initiate the attack he had not reckoned upon; and now to restrain them would be a herculean task.

"Back, back!" he shouted, meeting the crowd of charging savages who, shield and spear uplifted, were bearing down in full career upon the village.

In the headlong, exciting moment of their charge they hardly recognised him. Laurence Stanninghame's life hung upon a hair. Then, with a great burst of laughter, mocking, half defiant, they surged past him. They "saw red," and no power on earth seemed able to stop those human wolves now rushing upon their helpless prey.

"Back, back!" thundered Laurence again. "The village is dead, I tell you. It is the abode of death!"

This told. Barbarians have a shrinking horror of infectious disease. Thoughts of smallpox, cholera, what not, arose in the minds of these. No other consideration on earth could have restrained that charge, yet this one did. They stopped short.

"Lo! the stillness, the silence," went on Laurence, pointing to the lifeless village. "Would you, too, travel the voiceless and weaponless path of death?"

But mutterings both loud and deep went through the Wangoni ranks. What was this? They had been ordered to charge—been signalled to charge, and now they were forbidden to enter the village. "El Afà" (the serpent) had been absent from the expedition, and now turned up here, alone. Savages are ever suspicious, and these were no exception to the rule of their kind.

"*Whau*, what does it mean?" half sneered their leader, scowling resentfully upon Laurence as the warriors crowded around, growling like a pack of baffled wolves. "Had we not better send some in to see if these dogs are indeed all dead?"

"Not so, Mashumbwe," was the unconcerned reply. "Tarry until the others arrive, then will we act together."

But a furious clamour arose at the words. The Wangoni did not entirely believe the explanation; and to further their doubts there now arose from the inside of the huts the puling wail of infants which the mothers had not been entirely able to stifle.

"*Au*, we will add those to the death number, at least," said the chief, giving the signal to his followers to advance.

"Not so!" said Laurence decisively. "Hearken, Mashumbwe. You are chief of your own people but I am chief of all—*of all!* Not a man stirs until El Khanac comes up. Not a man, do you hear?"

Mashumbwe tossed back his ringed head, and his eyes glared. He was a tall, fine savage, with all the pride of mien inseparable from his rank and Zulu blood. Thus they stood, the savage and the white man, looking into each other's eyes; the one in a blaze of haughty anger, the other cool, resolute, and absolutely unflinching. How it would end Heaven alone knew.

But now the very thing that Laurence had been longing for happened. A hurried murmur ran through the Wangoni lines. The main body of the slave-hunters had emerged from the scrub, and had quietly surrounded the village. Laurence was satisfied. He had gained time so far, and with it his object.

"What astonishing freak is this, Stanninghame?" said Hazon, who, having taken in the situation at a glance, was promptly at his colleague's side, displaying, too, the piece of pencilled board. "What becomes of our pact when such a consideration as this comes in?" he continued, meaningly tapping the inscription on the board. "Have we obtained all we wanted on those terms up till now, or not?"

"No, we haven't; but now, having obtained almost all we wanted, we can afford to do this for once. If it had been your life instead of mine these people had saved twice, Hazon, I would willingly have spared theirs; now will you do less for me?"

"But it will breed a mutiny among our people," said Hazon doubtfully, with a half glance at the crowd of scowling Wangoni.

"Oh, a mutiny! By all means. We shall know how to deal with that, as we did before."

It seemed as though such knowledge were about to be called into requisition, for the announcement that all this "property" was to be relinquished absolutely was received by the more important section of the slave-hunters with a sullen silence more eloquent even than the wolfish growls of the Wangoni. The latter's disappointment lay in the fact that they were balked in giving vent to their instincts of sheer savagery—the delight of plunder and massacre. That of the former, however, was a more weighty factor to reckon with; for the smatter of civilisation in the Arab and Swahili element had brought with it the commercial instinct of cupidity. It speaks volumes, therefore, for the ascendancy which these two resolute white men had set up over their wild and lawless following, that the latter should have contented itself with mere sullen obedience.

Having gained his point Laurence returned within the village, and, calling Mgara, suggested that some of the people should carry forth food to their unwelcome visitors.

"I fear it may leave scarcity in your midst," he added; "but well-fed men are in better mood than hungry ones, Mgara, and are you not spared the slave-yoke and the spear?"

The head man, with many deferential expressions of gratitude, agreed, and soon a file of women and boys were told off, bringing goats and millet and rice for the slave-hunters. As they passed tremblingly among the ranks of the Wangoni the latter handled their great spears meaningly, and with much the same expression of countenance as a cat might wear when contemplating an inaccessible bird cage.

"Ho, dog!" cried Mashumbwe, as a youth passed before him without making obeisance. "Do you dare stand before me—before me! thou spawn of these man-eating jackals? Lo! lie prostrate for ever." And with the words he half threw, half thrust his great spear into the unfortunate lad's body. The blood spirted forth in a great jet, and, staggering, the boy fell.

"*Au!* And am I to be defiled with the blood of such as this," growled the chief, upon whom several red drops had squirted. "Let that carrion be removed."

Several of the Wangoni sprang forward, and, as the quivering body was dragged away, these savages gave vent to their pent-up ferocity by stabbing it again and again. Having tasted blood they rolled their eyes around in search of further victims. But the remaining Wajalu had withdrawn in terror; and well for all concerned that it was so, otherwise the Wangoni, inspired by the example of their chief, would certainly have commenced a massacre, which even the prestige and authority of Hazon and Laurence combined would have been powerless to quell. But there was no one outside to begin upon, and, though a truculent, unruly crowd, their interests in the long run lay in submitting to the authority of the white chiefs.

So the Wajalu rejoiced much, if tremblingly, as the last of the dreaded host disappeared. For good or for ill their village was spared—spared to continue its most revolting forms of savagery and cannibalism and parricide—spared for good or for ill in that it had entertained an angel unawares[2] in the person of that hard, pitiless, determined slave-hunter, Laurence Stanninghame.

CHAPTER XVII

DISSENSIONS

"WELL, I'm uncommonly glad I was out of that affair yesterday, Stanninghame. But it isn't like you, letting those poor devils off, eh?"

Thus Holmes, as the two were leisurely pursuing their way, somewhat on the rear flank of the slave party.

"I don't know. You see, they let me off, and I didn't want to be outdone in civility even by a lot of scurvy dogs who eat each other. There was no feeling about the matter."

Before the other could pursue the subject, the sound of faint groans, and pleading in an unknown tongue, was heard just ahead. With it, too, the sound of blows.

"Some devilish work going forward again," muttered Holmes, with savage disgust.

"You can't make omelettes without breaking eggs," was the indifferent reply. And then they came upon a not entirely unfamiliar scene.

On the ground crouched three human figures, wretched-looking and emaciated to the last degree. Disease and exhaustion had overpowered them, and they were begging to be left to die. Standing over them in threatening attitude was Lutali, with some half-dozen of the slavers.

"They are too far gone to feel the whip," Lutali was saying. "Clearly they are of no further use. You, Murad, shorten me the shadow of yonder dog. We shall see."

The man named, a savage-looking ruffian, stepped forward, grinning with delight. Just as he was swinging up his scimitar, Holmes burst forth—

"Hold on, Lutali. Give the poor devil another show."

Half turning his head at this interruption, there was that look upon the hawk-like features of the Arab which at times so strangely resembled that of Hazon. His keen eyes darted haughty reproof at Holmes, for he was a sort of supercargo of the slave department, and relished not this interference. Then, turning back, he once more gave the signal. Down flashed the great blade. There was a dull swooshing thud, and the headless trunk was deluging the earth.

The effect, however, upon the other two exhausted wretches was magical. With a despairing effort they raised themselves up and staggered on, to the accompaniment of not a few blows by way of recognition of their malingering. Lutali, who had uttered no word, and whose impassive countenance had not moved a feature, stalked gravely on.

"Why could we not have prevented this?" burst forth Holmes, whom a sort of morbid fascination seemed to root to the spot.

"Because it would have been the very acme of insanity to attempt such a thing. Lutali, in common with the rest, is in far too ugly a mood, after yesterday, to be fooled with needlessly. Besides, all that sentiment is simply thrown away. These people, remember, are atrocious brutes, who eat their own fathers and mothers. It is positively a work of charity to enslave them. Once they are off the march they are fairly well treated,—better, in fact, than they treat each other—and, of course, no more cannibalism."

"That may be. But I wish to Heaven I could blot out these two years as though they had never been. The recollection of the horrors one has been through will haunt me for life. I feel like blowing my brains out in sheer disgust. Why did I ever come?"

It was not the first time Holmes had burst forth in this fashion, as we have shown. Laurence looked keenly at him.

"There is a worse thing to haunt one's life than recollection," he said, "and that is anticipation."

"Of what?" asked Holmes shortly.

The other touched the muzzle of his rifle, then his own forehead.

"It's that—or this," he said, pointing to the ghastly trunk and the severed head which lay before them. "You don't suppose I should have adopted this sweet trade from choice, I suppose? No. Hard necessity, my dear chap. If anybody has to go under—and somebody always has to—I prefer that it shall not be me."

Holmes made no reply for a while, as they left the spot, walking in silence. Then Laurence went on—

"Now we are on the subject, I don't know that you would have come out any the better had we left you behind at Johannesburg. For you were going the wrong way. You were a precious sight too fond of hanging around bars, and that sort of thing grows. In fact, you were more than once a trifle—shall we say 'muddled.' Not to put too fine a point upon it, you were on your way to the deuce. I know it, for I've seen it so often before, and you know it too."

"I believe you're right there," assented Holmes.

"Well then, we owe our first duty to ourselves; wherefore, my soft-hearted young friend, it is better to spend a year or two raking in a fortune and ameliorating the lot of humanity, than to die in a state of soak and a disused shaft, on or around the Rand, even as did Pulman the day before we left."

"I don't believe that same fortune will do us any good," urged Holmes gloomily. "There is the curse of blood upon it."

"The curse of my grandmother," laughed the other.

There was no affectation about Laurence Stanninghame's indifference. It was perfectly genuine. Strong-nerved constitutionally, callous, hard-hearted through stress of circumstances, such sights as that just witnessed told not one atom upon him. In the sufferings of the miserable wretches he saw only a lurid alternative—his own. In them, toiling along, wearily, dejectedly, beneath the chain or yoke, he saw himself, toiling, grinding, at some sordid and utterly repellent form of labour, for a miserable pittance; no ray of light, no redeeming rest or enjoyment to sweeten life until that life should end. In them, cowering, writhing beneath the driver's brutal lash, he saw himself, ever lashed and stung by the torturing consciousness of what might have been, by the recollection of what had been. Or did they fall exhausted, fainting, to die, or to undergo decapitation to ensure that such exhaustion should not open even a feeble possibility of escape, there, too, he saw himself, sinking, borne down by the sheer blank hopelessness of Fate, taking refuge in the Dark Unknown, his end the grave of the suicide. It was himself or them, and he preferred that it should be them. Preyer or preyed upon—such was the iron immutable law of life, from man in his highest development to the minutest of insects; and with this law he was but complying, not in wanton cruelty, but in cold, passive ruthlessness.

Further, the sufferings of these people were only transitory. They would be much better off when the journey was ended and they were disposed of—better off indeed than many a free person in civilised and Christian lands. Besides, such races as these, low down as they were in the scale of humanity, suffered but little. It needs imagination, refinement, to accentuate suffering. To anything approaching such attributes, these were utter strangers. They were mere animals. Men dealt in sheep and cattle, in order to live, in horses and other beasts of burden, why not in these, who were even lower than the higher animals?

This theory of their sinister occupation Hazon thoroughly endorsed.

"Depend upon it, Stanninghame," he said, "ours is the right view to take of it—the only view. This is 'a world of plunder and prey,' as Tennyson puts it, and we have got to prey or be preyed

upon. You, for instance, seem to have fulfilled the latter rôle, hitherto, and it seems only right you should have your turn now. To
cite the latest instance, all this rotten scrip and market-rigging finished you off, and what was that but rascality?"

"Of course. I've been plundered, swindled, all along the line,
ever since I can remember. I'm tired of that damned respectability,
Hazon. It doesn't pay. It never has paid. This, however, does."

The other smiled significantly at the word.

"Respectability—yes," he said. "Look at your type of success,
your self-made man, swelling out of his white waistcoat in smug
self-complacency, your pattern British merchant, your millionaire
financier, what is he but a slave-dealer, a slave-driver, a blood-
sucker? What has become of your little all, swamped in those precious Rand companies, Stanninghame? Gone to bloat more unim-
peachable white waistcoats; gone to add yet more pillars to the
temple of pattern Respectability."

"That's so," assented Laurence, with something between a
sneer and a laugh, knocking the ashes out of his pipe." Yet that
same crowd of respectable swindlers would yelp in horror at us and
our enterprise. 'Piratical,' they'd call it, eh? A hanging matter!"

"Swindlers—no. Swindler is English for a convicted person.
Yet the percentage of the props and pillars of financial success and
mercantile respectability who, in the self-candour and secrecy of
their sleepless hours, are honestly unable to recall to mind one or
more occasions when Portland or Dartmoor, or Simonstown or
the Kowie¹ loomed more than near, cannot be a vast one; which,
for present purposes, may be taken to mean that if you have got to
make money you must make it anyhow, or not at all—'anyhow'
covering such methods as are involved in the conventional term
'rascality.' If you have got it you can run as straight as you like. We
haven't got it—at least not enough of it yet—and so we are making
it, and, like the rest of the world, making it anyhow. There's the
whole case in a nutshell, Stanninghame."

"Why, of course. But, if only we could bring Holmes round to
that pre-eminently sensible standpoint! I never could have believed
the fellow would turn out such an ass. I am more than sorry,
Hazon, that I should have influenced you to bring him along."

"Oh, Holmes is young, and hardly knows the meaning of the

term 'hard experience,' as we know it. Still, in his way, he's useful enough, and first-rate in a fight; and when he comes to bank his share he'll forget to feel over particular as to how he acquired it. That's mere ordinary human nature, and Holmes is far from being an abnormal unit."

"No, but he still affects a conscience. What if he goes back and takes on that blue-eyed girl he was smitten with, and, turning soft, incontinently gives us away?"

"Are *you* on the croak, Stanninghame? That's odd. Here, how's your pulse? Let's time it." And Hazon reached out his hand.

"Well, yes; it is unusual. But it's damned hot, and the steaminess of it depresses me at times," returned Laurence, with a queer, reckless laugh.

"He won't give us away, never fear," said Hazon carelessly. "He won't take on that girl, because she'll have forgotten him long ago; that, too, being ordinary human nature. And—nobody ever did give me away yet. I don't somehow think anybody is ever likely to."

Both sides of this remark struck a chord within Laurence's mind; the first, a jarring one, since it voiced a misgiving which had at times assailed himself, specially at such periods of depression as this under which he was now suffering. For the second, the tone was characteristic of the speaker and the subject. It seemed to flash forth more than a menace, in its stern, unrelenting ruthlessness of purpose, while the words seemed to recall the warning so darkly let fall by Rainsford and others regarding his present confederate. "Other men have gone up country with Hazon, but—*not one of them has ever returned.*" To himself the words contained no menace. He trusted Hazon, felt thoroughly able to take care of himself, and, moreover, was as little likely to violate the secrecy of their enterprise as Hazon himself. But what of Holmes? With all his hard, callous unscrupulousness, Laurence had no desire that harm should befall Holmes. In a measure, he felt responsible for him.

"Don't you worry about Holmes," said Hazon, as though reading his thoughts. "We can put him to all the show part of the business, reserving the more serious line for our own immediate supervision. And the time may come when we can do very well with Holmes, in short, when three white men may be better than two. We are very near the Ba-gcatya country, and an *impi* of them on the raid will give us as much trouble as we can do with; and I've seen signs of late which seem to point that way."

"Isn't it a crowded-on business this Ba-gcatya terror, eh?" said Laurence, lazily puffing out rings of blue smoke, which hung upon the hot, still atmosphere, as though they never meant to disperse. "I expect their strength is as exaggerated as their dash. Why, this part is not altogether unexplored, yet there is no record of an exceptionally strong tribe hereabouts."

Hazon smiled pityingly.

"That great god, the African explorer, don't know everything," he said—"no, not quite everything, although he thinks he does. Anyway, he frequently manages to get a pretty muddled-up idea of things and places hereabout—a muddle which the natives of this land would rather thicken than dispel. For instance, he will ask the name of a river or a mountain, and when the other party to the talk repeats his question, as natives invariably do to gain time for answering, he takes this for the answer, and forthwith the thing is dubbed by a word that simply means 'river' or 'mountain,' in one or other of the hundred and fifty tongues which prevail hereabout. No, the existence of the Ba-gcatya is not chronicled, simply because the explorer was fortunate enough not to fall in with them. Had he done so, he would probably never have returned to chronicle anything. But, get one or two of our Wangoni to talk, and he may, or may not, tell you something about them; for the Ba-gcatya are, like the Wangoni themselves, a Zulu off-shoot, only far more con-servative in the old Zulu traditions, and of purer blood. They are a much finer race; indeed I believe them to be as powerful and well-disciplined as the Zulus themselves were under Cetywayo. I was all through the war of '79, you know, and that pretty scar I carry about as an ornament represents the expiring effort of an awful tough customer, who had lost too much blood to be able to strike altogether home. I call it my Isandhlwana medal."

"That where you captured it, eh?" said Laurence, with interest, for the story was new to him. He remembered first noticing the great scar upon Hazon's chest the day he visited him when ill in bed at Johannesburg, but he had never asked its history; indeed, it was characteristic of the strange relations in which these two men stood to each other that, notwithstanding all this time of close comradeship, neither should ever have asked the other any question of a personal nature. Characteristic, too, was it of Hazon's method that this piece of information should have been vouchsafed as it was. Many an experience, strange and startling, had he narrated from time to time, but never for the sake of narrating it. If anything occurred to bring it forth, out it would come, carrying, perhaps, others in its train, but ever in due sequence. Even Holmes, the impulsive, who, being young, was the 'natural man' of the trio, had long since learned that to ask Hazon for a yarn was the direct way not to get one out of him.

"Yes," went on Hazon, "that's where I captured it. Speaking with some experience, Isandhlwana is the toughest thing that has ever travelled my way, and I don't hanker after any repetition of it with 'The People of the Spider'——Why, what does this mean?'

The words, quick, hurried, broke off. On the faces of both men was a look of keen, anxious alertness. For a wild and fierce clamour had suddenly arisen and was drawing nearer and nearer, loud, swelling, threatening.

CHAPTER XVIII

TWO PERILS

"JUST what I feared," said Hazon calmly, but with ever so faint a glance at his confederate. "Our people are in revolt."

Both men rose to their feet, but leisurely, and turned to confront the approaching tumult. And formidable enough this was. The Wangoni advanced in a compact mass, beating their shields with their spear-hafts, yelling in concert a shrill, harsh battle-song, into which they had managed to import an indescribable note of defiance, announcing their intention of returning to "eat up" those they had so weakly spared the previous day. On either side of them came the Arab and Swahili element, in silence, however, but a silence which was no less ominous than their sullen and scowling looks, and the almost significant gestures wherewith they handled their rifles.

"What do they want, Lutali?" said Hazon, turning to the Arab, who, with Holmes, had just joined the pair. But Lutali shrugged his shoulders, and his hawk-like features scarcely moved. Then he said—

"Who may think to strive against the hand of Allah and that of his Prophet? Yon foul dogs, even they—so great is the mercy of Allah—even they might have been turned into good Moslemin, even as other such have been before them. Yet we—we have left them to wallow in the mire of their cannibal abominations. Our people are not satisfied, El Khanac, and they fear that ill may come of it."

"A magnificent and comfortable hypocrisy that," said Laurence, in English. "Such combination of soul-saving and slave-selling is unique." Then, in Swahili, "But what do they want, Lutali?"

"They want to set right the error of yesterday,"

"But the Wangoni don't care a grain of rice for Allah and his Prophet," he went on. "Why then are *they* dissatisfied?"

"They are instruments in the hands of those who do. It is so written. Allah is great. Who may call in question his decrees?" replied the Arab, in the same level monotone. "Let the people do their will, which is also the will of Allah."

During this conversation the whole party had halted, and now stood in a great semicircle around the white leaders. Then Mashumbwe spoke, and his words, though fairly courteous, managed to cover an extremely defiant tone.

"Our people are dissatisfied, father," he said, addressing Hazon. "They desire to return home."

"Wherefore?" asked Hazon shortly.

"*Au!* they came forth to 'eat up' other tribes, not to spare such. They are dissatisfied."

"They'd better have their own way," muttered Hazon, in English. "You are sacrificing all we have done and obtained this trip to an empty whim. How does that pan out, Stanninghame?"

"I hate to go back on my word," was the reply; "still more to be bullied into it."

"Well said!" declared Holmes warmly.

The insurgents, reading the expression upon the countenances of these two, broke forth into tumult once more. Groans and mutterings arose among the Arab contingent, while the Wangoni uttered wild laughing whoops of defiance. Nothing would be easier than to slay the white leaders. A single volley would lay them low. The position was critical, perilous to a degree.

"We go then," cried Mashumbwe, waving his hand. "Fare ye well, El Khanac; Afà, fare ye well!"

But before his followers could form into marching rank, several men rushed from the forest, with every appearance of importance and alarm. Making straight to where stood their white leaders, they began hurriedly to confer with the latter.

"Your discontent was needless," cried Hazon, after a minute or two of such conference, turning to his rebellious followers, the whole body of whom had now paused to learn what tidings these had brought. "Your discontent comes a day too late. Those whom we spared have even now been eaten up, and their village given over to the flames."

The short, sharp gasp of amazement which greeted this announcement gave place to growls of renewed discontent. Some rival band of slave-hunters had fallen upon the village and taken that which they themselves had so weakly left. Such was their first thought.

"The Ba-gcatya have found them," continued Hazon calmly.

If there had been marvel before in the ejaculation now there was more. There was even a note of dismay. Forgetting their mutinous intentions now, all crowded around their white leaders, eager to learn full particulars. And in that moment Laurence, ever observant, was not slow to perceive, both in the looks and tones of the party, quite enough to confirm all that Hazon had said as to the terror inspired by the very name of the redoubtable Ba-gcatya. Even the savage and truculent Wangoni seemed for the moment overawed. It was striking, too, how, in the hour of impending peril, all turned to the white leaders, whom a moment before they had been entirely defying and more than half threatening.

"The Ba-gcatya are in great force," went on Hazon, as calmly as though he were merely announcing the proximity of one more well-nigh defenceless and slave-supplying village. "We shall have to fight, and that hard, but not here. We must fight them in the open."

A murmur of assent went up. Every head was craned forward, eager to hear more. Briefly and concisely Hazon set forth his commands.

Their then encampment was situate on the edge of the forest belt. Beyond the latter the country stretched away in vast, well-nigh treeless plains. Now a peculiar feature of these plains was the frequent recurrence of abrupt granite *kopjes*, at first glance not unlike moorland tors.[1] But more than one of them, when arrived at, wore the aspect of a complete Druidical ring—a circle of stones crowning the rise, with a slight depression of ground within the centre. One of these Hazon, who had been over the ground before, resolved should serve them as a natural fortress, whence to resist the fierce and formidable foe now advancing against them.

With surprising readiness the march began. Loads were shouldered and slaves yoked together extra firmly. Those who were too weak to keep up the pace—treble that of the normal one—at which they were hurried forward, were ruthlessly speared; but whether they were slain by their captors or by the pitiless Ba-gcatya mattered but little.

The *kopje* which Hazon had selected was situated about four miles from the forest belt. No better natural fortress could have been chosen; for it consisted of a complete circle of low rocks, of about two hundred yards' diameter, and commanded an open sweep of at least a mile on every side. Laurence and Holmes were loud in their admiration and interest.

"These are old craters, I reckon," said Hazon; "not volcanic, but mud-springs. This plain, you notice, is considerably below the level of the forest country. Depend upon it, the thing was once a big swamp, with great boiling, bubbling mud-holes."

No time was it, however, for speculations of a scientific nature; and accordingly the leaders proceeded to dispose their lines of defence. This was soon done, for the three white men and Lutali had arranged all that during the march. The Wangoni were of no great use, save in pursuit of a defeated enemy. They could hardly have hit a haystack once in six shots, nor did Hazon care to entrust with firearms such a turbulent and unruly crew. But the slavers were all fair marksmen—some indeed, among them Lutali, being not far short of dead shots. These were disposed around the circle of rocks so as to form a ring of fire; and the rocks themselves were heightened wherever necessary with some of the loads, or with such piles of loose stones as could be collected in time. The part allotted to the Wangoni was that of a reserve force, in the event of the enemy carrying any given point, and thus necessitating hand-to-hand conflict. The slaves, firmly secured, were placed in the centre of the great circle.

Hardly were these dispositions complete than a cry of astonishment, of warning, arose. Far away over the forest country, somewhat to the right and left of the route the party had been pursuing, several columns of smoke could be seen mounting to the heavens. There were other villages, then, besides the one spared, and now the Ba-gcatya, spreading over the land in their immense might, were firing all such and massacring the inhabitants. Many and various were the comments which arose as the party gazed intently upon the distant smoke columns.

"If only as a change from knocking on the head these defenceless devils, it's quite a blessed relief to have some real fighting," quoth Holmes.

"You'll get plenty of that, Holmes, within the next few hours," remarked Hazon drily.

It was near midday, and the heat was torrid and sweltering. The fierce vertical sun-rays seemed to pour down upon their unshaded position as in streams of molten fire. Even the quick excited murmurs of the men grew languid. And, having seen to all being in complete readiness, as Laurence Stanninghame sat there at his post in the torrid heat, smoking the pipe of meditation, did no thought of the home, such as it was, but which he would probably never see again, rise up before him? If it did, it was only to confirm him in the conviction that the present position of peril—whose chances he, at anyrate, was in no disposition to under-estimate—was the preferable of the two. Here freedom, activity, adventure; there galling bondage, stagnation, a ceasing to live. Yes, that time indeed seemed very, very far away. Even now he felt no shadow of inclination towards a recurrence thereof.

Then, suddenly, with magical swiftness, the whole party was astir, and it needed a sharp, hurried command or two from Hazon and Lutali to restrain some from leaping on the rocks in order to obtain a better view of what had caused the alarm.

Between the *kopje* and the forest belt the ground, save for an occasional roll, was entirely visible. Now, swarming out into the open, came masses of moving figures—fleeing figures. Hazon and Laurence, who each possessed a powerful glass, were able to master the situation in a twinkling.

Close on the rear of the fugitives pressed another multitude, to the naked eye like myriad ants upon the far plain, but to those who scanned them through the powerful glasses all detail was vividly distinct—the lines and lines of tufted shields, the gleam of spear blades, the streaming feather and cow-hair adornments.

And now the hum and roar of the wild onslaught and pursuit grows momentarily louder, drawing nearer and nearer. A great cloud of dust is whirling onward, and athwart it the gleam of steel, rising and falling, the distant death-scream, as the miserable fugitives fall ripped, hacked to fragments by their ferocious pursuers. And still the terrible wave pours on.

"This is going to be a hard business," muttered Laurence between his set teeth. "How many do you size them up at, Hazon?"

"Twenty thousand, rather more than less. That's just how Cetywayo's people came on at Isandhlwana, only there they took us more by surprise. Well, we're not a lot of soldiers here anyway to scatter all over the veldt. If they take this position they'll have to rush it, and rush it hard. Well, do you believe in the Ba-gcatya now, Stanninghame?"

Save a nod the other makes no answer, and now the attention of both men is upon the scene before them.

Some few of the fugitives, in the desperation of their terror, are gradually outstripping their pursuers. Against these whole flights of casting spears are launched, amid roaring shouts of bass laughter. Finally the last one falls.

And now the array of the enemy is but half a mile distant from the slaver's position. Far over the plain, in immense crescent formation, the barbarian host sweeps on, now in dead silence, not hesitating a moment, for the spoor[2] left by the slavers is broad and easy. Now it can be seen that these warriors are of splendid physique. Most of them are nearly naked save for their flowing war-adornments of hair or jackal-tails. Many are crowned with towering ostrich plumes, both black and white; others wear balls of feathers surmounted by the scarlet tuft of the egret; some, again, have round their heads bands of the hide of the spotted cat; but all flaunt some wild and fantastic adornment. And the great hide-shields, with their parti-coloured facings and tufted staves, are Zulu shields, and the broad stabbing spear is the Zulu *umkonto*.

There was a lurid fascination in gazing upon the awful splendour of this fierce and formidable battle-rank, which set even Laurence Stanninghame's schooled nerves tingling. As for Holmes, he could hardly remain still in his excitement. But in Hazon's piercing eyes there was a glow in which the lust of combat, despair of success, and the most indomitable resolve were about equally intermingled. The countenance of Lutali betrayed no change whatever. The bulk of the slave-hunters were scowling and eager; but the miserable slaves, realising that massacre awaited them, were moaning and trembling with fear. Under the slave-yoke they held their lives, at anyrate, but should the enemy without win the day, why, then, they would taste the steel in common with their present oppressors. The Ba-gcatya never spared.

Now the battle-rank of the latter underwent a change. From each end of the great crescent "horns" shot out, extending farther and farther. Still the numbers of the main body seemed in no wise to diminish. The rock-crowned mound was encircled by a wall of living men.

Then the silence was rent asunder, and that in most appalling fashion. From twenty thousand fierce throats in concert went up the war-shout—horrible, terrifying—combining the frenzied roars of a legion of maniacs with the snarls and baying of hounds tearing down their prey. One there had heard it before, but not in such awful, soul-curdling volume as this.

And then, with heads bent, shields thrust forward, broad spears in strong ready grip, the whole circle of the Ba-gcatya host came surging up the slope.

CHAPTER XIX

THE SIGN

CRASH! crash! A long, detonating roar, then crash! again. The rock-circle is a perfect ring of flame, sheeting forth in red jets athwart the hanging sulphurous smoke. Death-yells are mingling with the fearful war-shout. Shields are flung high in the air, and dark bodies, leaping, fall forward upon their faces, to be trampled into lifelessness as their own comrades tread them down, not pausing, rushing over them as they lie.

"No, no! no quicker," reproves Hazon, who is directing here, where the assailants' force is the strongest, namely, the main body, the *isifuba* or breast of the *impi*. "Fire steadily and low, as before, but no quicker."

His followers growl a ready assent. They are unmitigated ruffians, but terrible and determined fighters. The fanatical fatalism of the Mohammedan creed renders them utterly impervious to panic. They keep up a steady, quick-loading fire into the charging Ba-gcatya, and, aiming low, every shot tells, committing fearful havoc among the serried, onrushing masses. Yet those terrible warriors are dauntless. Whole lines go down; still, others surge over them, and now the charge is but two hundred yards from the line of rocks.

The fore ranks hesitate, then come to a halt, crumpling back upon those behind them. The slavers, with a shrill, ringing yell, seeing their opportunity, pour a frightfully raking volley into the momentarily confused mass. Shields are clashed together, spears wildly waving. For the moment it seems as though the Ba-gcatya were fighting with each other, striving to hew their way through their own ranks in their endeavours to escape beyond the reach of that awful and destructive fire.

"Give it them again!" growls Hazon, a lurid gleam in his deep-set, piercing eyes. "But, aim low—aim low!"

Again not a shot is thrown away. That side of the savage host falls back hurriedly, leaving the ground bestrewn with bodies,

dead, dying, crushed. A perfect storm of exultant cheers greets this
move.

But if a temporary retreat, it is no rout. In obedience to a
rapidly-uttered, whistling signal, fully one-half of the main body
swings round and hurls itself with incredible force and fury upon
another point of the rock-circle, seemingly the weakest point, for
here the rocks are low and apart, and have to be supplemented
with bags and bales.

Laurence Stanninghame is in command here. And now his dark
face flushes with the glow of a mad excitement, a perfectly transforming exhilaration. He would thunder his commands aloud, but
that a deadly coolness is as indispensable almost as accuracy of
aim. His orders are the same as Hazon's, and uttered as calmly—
but for a suppressed tremor—and as audibly.

The very earth seems to rock and reel beneath the detonating
roll of the volleys, the thunderous rumble of charging feet. The
dark, glaring faces of warring demons, the flinging aloft of shields,
the groaning and yells, the redness of the sheeting flames, all this
renders him mad—mad with the revel of conflict, with the herculean determination which is sublime above death. Here again
whole lines of the enemy are down. Here again those in front
would draw back if they could, but the immense weight behind
hurls them on. It is the work of but very few moments.

And now the whole of the Ba-gcatya host is circling around the
slavers' position, every now and again making a furious rush upon
what seems a weak point of the defences. But the defenders have
a way of massing upon each point thus attacked, and that with a
celerity which is truly marvellous, and the result is the same. Yet
with each repulse the terrible ranks leap forward immediately, and
every such charge brings them nearer than the last. Moreover, as
each of their fighting leaders is picked off, another springs forward
with unparalleled intrepidity to take his place. The while the
barking roar of their terrific slogan rends the air in its most demoniacal clamour.

Now an idea takes hold on the minds of these ferocious legionaries, and is passed like lightning round the ranks. Those in the
forefront haul up the bodies of the slain, and, holding them to
them, stagger forward, thinking to make a buckler of the dead for

the living. But the terrible rifles of the slavers drive their unerr-
ing missiles at that short range through dead and living alike, and
corpse is heaped upon corpse in ghastly intertwining.

In the thickest of the tumult Hazon is here, there, everywhere—directing, encouraging, restraining. But for the demon-
glow in the black eyes staring from the pale, set face, the man
might have been made of marble, so little trace of emotion of any
kind does he display. Laurence, too, is wary and self-contained,
though getting in here and there a telling shot. Holmes, on the
other hand, is firing away as fast as he can load. So far not a man
has been injured.

The assailants are not quite within spear-throwing distance yet.

"Ammunition hold out? Oh yes, we have plenty of that," is
Hazon's reply to a rapid, low-toned query on the part of Laurence.
"But it's time they turned tail. Isandhlwana was nothing to this."

But now, with a deafening, vibrating roar the Ba-gcatya,
massing suddenly, hurl fully one half of their force upon the point
directed by Lutali. They surge up the slope in one dense charge of
lightning swiftness. Bullets are hailed upon them. They waver not.
The hands of the defenders are skinned and blistered by contact
with the breeches of their own rifles, so hot have these become
through quick firing, and still the firing is not quick enough.
Stumbling, leaping, flying over the defences they come—a great
cloud of dark, grim faces, and bared teeth, and protruding eyeballs.
They spring upon the defences, then over them. The whole might
of the redoubtable foe is pouring into the natural fortress.

Now ensues a scene the like of which might be paralleled, but
hardly surpassed, by some lurid drama of hell. In jarring shock
they meet, those within and those, till now, without—the savage
legionaries of "The Spider," and the no less savage and equally
determined slave-hunters. The Wangoni, seeing their chance,
have sprung forward to meet and roll back the assailants. But they
themselves are beaten down by the broad shields, ripped with
the terrible stabbing spears of the ferocious Ba-gcatya, now mad-
dened to assuage their blood-thirst, and whose crushing might,
now pouring over in countless numbers, this handful shall never
hope to resist. The chief, Mashumbwe, is speared and ripped.
The struggle is fierce and hand-to-hand, but short. The Wangoni,

now a sorry remnant, are rolled back upon their allies.

Of these not a man but knows that the day is lost, that flight is impossible; that if the other half of the Ba-gcatya host has not swarmed over to take them on the rear, it is only because it is waiting to receive on its spear points all who flee. But there is no thought of flight. With all their indifference to human suffering, with all their brutality, their savagery, the slavers are as brave as any. They are indeed men picked for their desperate courage, and now, standing back to back, they begin to render the victory of the Ba-gcatya a dearly bought one indeed.

The war-shout no longer rends the air. There is a grim, fell silence in this hand-to-hand conflict, broken only by the snake-like hiss of the Ba-gcatya as an enemy goes down, by the slap and shock of shield meeting clubbed gun or stabbing knife, by the gasps of the combatants. The cloud of powder smoke hanging overhead partially veils the sun, which glowers, a blood-red ball, through this gloomy shroud. The whole space within the rock-circle is a very charnel-pit of corpses, among which the combatants stagger—victorious Ba-gcatya and vanquished slave-hunters alike—stagger and slip on a foothold of oozy gore; stab, and strike, and fall in their turn.

In the rush and the *mêlée* Laurence Stanninghame has become separated even farther from his comrades,—his white comrades, that is,—nor can he by any effort hope to rejoin them. Several Arabs are around him, his own followers, swarthy sons of the Prophet, their keen eyes flashing hate and defiance upon the foe, their long yataghans sweeping a circle of light around them. In their forefront is Lutali—Lutali, whirling a great scimitar, hewing down more than one of the too venturesome Ba-gcatya, and that in spite of broad bull-hide shield deftly wielded—Lutali, uttering a semi-religious war-cry, his erect form and keen haughty face, the very impersonification of absolute and dauntless valour. And he himself, wedged in by those around, can still get in now and again a telling shot from his revolver, and with every such shot one more warrior of "The Spider" has uttered his last battle-cry.

No, there is no hope. Swift as lightning, a mighty brain-wave surges through Laurence's mind, and in it he sees the whole of his past life. Yet not even this dismays him—rather does it engender a sort of half-bitter exultation. Life for him has been such a mistake, and that not through any fault of his own. It held no especial charm for him. All its sweetness has been concentrated within one short idyllic period; but even that could not have lasted—even to it would have come disillusionment. Lilith would never learn his fate. It, and that of those with him, would vanish, as others had done, into the mysteries of this great mysterious continent. All this and more—so lightning-like is the power of thought—passes through Laurence Stanninghame's brain at this dread and awful moment.

A casting spear strikes him on the left shoulder, penetrating the flesh. Infuriated by the sharp, sickening pang, he discharges his revolver at the supposed thrower, but his aim is uncertain. Again he draws trigger. The hammer falls with a harmless click; the chambers are empty. And now, hard pressed by the yelling Ba-gcatya, those of his followers yet between him and the enemy stagger back, fighting furiously, while the life-stream wells from many a gashed and gaping wound. No longer can he see either Hazon or Holmes, for the forest of waving, reeking spear blades. Then one of his own followers, a hulking Swahili, mortally wounded, reels and falls, and, doing so, bears back Laurence beneath his ponderous weight. The rock-rampart is immediately behind him, and is low here. It catches the back of his knees, and now, having lost all control over his balance, grasping at empty air in wild effort to recover himself, Laurence pitches heavily backward over the rocks, and lies half stunned upon the plain without.

Those of the Ba-gcatya host in waiting on that side surge tumultuously forward, uttering yells of savage delight. This is the first of the doomed slavers who has come over; and he a white man, and of course a leader. Each warrior is eager to bury his spear-head in this man's body, and they crowd around him, every right hand raised aloft for the downward stroke.

But the fatal stroke remains undealt. Broad blades quiver aloft in a ring of steel. Each grim, bloodthirsty countenance is set and staring, stony in its indescribable expression of mingled marvel and awe, and eyeballs seem to start from their sockets as their owners stand gazing down upon this prostrate white man. Then from each broad chest a gasp bursts forth—

"*Au!* The Sign! THE SIGN OF THE SPIDER!"

CHAPTER XX

TO WHAT END?

"THE Sign of the Spider!" Laurence Stanninghame lying there, his faculties half dazed by the shock of his fall and the pain of his wound, hearing the words—uttered as they were in pure Zulu—almost persuaded himself that the terrible events of that day had been a dream. But no, it was real enough. His half-unclosed eyes took in the sea of grim, dark faces pressing forward to gaze upon him. "The Sign of the Spider?" What did it—what could it mean, that it should be all-powerful to stay those devouring spears, to avert from him the grisly death of blood, whose bitterness even then was already past? Then, as for the first time, he suffered his glance to follow the direction of theirs, he saw a strange thing.

The metal box had come forth, either jerked from its resting-place during his fall, or unconsciously plucked thence by his own hand in the last moment of his extremity, and now, still secured by the steel chain, it lay upon his breast. And oh! marvel of marvels! Gazing thus upon it, focussed by his half-closed eyelids and confused senses—the straggling monogram, with its quaint turns and flourishes, lying brown upon the more shining metal, seemed to take exactly the form and aspect of a great sprawling tarantula. "The Sign of the Spider!" had been their cry! And these were "The People of the Spider!" What magic, what mystery was this? Lilith's last gift, Lilith's image; even her very name! It had indeed acted as a talisman, as a "charm" to stand between him and the most deadly of perils, as her aspiration had worded it. Verily, again had Lilith's love availed to stand between himself and a swift, sure, and bloody death! A marvel, and a stupendous one.

All this flashed through his mind as the Ba-gcatya crowded up around him, the hubbub of their excited voices sinking into an awestruck murmur as they gazed upon the man who wore "The Sign of the Spider." No wonder this man should have come forth alive from the ring of death, they decided,—he alone—wearing that sign. And he alone had come forth.

All sounds of conflict had now ceased, giving way to the exultant shouts and bass laughter of the victorious savages looting the property of the slavers. Not a man was left alive up there, Laurence knew only too well. He alone was spared, as the bearer of that mysterious sign; was spared, miraculously indeed, but—to what end?

Now he became conscious of a movement among the crowd, which parted, quickly, respectfully. Through the opening thus effected there advanced two men. Both were fine, tall warriors, elderly of aspect, for their short, crisp beards were turning grey, but apparently in the very prime of athletic strength and vigour. In outward adornment their appearance differed little from that of the bulk of the Ba-gcatya. Their shaven heads were surmounted by the *isicoco*,[1] or ring, exactly after the Zulu fashion, and on either side of this, but fastened so as not to interfere with it, nodded a tuft of magnificent white ostrich plumes. Laurence, who had now raised himself to a sitting posture, felt no doubt but that in these he beheld the two principal war-chiefs of the Ba-gcatya army.

"Who art thou, stranger, who wearest the Sign of the Spider?" began one of these in pure Zulu, after gazing upon him for a moment in silence.

Laurence at first thought to affect ignorance of the language, of which, indeed, he possessed considerable knowledge. He would the more readily get at their plans and intentions that way. But then it occurred to him he could hardly sustain his character as one to be favoured of the People of the Spider if professing an ignorance of their tongue, and he intended to work that fortunate incident for all it would carry. So he replied courteously—

"You see me, father. I alone am alive of those who fought up yonder. Even the spear which would slay me refused its work. It was turned aside," showing the wound in his shoulder, of which he realised he must make light, though, as a matter of fact, it was giving him considerable pain.

A deep murmur from the vast and increasing audience convinced the speaker that he had scored a point in making this statement. The chief continued—

"Rest now, while we rest, O stranger, and eat, for the way is far which lies before us."

"And whither does that way lie, O brave ones who command the valiant?" asked Laurence.

"Where dwelleth The Strong Wind that burns from the North." And with this darkly enigmatical rejoinder the speaker and his brother chief turned away, as a sign that the conference need proceed no further at present.

Some of those who had heard now beckoned Laurence forward, and, as he moved among that terrible host, many and strange were the glances which were cast at him. He, for his part, was not unmoved. This was an experience clean outside any he had ever known. The might and stature of these formidable warriors, lingering around in immense groups, many of them bleeding from ghastly wounds, yet devouring the dried food they carried, the while comrades were treating their hurts after a fashion which would have caused the civilised being to shriek aloud with agony; the ferocious volubility wherewith they discussed and fought the battle over again; and away beyond their lines, the earth black with corpses of the slain; while up yonder, though this he could not see, the rock circle was literally piled with those who had been his friends or followers for many a long day—all this impressed him to an extent which he had hardly deemed possible, though of any outward evidence thereof he gave no sign.

"Are all dead up yonder?" he asked some of the Ba-gcatya, as he joined them in their frugal fare.

A laugh, derisive but not discourteous to himself, greeted the question.

"Au! The bite of The Spider does not need repeating twice," was the reply. "None who have once felt it live."

The Ba-gcatya, heavy as had been their losses, were in high good-humour over their victory. After all, it was a victory, and a hard-fought one. They only lived for such. Losses were nothing to them. The spoils of the slavers' caravan—arms, ammunition, goods of all sorts, were distributed for transport among the younger regiments of the *impi*, which, its allotted period of rest over, at a mandate from its chiefs, prepared for departure. And now the solitary white man in its midst—captive or guest, he himself was hardly certain which—had an opportunity of admiring the stern and iron discipline of this splendid army of savages. That of the Zulu troops under the rule of Cetywayo, or even under that of Tshaka, might have equalled it, but could not possibly have surpassed it. Each company fell into rank with machine-like precision and celerity. The dead were left as they fell; those who were too grievously wounded to move received death from the swift, sure spear-stroke of a comrade; then, marching in five columns, the great army set forth on its return, striking a course to the northward.

Laurence Stanninghame's feelings were passing strange as he found himself thus carried captive, he knew not whither, by this mighty nation which had hitherto been to him but a name, as to whose very existence he had been until quite recently more than half-sceptical. Hazon had not exaggerated its strength or prowess; no, not one whit. Of that he had had abundant testimony. And Hazon himself? That strange individual, with his marked-out personality, his cold-blooded ruthlessness and dauntless courage? Well, his career was done. He lay in yonder circle, buried beneath the slain, fighting to the last with fierce and consistent valour. And Holmes? Even Laurence's hardened nature felt soft as he thought of the comrades with whom he had been so closely linked during these years of lawless and perilous enterprise. Well, they were gone, and he was spared, but—to what end?

Then the spirit of the true adventurer reasserted itself. What lay before him? What were the chances opening out to him in the dim, unknown land whither they were speeding? "You will return wealthy, or—you will not return at all," had been Hazon's words; and now their utterer would utter no more words of any kind— but he, Laurence, would he return at all? Would he?

And now, as they gained the edge of the great plain, the whole *impi* raised a mighty battle-song, improvised to celebrate their triumph. Its fierce strophes rolled like thunder along the ranks, to the tread of marching feet, and the multitude of hide-shields dappled the plain far and near, and the wavy lines of spear-points flashed and sparkled in the sunlight. And already over the wizard ring of the rock circle, piled with its slain, immense clouds of vultures were wheeling beneath the blue vault or swooping down upon their abundant feast. And the sun, flaming down upon the torrid earth, seemed to shed a pitiless, brassy glare upon this awful hecatomb, whose annals should ever remain unrecorded, swallowed up in the grim and gloomy mysteries of that region of cruelty and of blood.

For many days thus they journeyed—making rapid, but not forced marches. The aspect of the country, too, varied,—open, wavy plains, where giraffe and buffalo were plentiful, and were hunted in great numbers for the supply of the *impi*,—then gloomy forest tracts, which seemed to depress the Ba-gcatya, who hurried through them with all possible speed. Broad rivers, too, swarming with crocodiles and hippopotami,—and these the warriors would dash through in a mass, making the most hideous yelling and splashing. But ever the ground seemed gradually to ascend, and certain white peaks, for some time visible on the far skyline, were drawing nearer, growing larger with every march.

It may seem strange how readily Laurence Stanninghame adapted himself to this new turn in the tide of his affairs,—and indeed now and again he would faintly wonder at it himself. He had fought against these formidable savages in the most deter-mined and bloody hand-to-hand conflict that had ever befallen his lot, or, in all probability, ever would again. They had overwhelmed and massacred his comrades and whole following; sparing himself alone, and that by a miracle. And now not only was he subjected to no ill-treatment or indignity, but moved freely among them, and was even suffered to retain his arms. Yet there was a sort of stand-offishness about most of them, in which he thought to descry a mingling of awe and repulsion.

Now and again, however, a thought would occur to him,—a thought productive of a cold shiver. To what end was he thus spared? Was it to be sacrificed in some hideous and gruesome rite? The thought was not a pleasant one, and it would intrude more and more. The hot African glow, the adventurous life, replete with every phase of weird and depressing incident, had strangely affected this man's temperament. With all his coolness in emer-gencies—his readiness of resource—in times of rest he would grow moody and high-strung. A sort of surcharged, mesmeric property seemed to hold him at such times, and he would wonder whether the hideous experiences and iron self-repression which he had passed through of late had not begun, unknown to himself, actually to affect his brain.

Now during the heat of the midday halt, he would withdraw, and sit alone by the hour, contemplating the metal box, and at times its contents. More and more, since his wonderful escape, was it assuming in his eyes the properties of an amulet, or charm. It would reassure him, too, what time unpleasant thoughts would weigh upon him as to the end to which he had been reserved. Twice had Lilith's love stood between him and death. Would it not again? In truth the metal box was a possession beyond price.

All unconsciously his frequent and rapt contemplation of this object was standing him in valuable stead. The Ba-gcatya, furtively beholding him thus engaged,—for he was never beyond their watchful gaze,—were strengthened in their belief that he was a magician of The Spider, and feared him the more. He was thus, unconsciously, keeping up his character as such.

Yet, vivid as recollection was, as conjured up by the metal box, in other respects the old life seemed far away as a dream; misty, shadowy, vanishing. All its old conventionalities, its abstract notions of right and wrong, what were they? Dust. Even now, whither was he wending? Would he ever again behold a white face? It might be never.

"Have no white people ever visited your country, Silawayo?" he said one day while he and the two war-chiefs were talking together during the march.

"One only," was the reply, given with a shade of hesitation.

"And what became of him?"

"*Au!* He went to—— Well, he went——," answered the chief, with a curious look.

The reply smote upon Laurence with a cold fear. What grim and gruesome form of mysterious doom did it not point to? "One only," Silawayo had said. He himself was the second. It seemed ominous. But it would never do to manifest curiosity, let alone apprehension, on his own account, so he forebore further query as to the mystery, whatever it might be. Yet he thought it no harm to say—

"And what was this white man, Silawayo?"

"He was *Umfundisi*" (a preacher), answered the other chief, Ngumúnye. "The King loves not such."

Well, the King need have no objections to himself on that

score, at anyrate, thought Laurence, with a dash of grim humour. But he only said—

"The King? Tell me about your king, *Izinduna*.²—How does he look? What is his name?"

"*Hau!* Is it possible, O stranger, that you have never heard the name of the King?" said Ngumúnye, turning upon Laurence a blankly astonished face.

"Did not Silawayo but now say that only one white man had visited your country,—and even he had not returned?" said Laurence, in native fashion answering one query with another.

"Ha!" cried both chiefs, whom an idea seemed to strike. Then Ngumúnye went on impressively—

"Look around, O bearer of the Sign of the Spider. For days we have seen no man,—the remains of huts have we seen, but of people, none. You too were remarking upon it but yesterday."

"That is so," assented Laurence.

"The remains of huts, but of people, none," repeated the induna, with a wave of his hand. "Well, stranger, that is the name of the King, the Great Great One."

"The name of the King?"

"*E-hé.* I'Tyisandhlu."

"I'Tyisandhlu? The Strong Wind that burns from the North?" repeated Laurence, translating the name.

"*E-hé!*" assented both chiefs emphatically. "Now say,—hath not a broad belt around the land of the People of the Spider been burned flat?" with a wave of the hand which took in the desolated region.

They had gained the great mountain range whose snowy summits had been drawing nearer for days, and a noble range indeed it was apparently; moreover, of immense altitude. Laurence Stanninghame, who was well acquainted with the Alps, now gazed in wonder and admiration upon these snow-capped Titans whose white heads seemed to support the blue vault of heaven itself, to such dizzy heights did they soar. Walls of black cliff, overhung with ice cornices even as with gigantic white eyebrows, towered up from dazzling snow slope, and, higher still, riven crags, split into all fantastic shapes, frowned forth as though to menace the world. And all around, clinging about the feet of these stupendous heights, soft, luxuriant forests, tuneful with the murmur of innumerable glacier streams. A very Paradise of beauty and grandeur side by side, thought Laurence,—amid which the shields and spears, the marching column of the savage host, seemed strangely out of keeping.

"How are they called, those mountains, Silawayo?" he said.

"Beyond them lies the land of the People of the Spider," answered the induna evasively. And the other understood that he must not look for exuberant information on topographical subjects just then.

They entered the mountains by a deep, black defile which pierced the range. For a day and night they wound through this, hardly pausing to rest, for it had become piercingly cold. Moreover, as Silawayo explained, even when the weather was at its highest stage of sultriness elsewhere, in the mountains the changes were sudden and great. To be snowed up in this pass was too serious a matter to risk.

"Was it the only gate by which the country of the Ba-gcatya was, entered, then?"

But Silawayo did not seem to hear this question. He descanted learnedly on the suddenness of the mountain storms, and told tales of more than one *impi* which had set forth in all its warlike ardour, and had found here a stiff and frozen bed whereon its people might rest for all time.

The while, keenly alert to take in all the features of the route, Laurence affected the greatest interest in the conversation of those around him. But there was that about the dark ruggedness of this stupendous pass that weighed heavily upon his mind—that depressed, well-nigh appalled him. It were as though he were passing through some black and gloomy gate which should shut him forever from the outside world, as they wound their way, now where the cliffs beetled overhead so as to shut out the heavens, now along some dizzy ledge, with the dull roar of the mountain stream wafted up on icy gusts from far below. He suffered severely from the cold too, he who had breathed the moist, torrid heat of equatorial forests for so long,—and his wound became congealed and stiff. Yet he bore himself heroically, even as the Ba-gcatya themselves, who, their scanty clothing notwithstanding, seemed

to feel the cold not one whit, chatting and laughing and singing
while they marched. Finally the ground descended once more, and
at length—while he was nodding in slumber at the dawn of day,
during one of their brief rests—Ngumúnye touched him on the
shoulder and beckoned that he should accompany him. Laurence
complied, and when they had gained the brow of a gently rising
ridge beyond, an exclamation of wonder and admiration burst
from his lips.

"Lo!" said the induna, pointing down with his knob-stick.[3]
"Lo! there lies the land of the People of the Spider; there rests the
throne of The Strong Wind that burns from the North. Lo! his
dwelling,—Imvungayo."[4]

CHAPTER XXI

"THE STRONG WIND THAT BURNS FROM THE NORTH"

FROM where they stood the ground fell away in great wooded spurs
to a broad level valley, or rather plain,—shut in on the farther side
by rolling ranges of forest-clad hills. The valley bottom, green
and undulating, was watered by numerous streams, flashing like
bands of silver ribbon in the golden glow of the newly-risen sun.
Clustering here and there, five or six together, were kraals, circular
and symmetrical, built on the Zulu plan, and from their dome-
shaped grass huts blue lines of smoke were arising upon the still
morning air. Already, dappling the sward, the many-coloured
hides of innumerable cattle could be seen moving, and the long-
drawn shout and whistle of those who tended them rose in faint
and harmonious echo to the height whence they looked down.
Patches of broad, flag-like maize, too, stood out, in darker squares,
from the verdancy of the grass, and bird voices in glad note made
merry among the cool, leafy, forest slopes. Coming in contrast to
the steamy heat, the dank and gloomy equatorial vegetation,—
the foul and noisome surroundings of the cannibal villages, this
smiling land of plenty did indeed offer to him who now first beheld
it a fair and blithesome sight.

But another object attracted and held the attention of the spectator even more than all. This was an immense kraal. It lay on the slope at least ten miles away, but with the aid of his glass, which had been returned to him from among the slavers' loot, Laurence could bring it very near indeed. The yellow domed huts lay six or seven deep between their dark, ringed fences, the great circular space in the middle—the *isigodhlo*, or enclosure of royal dwellings partitioned off at the upper end—why, the place might have been the chief kraal of Cetywayo or Dingane miraculously transferred to this remote and unexplored region.

"Lo! Imvungayo. The seat of the Great Great One—the Strong Wind that burns from the North," murmured Ngumúnye, interpreting his glance of inquiry. "Come—let us go down."

As the great *impi*, which up till now had been marching "at ease," emerged upon the plain, once more the warriors formed into rank, and advanced in serried columns—singing a war-song. Immediately the whole land was as a disturbed beehive. Men, women, and children flocked forth to welcome them, the latter, especially, pressing forward with eager curiosity to obtain a glimpse of the white man, the first of the species they had ever seen, and the air rang with the shrill, excited cries of astonishment wherewith they greeted his appearance, and the calm, unruffled way in which he ignored both their presence and amazement. Much singing followed; the stay-at-homes answering the war-song of the warriors in responsive strophes,—but there was little variety in these, which consisted largely, as it seemed to Laurence, of exuberant references to "The Spider" and praise of the King.

As they drew near the great kraal, two companies of girls, arrayed in beaded dancing dresses, advanced, waving green boughs, and, halting in front of the returning *impi*, sang a song of welcome. Their voices were melodious and pleasing to the last degree, imparting a singular charm to the somewhat monotonous repetition of the wild chant—now in a soft musical contralto, now shrilling aloft in a note of pealing gladness. Laurence, who was beginning to feel vividly interested in this strange race of valiant fighters, failed not to note that many of these girls were of extraordinarily prepossessing appearance, with their tall, beautiful figures and supple limbs, their clear eyes, and white teeth, and bright, pleasing faces. Then suddenly song and dance alike ceased, and the women, parting into two companies, the whole *impi* moved forward again, marching between them.

The huge kraal was very near now, the palisade lined with the faces of eager spectators. But Laurence, quick to take in impressions, noticed that here were no severed heads stuck about in ghastly ornament. This splendid race, as pitiless and unsparing in victory as it was intrepid in the field, was clearly above the more monstrous and revolting forms of savage barbarity. Then all further reflections were diverted into an entirely new channel, for the whole *impi*—tossing the unarmed right hand aloft—thundered aloud the salute royal, then fell prostrate—

"*BAYÉTE!*"[1]

The roar—sudden, and as of one man—of that multitude of voices was startling, well-nigh terrifying. Laurence, unprepared for any such move, found himself standing there—he alone, erect—while around him, as so much mown corn, lay prostrate on their faces this immense company of armed warriors. Then he took in the reason.

Just in front of where the *impi* had halted rose a small cluster of trees crowning a knoll. Beneath the shade thus formed was a group of men, in a half-squatting, half-crouching attitude—all save one.

Yes. One alone was standing—standing a little in advance of the group—standing tall, erect, majestic—in a splendid attitude of ease and dignity, as, with head thrown slightly back, he darted his clear expressive eyes proudly over the bending host. A man in the prime of life—a perfect embodiment of symmetry and strength—he wore no attempt at gew-gaws or meretricious adornment. His shaven head was crowned with the usual *isicoco*, or ring, whose jetty blackness seemed to render the rich copper hue of the smooth skin even lighter, and for all clothing he wore a *mútya* of lion-skin and leopards' tails. Yet Laurence Stanninghame, gazing upon him, recognised a natural dignity—nay, a majesty enthroning this nearly naked savage such as he had never seen quite equalled in the aspect or deportment of any other living man. Clearly this was the King—Tyisandhlu—"The Strong Wind that burns from the North." Removing his hat with one hand he raised the other above his head, and repeated the salute-royal as he had heard it from the warriors.

The King acknowledged his greeting by a brief murmur. Then he called aloud—

"Rise up, my children."

As one man that huge assembly sprang to its feet,—and the quivering rattle of spear-hafts was as a winter gale rushing through a leafless wood. With one voice it began to thunder forth the royal titles.

"O Great Spider! Terrible Spider! Blood-drinking Spider, whose bite is death! O Serpent! O Elephant! Thunder of the heavens! Divider of the Sun! House Burner! O Destroyer! O All Devouring Blast!" These were some of the titles used—but the praisers would always bring back the *bonga*² to some attribute of the spider. Laurence, who understood the system, noted this peculiarity, differing, as it did, from the Zulu practice of making the serpent the principal term of praise. Finally, as by signal, the shouting ceased, and the principal leaders of the *impi*, disarming, crept forward, two by two, to the King's feet.

Laurence was too far off to hear what was said, for the tone was low, but he judged, and rightly, that the chiefs were giving an account of the expedition. At length the King dismissed them, and pointing with the short knob-stick he held in his hand, ordered that he himself should be brought forward.

The ranks of the warriors opened to let him through, and as, having been careful to disarm in turn, he advanced, Laurence could not repress a tightening thrill of the pulses as he wondered what fate it was, as regarded himself, that should now fall from the lips of this despot, whose very name meant a terror and a scourge.

Tyisandhlu for some moments uttered no word, but stood gazing fixedly upon his prisoner in contemplative silence. Laurence, for his part, was studying, no less attentively, the King. The finely-shaped head and lofty brow—the clear eyes and oval face, culminating in a short beard, whose jetty thickness just began to show here and there a streak of grey,—the noble stature and erect carriage, impressed him even more, thus face to face, than at a distance.

"They say thou bearest the Sign of this nation, O stranger," began the King, speaking in the Zulu tongue, "and that to this thou owest thy life."

"That is true, Great Great One," answered Laurence.

"But how know we that the Sign is genuine?" continued Tyisandhlu.

"By this, Father of the People of the Spider. Not once has it stood between me and death, but twice, and that at the hands of your people."

A murmur of astonishment escaped his hearers. But the King said—

"When was this other time?—for such would, in truth, be something of a test."

Then Laurence told the tale of his conflict with the Ba-gcatya warriors beneath the tree-fern by the lagoon—and the murmur among the listeners deepened.

"I was but one man, and they were twelve," he concluded. "Twelve of the finest warriors in the world, even the warriors of the People of the Spider. Yet they could not harm me, see you, Great Great One. They could not prevail against the man who held—who wore—the Sign of the Spider."

Now an emphatic hum arose on the part of all who heard—and indeed there had been a silence that might be felt while he had been narrating his tale. More than ever was Laurence convinced that in deciding to tell it he had acted with sound judgment. He had little or nothing to fear from the vengeance of the relatives of those he had slain—for he had seen enough of these people to guess that they did not bear a grudge over the fortunes of war—over losses sustained in fair and open fight. And, on the other hand, he had immensely strengthened his own case.

"Yet, you made common cause with these foul and noisome Izímu,"* said the king, shifting somewhat his ground. "These carrion dogs, who devour one another, even their own flesh and blood?"

"I spared but one of their villages, O Great North Wind. For the rest, how many have I left standing?"

"That is so," said Tyisandhlu, still gazing fixedly at his prisoner. Then he signed the latter to retire among the warriors, and, turning, gave a few rapid directions in a low voice to an attendant.

In the result, a group of armed warriors was seen hurrying forward, and in its midst a man, unarmed—a man ragged and

---

* Cannibals.—Mitford's note.

covered with dried blood, and with his arms ignominiously bound behind him. And wild amazement was in store for Laurence. He had reckoned himself the sole survivor of the massacre. Yet now in this helpless and ill-treated prisoner he recognised no less a personage than Lutali.

His body and limbs slashed with many spear-wounds—his clothing cut to ribbons—his half-starved and filthy aspect—as he was hustled forward into the king's presence, the Arab would have looked a pitiable object enough but for one thing. The dignity begotten of high descent and indomitable courage never left him—not for one moment. Weak as he was with loss of blood and the pain of his untended and mortifying wounds, the glance of his eyes, no less than the set of his keen, hawklike face, was as proud, as fearless, as that of the King himself.

"Down, dog!" growled the guards, flinging him forward on his face. "Lick the earth at the feet of the Great North Wind, whose blast kills!"

But immediately Lutali staggered to his feet, and the hell blast of hate and fury which shone from his eyes was perfectly demoniacal.

"There is but one God, and Mohammed is the Prophet of God!" he roared. "Am I to prostrate myself before an infidel dog—the chief dog of a pack of dogs? This for the scum!" And he spat full towards Tyisandhlu.

An indescribable shiver of awe ran through the dense and serried ranks of armed warriors, followed by a terrible tumult.

"Au! he is mad!" cried some; while others clamoured: "Give him to us, Great Great One. We will put him to the fiery death!"

But the King returned no word. It is even possible that his own intrepid soul was moved to admiration by the sublime courage of this man—his prisoner, bound, helpless, weakened—standing thus before him—before him at whose frown men trembled—face to face, and thus defying him. One other who beheld it, the sight must have powerfully moved, for with a lull in the tumult a voice rose clear and distinct—

"Spare him, O Great Great One, for he is a brave man."

If anyone had told Laurence Stanninghame but an hour earlier that he was about to commit so rash and suicidal an act as to beg the life of another at the hands of a grossly insulted despot, and in the face of an enraged nation, he would have scouted the idea as too weakly idiotic for words. Yet, in fact, he had just committed that very act. Deep and savage were the resentful growls that greeted his words. "*Au!* he presumes! He shares in the insult offered to the majesty of the King," were some of the ominous mutterings that went forth.

The King merely glanced in the direction of the speaker, and said nothing. But Lutali, becoming aware for the first time of the presence of his former confederate, turned towards the latter.

"Ask not my life at the hands of these dogs, these unclean swine, Afâ," he cried;—"Lo, Paradise awaits to receive the believer. I hasten to it; I enter it;" and he threw back his head fearlessly, while his eyes shone with a fanatical glare.

"Spare him, O King, for he is a brave man," urged Laurence again.

"And so art thou, I think," replied Tyisandhlu, turning a somewhat haughty stare upon the speaker. Then he muttered, "Yet, not this one."

An interruption occurred; gruesome, grotesque. A number of figures, seeming to spring from no one knew where, were seen gliding forward. They were coal black from head to foot, and their faces were more like masks than the human countenance, being bedaubed with some pigment that gave each of them the aspect of possessing two huge goggle eyes. But these horrible beings seemed at first sight to have no arms and no legs, their whole anatomy being encased in a sort of black, hairy sacking, whence tails and streamers, also hairy, flapped in the air as they moved. Hideous, indeed, they looked,—hideous and grotesque, half reptile, half devil.

They surrounded Lutali—all in dead silence, the guards precipitately falling back to give them way. Then the King spoke, and his words were gentle and mocking—

"Go now to thy Paradise, O believer. These will show thee the way. *Hamba-gahle!*"³

He waved his hand, and, in obedience to the signal, the whole group of black horrors fastened upon the Arab and dragged him away. And from all who beheld there went up a deep, chest note of exclamation that was part satisfaction, part awe.

The King, having received further reports and attended to other business connected with the army, withdrew. Laurence, watching the stately personality of this splendid savage retiring amid the groups of indunas towards the gate of the great kraal, felt his ever-present conjectures as to his own fate merge in a vivid sense of interest. But Tyisandhlu seemed to have forgotten his existence, for he bestowed no further word upon him; however, he was taken charge of by Ngumúnye, who assigned him a large hut within the royal kraal.

CHAPTER XXII

THE SHADOW OF THE MYSTERY

THE next few days were spent by the Ba-gcatya in dancing and ceremonial—and by Laurence Stanninghame in trying to find out all he could about the Ba-gcatya. He laid himself out to make friends with them, and this was easy, for the natural suspiciousness wherewith the savage invariably regards a new acquaintance once fairly laid to rest, the Ba-gcatya proved as chatty and genial a race of people as those of the original Zulu stock. But on one point the lips of old and young alike were sealed, and that was the fate of Lutali. No word would they ever by any chance let fall as to this; but the awed silence wherewith they would treat all mention of it, and their hurried effort to change the subject, added not a little to the impression the last glimpse of his Arab confederate had made upon Laurence. What awesome, devilish mystery did not those hideous beings represent?

For the rest, he learned that these people were of Zulu stock, and having opposed the accession of Tshaka, when that potentate usurped the royal seat of Dingiswayo, had deemed it advisable to flee. They had migrated northward, even as Umzilikazi and his followers had done, though some years prior to the flight of that chieftain. But they were nothing if not conservative, and so intent was the King on preserving the pure Zulu blood, that he was chary of allowing any slaves among them. As it was, the issue of all slaves had no rights, and could under no circumstances whatever rise above the condition of slavery. And Laurence, noting the grand physique, and even the handsome appearance, of the sons and daughters of this splendid race, had no doubt as to the wisdom of such a restriction.

Now, as the days went by, there began to grow upon Laurence a sort of restfulness. The terrible conflict and merciless massacre of his friends and followers had impressed him but momentarily, accustomed as he was to scenes of horror and of blood—and indeed in direct contrast to such did he the more readily welcome the peaceful tranquillity of his present life. For the dreaded Ba-gcatya at home were a quiet and pastoral race, owning extensive herds of cattle, also goats and a strange kind of large-tailed sheep—though, true to their origin, horned cattle formed the staple of their possessions—and the land around the king's great place was dappled with grazing stock, and the air was musical with the singing of women hoeing the millet and maize gardens.

Then again, the surrounding country swarmed with game, large and small, from the colossal elephant to the tiny duikerbuck. To Laurence, passionately fond of sport, this alone was sufficient to reconcile him to his strange captivity—for a time. He would be the life and soul of the Ba-gcatya hunting-parties, and his skill and success, together with his untiring energy and philosophical acceptance of the hardships and vicissitudes of the chase, went straight to the hearts of these fine, fearless barbarians. He became quite a favourite with the nation.

The female side of the latter, too, looked upon him with kindly eyes. He would chaff the girls, when he came upon them wandering in bevies, as was their wont, and tell them strange stories of other conditions of life, until they fairly screamed with laughter, or brought their hands to their mouths in mute wonder.

"*Whau*, Nyonyoba,—why do you not *lobola** for some of these?" said Silawayo one day, coming upon him thus engaged. Then you could dwell among us as one of ourselves."

"One might do worse, induna of the King," he returned tranquilly, with a glance at the group of bright-faced, merry, and extremely well-shaped damsels whom he had been convulsing with laughter.

---

* Payment of cattle made to the father of a girl sought in marriage.— Mitford's note moved from a later place in the text.

"*Yau!* Listen to our father," they cried. "He is joking, indeed. *Yau!* Farewell, Nyonyoba. Fare thee well." And they sped away, still screaming with laughter.

The old induna looked quizzically after them, then at Laurence. Then he took snuff.

"One might do worse, Silawayo," repeated Laurence. "I have known worse times than those I have already undergone here. But all I possess, I have lost. My slaves your people have killed, and my ivory and goods the King has taken, leaving me nothing but my arms and ammunition. Tell me, then. Do the Ba-gcatya give their daughters for nothing, or how shall a man who is so poor think to set up a kraal of his own?"

The induna laughed drily.

"We are all poor that way," he said, "for all we own belongs to the King. Yet the Great Great One is open-handed. He might return some of your goods, Nyonyoba."

This, by the way, was Laurence's sobriquet among these people, bestowed upon him by reason of his skill and craft in stalking wild game.[1]

It was even as Laurence had said. This raid had gone far towards undoing the results of their lawless and perilous enterprise. A portion of his gains were safe, but this last blow was of crippling force. And only a day or so prior to it he had been revelling in the prospect of a speedy return to civilised life, to the enjoyment of wealth for the remainder of his allotted span. He recalled the misgivings uttered by Holmes, that wealth thus gained would bring them no good, for the curse of blood that lay upon it. Poor Holmes! The prophecy seemed to have come true as regarded the prophet—but for himself? well, the loss reconciled him still more to his life among the Ba-gcatya.

Of Tyisandhlu he had seen but little. Now and then the King would send for him and talk for a time upon things in general, and all the while Laurence would feel that the shrewd, keen eyes of this barbarian ruler were reading him like a book. Tyisandhlu, moreover, had expressed a wish that a body of picked men should be armed with the rifles taken from the slavers, and instructed in their use—and to this Laurence had readily consented.

"Yet consider, Ndabezita,"* he had said. "Is it well to teach them reliance on any weapon other than the broad spear? For had your army possessed fire-weapons, never would it have eaten up our camp out yonder. It would have spent all its time and energy shooting, and that to little purpose. It would have had time to think, and then the warriors would have brought but half a heart to the last fierce charge.

"There is much in what you say, Nyonyoba," replied the king. "Yet, I would try the experiment."

So the indunas were required to select the men, and about three hundred were organised, and Laurence, having spent much care in their instruction, soon turned out a very fair corps of sharp-shooters. No scruple had he in thus increasing the fighting strength of this already fierce and formidable fighting race, to which he had taken a great liking. He began even to contemplate the contingency of ending his life among them, for of any return to civilisation there seemed not the remotest prospect; and, indeed, rather than return without the wealth for which he had risked so much, he preferred not to return at all.

Even the memory of Lilith brought with it pain rather than solace. After all this time—years indeed, now—would not his memory have faded? The life he had led tended to foster such memory in himself, but with her it was otherwise. All the conditions of her daily life tended rather to dim it. That sweet, short, passionate episode had been all entrancing while it lasted; yet was it not counterpoised by the certainty that with women of her temperament such episodes are but episodes? All the bitter side of his philosophy cried aloud in the affirmative.

He had now been several months among the Ba-gcatya; and had long since ceased to feel any misgiving as to his personal safety at their hands. But his sense of security was destined to receive a rude shock, and it came about in this way.

Returning one day from a hunt, at some distance from Imvungayo, he had marched on ahead of his companions, and, the afternoon being hot, had lain down in the shade of a cluster

---

* A term of deference frequently used in addressing one of the royal family.—Mitford's note.

of trees for a brief nap. From this the buzz of muttering voices awakened him.

At first he paid no attention, reckoning that the remainder of the party had come up. But soon a remark which was let fall started him very wide awake indeed, and at the same time he recognised that the voices were not those of his present companions, but of strangers. From a certain quaver or hesitancy in the tones, he judged them to be the voices of old men.

"*Whau!* The Spider must be growing hungry again. It is long since he has drunk blood."

"Not since the son of Tondusa assumed the head-ring," answered another.

"And now a greater is about to assume the head-ring," went on the first speaker, "even Ncute, the son of Nondwana."

"The brother of the Great Great One?"

"The same," assented the first speaker, in that sing-song hum in which natives, when among themselves, will carry on a conversation for hours.

Now the listener was interested indeed. On the mysterious subject of "The Spider" the Ba-gcatya had been as close as death. No hint or indication tending to throw light upon it would they let fall in reply to any question, direct or indirect. Now he was going to hear something. These men, unaware of his presence, and talking freely among themselves, would certainly afford more than a clue to it. Nondwana, the king's brother, he suspected of being not over favourably disposed towards himself, possibly through jealousy.

"That will be when the second moon is at full?" continued one of the talkers.

"It will. Ha! The Spider will receive a brave offering. Yet how shall it devour one who bears its Sign?"

"It may not," rejoined the other. "*Hau!* that will in truth be a test—if the Sign is real."

One who bears its Sign! The listener felt every drop of blood within him turn cold, freeze from head to foot. What sort of devil-god could it be from which this nation derived its name, and which these were talking about as one that devoured men?

He that bears its Sign! The words could apply to none other than

himself. He had deduced that, although the Ba-gcatya held cannibalism in abhorrence, yet from time to time human sacrifices
of a very awesome and mysterious nature took place, and that on
certain momentous occasions—the accession or death of a king, of
an heir to any branch of the royal house, or such a one as this now
under discussion—the admission to full privileges of manhood of a
scion of the same. And the sacrifice on this occasion was to consist
of himself? To this end he had been spared—even honoured.

"It will in truth be a test, for some doubt that the Sign as worn
by this stranger hath any magic at all," continued one of the talkers.
"If he comes out unharmed—*Hau!* that will be a marvel, indeed—a
marvel, indeed."

"*E-hé!*" they assented. Then they fell to talking of other things,
and soon the concealed listener heard them rise up and depart.

Laurence decided to wait no more for his companions. He
wanted to be alone and think this matter out. So when the voices
of the talkers had fairly faded beyond ear-shot he left the cluster
of trees on the farther side and took his way down the mountain
slope.

A ghastly fear was upon him. The horror and mystery of the
thing got upon even his iron nerves—the suddenness of it too,—just
when he had lulled himself into a complete sense of security. Had
he learned in like fashion that he was to be slain in an ordinary way
at a given time it would not have shaken him beyond the ordinary.
But this thing—there was something so devilish about it. What
did it mean? Was it some grotesque idol worked by mechanism,
even as in the old pagan temples—to which human sacrifices were
offered? Or—for he could not candidly discredit all the weird and
marvellous tales and traditions of some of these up-country tribes,
degraded and man-eating as they were—was it some unknown
and terrifying monster inhabiting the dens and caves of the earth?
Whatever it was, he knew too well, of course, that the coincidence
which had so miraculously resulted in the sparing of his life at the
hands of the victorious Ba-gcatya, reeking with slaughter, would
stand him in nowhere here. He remembered the mystery hanging
over the fate of Lutali, and those horrible beings who had haled
the Arab to his doom, whatever it was, who indeed might well
constitute the priesthood of an unknown devil-god.

Surely never indeed had earth presented a fairer scene than this upon which the adventurer's eyes rested, as he made his way down the mountain-side. The calm peaceful beauty of the day, the golden sunlight flooding the plain beneath, the great circle of Imvungayo, and the—by contrast—tiny circles of lesser kraals scattered about the valley or crowning some mountain spur, and, mellow upon the stillness, the distant low of cattle—the singing of women at work mingling with the soft voices of a multitude of doves in corn-lands and surrounding forest-trees. Yet now in the white peaks towering to the cloudless heavens, in the black and craggy rifts, in the wide, rolling, partially-wooded plains—the hunter's paradise—this man saw only a gloomy wizard circle enclosing some horrible inferno—the throne of the frightful demon-god of this extraordinary race.

Then it occurred to Laurence that he had better not let this thing get too much upon his nerves. It was the result of inaction, he told himself. Several months of rest and tranquillity had begun to turn him soft. That would not do. He had got to look matters in the face fairly and squarely. The ceremony which was to bring him to what would almost certainly be a fearful fate was set for the full of the second moon, the talkers had said; but of this he had been already aware, for the chief Nondwana and his son were both well known to him. That would give him a little over six weeks. Escape? Nothing short of a miracle could effect that—he told himself—remembering the immense tract of desolate country surrounding the fastnesses of the Ba-gcatya, and the ferocious cannibal hordes which lay beyond these, and who indeed would wreak a vengeance of the most barbarous kind upon their old enemy and scourge, the slaver-chief, did they find him alone, and to that extent no longer formidable, in their midst.

The friendship of the King? No. That was based on superstition, even as the friendship of the entire nation. Even it was assumed for an end. Again, should he boldly challenge the pretensions of the demon-god, whatever it might be, and asserting himself to be the real one, offer to slay the horror in open conflict? Not a moment's reflection was needed, however, to convince him of the utter impracticability of this scheme. The cherished superstition of a great nation was not to be uprooted in any such rough-and-ready fashion. The only way of escape left open to him was that of death—death swift and sudden; the death of the suicide—to escape the greater horror. But from this he shrank. The grim hardness of his recent training had nerved him rather to face peril than to avoid it. He did not care to contemplate such a way out of the dilemma. He was cornered. There was no way of escape.

And then, as he walked thus, thinking, and thinking hard, in the fierce, desperate, clear-headedness of a strong, cool-nerved man, face to face with despair, a voice—a female voice—lifted in song— sounded across his path, nearer and nearer. And now a wave of hope, of relief, surged through Laurence Stanninghame's heart, for there flooded in upon him, as with an inspiration, a way out of the situation. For he knew both the voice and the singer, and at that moment a turn in the bushes brought the latter and himself face to face.

CHAPTER XXIII

LINDELA

A WOMAN—young, tall, perfectly proportioned, light of colour, and with the bright and pleasing expression common among the well-born of the Ba-gcatya maidens, enhanced by large lustrous eyes, lips parted in a smile half-startled, half-coquettish, revealing a row of teeth of dazzling whiteness and unrivalled evenness. She wore a *mútya* or skirt of beautiful beadwork, and a soft robe of dressed fawn-skin also richly beaded but half concealed the splendid outlines of her frame. Withal there was an aspect of dignity in her erect carriage, and the pose of her head, which the Grecian effect of the *impiti*, or cone into which her hair was gathered above the scalp, went far to enhance. She was not alone; two other young women, also attractive of aspect, being in attendance upon her, though these held somewhat in the background.

"Greeting, Nyonyoba," she began, in a sweet and musical voice. "I was startled for a moment—here where I expected to find none."

"To thee, greeting, daughter of the great," returned Laurence, for this girl was a princess of the highest rank in the nation, being, in fact, a daughter of Nondwana, the King's brother—that same chief whose son's accession to manhood was to be the occasion of his own departure to another sphere. Nor was it, indeed, the first time these two had talked together.

"And why are you sad and heavy of countenance, Nyonyoba? Was the hunt bad—the game scarce?" she went on, with a quick searching glance into his eyes.

"Not so," he answered. "Those who are with me bring on much ivory for the King's treasury. For yourself, Lindela, I found a bright-plumaged and rare bird, which I will stuff and set up for you."

The girl uttered a cry of delight, and her face brightened. It so happened that Laurence was something of a taxidermist, and had already stuffed a few birds and small animals for the chief's daughter, who was as delighted with her increasing "museum" as any child could have been. Now, in her unfeigned glee over the prospect of a new specimen, Lindela looked extremely attractive; and noting it, an unconscious softness had crept into the man's tone. Even the girls behind observed it, and whispered to each other, sniggering—

"*Hau! Isityeli!* Quite a wooer! Nyonyoba is hoeing up new land."

"Withdraw a little from these, Lindela," he said in a lowered tone;—"I would talk."

The chief's daughter made a barely perceptible sign, but her attendants understood it, and remained where they were standing.

"The success or failure of a hunt is a small thing. Such does not render a man heavy of countenance," he went on, when they were beyond earshot.

"What does, then?" said the girl, raising her large eyes swiftly to his.

"Sorrow.—Parting.—Such are the things which make life dark. I have dwelt long among your people, and at the prospect of leaving them my heart is sore."

As the last words left his lips, Laurence learned in just one brief flash of a second exactly what he wanted to know. But the look of startled pain in Lindela's face gave way to one of surprise.

"Of leaving them?" she echoed. "Has the Great Great One, then, ordered you to begone, Nyonyoba?"

"Not yet. But it will be so. Listen! At the full of the second moon."

A cry escaped her. She understood. For a moment the self-control of her savage ancestors entirely forsook her. She became the child of nature—all human.

"It shall not be! It shall not be!"

The passion, the abandonment in the soft, liquid Zulu tone—in the large eyes, transforming the whole attractive face—touched even him—penetrated even the scaly armour which encased his hardened heart. Considerations of expediency no longer reigned there alone as he stood face to face with the chief's daughter. She was a magnificent specimen of womanhood, he decided, gazing with unfeigned admiration upon her splendid frame, upon the unconscious grace of her every movement.

"If I go, I return not ever," he went on, resolved to strike while the iron was hot—to strike as hard as he knew how. "Yet how to remain—for the brother of the King is so great a chief that he who would approach him with *lobola* would need to own half the wealth of the Ba-gcatya people? Now I, who owned much wealth, am yet poor to-day, for the Ba-gcatya have killed all my slaves, and the King has taken my ivory and goods."

The girl's eyes sparkled. Perhaps she too had learned something she wanted to know; indeed, it must have been so, for her whole face was lit up with a gladsome light, a wonderfully attractive light.

"Perchance the King will return some of it," she said. "Yet you are a white man, and strong, Nyonyoba—are all white men like you, I wonder?—and can overcome all difficulties. Listen! You shall not leave us at the full of the second moon. Now, farewell—and—forget not my name."*

There was a grandeur of resolution in her tone, in her glance, as she uttered these last words; her lustrous eyes, wide and clear, meeting his full. Laurence, standing there gazing after the tall, retreating form of the chief's daughter, felt something like a sense of exultation stealing over him. His scheme seemed already to

---

* "Lindela" means to "wait for"—in the sense of "to watch for," hence the full significance of the parting remark.—Mitford's note.

glow with success. He had suspected for some time that Lindela regarded him with more than favour; and indeed, while weighing the prospect of casting in his lot with the Ba-gcatya, he had already in his own mind marked her out to share it. Now, however, the thing had become imperative. In order to save not merely his life,—but to escape a fate which brooded over him with a peculiarly haunting horror,—he had got to do this thing, to take to wife, according to the customs of the Ba-gcatya, the daughter of Nondwana, the niece of the King. Then not a man in the nation dare raise a hand against him, and the dour priesthood of the Spider might look further for their victim—and might find in their selection one much more remote from the throne.

And now that he was face to face with the prospect, it struck him as anything but an unpleasing one. Such an alliance would place him among the most powerful chiefs in the land. All the ambition in the adventurer's soul warmed to the prospect. To be high in authority among this fine race, part-ruler over this splendid country, sport in abundance, and that of the most enthralling kind—war occasionally; to dwell, too, in the strong revivifying air of these grand uplands;—why, a man might live for ever under such conditions.

And the other side of the picture—what was it? Even if he returned to civilisation—even if it were possible—he would now return almost as poor as he had quitted it,—to the old squalid life, with its shifts and straits. His whole soul sickened over the recollection. Nothing could compensate for such—nothing. Besides, put nakedly, it amounted to this. His experiences of respectability had been disastrous. They had been such as to draw out all that was latently evil in his nature, and, indeed, to implant within him traits which at one time he could never have suspected himself capable of harbouring. Physically it had reduced his system to the lowest. All things considered, he could not think that the adventurous life—hard, unscrupulous, lawless as it was—had changed him for the worse. It had developed some good traits, and had enabled him to forget many evil ones.

"I would have speech with the King."

Those who sentinelled the gate of the great kraal, Imvungayo, conferred a moment among themselves, and immediately two men were sent to learn the royal pleasure as to the request. Laurence Stanninghame, awaiting their return, was taciturn and moody, and, as he gazed around, his one thought was lest his scheme should miscarry. The sun had just gone below the western peaks, and a radiant afterglow lingered upon the dazzling snow ridges, flooding some with a roseate hue, while others seemed dyed blood-red. Long files of women, calabash on head, were wending up from the stream, singing as they walked, or exchanging jests and laughter, their soft, rich voices echoing melodiously upon the evening stillness. Even the shrill "moo" of cattle, and the deep-toned voices of men—mellowed by distance, came not inharmoniously from the smaller kraals which lay scattered along the hillside,—and but for the shining spearheads and tufted shields of the armed guard in the great circle of Imvungayo, the scene was a most perfect one of pastoral simplicity and peace. And then, as the grey, pearly lights of evening, merging into the sombre shades of twilight, drew a deepening veil over this scene of fair and wondrous beauty, once more the words of Lindela, in all their unhesitating reassurance, seemed to sound in this man's ears, rekindling the fire of hope within his soul,—perchance rekindling fire of a different nature.

"The Great Great One awaits you, Nyonyoba."

Laurence started from his reverie, and, accompanied by two of the guards, proceeded across the great open space in silence. At the gate of the *isigodhlo*, an enclosure made of the finest woven grass, and containing the royal dwellings, he deposited his rifle on the ground, and, deliberately unbuckling the strap of his revolver holster, placed that weapon beside the other; and thus unarmed, according to strict Zulu etiquette, he prepared to enter. An *inceku*, or royal household servant, received him at the gate, and the guards having saluted and withdrawn, he was ushered by the attendant into the King's presence.

The royal house, a large dome-shaped, circular hut, differed in no respect from the others, save that it was of somewhat greater size. Laurence, standing upright within it, could make out three seated figures, the shimmer of their head-rings and the occasional shine of eyeballs being the only distinct feature about them. Then somebody threw an armful of dry twigs upon the fire which burned in the centre, and as the light crackled up he saw before him the King and the two fighting indunas, Ngumúnye and Silawayo.

"*Bayéte!*" he exclaimed, lifting his hat courteously.

"I behold you,[1] Nyonyoba," replied the King. "Welcome—be seated."

With a murmur of acknowledgment, Laurence subsided upon the grass mat which had been placed for him by the inceku, who had followed him in. Then there was silence for a few moments, while a couple of women entered; bearing large clay bowls of *tywala*,[2] or native beer; and the liquor having been apportioned out according to etiquette, the attendants withdrew, leaving Laurence alone with the King and the two indunas.

"And the hunt, has it been propitious?" began Tyisandhlu presently.

"It has. Ten tusks of ivory are even now being brought in," replied Laurence. "Also an unusually fine leopard skin which fell to my bullet, and which I would beg the King to accept."

"You are a great hunter, Nyonyoba—a very great one. *Whau!* The Ba-gcatya will become too rich if you tarry long among us," said Tyisandhlu quizzically, but evidently pleased at the news. "We shall soon be able to arm the whole nation with the fire weapons, now that we have so much ivory to trade with the northern peoples."

Something in the words struck Laurence. "If you tarry long among us," the King had said. Even these were ominous, and made in favour of the sinister design he had so accidentally discovered. Yet could this courtly hospitality, of which he was the object, indeed cover such a horrible purpose? Well, he dare not bolster himself up with any hope to the contrary, for now many and many an incident returned to his mind, little understood at the time, but, in the light of the conversation he had overheard, as clear as noonday. The fear, the anxiety, too, which had flashed over the face of Lindela at his significant words, proved that the ordeal through which it was designed to pass him was a real and a terrible one. Through her, and her only, lay his chance of escaping it.

"I am glad the King is pleased," he went on, "for I would fain tarry among the Ba-gcatya for ever. And, becoming one of that

people, shall not all my efforts turn towards rendering it a great
people?"

A hum of astonishment escaped the two indunas, and Laurence
thought to detect the same significant look on both their faces
Then he added—

"And those whom I have already taught in the use of the fire
weapon, they are strong in it, and reliable?"

"That is so," assented Tyisandhlu.

"And I have taught many the ways of the chase, no less than
the more skilled ways of war—that too is true, O Burning Wind?"

"That too is true," repeated the king.

"Good. And now I would crave a boon. While the People of
the Spider have become more formidable in war, while the ivory
comes pouring into the King's treasury, faster than ever it did
before, so that soon there will be enough to buy fire weapons for
the whole nation, I who brought all this to pass remain poor—am
the poorest in the nation—and—the daughters of the Ba-gcatya
are fair—exceeding fair."

"*Whau!*" exclaimed the two indunas simultaneously, with their
hands to their mouths. But Tyisandhlu said nothing, though a
very humorous gleam seemed to steal over his fine features in the
firelight.

"The daughters of the Ba-gcatya are exceeding fair," repeated
Laurence, "but I, the poorest man in the nation, cannot take
wives.—For how shall I go to the father of a girl and say, 'Lo, I
desire thy daughter to wife, but my slaves have been killed, and
my other possessions are now the property of the King; yet inas-
much as I cannot offer *lobola*, having nothing, give her to me on
the same terms?'—My house will not grow great in that way. Say
now, Ndabezita,—will it?"

"I think not, Nyonyoba," answered the King, struggling to
repress a laugh. "Yet perhaps a way may be found out of that difficulty, for in truth thou hast done us good service already. But
we will talk further as to this matter in the future. For the present,
there waits outside one who will show thee what thou wilt be glad
to see."

Quick to take this hint of dismissal, Laurence now arose,
saluted the king, and retired, not ill-pleased so far with the results

of his interview. For in the circumlocutory native way of dealing
with matters of importance, Tyisandhlu had received with favour
his request, preferred after the same method, that some of his possessions should be restored to him. Then he would offer *lobola* for
Lindela, and—

"I accompany you farther, Nyonyoba, at the word of the Great
Great One, by whose light we live."

The voice of the *inceku* who had ushered him forth broke in
upon his meditations. This man, instead of leaving him at the gate
of the *isigodhlo*, still kept at his side, and Laurence, manifesting no
curiosity, having picked up his weapons where he had left them,
accompanied his guide in silence.

They passed out of Imvungayo, and after walking nearly a
mile came to a large kraal, which Laurence recognised as that of
Nondwana, the King's brother. And now, for the first time, he
felt a thrill of interest surge through him. Nondwana's kraal! Had
Tyisandhlu, divining his wishes, indeed forestalled them? But this
idea was as quickly dismissed as formulated. The King had probably ordered that one or two of the Ba-gcatya girls should be allotted to him—possibly chosen from those in attendance upon the
royal wives. His parting remark seemed to point that way.

"Enter," said the *inceku*, halting before one of the huts. "Enter,
and good go with thee. I return to the King. Fare thee well!"

Laurence bent down and pushed back the wicker slab that
formed the door of the hut, and, having crawled through the
low, beehive-like entrance stood upright within, and instinctively
kicked the fire into a blaze. And then, indeed, was amazement—
wild, incredulous, bewildering amazement—his dominant feeling,
for by the light thus obtained he saw that the hut was tenanted
by two persons. No feminine voice, however, was raised to bid
him welcome in the soft tongue of the Ba-gcatya, but a loud, full
flavoured, masculine English one—

"Stanninghame—by the great Lord Harry! Oh, kind heavens,
am I drunk or dreaming?"

CHAPTER XXIV

AS FROM THE DEAD

"There, there, Holmes. Do you quite intend to maim a chap for life, or what?" exclaimed Laurence, liberating, with an effort, his hand from the other's wringing grasp. "And Hazon, too? In truth, life is full of surprises. How are you, Hazon?"

"So so," was the reply, as Hazon, who had been biding the evaporation of his younger friend's effusiveness, now came forward. But his handshake was characteristic of the man, for it was as though they had parted only last week, and that but temporarily.

"And is it really you yourself, old chap?" rattled on Holmes. "It's for all the world as if you had risen from the dead. Why, we never expected to set eyes on you again in life—did we, Hazon?"

"Not much," assented that worthy laconically.

"Well, I can say the same as regards yourselves," rejoined Laurence. "What in the world made them give you quarter?"

"Don't know," answered Hazon. "We managed to get together, back to back, we two, and were fighting like cats. Holmes got a shot on the head with a club that sent him down, and I got stuck full of assegais till I couldn't see. The next thing I knew was that we were being carted along in the middle of a big *impi*—Heaven knew where. One thing, we were both alive—alive and kicking, too. As soon as we were able to walk they assegaied our bearers, and—made us walk."

"Don't you swallow all that, Stanninghame," cut in Holmes. "He fought, standing over me—fought like any devil, the Bagcatya say—although he makes out now it was all playful fun."

"Well, for the matter of that, we had to fight," rejoined Hazon tranquilly. "Where have you been all this time, Stanninghame?"

"Here, at Imvungayo. And you two?"

"Shot if I know. They kept us at some place away in the mountains. Only brought us here a few days back."

"They won't let us out in the daytime," chimed in Holmes.

"And it's getting deadly monotonous. But tell us, old chap, how it is they didn't stick you."

This, however, Laurence, following out a vein of vague instinct, had decided not to do, wherefore he invented some commonplace solution. And it was with strange and mingled feelings he sat there listening to his old confederates. For months he had not heard one word of the English tongue, and now these two, risen, as it were, from the very grave, seemed to bring back all the past, which, under novel and strange conditions, had more and more been fading into the background. He was even constrained to admit to himself that such feelings were not those of unmingled joy. He had almost lost all inclination to escape from among this people, and now these two, by the very associations which their presence recalled, were likely to unsettle him again, possibly to his own peril and undoing. Anyway, he resolved to say nothing as to the incident of "The Sign of the Spider."

"Well, you seem to have got round them better than we did, Stanninghame," said Hazon, with a glance at the Express rifle and revolver wherewith the other was armed. "We have hardly been allowed so much as a stick."

"So? Well, I've been teaching some of them to shoot. That may have had a little to do with it. In fact, I've been laying myself out to make thoroughly the best of the situation."

"That's sound sense everywhere," rejoined Hazon. "You can't get Holmes here to see it, though. He's wearing out his soul-case wanting to break away."

This was no more than the truth. Laurence, seated there, narrowly watching his old comrades, was swift to notice that whereas these months of captivity and suspense had left Hazon the same cool, saturnine, philosophical being he had first known him, upon Holmes they had had quite a different effect. There was a restless, eager nervousness about the younger man; a sort of straining to break away, even as the more seasoned adventurer had described it. The fact was, he was getting desperately home-sick.

"I wish I had never had anything to do with this infernal business," he now burst forth petulantly. "I swear I'd give all we have made to be back safe and snug in Johannesburg, with white faces around us,—even though I were stony-broke."

"Especially one 'white face,'" bantered Laurence. "Well, keep up your form, Holmes. You may be back there yet, safe and sound, and not stony-broke either."

"No, no. There is a curse upon us, as I said all along. No good will come to us through such gains. We shall never return—never."

And then Laurence looked across at Hazon, and the glance, done into words, read: "What the mischief *is* to be made of such a prize fool as this?"

The night was spent in talking over past experiences, and making plans for the future, as to which latter Hazon failed not to note, with faint amusement, blended with complacency, that the disciple had, if anything, surpassed his teacher. In other words, Laurence entered into such plans with a lukewarmness which would have been astonishing to the superficial judgment, but was not so to that of his listener.

Nondwana, the brother of the king, was seated among a group of his followers in the gate as Laurence went forth the next morning to return to his own quarters. This chief, though older than Tyisandhlu in years, was not the son of the principal wife of their common father, wherefore Tyisandhlu, who was, had, in accordance with native custom, succeeded. There had been whisperings that Nondwana had attempted to oppose the accession, and very nearly with success; but whether from motives of policy or generosity, Tyisandhlu had forborne to take his life. The former motive may have counted, for Nondwana exercised a powerful influence in the nation. In aspect, he was a tall, fine, handsome man, with all the dignity of manner which characterised his royal brother, yet there was a sinister expression ever lurking in his face—a cruel droop in the corner of the mouth.

"Greeting, Nyonyoba. And is it good once more to behold a white face?" said the chief, a veiled irony lurking beneath the outward geniality of his tone.

"To behold the face of a friend once more is always good, Branch of a Royal Tree," returned Laurence, sitting down among the group to take snuff.

"Even when it is as that of one risen from the dead?"

"But here it was not so, Ndabezita. My 'Spider' told me that these were all the time alive," rejoined Laurence, with mendacity on a truly generous scale.

"Ha! thy Spider? Yet thou art not of the People of the Spider."

"But I bear the Sign," touching his breast. "There are many things made clear to me, which may or may not be set forward in the light of all at the full of the second moon. Farewell now, son of the Great. I return home."

The start of astonishment, the murmur which ran round the group, was not lost upon him. It was all confirmatory of what he had heard. And then, as he walked back to his hut in Silawayo's kraal, it occurred to Laurence that he had probably made a false move. Nondwana, who, of course, was not ignorant of his daughter's partiality, would almost certainly decide that Lindela had betrayed the secret and sinister intent to its unconscious object; and in that event, how would it fare with her? He felt more than anxious. The King might take long in deciding whether to restore his property or not, and etiquette forbade him to refer to the matter again—at anyrate for some time to come. That Nondwana might demand too much *lobola*, or possibly refuse it altogether, as coming from him, was a contingency which, strange to say, completely escaped Laurence's scheming mind.

"Greeting, Nyonyoba. Thy thoughts, are deep—ever deep."

The voice, soft, rich, bantering, almost made him start, as he raised his eyes to meet the glad laughing ones of the object of his thoughts at that moment, the chief's daughter.

"What do you here, wandering alone, Lindela?" he said.

"Ha—ha! Now you did well to say my name like that—for—does it not answer your question, 'to wait, to watch for'? And what is meant for two ears is not meant for four or six. I have news, but it is not good."

They were standing in the dip of the path, where a little runlet coursed along between high bush-fringed banks, and the tall, graceful form of the girl stood out in splendid relief from its background of foliage. Not only for love had she awaited him here, for her eyes were sad and troubled as she narrated her discoveries, which amounted to this: It was next to impossible for Laurence to escape the ordeal—whatever it might be. All of weight and position in the nation were resolved upon it, and none more thoroughly so than

Nondwana. The King himself would be powerless to save him, even if he wished, and, indeed, why should he run counter to the desire of a whole nation, and that on behalf of a stranger, some time an enemy?

Laurence, listening, felt his anxiety deepen. The net was closing in around him, had indeed already closed, and from it there was no outlet.

"See now, Lindela," he said gravely, his eyes full upon the troubled face of the girl. "If this thing has got to be, there is no help for it. And, however it turns out, the world will go on just the same—and the sun rise and set as before. Why grieve about it?"

"Because I love you—love you—do you hear? I know not how it is. We girls of the Ba-gcatya do not love—not like this. We like to be married to men who are great in the nation—powerful indunas if not too old,—or those who have much cattle, or who will name us for their principal wife; but we know not how to love. Yet you have taught me, Nyonyoba. Say now, is it through the magic of the white people you have done it?"

"It may be so," replied Laurence, smiling queerly to himself, as he thought how exactly, if unconsciously, this alluring child of Nature had described her civilised sisters. Then his face became alert and watchful. He was listening intently.

"I, too, heard something," murmured Lindela, scarcely moving her lips. "I fear lest we have been overlooked. Now, fare thee well, for I must return. But my ears are ever open to what men say, and my father talks much, and talks loud. It may be that I may learn yet more. But, Nyonyoba, delay not in thy first purpose, lest it be too late; and remember, Nondwana has a covetous hand. Fare thee well."

Left alone, Laurence thought he might just as well make sure that no spy had been watching them. Yet though he examined the banks of the stream for some little distance around, he could find no trace of any human presence, no mark even, however faint, of human foot. Still, as he gained his own quarters in Silawayo's kraal, a presentiment lay heavy upon him—a weird, boding presentiment of evil to come—of evil far nearer at hand than he had hitherto deemed.

Long and hard he slept, for he was weary with wakefulness and anxiety. And when he awoke at dusk, intending to seek an interview with the King, he beheld that which in no wise tended to allay his fears. For as he drew nearer to Imvungayo there issued from its gate a crowd of figures—of black, grotesque, horrible figures, and in the midst a man, whom they were dragging along in grim silence, even as they had haled Lutali to his unknown doom. And as they disappeared into the gathering darkness, Laurence knew only too well that here was another victim—another hideous sacrifice to the grisly and mysterious demon-god. No wonder his blood grew chill within him. Would he be the next?

"And you would still become one of us, Nyonyoba?"

"I would, Great Great One; and to this end have I sent much ivory, and many things the white people prize, including three new guns and much ammunition, to Nondwana."

"Ha! Nondwana's hand is large, and opens wide," said the King, with a hearty chuckle. "Yet Lindela is a sprig of a mighty tree. And I think, Nyonyoba, you yourself are sprung from such a root."

"That is no lie, Ruler of the Wise. As a man's whole height is to the length of half his leg, so is the length of my house to that of the kings of the Ba-gcatya, or even to that of Senzangakona* himself."

"Ha!—That may well be. Thou hast a look that way."

This conversation befel two days after the events just described. The King had refused him an audience on that evening, and indeed since until now. But in the meantime, by the royal orders, a great portion of the plunder taken from the slave-hunters' camp had been restored to him, considerably more, indeed, than he had expected. And now he and Tyisandhlu were seated once more together in the royal dwelling—this time alone.

"But to be sprung from an ancient tree avails a man nothing in my country if he is poor," went on Laurence. "Rather is it a disadvantage, and he had better have been born among the meaner sort. That is why I have found my way hither, Ndabezita."

"That is why? And have you gained the desired riches?" said Tyisandhlu, eyeing him narrowly.

---

* Founder of the Zulu dynasty, and of course patriarchally greater than the royal house of this Zulu-originated tribe.—Mitford's note.

"I had—nearly, when the Ba-gcatya fell upon my camp, and killed my people and my slaves. Now, having lost all, I care not to return to my own land."

"But could you return rich you would care so to return?"

"That is so, Root of a Royal Tree. With large possessions it is indeed a pleasant land to dwell in—with no possessions a man might often think longingly of the restful sleep of death."

"That may well be," said Tyisandhlu thoughtfully. "The cold and the gloom and the blackness, the fogs and the smoke—the mean and horrible-looking people who go to make up the larger portion of its inhabitants—*Whau*, Nyonyoba, I know more of you white people and their country than anyone here dreams, and it is as you say. Without that which should raise him above such horrors as this, a man might as well be dead."

"Wherefore I prefer to live in the land of the Ba-gcatya rather than die in my own. But whoever brought hither that description of our land told a wonderfully true tale, Ruler of the Great."

Tyisandhlu made no reply, but reaching out his hand he took up a whistle and blew a double note upon it. Immediately there entered an *inceku*.

"Let no man approach until this note shall again sound," said the King. "Preserve clear a wide space around, lest the ear that opens too wide be removed from its owner's head. Go."

The man saluted humbly and withdrew. And then, for long did they sit together and talk in a low tone, the barbarian monarch and the white adventurer—and the subject of their talk seemed fraught with some surprise to the latter, but with satisfaction to both.

"See now, Nyonyoba," concluded the King. "They have brought you here, here whence no man ever returned; and you would become one of us. Well, be it so. There is that about you which I trust."

"Whence no man ever returned?" echoed Laurence.

"Surely. Ha! A white man found his way hither once, but—he was a preacher—and I love not such. He never returned."

"But what of my two friends? You will not harm them, Ndabezita, because they are my friends, and we have fought together many a long year," urged Laurence.

"I will spare them for that reason. They shall be led from the country with their eyes covered, lest they find the way back again. But—if they do—they likewise shall never depart from it. And now, Nyonyoba, all I have told you is between ourselves alone. Breathe not a whisper of it or anything about me even to your friends. For the present, farewell, and good fortune be yours."

CHAPTER XXV

HIS LIFE FOR HIS FRIEND

Now, if Laurence Stanninghame's prospects were brightening, and his lines beginning to fall in pleasant places—relatively speaking, that is, for everything is relative in the conditions of life—the same held not good as regarded the other twain of our trio of adventurers. Both were kept prisoners in Nondwana's kraal, and, save that they were not ill-treated, no especial consideration was shown them. They were allowed to wander about the open space outside, but watchful eyes were ever upon them, and did they venture beyond certain limits, they were speedily made aware of the fact. No such distractions as joining in the hunting-parties, or coming and going at will such as their more fortunate comrade enjoyed, were allowed them, and against the deadly monotony of the life—in conjunction with a boding suspense as to their ultimate fate—did Holmes's restless spirit mightily chafe; indeed, at times he felt sore and resentful towards Laurence. At such times Hazon's judicious counsel would step in.

"Shall we never make a philosopher of you, Holmes?" he would say. "Do you think, for instance, that Stanninghame faring no better than ourselves, would improve our own lot any? No. Rely upon it his standing in with the King and the rest of them is doing us no harm in the long-run."

"I suppose you're right, Hazon; and it's beastly selfish of one to look upon it any other way," poor Holmes would reply wearily. "But, O Lord, this is deadly work. Is there no way of getting away from here?"

"Not any at present. Yet you don't suppose I'm keeping my eyes or ears shut, do you? We must watch our chances, and see and hear all we can. I believe Tyisandhlu is a decent fellow all round, and mind, you do come across plenty of pretty good fellows even among savages, whatever bosh some men may talk to the contrary. But I don't care for Nondwana. I believe he'd make short work of us if he dared. Possibly the King may be watching his opportunity of smuggling us out of the country. At any rate, I don't think he means us any harm, if only by reason of the astonishing fancy he seems to have taken to Stanninghame!"

This, as we know, was very near the truth, though far more so than the speakers guessed. For Laurence, moved both by inclination and expediency, had rigidly adhered to his promise of secrecy. If it seemed hard that he should be compelled to shut his companions out of his entire confidence, he consoled himself with the certainty that their admission into it, though it might encourage them mentally, could in no wise benefit them materially—very much the reverse, indeed, for it would probably bring about their destruction.

"Well, if anything is going to be done, it had better be soon or not at all. It wouldn't take much to send me clean off my chump," said Holmes dejectedly. "Every day I feel more inclined to break out—to run amuck in a crowd, if only for the sake of a little excitement. Anything for a little excitement!"

The two were strolling up and down outside Nondwana's kraal. It was a still, hot morning; oppressive as though a storm were brooding. A filmy haze lay upon the lower valley bottom, and the ground gave forth a shimmer of heat. Even the amphitheatre of dazzling snow-peaks omitted to look cool against the cloudless blue, while the coppery, terraced cliffs seemed actually to glow as though red hot.

"I hate this,"—growled Holmes, looking round upon as magnificent a scene of Nature's grandeur as the earth could show—"positively hate it. I shall never be able to stand the sight of a mountain again as long as I live—once we are out of this. Oh Heavens, look! *What* a brute!"

His accents of shuddering disgust were explained. Something was moving among the stones in front—something with great hairy, shoggling legs, and a body the size of a thrush, and much the same colour. A spider, could it be, of such enormous size? Yet it was; and as truly repulsive and horrible-looking a monster as ever made human flesh creep at beholding.

Whack! The stone flung by Holmes struck the ground beside the creature; struck it hard.

"Hold, you infernal fool," half snarled, half yelled Hazon. But before he could arrest the other's arm, whack!—went a second stone. The aim was true. The grisly beast, crushed and maimed, lay contracting and unfolding its horrible legs in the muscular writhings of its death throes.

"What's the row, eh?" grumbled Holmes, staring open-mouthed, under the impression that his comrade had gone mad, and at first sight not without reason, for Hazon's face had gone a swarthy white, and his eyes seemed to glare forth from it like blazing coals.

"Row? You fool! You've signed our death-warrant, that's all. Here, quick, pretend to be throwing stones on to it, as if we were playing at some game. Don't you see? The name of this tribe— People of the Spider! They venerate the beast. If we have been seen, nothing can save us."

"O Heavens!" cried Holmes, aghast, as the whole ugly truth dawned upon him, setting to with a will to pile stones upon the remains of the slain and shattered monster.

"Too late!" growled Hazon. "We have been seen! Look."

Several women were running stealthily and in alarm towards the gate, and immediately a frightful uproar arose from within. Armed with sticks and spears, the warriors came pouring forth, and in a moment had surrounded the two—a howling, infuriated, threatening mob.

Although expecting nothing less than instant death, with the emergency Hazon's coolness had returned. He stood in the midst of the appalling uproar, apparently unmoved. Holmes, on the other hand, looked wildly around, but less in fear than in desperation. He was calculating his chances of being able to snatch a weapon from one of them, and to lay about him in a last fierce battle for life. "Anything for a little excitement!" he had said. In very truth his aspiration was realised. There was excitement enough in the brandished spears and blazing eyeballs, in the infuriated demonia-cal faces, in the deafening, roaring clamour.

"This is no matter for you," cried Hazon in firm, ringing tones. "Take us to the King. We can explain. The affair is an accident."

At this the ferocious tumult redoubled. An accident! They had lifted their hand against the great tutelary Spider that guarded Nondwana's house! An accident!

"Hold! To the king let them be taken!" interposed a strong, deep voice. And extending his hands, as though to arrest the uplifted weapons, Nondwana himself stalked into the circle.

There was no gainsaying the mandate of one so great. Weapons were lowered, but still vociferating horrible threats, the crowd, with the two offenders in its midst, moved in the direction of Imvungayo.

But it seemed as though the wild, pealing shouts of rage and consternation were a very tocsin; for now from every kraal, near and far, the inhabitants came surging forth, streaming down the hillsides, over the face of the plain like swarming ants—and before they reached Imvungayo the two whites seemed to move in the midst of a huge sea of gibing, infuriated faces, as the dark crowd, gathering volume, poured onward, rending the air with deafening shouts of execration and menace. But the royal guards barred the gate, suffering no entrance save on the part of the two white men, together with Nondwana and a few of the greater among the people.

"This is the tightest place we have been in yet," murmured Hazon. "To tread on the superstitions of any race is to thrust one's head into the jaws of a starved lion."

"Damn their filthy superstitions!" said Holmes, savagely desperate. "Well, I did the thing, so I suppose I shall be the one to suffer."

The other said nothing. He had a shrewd suspicion that more than one life would be required in atonement. But he and death had stared each other in the face so frequently that once more or less did not greatly matter.

On learning the cause of the tumult, Tyisandhlu had come forth, and now sat, as he frequently did to administer justice, at the head of the great central space. When the shouts of *bonga* which greeted his presence had subsided, he ordered that the two whites should be brought forward.

This was the first time the latter had seen the King, and now, as they beheld his stately, commanding bearing, calm and judicial, both of them, Holmes especially, began to hope. They would explain the matter, and offer ample apologies. The owner of that fine, intellectual countenance, savage though he might be called, he, surely, had a soul above the debased superstitions of his subjects. Hitherto he had spared their lives,—surely now he would not sacrifice them to the clamour of a mob. Yet, as Hazon had said, to tread on the superstitions of any race was the most fatal thing on earth.

"What is this that has been done?" spoke the King, when he had heard all that the accusers had to say. "Surely no such deed has been wrought among us since the Ba-gcatya have been a nation."

There was a sternness, a menace even, in the full, deep voice, that dispelled all hope in the minds of the two thus under judgment. They had committed the one unpardonable sin. In vain Hazon elaborately explained the whole affair, diplomatically setting forth that the act being accidental, and done by strangers and white people, in ignorance, no ill-luck need befall the nation, as might be the case were the symbol of its veneration offended by its own people. The voice of the King was more stern than before—almost jeering.

"Accidental!" he repeated. "Even though it be so, accidents often bring greater evil in their results than the most deliberate wrong-doing—for such is the rule of life."

"That is so!" buzzed the indunas grouped on either side of the King. "*Au!* hear the wisdom of the Burning North Wind!"

Well then, in this matter atonement must be made. It appears that one only was concerned in it, and that one is Nomtyeketye."

This was the somewhat uncomplimentary nickname by which Holmes was known, bestowed upon him on account of his talkative tendencies as contrasted with the laconic sententiousness of Hazon.

"I rule, therefore," went on the King, "that Nomtyeketye *be taken hence to where atonement is offered.* The other may depart from among us to his own land."

A shout of approval rose from the vast crowd without as the decision became known. Some there were who clamoured for two victims,—but the King's decision was not lightly to be questioned. And before the shout had died into a murmur the whole multitude of hideous black figures in their weird disguise came bounding across the open space to seize their victim. But before they could surround the latter an unlooked-for interruption occurred.

"Hold!" cried a loud voice. "I have a favour to ask the King. I, who bear the Sign!" And Laurence, who in the midst of one of the listening groups had been unseen hitherto, now came forward, none hindering, and stood before the King.

A deep silence was upon all. Every head was bent forward. The frightful priesthood of the demon paused, with staring eyes, to wait on what new turn events would take.

"Say on, Nyonyoba," said Tyisandhlu shortly, looking anything but pleased at the interruption.

"It is this, O Burning Wind. Let Nomtyeketye return to his own people. I will take his place."

"You?" exclaimed the King, as a gasp of amazement shivered through the listeners.

"Yes, I. Hearken, Ndabezita. I it was who brought him hither. He is young, and his life is all before him. Mine is all behind me, and has been no great gain at that. I will proceed with these"— with a glance in the direction of the blackly horrible group—"to where atonement is offered. But let the two return together to their own land."

"Pause, Nyonyoba! Pause and think!" said the King, speaking in a deep and solemn voice. "That which awaits you, if I grant your request, is of no light order. Men have sought their own death rather than face it. Pause, I say." Then rapidly, and speaking very low—"Even I cannot save you there. It may be that the Sign itself cannot."

Now, what moved him to an act of heroic self-sacrifice, Laurence Stanninghame hardly knew himself. It may have been that he did not appreciate its magnitude. It may have been that he held more than a lingering belief that the King would find some secret means for his deliverance, whereas to his younger comrade no such way of escape lay open. Or was it that at this moment certain words, spoken long ago in warning, now stood forth clear, and in flaming letters upon his brain: *"Other men have*

gone up country with Hazon, but not one of them has ever returned!"
He himself, abiding henceforward among the Ba-gcatya, and
Holmes consigned to the mysterious doom, would not those
warning words be carried out in all their fell fatality? But that
after these years of hardening in the lurid school of bloodshed
and ruthlessness he should be capable of sacrificing himself for
another, through motives of impulsive generosity, Laurence
could not have brought himself to believe. Indeed, he could not
have defined his own motives.

"Give me your word, Great Great One, in the sight of the
whole nation," he said in a loud voice, "that these two shall be
suffered to depart unharmed—now, at once—and I will take the
place of Nomtyeketye."

"That will I readily do, Nyonyoba, for I have no need of strangers here such as these," answered Tyisandhlu. Then, sadly—
"And—you are resolved?"

"I am."

"Then it must be. For ye two, go in peace;—enough shall be
given you for your journey."

Holmes, who understood the language very imperfectly, had
no clear notion, even then, of what had taken place. But when he
saw the gigantic forms in their black disguise bounding forward
to surround Laurence, he, being otherwise unarmed, instinctively
threw himself into a boxing attitude, which was, under the circumstances, ridiculous, if natural.

"Keep cool, you young idiot," snarled Hazon. "We're out of
this mess better than we deserve."

"Why, what's happened?"

"Stanninghame is acting substitute for you, and we are to be
fired out of the country, which is good news to you, I take it."

"But I can't allow it!" cried Holmes bewilderedly, as the truth
began to dawn upon him. "No, hang it, I can't! Tell the King,
I——"

"No good. Keep your hair on. And remember, too, it's more
than probable he won't come to any harm. He stands in with them
too well."

Holmes, more than half reassured, suffered himself to be persuaded,—especially as he was powerless to do anything at all.

But whether Hazon believed or not in what he had just advanced must remain for ever locked up as a mystery in the breast of that inscrutable individual. One thing, however, he did not believe in, and that was in he himself suffering for the foolishness of other people.

Meanwhile Laurence, in the midst of his disguised executioners, was pursued by the howling and execrations of the crowd, which parted eagerly to make way for their passage. Outside on the open plain a vast mob of women had collected, yelling shrilly at him,—and even pelting him with earth and sticks. One of the latter, thrown at close quarters, hurtling over the heads of his guards, struck him on the shoulder, painfully and hard. He looked up. It had been hurled by the hand of Lindela; and as he met her eyes full, the face which he had last looked upon softening and glowing with the wondrous light of love, was now wreathed into a horrible grin of hate and savagery.

"*Yau!* The Spider is hungry! Fare thee well, Umtagati,"* jeered the chief's daughter' shrilly.

CHAPTER XXVI

THE PLACE OF THE HORROR

Was he awake—asleep and dreaming—or dead?

All these questions did Laurence Stanninghame ask himself by turn as he recovered his confused and scattered senses; and there was abundant scope for such conjecture, for, in truth, the place wherein he found himself was a strange one.

A wall of rock arose on either side of him—one straight, perpendicular, the other overhanging, arching out above the first. As he lay there in semi-gloom, his first thought was that he was in a cave; a further glance, however, convinced him that the place was a gigantic fissure or rift. But, how had he come there?

With an effort, for he still felt strangely languid and confused, he sent his mind back to the events of the previous day. Stay, though—was it the previous day? Somehow it seemed much

---

* Doer of witchcraft.—Mitford's note.

longer ago. He remembered the long hurried march into the heart
of the mountains with his gruesome escort. He remembered par-
taking of a plentiful meal and some excellent corn-beer; this he had
done with a view to keeping up his strength, which he might need
to the full. Then he remembered no more. The liquor had been
drugged, he decided.

But to what end? To what end, indeed, was he there? How had
he been brought there? He raised himself on his elbow and looked
around.

He started. A large bundle lay beside him—something rolled
up in a native blanket. Speedily undoing this, he discovered several
grass-baskets with lids. These contained pounded corn, such as is
eaten with *amasi*, or curdled milk—and, indeed, a large calabash
of the latter, tightly stoppered, was among the stores. Well, whatever was to become of him, he was not to starve, anyhow. But was
he only being fattened for a worse fate?

Then a thought struck him, which set all his pulses tingling
into renewed life. He, too, had been sent out of the country, and
these stores were to last him for, at anyrate, part of his journey.
True, the prospect was anything but an exhilarating one, seeing
that he was unarmed, and had but the vaguest idea which way to
turn, and that the Ba-gcatya country was surrounded by ferocious
and hostile races. But then, everything is relative in this world, and
to a man who had spent hours of a long day journeying towards
a mysterious, horrible, and certain death, the discovery of release
and life, even with such slender chances, was joy after the boding
dread which those long hours had held for him. Yes, that was
it, of course. Tyisandhlu had not been faithless to the friendship
between them. While openly consenting to his sacrifice, for even
the King dare not, in such a matter, run counter to the feeling of
the nation, Tyisandhlu had given secret orders that he should be
smuggled out of the country.

Having arrived at this conclusion, it occurred to Laurence that
he might as well explore a little. He would leave his stores here
for the present; for a glance served to show that the rift or fissure
ended there, so taking only a handful of the pounded corn, to eat
as he walked, he started at once.

But there was a something, a cold creepiness in the air perhaps, that quelled much of his new-born hope. The rift seemed to form a kind of circle, for he walked on and on, ever trending to the right, never able to see more than a short distance in front; never able to behold the sky. There was something silently, horribly eloquent in the grim sameness of those tomblike walls. Just then, to his relief, the semi-gloom widened into light. The cliffs no longer overhung each other. A narrow strip of sky became visible, and, in front, the open daylight.

But with the joy of discovery another sight met his gaze, a sight which sent the blood tingling through his veins. Yet, at first glance, it was not a particularly moving one. On the ground, at his feet, lay two unobtrusive-looking pebbles of a bluish grey. But as the next moment he held them in his hands, Laurence knew that he held in a moment what he had gone through years of privation and ruthless bloodshed to obtain—wealth, to wit. For these two unobtrusive pebbles were, in fact, splendid diamonds.

More of them? Of course there were. The exploration could wait a little longer. An accident might cut him off from this spot—might cut him off from such a chance for ever. The hands of the seasoned adventurer trembled like those of a palsied old woman as he turned over the loose soil with his foot, for instrument of any kind he had none; and, indeed, his agitation was not surprising, for in less than an hour Laurence was in possession of eight more splendid stones as large as the first, besides a number of small ones. He knew that he held that which should enable him to pass the remainder of his life in wealth and ease, could he once get safe away.

Could he? Ah, there came in the dead weight—the fulfilling of that strange irony of Fate which well-nigh invariably wills that the good of life comes to us a trifle too late. For his search had brought him quite into the open day once more. Before him lay a valley—or rather hollow—of no great size, and—it was shut in—completely walled in by an amphitheatre of lofty cliffs.

Cliffs on all sides—at some points smooth and perpendicular, at others actually overhanging, at others, again, craggy and broken into terraces; but, even with the proper appliances, probably unscalable; that detail his practised eye could take in at a glance. How, then, should he hope to scale them, absolutely devoid, as he was, of so much as a stick—let alone a cord.

A cord? How had he been brought there? Had he been let down by a cord—or brought in by some secret entrance? The latter appeared more probable; and that entrance he would find,—would find and traverse, be its risks, be its terrors what they might. He had that upon him now which rendered life worth any struggle to preserve.

He stepped forth. The sky was over his head once more, clear and blue. That was something. By the slant of the sun-rays he judged it must be about the middle of afternoon. The floor of the hollow was humpy and uneven. Sparse and half-dry grass bents sprung from the soil, but no larger vegetation—no trees, no brush. Stranger still, there was no sign of life—even of bird or insect life. An evil, haunted silence seemed to brood over the great, crater-like hollow.

The silence became weighty, oppressive. Laurence, in spite of himself, felt it steal upon his nerves, and began to whistle a lively tune as he walked slowly around, examining the cliffs, and every crack and cranny, with a critical eye. The echoing notes reverberated weirdly among the brooding rocks. Suddenly his foot struck something—something hard. He looked down, and could not repress a start. There at his feet, grinning up at him, lay a human skull—nay, more, a well-nigh complete skeleton.

It was a gruesome find under the circumstances. Laurence, his nerves unstrung by the effects of the drug, and recent alternations of exultation, and what was akin to despair, felt his flesh creep. What did it mean? Why, that no way of escape did this valley of death afford? This former victim—had he been placed there in the same way as himself, and, all means of exit failing, had succumbed to starvation when his provisions were exhausted? It looked that way. Bending down, he examined this sorry relic of humanity—examined it long and carefully. No bone was broken, the skeleton was almost complete; where it was not, the joints had fallen asunder without wrench; and the smooth round cranium showed not the slightest sign of abrasion or blow.

With sinking heart he pursued his search; yet somehow his attention now was given but languidly to potential means of exit which the faces of the cliffs might afford. Something seemed irresistibly to draw it to the ground. Ha! that was it. Again that horrid gleam of whitened bones. Another skeleton lay before him—and look, another, and another, at short distances apart. All these, like the first, were unshattered, uninjured; but—the whole area here was strewn with skulls, yellow and brown with age,—was strewn with bones also, mossy, mahogany-hued, and which crackled under his tread.

No one could be more ruthless, more callous; no man could view scenes of cruelty and bloodshed more unmoved than Laurence Stanninghame,—as we have shown,—or bear his part more coolly and effectively in the fiercest conflict; yet there was something in these silent human relics lying there bloodless; in the unnatural, haunted silence of this dreadful death-valley that caused his flesh to creep. Then he noticed that all were lying along the slope of a ridge which ran right across the hollow, dividing the floor of the same into two sections. He must needs go over that ridge to complete his explorations, yet now he shrank from it with an awe and repugnance which in any other man he would have defined as little short of terror. What would await him on the other side?

Well, he must go through with it. Probably he would find more of such ghastly relics—that was all. But as he stood upon the apex of the ridge, with pulses somewhat quickened, no whitening bones met his gaze—fixed, dilated as that gaze was. The cliff in front—he thought to descry some faint chance of escape there, for its face was terraced and sloping backward somewhat. Moreover, it was rent by crannies and crevices, which, to a desperate and determined man, might afford hand and foothold.

And now for the first time it flashed upon Laurence that the mystery of "The Spider" stood explained. This horrible hole whence there was no escape—where men were thrust to die by inches as all of these had died before him—the repulsive and blood-sucking insect was in truth a fitting name allegorically for such a place, which swallowed up the lives of men. Besides, for all he knew, the configuration of the crater might, from above, resemble the tutelary insect of the Ba-gcatya. Yes; he had solved the mystery, as to that he was confident; the next thing to do was to find some way out, to break through the fatality of the place.

For the first time now his shoulder began to feel stiff and sore, where the stick hurled by Lindela had struck him. That was a bad preparation for the most perilous kind of cliff climbing. Then the incident recalled to mind Lindela herself. Her sudden change of front was just such an oddity as any of the half-ironical incidents which go to make up the sum of life's experiences. Well, savage or civilised, human nature was singularly alike. A touch of superstition, and the god of yesterday became the demon of to-day.

Thus musing he came, suddenly and unexpectedly, upon another skeleton. But the effect of the discovery of this was even more disconcerting than that of the first. For, around, lay rotting rags of clothing, and a gold ornament or two. These remains he recognised at a glance. They were those of Lutali.

Yes, here was a broad bracelet of gold, curiously worked with a text of the Koran, which he had seen last on the Arab's sinewy wrist. Now that wrist was but a grisly bone. There, too, were parchment strips, also inscribed with Koran passages, and worn in a pouch as amulets. The identity of these remains was established beyond a doubt.

But the discovery inspired within him a renewed chill of despair. If Lutali had been unable to find means of escape, how should he? The Arab was a man of great readiness of resource, of indomitable courage, and powerfully built. If such a one had succumbed, why should he, Laurence, fare any better? He sat down once more, and, gazing upon the sorry remnant of his late confederate, began to think.

What a strange, vast, practical joke was that thing called life. Here was he at the end of it, and the very means of ending it for him had, at the same time, put him into possession of that which rendered it worth having at all. He felt the stones lying hard and angular in his pockets, he even took out one of them and turned it over sadly in his hands. He would gladly give a portion of these to be standing on the summit of yonder cliff instead of at the base; not yet had he come to feel he would gladly give them all. It was only of a continuance with what life had brought him that he should be there at all. He had sacrificed himself for another. The sublimity of the act even yet did not strike him. He regarded it as half-humorous, half-idiotic,—the first because his cynical creed was bolstered up by the consciousness that Holmes would never more than half appreciate it; the last, because—well—all unselfishness, all consideration, was idiotic.

Then it occurred to him that it would be time enough to sit down and dream when he had exhausted all expedients, and he had not explored that side of the hollow at all yet. To this end he moved forward. A very brief scrutiny, however, of the face of the cliff sufficed to show that for climbing purposes the cracks and crannies were useless.

Ha! What was this? A cave or a rift? Right in front of him the cliff yawned in just such a rift as the one in which he had awakened to find himself, only not on anything like such a large scale. Eagerly Laurence plunged into this. Here might be a way to the outer world—to safety.

He pressed onward in the semi-gloom. The rocks darkened overhead, forming, in effect, a cave. And now it seemed that he could hear a strange, soft, scraping, a kind of sighing noise. A puff-adder—was his first thought, looking around for the reptile. But no such reptile lay in his path, and he had no means of striking a light. With a dull shrinking, his flesh creeping with a strange foreboding, as with the consciousness of some fearful prescience, he decided to push on; being careful, however, to tread warily. This was no time for sticking at trifles.

But, as he advanced, the air became fœtid with a strange, pungent, nauseous odour. There were lateral clefts branching off the main gallery, but of no depth, and to these he had given but small notice. Now, however, something occurred of so appalling a nature that he stood as one turned to stone.

There shot out from one of these lateral recesses two enormous tentacles—black, wavy as serpents, covered with hair, armed at the extremity with a strong double claw. They reached forth noiselessly to within a couple of yards of where he stood, then two more followed with a quick, wavy jerk. And now behind these, a head—as large as that of a man, black, hairy, bearing a strange resemblance to the most awful and cruel human face ever stamped with the devil's image—whose dull, goggle eyes, fixed on the appalled ones of its discoverer, seemed to glow and burn with a truly diabolical glare.

Laurence stood—staring into the countenance of this awful thing—his blood curdled to ice within him, his hair literally standing up. Was it the Fiend himself who had taken such unknown and fearful shape to appear before him here in the gloom of this foul and loathsome cavern? Then, as his eyes grew more and more used to the dim shades, he made out a huge body crouched back in the recess, half hidden by a quivering mass of black, hairy tentacles.

For a few moments thus he stood—then with a cry of horror he threw out his hand as though instinctively to ward off an attack. The four tentacles already protruded were quickly withdrawn, and the fearful creature, whatever it was, seemed to shrink back into the cranny. One last look upon the hairy heap of moving, writhing horror—upon those dreadful demon eyes—and this man, who had faced death again and again without shrinking, now felt it all he could do to resist an impulse to turn and flee like a hunted hare. He did, however, resist it—yet it was with flesh shuddering and knees trembling beneath him that he withdrew, step by step, backwards, until he stood once more in the full light of day.

CHAPTER XXVII

THE HORROR

VAMPIRE—insect—devil—what *was* the thing? From the length and thickness of those frightful tentacle-like legs, stretching forth from the cranny—Laurence—who had not halted until he had gained the ridge dividing the hollow—estimated that the creature when spread out must be eight or ten feet in diameter.

He looked back. It had not followed him from the cave. Why had it not? Was it waiting for night—to steal upon him in the darkness, to wreathe around him those terrible tentacles, and to drain his life-blood?

Now, indeed, all stood clear. "The Spider" was no allegorical term, but literal fact. That frightful monster with which he had just come face to face was indeed the demon-god of the Ba-gcatya! It was actually fed with living men, in accordance with some dark and mysterious superstition held by that otherwise fine race. Now the fate of those whose skeletons lay around stood accounted for. They had been devoured by this unimaginable horror. Alive? It was almost certain—possibly when weakened by starvation. Yet a gruesome thought entered his mind. Why had an abundance of food been lowered with him into this hell-pit? Did not the circumstance make as though it was in their full vigour that the monster was designed to seize its victims—and in that event, with what an extent of strength and fell ferocity must it not be endowed?

But what *was* this thing? Laurence had seen spiders of every variety, huge and venomous, and of grisly size, yet nothing like this. Why, the creature was nearly as large as a bear.—It must be some beast hitherto unknown to natural history; yet those awful tentacles—joints, hair, everything—could not but belong to an insect—were, in fact, precisely as the legs of a huge tarantula, magnified five hundred-fold. What ghastly and blood-curdling freak of Nature could have produced such a monstrosity as this? Why, the very sight of the awful thing, huddled up, black, within the gloom of the cranny, the horrid tentacles—a hundred-fold more repulsive, more blood-curdling than though they actually were so many serpents—moving and writhing in a great quivering, hairy, intertwined mass—was in itself a sight to haunt his dreams until his dying day, did he live another fifty years. What must it mean, then, to realise that he was actually shut in—escape impossible—with the deliberate purpose of being devoured by this vampire, this demon, even as all these others had been devoured before him?

At this juncture of his meditations his mind became alive to two discoveries—one, that he had gained the farther end of the ridge than that by which he had crossed; the other, that immediately before and beneath him, just over the slope of the ridge, lay the body of a man.

Yes—the body of a man, not the skeleton of one. That it was that of a dead man he could see at a glance—also that it was one of the Ba-gcatya. With a shudder he remembered the luckless wretch he had seen dragged away but a day or two before his own seizure—whether for evil-doing or as a customary sacrifice he had been condemned to this, Laurence had not inquired at the time. Casting one more look at the cave, and satisfying himself that the monster had not emerged, Laurence went down to examine the body.

It was that of a man in the prime of life—and wearing the head-ring. It was lying on its back, the throat upturned and protruding.

And then Laurence, shudderingly, noticed two round gaping orifices at the base of the throat, clearly where the great nippers of the monster had punctured. The limbs, too, were scratched and scored as though with claws; and upon the dead face was such an awful expression of the very extremity of horror and dread, as the spectator, accustomed as he was to such sights, had never beheld stamped on the human countenance before. And beholding it now, Laurence Stanninghame felt that the perspiration was oozing upon him at every pore, for he realised that he was looking upon a foresight of his own fate; for was he not that most perfectly and completely helpless of all God's creatures—an unarmed man!

He had not so much as a stick or a pocket-knife to resist the onslaught of this blood-drinking monster—no, not even a boot, for it flashed across his mind at that moment that a good iron-shod heel might be better than nothing.—He was wearing only a low-soled pair of ordinary *velschoenen*—hide-shoes, to wit. There were not even stones lying about the ground, save very small ones, and he had no means of loosening rock slabs large enough to serve as weapons. There was no place of refuge to climb into afforded by ledges or pinnacles of rock, and even were there, why, the thing could surely come up after him as easily as the common tarantula could run up a wall. Nothing is more completely demoralising than the helplessness of an unarmed man. With his Express—or his six-shooter—this one would have regarded the situation in the light of a wholly new and adventurous excitement; with even a large strong-bladed knife he would have been willing to take his chances. But he was totally unarmed. It seemed to Laurence that in that brief while he had lived a lifetime of mortal fear.

Then with a mighty effort he pulled himself together. He would return to where he had left his stores ere commencing the exploration. Nobody ever yet improved a situation of peril by starving himself. Yet as he wended his way up the long chasm wherein he had first awakened to life, it was with a feeling of shuddering repulsion. The place bore such a close resemblance now to that other cave; yet here, at anyrate, he knew there was nothing.

He opened the corn baskets and the calabash of *amasi*, and made a fairly good meal. Then, by the glooming shades of the overhanging rock, he judged that daylight was waning. Out into the open once more. The open air might render such a life-and-death struggle with the monster a trifle less horrible than here, shut in by these tomb-like rock walls.

The grey of the brief twilight was upon the faces of the surrounding cliffs, which soon faded into misty gloom. Only the stars, leaping forth into the inky sky, shed an indistinct light into this vault of horror and of death. He was shut in here—and shut in with this awful thing which should find him out during the hours of darkness. And, marvellous to tell—a sudden drowsiness came upon him—and whether the effects of the drug still lingered about him, or was it the reaction from an overstrained mind? he actually slept—slept hard and dreamlessly.

Suddenly he awoke—awoke with the weight of an indefinable terror upon him. A broad moon in its third quarter was sailing aloft in the heavens, flooding the hollow with its ghostly light. Instinctively he sprang to his feet. As he did so there came upon him a resistless and shuddering fear akin to that which had paralysed him in the cave. What was it? The magnetic proximity of the awful Thing stealthily stalking him? No. The reason now lay clear.

In the moonlight he could make out, shadowy and indistinct, the corpse he had found during the afternoon. But, as he gazed, a change seemed to have come over it. It had increased in size—had more than doubled its bulk. Heavens! the dark mass began to move—to heave—and then he thought the very acme of horror was reached. Not one body was there, but two. Spread out over the human body was that of the monster. Now he could make out almost every detail of its hideous shape, the convulsive working of the frightful tentacles as it devoured its lifeless prey. He could stand it no longer. His brain was bursting; he must do something. Raising his voice he shouted—shouted as assuredly he had never shouted in his life. There was a maniacal ring in his tone. He felt as though he must rush right at this thing of fear. Was he really going mad? Well, it began to look like it.

But the effect was prompt. The awful vampire, gathering its horrible legs under it, sprang clear of the carcase. It stood for a moment in rigid immobility, then ere the maniacal echoes of that shout had quavered into silence among the cliffs, it shoggled over the ridge and was lost to view.

The night wore through somehow, and if ever mortal eyes were rejoiced by the light of dawn, assuredly they were those of Laurence Stanninghame, as once more he found himself the sole living tenant of that ghastly place of death. Yet, to what end? One more dreary day in his rock prison, another night of dread—and—the same brooding fate awaiting!

He could not remain awake for ever. Even though the sound of his voice thus unexpectedly lifted up had alarmed the vampire, it would not always do so. Still, with the light of the new-born day after the night of terror came some modicum of relief.

Once more he drew upon his provision stores. While repacking them his gaze rested on the native blanket with a wild idea of manufacturing therefrom a cord. But to do this he needed a knife. The stuff was of material too stout for tearing.

A knife! Ha! With the thought came another. It was not worth much, but it was something,—and with it came a hard, fierce, desperate hope. The broad gold bracelet which still encircled Lutali's skeleton wrist—could not that be banged and flattened into something sharp and serviceable? It was hard metal, anyway.

The day wore on, and still the grim horror lurked within its cave—still it came not forth. It was waiting until another night should embolden it to seize its defenceless human prey. He glanced upward. There were still from two to three hours of daylight. In a very few moments he had reached the skeleton of the Arab, and, snapping off the bony wrist without hesitation, the bracelet was within his grasp.

But as he looked around for some means of flattening it, there flashed in upon him another idea—a perfectly heaven-sent idea, grisly, under ordinary circumstances, as it might be. The bracelet was large and massive, and for it a new use suggested itself. Critically examining the skeletons, he selected two with the largest and strongest leg-bones. These he soon wrenched off, and, running one through the gold bracelet, he jammed the latter fast against the thicker end—binding it as tightly as he could to the bulging joint with a strip torn from his clothing. With a thrill of unutterable joy he realised that he was no longer unarmed. He had manufactured a tolerably effective mace. He swung it through the air two or three times with all his force. Such a blow would strike a human enemy dead;—was this fearful thing so heavily armour-plated as to be proof against a similar stroke?

With one idea came another. These bones might be further utilised. They might be splintered and sharpened into daggers. No sooner thought of than carried out. And now the skeletons underwent the most ruthless desecration. Several were wrenched asunder ere he had selected half a dozen of the most serviceable bones—and these he hammered to the required size with his newly constructed mace—sharpening them on the rough face of the rock. And then, as with a glow of satisfaction he sat down to rest and contemplate his handiwork, he almost laughed over the grim whimsicality of it. Did ever mortal man go into close conflict armed in such fashion—he wondered—with club and dagger manufactured out of the bones of men?

Should he take the bull by the horns, and advance boldly to attack the monster in its own den? He shrank from this. The gloom of the cavern invested the thing with an additional element of terror, besides the more practical consideration that a confined space might hinder him in the use of his bizarre and impromptu weapons. He would need all the freedom of hand and eye. Once more he took out the metal box, and fed his eyes long and earnestly upon its contents. The Sign of the Spider! Was there indeed an influence about this trinket—or rather, the love which had hallowed it—which was potent to stand between him and peril in the direst extremity, even as it had stepped between him and certain death at the spears of the victorious Ba-gcatya? Slightly improved as was his helpless condition, yet he could not hope. Even if he succeeded in slaying the monster, how should he escape from this death-trap, this rock-prison? The second day closed.

How many hours of darkness should precede moon-rise, he could but feebly guess. Grasping his strangely fashioned club in his right hand, and the strongest and sharpest of his bone daggers in the left—he stood, his back to the rock wall, so as not to be taken in the rear; never relaxing for a moment in vigilance, his ears strained to their utmost tension, his eyeballs striving to pierce the black gloom. More than once a sound as of stealthy, ghostly scrapings caused his heart to beat like a hammer; and he seemed to see the horrible eyes of the monster flaming luridly out of the darkness; but still the silent hours went by unbroken by any disturbance.

Ha! The gloom of the hollow was lightening—and soon the rim of the great moon peeped over the cliff behind him. But his attention was riveted now upon something before him—a Something, huge and black and shadowy—which moved. The Horror was coming over the ridge.

It came,—running stealthily a few yards,—then halting,—then running again. It passed the body of its last victim, and came running on. Laurence stood transfixed, spellbound, with loathing and repulsion, as he gazed upon the huge hairy legs, as he listened to the scraping patter of their claw-armed extremities. But he had no doubt now as to its intentions. It was coming straight for him. It stopped—within a bare forty yards, and now as for the first time, he got a clear view of it in the bright moonlight, Laurence felt his heart fail him for the very hideousness of the beast. It had the head of a devil, the body and legs of a spider, and the black hairy coat of a bear; and, indeed, it was nearly as large as a fair-sized specimen of the latter. No, it was no ordinary thing this fearsome monster.

It advanced a little nearer,—stopped again,—then rushed straight at him.

Laurence stepped aside just in time to avoid the open jaws, but too late entirely to escape the great flail-like tentacle, which swept him from his feet, right under the Horror, pinioning for a moment his arms. Then, by a tremendous effort, he threw himself partly upward. The formidable nippers descended—but, missing his throat—descended to his chest, and met there, with a metallic, crunching sound.

Yet he was unhurt. Even in that unspeakably awful moment—crushed in the wreathings of the huge tentacles,—the frightful head and devilish eyes of the vampire within a few inches of his own—he realised what had happened. Instead of penetrating his body, the nippers of the monster had struck upon the metal box. The thought nerved him. Wrenching his arm partly free beneath the Horror, he sought a joint in the horny armour, and drove the bone dagger into its body—drove it in to the very butt.

Throwing up its head convulsively, the fearful creature began to spin round and round, and its would-be victim realised some-

what of its enormous muscular strength, for wiry and in hard training as he was, he was dragged with it, rolled over and over in the
wreathings of the black, hairy tentacles. Was he being dragged off
to its den? The very terror of the thought nerved him once more—
revived his fast-failing strength. Drawing forth another of his bone
daggers, he plunged it, too, deep into the body of the beast.

For a moment the sinewy, struggling tentacles relaxed, and
just that moment the man was able to seize, or he had been lost.
With a violent effort he flung himself free, and, having once more
gained his feet—his breath coming in hard, panting gasps,—stood
awaiting the next attack.

Thus they stood, a strange group indeed, in the brilliant moonlight. The man, his rudely constructed mace uplifted—his head
bent forward, a lurid glow in his eyes—the glow of the fell fury
of desperation; the hideous Spider-devil—swaying itself on its
horrible tentacles as though for another spring upon its intended
victim. Ha! it was coming!

The man stood ready. A tightening of the muscles of the arm
that held the club, a lowering of the brows. On the part of the
demon, a spasmodic contraction. Again it came at him.

Half rearing itself from the ground, its feelers waving in the
air on a level with his face, propelling itself slowly forward, as
though to make sure of its final rush, emitting the while a kind
of soft breathing hiss—the aspect of the creature was so truly
fearful, that the man, gazing upon it, was conscious of a kind of
blasting influence stealing over him, beginning to paralyse nerve
and effort alike,—a feeling that it was useless to continue the
struggle. The metal box could not save him twice. Yet, through
all, was the certainty that to lose nerve for one moment was to
lose life.

His will-power triumphed. He knew that did he once again
get within grip of those ghastly tentacles, he would never emerge
alive. He swung up his improvised mace. The creature was now
within twelve yards of him. He hurled the club. With terrific force
it cleft the air, the massive band of gold which constituted its
head lighting full upon one of the demon's eyes. For one moment
the Horror contracted into a heaving, writhing heap, frightful to
behold, then throwing out its grisly tentacles it spun round and

round as it had done before. The man's heart was beating as though it would burst. Was the thing slain, or in its vampire tenacity of life would it renew the combat? Ha!—was it coming again? Was it? One moment of the most unutterable suspense, and then——and then—the fearful Thing drew back, turned round, and shoggled away in the direction whence it had come. It was worsted.

Save for a few scratches, Laurence was unhurt. He had almost miraculously escaped the creature's nippers. Yet now that he had won his hard-fought victory, a sort of rage took possession of him, an impulse to follow it up, to destroy this fell horror utterly. Growling a savage curse, he started in pursuit of the retreating monster, but hardly had he taken two steps forward than there floated to his ear a sound—a voice, which seemed to fall from the sky itself. He stopped short in his tracks and stood immovable, statuesque, listening.

CHAPTER XXVIII

"ONLY A SAVAGE!"

"NYONYOBA!"

Clear, distinct, the name sounded, floating down from above.

"What the devil is that?" was the characteristic exclamation that burst from Laurence,—and there was something of a quaver in the tone. For his nerves were quite overstrung, and no manifestation of things unknown would have surprised him now.

"Nyonyoba! Ho, Nyonyoba!" again called the voice in soft, rich Zulu tones, low but penetrating. "Move now some thirty paces to where the cliff juts. There is that by which you may return to earth again—and the Spider may go hungry."

"The Spider has got enough to fill him up for some long time," answered Laurence, with excusable pride. "But who speaks?—The voice is like that of Lindela."

"It is that of Lindela," came the soft-toned reply. "Climb now, and tarry not. I see the Spider. Climb before it is too late."

With all his elation, now that the first flush of victory was over, Laurence could not recall without a shiver the grasp of those horrible tentacles, the fiend-like glare of that dreadful face. He vastly preferred flight to renewed fight, now.

Following the voice, he came to the point indicated. A rope of twisted raw-hide thong lay against the rock. His heart leaped within him. Soon he would be free from this fearful place. The cliff here formed a projecting angle, all jagged like the teeth of a saw. He remembered noticing this, remembered balancing its capabilities of forming a natural ladder. He had even climbed a few steps, and then had been forced to own that it was impracticable. Now, however, with the aid of the raw-hide rope, the thing could be done—done with comparative ease.

As a preliminary he stepped back, and, gazing upward, went over the climb in his mind, carefully noting every step, every handhold. The cliff was terraced here, and the nearest resting-place, whence, indeed, the rope hung, he estimated to be about sixty feet. Without this aid, however, it might as well have been sixty hundred.

Seizing the rope he began his ascent, the mace and the remainder of his bone daggers still slung around him. The task was more difficult than it looked. Contact, often sudden and violent, with the rock face bruised his knuckles, inflicting excruciating pain, once indeed so as to turn him sick and faint. But a glance down into the grisly hollow, as he hung thus suspended by a thread—the glint of the white skeletons in the moonlight, and, above all, the vague, shadowy outline, black and frightful, of the Horror, which still lingered outside its den, as though meditating return—nerved him once more. What if he were to fall, maimed, battered, helpless—would not the frightful thing hold him entirely at its mercy, and return and drain his life-blood at its pleasure? Summoning all his will-power, all his strength, he resumed his climb, and soon a firm, resolute hand, grasping his, drew him up for the time being into safety. For they were on a ledge.

"Rest now, beloved," said the chief's daughter softly, as she turned to draw up the rope. "I have saved thee so far."

"But—to what end, Lindela? Did you not fling a stick at me, and strike me hard? See, I am bruised with it yet. It has even hindered my climbing powers. That is a strange way of showing love."

"But is this a stranger way?" said the girl sadly, displaying the rope she had just drawn up. "See now. They suspected me, as it was. Had I not shown myself the first and the fiercest to turn against you, should I have been here now? But come. We are not yet in safety. When we are it will be time enough for talk, and for——love."

She led the way to a steep, narrow cranny. Up this they climbed some fifty feet without difficulty, emerging upon another terrace. Here another rope hung from the cliff above, about the same height.

"Go first, Nyonyoba, while I hold the rope to steady it," said the girl. "Then, too, if your strength should give way, perhaps I may catch you and break your fall. I am as strong as any of the women of the Ba-gcatya—and that is saying much."

For answer, Laurence uttered a derisive laugh. But there must have been that in its tone which pleased the chief's daughter, for she repeated the request, more softly, more entreatingly.

"See now, Lindela," he answered, placing a hand on each of the shapely shoulders, which glistened light bronze in the moonlight. "You don't know me yet if you think I will leave the post of danger to you. Obey me instantly. Go first up that rope, or I return and do combat once more with the Spider."

"Once more? Have you then—actually fought with that—with that which is down there?" And her eyes were round with amazement.

"I have, and the thing has two of these sticking in it to their full length," showing the bone daggers. "I have a recollection, too, of smiting hard with this noble knob-stick, but it was like smiting the largest kind of tortoise shell. Not yet, however, is the time to talk. Go first, Lindela,—go first."

She obeyed him now without further demur, and soon he had joined her, for this climb was neither so long nor so difficult as the first.

Laurence now saw that they were high up on a mountain top. Great peaks, some snow-capped, towered aloft—and far away beneath stretched a billowy expanse of rolling country, dim, misty in the moonlight. The air was keen and chill, and with something of a shiver Lindela resumed her light upper covering, which she had laid aside in order to give full freedom to body and limbs.

"And you have met and fought with that"—she began, pointing downwards, "and are still alive? Why, Nyonyoba, you have done that which no man has ever done before. How did you do it? With the bones of dead men? Ha! you are indeed great, Nyonyoba,— great indeed. Yet—what a thought!"

"A good thought truly. Still, had it occurred to those who went before me they might have done the same. Yet not—for there was another force that saved me which they lacked."

"Ha! Another force?"

"Yes. The Sign of the Spider. The Spider itself was powerless against that."

He drew forth the metal box, and for the first time examined it. By the light of the moon he could discern two slight dents; one upon the border of the quaint sprawling initials, where the nippers of the monster had struck. For the moment he forgot Lindela, forgot the surroundings, forgot where he was, remembering only Lilith. Three times had Lilith's love interposed between him and certain death—three times most unequivocally. And this third time, from what unutterably horrible form of death? Those poisoned fangs! The very thought made him shudder.

"You are cold, beloved. See, here are coverings. I have thought of everything."

The voice, the touch upon his arm, recalled him to himself. If the love of the one woman had stood between him and death—no less had that of the other borne its part. And this other now stood before him, soft-eyed, pleading,—grand in her statuesque and perfect proportions, in her splendid strength and courage—that strength and courage which had nerved her to set aside the most awesome traditions of her race, to brave its gloomy superstitions, to venture alone and unaided into the haunt of mysterious terror, for love of this stranger and alien. This, too, was the sublimity of love in all its indomitable quenchlessness. And she who gave so freely, who gave all, indeed, of this rich, this inestimable gift was—only a savage!

Only a savage! It is probable that some of the most golden-lined, well-nigh divine phases of mind that ever had dawned upon him in his life were shed over Laurence Stanninghame then, as he stood upon that lofty mountain top at midnight in the flooding light of the moon, his gaze meeting the sweet responsive one from the wide opened eyes of this——savage.

"Say, Nyonyoba?" and the voice was full and rich,—"say, Nyonyoba, what will you give me if I show you that which will delight your eyes? Will you love me very much—very much?" and the soft musical Zulu word "*Ka-kúlu*"¹ thus repeated was as a caress in itself. "Well then,—come."

She led the way a few yards, then halted. A bundle lay upon the ground, and this Lindela proceeded to undo. It consisted of a couple of strong native blankets, enclosing several round baskets of woven grass similar to those which had contained the food which had been let down in cruel mercy into the place of the Horror by the mysterious hands which had lowered himself. But that upon which Laurence's eyes rested, upon which he almost pounced, was a short carbine and a well-stocked cartridge-belt. It was a vastly inferior weapon to his own trusty Express, but still it was a firearm.

"That is not all," cried the girl, laughing gleefully. "See this."

She thrust another bundle into his hands. Almost trembling he opened it. A revolver—his own; also another of smaller calibre. And with both was a quantity of ammunition. As he seized these, he realised that he would have given half his diamonds, up till then well-nigh forgotten, for just such an armoury. Now he felt equal to anything, to anybody. He was once more the dominant animal,— an armed man—nay, more—a well-armed man.

"Ha!—now you are once more as you ought to be," cried Lindela, gleefully clapping her hands together. "You who are stronger than—that which is down there," falling into the Zulu custom of refraining directly to mention that which is held in awe, "without weapons, what are you now with them? Great,—great! To defeat The Spider—armed only with the bones of men. *Whau!* That was great—indeed magnificent!"

"Yet I think I will silence for ever that horror," said Laurence, stepping to the brink of the cliff and peering down into the awful hollow. "Yes, there the beast is; I will risk a long shot," and he sighted the carbine.

But in a moment Lindela's arms were around him, pinioning his to his sides.

"Not so, beloved," she whispered earnestly. "Not so. The Black Ones who wait on The Spider frequently come to look down into his haunt, even when they do not bring offerings of men. If they find him slain they will know you have escaped, and will pursue; for which reason it is well,—well, indeed, that you did not quite slay him with those marvellous weapons, the bones of men. Further, they might hear the sound of the fire-weapon, and know where to find us. Come; we have far to travel."

This was unanswerable. Laurence stood for a few moments gazing down into the fearsome place which held this shuddering mystery. Was it real? Was he dreaming? Were those hours of terror and despair spent down there but some gigantic nightmare? He passed his hand over his eyes—then looked again. The thing was real. But now he could no longer see the horrid shape—black and grisly. The creature must have withdrawn into its ghastly den—to die. The wounds which he had inflicted upon it were surely too deep, too strongly dealt, to be aught but mortal. The Spider would no more drink the blood—feed on the flesh—of men. Then he turned to follow Lindela.

The latter had already loaded herself with the bundle of wraps and provisions. To his suggestion that they should, at anyrate, halve the load, Lindela laughed in scorn.

"A man's work is to carry his weapons, and, when needed, use them," she answered. "To bear loads—and this is a light one indeed—is woman's work—not work for one who has proved too great even for The Spider."

Then, as they travelled down the mountain side in the fresh cool night air, she told him of all that had befallen since he had been haled to his mysterious and awful doom. The thoughtless act of Holmes had necessitated the destruction of Nondwana's kraal there and then; and, indeed, the King's brother was more than dissatisfied with the clemency extended to the other two white men. But the word of Tyisandhlu, once given, stood. They had been sent out of the country under a strong armed escort, which was under orders to conduct them to the great town of an Arab chief, with whom El Khanac had blood brotherhood.

How had she found out the mystery of The Spider? Was it known to all the nation? It was known to very few, she explained.

The Black Ones, who waited upon The Spider, were a mysterious order—so mysterious, indeed, that none knew exactly who were members of it and who were not. Nor could she tell how the strange and gruesome cult first originated, save that it was dimly whispered that the Ba-gcatya had taken it over from the nation they had driven out, and that in accordance with an ancient prophecy uttered by a famous magician at the time of their flight from Zululand. But as she told of her resolve to rescue him at all risks, even so long ago as when, by overhearing her father's talk, she learned that this doom was to be his in any case, Laurence felt himself grow strangely soft towards her. Savage or not, Nondwana's daughter was a splendid character in the whole-hearted devotion of her love. Heroic was hardly the word for it. And as she went on to tell how she had devoted herself entirely to finding out the locality of the dreaded spot, learning the way to it by stealthily following on the footsteps of that grim order when it was actually engaged in conveying thither another human victim, risking her life at every step,—and not her life merely, but incurring the certainty of the same fearful doom in the event of discovery,—telling it, too, in the most simple way, and as though the act was the most natural thing in the world, Laurence realised that he might have done worse than throw in his lot with this loftily-descended daughter of a splendid race of kingly barbarians, had circumstances been ordered otherwise.

But even while thus listening, while thus thinking, another vein of thought was running parallel in his mind. Those insignificant-looking stones, which he had picked up down there, represented wealth—ample wealth; and with it had come a feverish longing to enjoy the comforts, the pleasures, the delights which civilisation afforded to those who possessed it. Yet, his entering upon such enjoyment, if it were ever effected—as at that moment it seemed in a fair way to be—he owed to Lindela. What was to become of her, for she could never return to her nation? She had thrown away everything, this high-born daughter of a race of kings; had risked her life daily, to save the life of a stranger—and that for love. Yes, that was love indeed! he thought. She was a brown-skinned savage, but she was a splendid woman—with mind and character as noble as her own magnificent physique. She would be a delightful, a perfect companion during those wild, free forest marches—day after day, night after night, fraught with peril and hardship at every step, but—how would civilisation affect her? Would it not ruin that grand character, even as it had ruined really noble natures before her,—for there is such a thing as the "noble savage," although we grant the product to be a scarce one! And with all this was entwined the thought of Lilith Ormskirk.

Well, sufficient for the day is the evil thereof, had always been his guiding maxim, and for the present, as he took his way down the mountain side—the great crags rising higher and higher to the moon, the black billowy roll of the forest country drawing nearer and nearer, the voices of the wild creatures of the waste, raised weird and ravening on the night, the thunderous boom of the voice of the forest king ever and anon dominating all others—Laurence felt conscious of a wild, exhilarating sense of freedom. There was music in these sounds after the ghastly, awed silence of the horrible place from which he had been delivered. And, was it due on his part to the frame of mind of the hardened adventurer—trained to take things as they come, the good with the ill—but never, during the days and weeks that followed, did the daughter of the line of the Ba-gcatya kings feel moved to any qualm of regret over the sacrifice of name and home and country which she had made for this man's sake.

CHAPTER XXIX

"A DEEP—A SOLITARY GRAVE"

THEY were now on the outer slope of the great mountain chain which shut in the Ba-gcatya country on that side, and, judging by the landmarks, it seemed to Laurence that the surroundings wore an aspect not absolutely unfamiliar, and that they could not be far out of the way by which he had been brought in a captive. There was the same broad belt of desolate land which took many days to traverse—a land of gloomy forest, and sluggish river, reed-fringed, crocodile-haunted—and, night after night they would build their camp-fire, resting secure in the red circle of its cheery flame, while the howling of ravening beasts kept up dismal chorus in the outer darkness beyond. It was a primeval idyll, the wandering of these two—the man, the product of the highest *fin-de-siècle* civilisation; the woman, the daughter of a savage race. Yet in such wandering, savage and civilised were curiously near akin. They were free as air—untrammelled by any conventionality or artificial needs. The land furnished ample subsistence, animal and vegetable. The wild game which supplied them with food could not have been more free.

"Would you rather have been rescued some other way, Nyonyoba?" said the girl one evening, as they were sitting by the camp-fire.

"No. There is no other way I should have preferred. See now, Lindela. What if we were to return to your people? Surely they would believe now in The Sign of the Spider—and that the conqueror is greater than the conquered?"

"Not so," she answered, and her eyes, which had brightened at the first words of his reply, became clouded and sad. "They would put us to death now—both of us. But were it otherwise—would you really desire to return?"

"One might do worse. I don't know that the blessings of civilisation are such blessings after all, which to you is a riddle."

He relapsed into silence and thought. There were times when, with the riches upon him, he was consumed with a perfectly feverish longing to return to civilisation. There were other times, again, when he looked back with more than a lingering regret to the pleasant land of the Ba-gcatya. Furthermore, Lindela had entwined herself around his heart more than he knew. Not an atom of the intrepidity of devotion she had displayed in order to compass his final rescue was thrown away upon him—any more than her deportment since. Through the toilsomeness and peril of their journeying no word of complaint or despondency escaped her. She was always sunny-natured, cheerful, self-sacrificing, resourceful—in short, a delightful companion. Yet—she was a savage, he thought, with a curl of the lip, as before his mind's eye arose the contrast between her and her civilised sisters, with their artificiality and moods and caprices, and petty spites and fictitious ailments, and general contentiousness all round. It was by no means certain he would not have returned to dwell with her among her own people, had that course been open—but it was not. Only the return to civilisation lay before him, and—what to do with Lindela,—for he had not the slightest desire to part with her?

Meanwhile they had reached the perilous phase of their wanderings. Ruins of multitudinous villages lay in their path at every turn, but, what was worse, signs of human occupation began to show once more, and human occupation meant hostile occupation. It was fortunate that the land had been doubly raided—by the slave-hunters and the Ba-gcatya—because in its depopulation lay their safety. But those who had escaped would not be likely to view with any friendly glance a representative of each despoiling factor, as exemplified in these two. So they avoided villages, which was easy enough by careful observation ahead. What was less easy, however, was to avoid wandering parties.

Nor was it always practicable. Once they came right into such a horde—near enough, that is, for their presence to be discovered, and for a whole day were they stealthily followed, their pursuers only drawing off owing to nightfall and the proximity of other tribes hostile to themselves. Another time they nearly walked into the midst of an encampment while a cannibal feast was in progress. At sight of the human limbs hung up, the filed teeth and tattooed faces of these savages tearing at their horrible repast, Lindela shuddered with repulsion and anger.

"See there, Nyonyoba," she said, when they had withdrawn beyond hearing, "do not the Ba-gcatya act rightly in stamping out these foul *Izimu*—who devour the flesh of their own kindred, like wild dogs?"

"I think so. And we, who capture them to sell them, do we not send them to a better fate, where they can no more indulge in such repellent appetites?" And this she did not attempt to gainsay.

For months they journeyed on thus, peril their companion at every step, the more so as they gained the more inhabited tracts. Once they fell in with a petty Arab chief and his following. This man was known to Laurence, and treated them well and hospitably while they remained at his camp. But before they departed he said—

"What sum will purchase this girl, my friend, for by now thou

must have had enough of her? She would fetch large money at
Khartoum, whither I can forward her, and I will deal with thee
fairly. Yes, Allah is great. I will only make my profit on her. The
price shall be liberal."

Then Laurence Stanninghame, the renegade, the man who
had thrown all considerations of duty and feeling to the winds
as so much lumber, so much meaningless conventionality, felt
as shocked and disgusted as ever he could have done in his most
foolish days, what time illusions were as vivid, as golden as ever.
But, remembering himself, he replied in an even tone—

"No sum will purchase her, Rahman bin Zuhdi.—Were I dying
at this moment, and large wealth could bring me fifty years more
of life, I would not sell her. All that the world contains could not
purchase her, for she has restored me to life at the peril of her own,
again and again,—nay, more, has restored me to that which alone
renders life a possession of any value. I have dealt in slaves, but this
is a daughter of a race of kings."

"The People of the Spider," said the Arab thoughtfully, flashing a curious glance at Lindela, who stood some little way apart.
"They grow their women fine, if they are all as this one. Well, I did
but make thee the offer, my brother; but if a man values anything
above gold, all the gold in the world will not induce him to part
therewith. Fare thee well. We part friends."

"As friends indeed do we part, O Rahman," replied Laurence.
And then they resumed their respective ways.

As time went on, Lindela's manner seemed to undergo a
change—her spirits to flag. Was it the fearful malarial heat of the
low-lying forest country, often swampy, which was affecting her,
thought Laurence with concern. He himself was inured to it, but
this daughter of a healthy upland race, accustomed to the breezy,
equable climate of her mountain-girt home—on her the steaming
heat of the rotting vegetation and marshy soil might conceivably
be beginning to tell.

They were resting one day during the noontide heat. No
burning rays from the outside sun could scorch here, for the place
was dim with thick foliage and creepers trailing from the limbs of
great forest trees. Both had fallen asleep.

Suddenly Lindela started up. A sharp wringing pain, seeming

to begin on the left shoulder, went through her frame. It spread—down her arm—then through to the other shoulder—down the other arm. What was it? A cramp caught from the treacherous chill of the humid soil? Perhaps. Well, it would soon pass. Then Laurence began to stir in his sleep. The sight made her forget her pain. He must not awaken; he needed rest. Noiselessly plucking a leafy branch she went over to him and began softly to fan him. This was effective. His even, regular breathing told that he slumbered peacefully, restfully, once more. Soon she became aware that her powers were failing her. Her arm seemed to become cramped, paralysed, and a mist floated before her eyes. What did it mean? Her lips opened to call aloud—then closed, uttering no sound. Why should he be disturbed because she was suffering a little pain? thought this "savage"—this daughter of a line of savage kings.

But the mist deepened before her failing vision. She swayed where she sat, then fell heavily forward—upon him—the branch wherewith she had been fanning him striking him sharply across the face.

Laurence sprang to his feet, unconsciously throwing her from him. His first impression was that he had been surprised in his sleep by an enemy.

"Lindela! What is it?" he cried, raising her up and supporting her. And then his dark face turned a livid ashen white—for with the dull stupor which lay heavy in the usually bright eyes, his own eyes had rested upon something else. The shapely shoulder was swollen to an abnormal size, and at the back of it were two small round punctures.

"She has been bitten. A snake, of course," he muttered. "And it is too late."

"Yes, it is too late, Nyonyoba," she murmured. "Yet I do not think I have been bitten—not by a snake, or I should have known it."

"But you have been. When was this? Why did you not awaken me?" And his voice startled even himself, so fierce—was it in its grief.

"Why should I awaken you, beloved, you who needed rest?" she murmured, groping for his hand. "Yes, it is too late. It was some time ago. I thought it was a cramp, but I must have been bitten."

Laurence was thinking—and thinking hard. What remedy was there? None. It was even as she had said—too late. The poison had permeated her whole system.

"I am dying, beloved—and shall soon go into the Dark Unknown——," she murmured, more drowsily than before. "Yet it matters nothing, for those of our nation do not fear death. And listen. I heard the Arab's proposal to you, and your answer thereto—yet, when you returned to your own people, what would have become of me?"

She was but voicing his own thoughts of many and many a time before. Yet now Laurence felt almost startled. Was it the clear intuition which rightly or wrongly is believed to accompany the hour of dissolution? Then he remembered she could have learned much about civilised peoples through the talk of Tyisandhlu and her father.

"I die, beloved, but I welcome death," she went on,—"for I have lived—ah, yes, I have lived. I feel no pain now, and I die in your arms. Surely my *itongo** will not weep mournfully on the voices of the night as others do,—surely it will laugh for very joy, for very love, because of this my end, until time shall die—will it not, Nyonyoba, my beloved? Say—will it not?"

But Laurence could not say anything, for, lo—a marvel. This man, deadened for long years to feeling or ruth; this coldly pitiless trafficker in the sufferings of human beings; in whose cynical creed now such a love as that of this savage girl held no place—felt now as though a hand were gripping him by the throat, choking all power of reply. And the call of birds, high among the tree-tops, alone broke the silence, in the semi-gloom of the forest aisles.

Lindela's voice had sunk until it was well-nigh inaudible, and Laurence was constrained to bend his head to hers in order to catch her every word. Then—a flash of gladness seemed momentarily to light up the drowsy eyes, and she spoke no more. Her eyelids closed, her breathing grew fainter and fainter, and soon Laurence knew that that which lay heavy within his arms was no longer a living woman. Lindela had passed.

For long he sat thus. Then a faint rustling sound in the dry wood of an immense fallen tree-trunk caught his ear. Ha!—the snake

---

* Tutelary spirit.—Mitford's note.

which had been the cause of her death! It, at anyrate, should die. Gently he laid her down, then snatching up a stick which had been used to carry one of the loads he advanced towards the sound.

Something was struggling among the dry bark. With the stick he broke this away. There fell out an enormous spider.

He started back in horror and loathing. The hairy monster brought back too gruesome a reminiscence. Then he noticed that it looked as if it had received injury through crushing, two or three of the hideous tentacles being partially or wholly broken off.

Then, as he gazed with loathing upon the sprawling thing, it seemed that the missing link was supplied. Lindela, in her sleep, must have moved over on to this horror, though not heavily enough to crush it. It had buried its venomous nippers in her shoulder, prior to crawling away to die.

A shiver ran through his frame as he beat to death the great noisome insect—and his blood seemed to chill with a superstitious fear. It seemed too strange, too marvellous to be a mere coincidence. Lindela had defied the traditions of her race,—and now she had met her death through the agency of the very embodiment of those traditions. She, a daughter of the Kings of The People of the Spider—had met her death through the Spider's bite. It was horrifying in its sinister appropriateness. Was it really a thing of witchcraft? Did the Fiend have actual bodily power here, in "the dark places of the earth"? Had this demoniacal influence followed her to wreak its vengeance here, at such a distance from the home and country to which she would return no more?

When Laurence Stanninghame resumed his journey the next day he left behind him a grave—a deep, secure grave—a solitary grave in the heart of the untrodden forest. His journeyings henceforth must be alone; but ofttimes his thoughts would go back to that nameless grave, and to her who rested for ever therein. Only a savage! Only a heathen! Yes—but if brave, devoted, self-sacrificing love is of any account at all in the scheme of Christian virtues, where would this savage, this heathen, come in at the day of awards? Where, indeed, among the multitude of gold-worshipping, form-adoring Pharisees? Truth to tell, Laurence believed but dimly in the day of awards. Yet, did it exist, he thought he knew the answer to his own question.

CHAPTER XXX

"GOOD-BYE—MY IDEAL!"

JOHANNESBURG once more.

The great, restless gold-town had passed through many changes, many booms and rumours of booms—the latter for the most part—since that quiet *trek* now four years ago. Many of those who then were among its busiest inhabitants had departed, some to a land whence there is no return, others to the land of their respective births. Many, who then had been on the verge of millionaires, "buzzing" their rapidly acquired gains with a lavish magnificence which they imagined to be "princely"—were now uncertificated bankrupts, or had blown their brains out, or had come within the meshes of the law and the walls of a convict prison; while others, who at that time lived upon hope and the "whiff of an oiled rag," now fared sumptuously every day, and would do so unto their lives' end. But for those who had held on to the place through good and evil report since the time we last pioneered our reader through its dust-swept streets and arid surroundings, something of a surprise was in store. For the old order of things was reversed. Instead of Hazon returning without his travelling companions, the latter had returned without Hazon.

"Bless my soul, Stanninghame, is that you?" cried Rankin, running right into Lawrence one morning just outside the new Exchange. "And Holmes too? Why, you're looking uncommonly well, both of you. What have you done with the Pirate, eh?"

"Oh, he's coming on!" replied Laurence, which in substance was correct, though it might be weeks before he came on; for, as a matter of fact, Hazon had remained behind at a certain point to collect and reduce to cash such gains as were being custodied for him—and the joint undertaking—by sundry of his blood-brethren the Arab chiefs.

"Coming on, is he? Well, well! I think we've been libelling the Pirate after all, eh Rainsford?" as that worthy just joined them.

"Here's Hazon's *trek* come back without Hazon, instead of the other way about."

Laurence thought how nearly it had been a case of the other way about. Had he not offered himself instead of Holmes, it would have been, for he would have remained with the Ba-gcatya, and Hazon would have returned alone. Of the fate of Holmes—well—he knew what that would have been. Holmes, however, did not, for the simple reason that Laurence had refrained from communicating a word relating to that horrible episode to either of his associates—when, shortly after parting with Rahman bin Zuhdi, and the death of Lindela, he had found the two, safe and well, at the principal town of a prominent Arab chief. And Holmes, possibly through ignorance of its nature or magnitude, never did fully appreciate the sacrifice which the other had made for him.

"What do you think?" went on Rankin, when the requisite amount of greeting and chaff had been exchanged. "This fellow Rainsford has gone and got married; has started out in the nursery department for all he's worth."

Laurence laughed.

"Why, Rainsford, you were as stony-broke as the rest of us when I left. Things looking up, eh?"

"Of course. I told you it was a case of 'down today, up to-morrow'—told you at the time. And it's my belief you'd have done better to have remained here." Then lowering his voice: "Where's the Pirate?"

"Coming on."

Rainsford whistled, and looked knowing.

"What do you say?" cut in Rankin. "A drop of gin and soda wouldn't hurt us, eh?" Then while they moved round to the Exchange bar, he went on "I've got a thing that would suit you to a hair, Stanninghame. I'd take it up myself if I could, but I'm only an agent in the matter."

"Shares, eh?"

"Yes—Skinner and Sacks."

"Dead off. See here, Rankin—you must off-load them on somebody else. If I were next door to certain of making half a million out of it, even then I wouldn't touch any sort of investment connected with this place. No, not, to save my immortal soul—if I've got one, which at times seems doubtful." And there was something in Laurence's laugh—evoked by old time recollections—which convinced the other that no business was to be done in this quarter at anyrate.

There was method in the way in which Laurence had sought to dawdle away the morning. He had arrived late the night before, and as yet had made no inquiries. How strange it all seemed. Surely it was but yesterday that he was here last. Surely he had slept, and had dreamed the portentous events which had intervened. They could not have been real. But the stones—the great diamonds—they were real enough; the metal box too—the "Sign of the Spider."

How was he thus transformed? Later in the day, as he stood on the *stoep*, knocking at the door of Mrs. Falkner's house, he was conscious that his heart hardly beat quicker, that his pulses were as firm and even as ever. Four years of a hard, stern schooling had done it.

Yes, Mrs. Falkner was at home. He was ushered into the drawing-room, which was empty. There was the same ever-clinging scent of roses, the same knick-knacks, the same lounge on which they had sat together that night. Even the battery stamps across the kloof[1] seemed to hammer out the same refrain.

The door opened. Was it Lilith herself? No,—only Lilith's aunt.

"Why, Mr. Stanninghame, I am glad to see you. But—how you have changed."

"Well, yes, Mrs. Falkner. Time has knocked me about some. I can't say the same as regards yourself, though. You haven't changed an atom."

She laughed. "That can't be true. I'm sure I feel more and more of an old woman every day. But sit down, do, and tell me about your adventures. Have you had a successful trip?"

"Pretty well. It has proved a more paying concern, at anyrate, than the exhilarating occupation known as 'waiting for the boom.'"

"I am very glad to hear that. And your friends—have you all returned safe and sound?"

Laurence replied that they had. But for all his outward equability, his impatience was amounting to torment. Even while he talked his ears were strained to catch the sound of a light step without. How would Lilith look, he wondered?

Would these four years have left their mark upon her?

"And how is your niece, Miss Ormskirk?" he went on.

"Lilith? Oh, but—by the way, she is not 'Miss Ormskirk' now. She is married."

"Oh, is she? I hadn't heard. After all, one forgets how time slips by."

That was all. It was a shock—possibly a hard one—but of late Laurence Stanninghame had been undergoing a steady training for meeting such. Mrs. Falkner, who had made the communication not without some qualm, for she had been put very much up to the former state of things, both by her nephew, George, and certain "signs of the times," not altogether to be dissimulated, however bravely Lilith had borne herself, after that parting now so far back—felt relieved and in a measure a trifle disappointed, for, womanlike, she dearly loved romance. But the man before her had not turned a hair, had not even changed colour at the intelligence. It could not really matter, she decided—which was as well for him, but for herself disappointing.

"Yes—she married her cousin George, my nephew. You remember him," she went on. "I was against it for a long time; but, after all, I believe it was the saving of him, poor fellow, he was so wildly in love with her. He was simply going to the dogs. Yes, it was the saving of him."

"That's satisfactory, anyway," said Laurence, as though he were discussing the fortunes of any two people whose names he had just heard for the first time. But meanwhile his mind was inwardly avenging itself upon its outward self-control. For vividly, and as though spoken into his ears, there seemed to float fragments of those farewell words uttered there in that room: *"You have drawn my very heart and soul into yours. . . . Oh, it is too bitter! Laurence, my darling—my love, my life, my ideal, good-bye—and good-bye!"*

Well, the foolish dream had been a pleasant one while it lasted. Nay, more,—in all seriousness it had borne momentous fruit,—for no less than three times had that episode—yes, now it seemed a mere episode—intervened between him and death.

"Lilith will be so glad to see you when you are passing through; for of course you will be returning home again. They have taken a bungalow at Kalk Bay² for the summer. I'll find you the address."

They talked on a little longer, and then Laurence took his departure.

As he gained the outer air once more there was that about the shimmer of the sunlight, the hum of the battery stamp, the familiarity of the surroundings, which reminded him of that former time when he had thus stepped forth, having bidden a good-bye which was not a good-bye. Yet the same pain did not grip around his heart now—not in its former acuteness. Rather was it now a sense of the falling away of all things. By a freak of psychology his mind reverted to poor Lindela, dying in his arms in the steamy gloom of the equatorial forest: dying slowly, by inches, in pain; yet uttering no cry, no complaint, lest she should rob him of a few minutes more or less of sleep. That was indeed love. Still, even while making it, his sense of philosophy told him the comparison was not a fair one.

Well, that was over—another chapter in his life to shut down. Now to make the best of life. Now, with the means to taste its pleasures, with hard, firm health to enjoy them; after all, what was a mere sentimental grievance? Perhaps it counted for something, for all he told himself to the contrary. Perhaps deep down there gnawed a restless craving, stifle it as he would. Who can tell?

"The R. M. S. *Alnwick Castle* leaves for England at 4 P.M."

Such was the notice which, posted up in shipping office, or in the short-paragraph column of the Cape Town newspapers, met the public eye.

It was the middle of the morning. Laurence Stanninghame, striving to kill the few hours remaining to him on African soil, was strolling listlessly along Adderley Street. A shop window, adorned with photographic views of local scenery and types of natives—mostly store-boys rigged up with shield and assegai to look warlike for the occasion—attracted his attention, and for a while he stood, idly gazing at these. His survey ended, he backed away from the window in a perfectly irrational and British manner on a busy thoroughfare, and——trod hard on somebody's toes.

A little cry of mingled pain and resentment, then he stood—profusely apologising.

But with the first tones of his voice, she whom he had so awkwardly, if unintentionally damaged, seemed to lose sight of her injuries. Her face blanched, but not with physical pain, her lips parted in a sort of gasp, and the sweet eyes, wide and dilated, sought his in wonder—almost in fear.

"Laurence!"

The name was hardly audible, but he heard it. And if his steely philosophy had stood him in good stead before, assuredly at this moment his guard was down; as he recognised that he had last beheld this serene vision of loveliness, arrayed as now in cool white, strained to him in farewell embrace alone in the solemn night, those parted lips pressed to his in heart-wrung pain, those sweet eyes, starry, humid with love, gazing full into his own. And now they met again, four years later—by chance—in a busy thoroughfare.

"Pray excuse my inexcusable awkwardness; I must have hurt you," he said, as they clasped hands; and the tone was even, almost formal, for he remembered they were in public.

"You—you—have changed. I should hardly have known you but for your voice," she said unsteadily—for he had turned to walk up the street with her. "But—when did you return? I—had not heard."

"Had you not? I called on your aunt in Johannesburg on the way through. She was telling me all about you."

Something of relief seemed to manifest itself in Lilith's tone as she rejoined—

"But you—are you staying here?"

"Well, no. I have been trying to kill time until this afternoon. I am leaving by the *Alnwick Castle*."

"Oh! By the *Alnwick Castle*?" she repeated again—and in the catch in her voice, and the quickness of utterance, he knew she was talking at random, for the sake of saying something, in fact.

"Do you care to hear a little of what has befallen me since I went?" he said. "Then let us turn in here," as she made a mute but eager gesture of assent.

They had gained the entrance to the oak avenue at the back of

Government House. Strolling up this, they turned into the beautiful Botanical Gardens. Nobody was about, save a gardener or two busied with his work.

"What I am going to tell you is so marvellous that you will probably refuse to believe it," he said, after narrating the incident of the Sign upon the metal box which had arrested the uplifted weapons of the unsparing Ba-gcatya, and, of course, editing out all that might have revealed the real nature of the expedition. "I have never breathed one word of it to any living being—not even to those who were with me. I would rather you did not either, Lilith, because it is too strange for anybody to believe, and—for other reasons."

She gave the required promise, and he drew forth the box. At sight of this relic of the past, that sweet, entrancing, if profitless past—Lilith could no longer quite keep herself in hand. The tears welled forth, falling upon the metal box itself—hallowing, as it were, the sweet charm of its saving power.

"Your love had power to save one life, you see," he went on in a cold, even voice, intended to strengthen him against himself. "But look, now. See those marks on the lid, just discernible? Now—listen."

And Lilith did listen; and at the description of the awful rock prison, with its skeleton bones, the long hours of helpless suspense and despair—and the final struggle in the ghastly moonlight; the struggle for life with the appalling monster that tenanted it, her eyes dilated with horror, and with pallid face and gasping lips she begged him not to go on, so great a hold did the incident take upon her imagination, even there, in the blaze of the broad midday sunlight.

"I have done now," he said. "Well, Lilith—you see what that token of your love has rescued me from.—It was given as an amulet or charm, and right well has it fulfilled its purpose. But—to what end?"

"Did you—did you come back with what you went for," she broke forth at last, as with an effort.

"Yes. Therein, too, you proved yourself a true prophet. And now tell me something about yourself."

"Were you—angry with me when you heard what I had done, Laurence?" she said, raising her eyes full to his.

"Angry? No. Why should I be? Your life is your own, though, as a rule, sacrificing oneself to save somebody else, as your aunt rather gave me to understand was the case here—is lamentably apt to turn out a case of throwing away one's life with both hands. It is too much like cutting one's own throat to save somebody else from being hanged."

"And is that your way of wishing me well, Laurence?" she said reproachfully.

"No. I wish you nothing but well. It would be futile to say 'happiness,' I suppose."

"The happiness of doing one's duty is a hard kind of happiness, after all," she said, with a sad little smile.

"Yes. An excellent copybook maxim, but for all purposes of real life—bosh. Am I not in my own person a living instance to that effect? As soon as I pitched 'duty' to the dogs, why then, and only then, did I begin to travel in the contrary direction to those sagacious animals myself—which, of course, is simply appalling morality, but—it's life. Well, child, make the best of your life, and prove a shining exception to the dismal rule."

"Do you remember our talk on board the dear old *Persian*? Yes, we had so many, you were going to say,—but I mean our first one, the first serious one—that night, leaning over the side. I asked you: 'Shall I make a success of life?' Do you remember your answer?"

"As well as though it were yesterday. I replied, that the chances were pretty even, inclining, if anything, to the negative. Well, and was I right?"

Lilith turned away her head. He could see that the tears were not far away. Her lips were quivering.

"I likewise told you you were groping after an ideal," he went on.

"And I found it. Perhaps I had already found it when I asked the question. O Laurence, life is all wrong, all horribly wrong and out of joint," she burst forth, with a passionate catch in her voice, as she turned and faced him once more.

"Yes, I know it is. I came to that conclusion a goodish while ago, and have never seen any reason since to doubt its absolute accuracy."

"All out of joint!" she repeated hopelessly. "It is as if our lives had been placed opposite each other on parallel lines, and then one of the lines had been moved. Then our lives lay apart forever."

"That's about it."

She was not deceived. His tone was hard; to all appearances indifferent. Yet not to her ear did it so ring. She knew the immensity of effort that kept it—and what lay behind it—under control. Then she broke down entirely.

"Laurence, my love—my doubly lost love!" she uttered through a choking whirlwind of sobs. "Teach me some of your strength—some of your hardness. Then, perhaps, I can bear things better."

"A chain is no stronger than its weakest link, remember, and perhaps you have shown me the weak link here. That for my 'hardness.' Child, I would not teach you an iota of it, if I could. It is good for me, but no woman was ever the better for it yet. But keep yourself in hand now. We are in a public place, although a comparatively secluded one. For your own sake, do not give way. And for the very reason that I feared to stir up old memories, I had intended to go through without attempting to see you once more. Tell me one thing,—Would it have been better had I done so?"

"Better had you done so? No—no. A thousand times no—Laurence, my darling. I shall treasure up this last hour we have spent together—shall treasure it as the sweetest of memories as long as life shall last."

"And I shall treasure up that reply. Listen. Twice has your love stood between me and death, as I have told you. Yet of the third time I have never told you. It was the day I decided to go up country. I had done with life. The pistol was pressed hard against my forehead. I was gradually trying how much more pressure the trigger would bear. A hair's-breadth would have done it. Then it seemed that your voice was in my ear, your form stood before me. I tell you, Lilith, you saved me that day as surely as though you had actually been within the room. I put the pistol down."

"I did this?" wonderingly. "Why, that must have been the day I had that awful dream."

"It was. Hazon came in just after, and we made our plans for the expedition. I remember telling you of it that same afternoon."

"Why, then, if this is so, it must have been with some great purpose," she cried, brightening up, a strange, wistful smile illumining her face. "Oh, how glad I am you have told me this, for now I can see comfort—strength. In some mysterious way it seems as if our two lives were intertwined, that it would ever be in my power in some dim way to watch over yours. My darling, my darling—until this moment I had not the strength to part with you—now I have. Let me do so before it leaves me, for we have been here a very long time. I would have seen you off on board, but that I dare not. I simply lack the strength of will to bear that, Laurence, my dear one. We had better say good-bye here—not in the crowded street. Then I will go——alone."

Both had risen, and were holding each others' hands, were gazing into each others' eyes. Thus they stood for a moment. Nobody was in sight. Lilith lifted her lips, and they moved in a barely audible murmur.

"Good-bye, my—ideal!"

One long, close, farewell kiss, and she was gone. And the man, as he flung himself back on the garden seat, with his eyes fixed dreamily on the jutting end of the massive rock wall of Table Mountain towering on high to the cloudless blue, realised at that moment no elation such as one might feel who had found considerable wealth, and was returning full of hard, firm health to enjoy the same. More than ever at that moment did life seem to him all out of joint—more than ever—if possible; for his had been one of those lives which, from the cradle to the grave, never seems to be anything else.

CONCLUSION

"WELL, Fay, I think that's about enough for one lesson. Down you get."

"Just once more round the park, father," was the pleading rejoinder. "I'm quite beginning to feel at home on Tricksie now."

Laurence gave way, and Tricksie darted off, perhaps a trifle too vivaciously for a learner of the noble art of horsemanship. But the girl kept her seat bravely, and the conceded scamper being brought to a close—she came round to where Laurence awaited, and slid from her saddle.

"Father, I won't have you call it 'lessons' any more," she cried. "I can ride now; *can* ride—do you hear!"

"Oh, can you?" laughed Laurence, thinking what a pretty picture she made standing there with the full light of the setting sun tinting the golden waves of her hair, playing upon the great dark eyes. Indeed, he owned inwardly to a weakness, a soft place as strange as it was unwonted, for this child of his. Yet she was something more than a child now, quite a tall slip of a girl, at the angular age; but there was nothing awkward or angular even then about Fay Stanninghame.

"Well, hitch up the pony to the rail there," he went on. "Those two scamps can take him in when they are tired of careering around and whooping like Sioux on the war-path."

The two boys, also happy in the possession of a pony apiece, had lost no time either in learning to ride it.

"There's no part of a fool about either of those chaps," said Laurence more to himself than to the girl, as he watched the two circling at full gallop in and out among the trees, absolutely devoid of fear. "Let's stroll a little, Fay; or would you rather go in?"

"Of course, I wouldn't," linking her arm in his. "Father, are we very rich now?"

"Oh, pretty warm. Think it fun, eh, child?"

"Fun? Why, it's heavenly. This lovely place! Oh, sometimes I dream that this is all a dream, and then—to wake up and find it real!"

"Well, dear, be as happy as you like now—all day and every day. You have had enough of the other thing to last you a precious long time."

They strolled on through the sweet May evening—on beneath a great beech hanger, where cushats cooed softly among the green mast,—and the air was musical with the sweet piping of thrushes and the caw of homing rooks. Here and there a gap in the hawthorn hedge disclosed a glimpse of red-tiled roof and farm stack—and, nestling among the trees of the park, the chimneys of the Hall.

Laurence Stanninghame had found this place by a mere chance. He might have purchased it for a third of its value, but he preferred not. Possibly he distrusted the wandering blood within him, possibly he did not lose sight of the fact that where he had found the great diamonds he had certainly left behind many more, to be found or not at some future time. So he rented the house and park, and extensive shooting and fishing rights. No more pinching and scraping now. To the children this change was, as Fay had said, "heavenly."

"How do people get rich in Africa, father?" said the latter, as they turned homeward.

"In various ways. They find gold-mines with no gold in them, and then sell shares in them to a pack of idiots for a great deal of money. Or they perhaps find a few diamonds themselves. Or they trade in all sorts of things—ivory, and so forth."

He had stopped to light a pipe; Fay, intently watching his face through the clouds of smoke he was puffing forth, detected a lurking quizzical expression in his eyes, which roused her scepticism.

"I never quite know whether you are serious or not, father," she said. "But you never tell us any stories about Africa."

"I've got out of practice for story-telling, little one."

"But Colonel Hewett tells us plenty,"—naming a neighbour,— "and yet he hasn't been so much in Africa as you have."

"Ah, he'll never get out of practice in that line," returned Laurence, with the same quizzical laugh.

"What a lot of adventures you must have had, father," went on Fay wistfully; for this was a sore subject both with herself and her brothers. They had expected tale upon tale of hair-raising peril— of lions and crocodiles and snakes and fighting Zulus. But woful disappointment awaited. The last topic the returned wanderer seemed to care to talk upon was that of his wanderings.

Before they regained the house they were joined by the two boys, happy and healthy with their recent gallop, and full of the trout they were going to catch on the morrow under the tuition of the keeper. Laurence, dismissing them for a while, entered quietly by a back way. The post had come in, and with it an African mail letter. This he carried into his private sanctum. It was from Holmes.

"I hope the fellow isn't going to make trouble," he said to himself with a slight clouding of the brow. "He's idiot enough to turn pious—repentant, I suppose, they would call it—and give the whole thing away. 'Nothing but a curse can come of it—the curse of blood,' the young fool said, or words to that effect. I wonder what sort of a 'curse' it is that puts one in possession of all this," looking out upon the soft, peaceful English landscape, hayfield and wooded hill slumbering in the gathering dusk. "As if there could be a greater curse anyhow than being condemned to go through life that most pitiable object—a pauper with sixteen quarterings. No—no!"

He tore open the envelope, and in the fading light ran rapidly over its contents. Hazon had returned to Johannesburg, and had wound up all their affairs, and each of them was in possession of more than a small fortune. There was nothing, however, of the remorseful or the morbid about the writer now, and, turning over the page, Laurence broke into a short half-laugh, for there followed the announcement of Holmes's engagement to Mabel Falkner of the blue eyes, and the usual transports and rhapsodies attendant upon such communication. Skipping the bulk of this, Laurence returned the missive to his pocket with another sneering laugh.

"We shall hear no more about a 'curse' on our good fortune now, friend Holmes," he said to himself, "for you are entering upon an institution calculated to knock out all such Quixotic niceties. Ha, ha! I shouldn't be in the least surprised if in a little while you didn't hanker to start up-country again, upon another 'ivory' trade."

But Holmes's letter had, as it were, let in a waft of the dark cloud of the Past upon the fair and smiling peacefulness of the Present, and he fell to thinking on what strange experiences had been his—of the consistent and unswerving irony of life as he had known it. Every conventionality violated, every rule of morality, each set aside, had brought him nothing but good—had brought nothing but good to him and his. Had he grovelled on in humdrum poverty-stricken respectability, what would have befallen him—and them? For him the stereotyped "temporary insanity" verdict of a coroner's jury—for them, well, Heaven only knew. Whereas now—?

At this stage an impulse moved him, and opening a locked cabinet he took forth something, and as he examined it the associations of the thing, and the fast darkening room, brought back the vision of glooming rock walls and a perfectly defenceless man weighed down with horror and dread.

"May I come in, father? But you are in the dark."

It was Fay's voice. He half started, so rapt was he in his meditations.

"That's soon remedied," he said, striking a light. "Yes, come in, little one. You were asking about this thing once. Look at it. Queer sort of weapon, isn't it?"

"It is, indeed," she answered. "Is it a Zulu war club? Why, the head is made of brass, or is it gold? And look, there is some strange writing on it."

"And the handle is a bone. Yes, the head is gold, and I put the thing together when I had no other weapon—ay—and used it, too, in the ghastliest kind of fight I ever was in. Come, now. We will put it away again."

"Not yet, father. Show me some more queer things," she pleaded—nestling to his side.

Then he got out other trophies and curios, and Fay spent a good hour of unalloyed delight turning them wonderingly over, and drinking in the incident, more or less stirring, which related to each.

But there was one thing he did not show her—one thing upon which no eye save his own might ever again rest,—one thing he treasured up in the greatest security under lock and key—which was enshrined within his mind as a hallowed "charm," and that was the metal box and its contents—the "charm" which twice had stood between him and death—death violent and horrible——The Sign of the Spider.

NOTES

CHAPTER I

1 (p. 8) A traditional English puppet show of loud, action-packed farcical comedy. The oddly likeable anti-hero Punch is a hook-nosed cowardly rascal who frequently beats his wife Judy with a stick and is served in return as good as he gives.

CHAPTER II

1 (p. 13) Obeisance; used frequently for the political acknowledgment of allegiance.

CHAPTER III

1 (p. 26) "Grant us peace," from the *Agnus Dei* in the Mass.

2 (p. 27) "Argument" comes from the Latin *arguere*, "to clarify."

3 (p. 28) The term "child" is an affectionate diminutive denoting the male's more worldly status, not her youth *per se*; perhaps, "you who are wholly guiltless."

CHAPTER IV

1 (p. 32) "Also"; Mitford occasionally uses obsolete forms, perhaps to call attention to the constructedness of his narration.

2 (p. 34) Thomas Pringle (1789-1834) first published "Afar in the Desert" in 1824; collected in his *African Sketches* (1834). S. T. Coleridge greatly admired this poem. In R. M. Ballantyne's *The Settler and the Savage* (1877) there is a complimentary description of Pringle as a leader of the settlers and also, curiously, a reference to the African branch of Mitford's own family, the Bowkers, "who afterwards played a prominent part in the affairs of the colony."

3 (p. 36) Any fast train, so-called after the "Flying Watkin Express."

4 (p. 37) Mark Twain, *Roughing It* (1872): "Horace Greeley went over this road once. When he was leaving Carson City he told the driver, Hank Monk, that he had an engagement to lecture at Placerville and was very anxious to go through quick. Hank

Monk cracked his whip and started off at an awful pace. The coach bounced up and down in such a terrific way that it jolted the buttons all off of Horace's coat, and finally shot his head clean through the roof of the stage, and then he yelled at Hank Monk and begged him to go easier—said he warn't in as much of a hurry as he was awhile ago. But Hank Monk said, 'Keep your seat, Horace, and I'll get you there on time'—and you bet you he did, too, what was left of him!" (Chap. XX).

CHAPTER V

1   (p. 38) Stock certificates or (more frequently) receipts for fractional shares of stock.

2   (p. 39) From *Witwatersrand*, a rich gold-bearing ridge of rock in South Africa's Transvaal region.

3   (p. 40) Angostura bitters, a concentrated herbal flavoring famous as a cure-all; a few drops in gin, not vice versa, is the recipe.

4   (p. 41) *Te Deum Laudamus*: "We praise you God." A liturgical chant and song at the end of the service.

5   (p. 41) John ("Johnnie") Walker's Scotch whisky had been produced at Kilmarnock since 1820.

6   (p. 44) A suburb south of inner city Johannesburg.

7   (p. 45) Carlyle condemns the people for being full of wealth but dying of lethargy; for worshiping false gods and wasting away for better men to emulate; he did not originate the phrase, "a nation of shopkeepers."

CHAPTER VI

1   (p. 47) Matthew 3:5.

2   (p. 48) The front step(s) of a dwelling, part of its verandah.

3   (p. 54) Quinine, extracted from the bark of a tree, was the first effective treatment for "up-country fever," i.e., malaria.

CHAPTER VII

1   (p. 57) Saw / cutting. This sort of writing was typical of Mitford's journalistic background.

2   (p. 58) 2 Kings 2:12.

CHAPTER VIII

1 (p. 66) Entirely; 100%.

CHAPTER IX

1 (p. 78) Diamonds.

CHAPTER XI

1 (p. 88) The Crown Mine and its battery of rock-crushing "stamps" was one of the earliest and most important excavations atop Johannesburg's Main Reef.

2 (p. 89) From the Irish ballad "Kathleen Mavourneen" (1835) by Julia Crawford.

CHAPTER XII

1 (p. 99) Mitford's allusion to Psalms 74:20 also clearly later echoes in Conrad's "heart of darkness" motif, as do the themes of slavery and cannibalism.

2 (p. 103) The Wangoni, a branch of the Zulu originally from Natal, South Africa, spread progressively northward to the central and eastern regions around Lake Nyasa.

CHAPTER XIII

1 (p. 106) An Express rifle is designed to be super-accurate, having a light bullet with a heavy charge of power, a high muzzle velocity, a flat trajectory, and adjustable rear sight.

2 (p. 106) In January of 1879, a column of British and native troops invading Zululand were attacked by about 10,000 Zulus under Cetewayo and wiped out in the first battle of the Zulu War.

3 (p. 107) A large headstream of the Congo River rising in the southeast Congo, flowing north.

4 (p. 110) To indicate to Stanninghame their direction.

CHAPTER XIV

1 (p. 114) Vesta safety matches, named after a Roman goddess of fire.

CHAPTER XV

1 (p. 121) Tshaka (or Shaka, Chaka) founded the Zulu empire.

During this period of unrest, Mitford imagines the Ba-gcatya as a prototype break-away clan, similar to the historical flight of Umzilikazi, founder of the Ndebele nation. Tshaka, Dingane, Panda, Cetywayo successively ruled the Zulus until, provoked by the invading British, they attacked them at Isandhlwana, winning that battle but losing the Zulu War.

2   (p. 122) Army.

CHAPTER XVI

1   (p. 126) Arabic, "sir" or "lord."
2   (p. 130) Hebrews 13:2.

CHAPTER XVII

1   (p. 134) Portland and Dartmoor, British prisons; Simonstown and the Kowie, Cape prisons.

CHAPTER XVIII

1   (p. 139) *Kopjes* are small bouldered hillocks (Dutch: literally, "little head"); moorland tors, as in the UK upland area of Dartmoor, are the product of molten rock that cooled, shrank, and eroded.
2   (p. 142) Any vestige, such as footprint, scent, or broken plant, showing the path taken by man or beast.

CHAPTER XX

1   (p. 150) Head-ring of hair stiffened with gums, indicative of senior-warrior status.
2   (p. 155) Noble advisers or military commanders ("izin-" plural noun prefix); *induna* is the singular.
3   (p. 157) Also knobkierie (from the native word *kerrie, kiri*, stick), a short, round-headed club, swung to crush or thrown to immobilize.
4   (p. 157) *-vunga (im-)* "Sound of a low singing or humming" + *-yo* a suffix (from verb *ya*) denoting a state or condition of continuing action.

CHAPTER XXI

1   (p. 159) A salute exclusive to his royal majesty, adopted from

northern non-Zulu tribes and probably connoting "we are under your feet."

2   (p. 160) Praise and/or titles, as applied to the King; "hail to the chief."

3   (p. 163) "Go in peace" (*gahle*, also "gently"), an ironic use of a polite phrase, here akin to the tombstone "rest in peace."

CHAPTER XXII

1   (p. 166) His name is a verb, *nyonyoba*, from *nyo-nyo*, soft, and *uba*, to step forth; therefore, to stalk quietly in order to catch something.

CHAPTER XXIII

1   (p. 176) The polite Zulu hello, *Sawubona*, literally translated means "I see you."

2   (p. 176) Or *twala*, *tshwala*. A fermented grain-sorghum beer, both nutritious and alcoholic, best served cool and drunk from large pots.

CHAPTER XXVIII

1   (p. 212) Greatly; very much (*ka* as prefix renders the adjective noun an adverb + *kulu*, great).

CHAPTER XXX

1   (p. 224) Deep, usually wooded, ravines (Dutch).

2   (p. 226) A seaside resort and fishing village on the Cape Peninsula, near Cape Town.

APPENDIX

"**About Men and Women,**" *Eastern Daily Press*, **17 November 1896.**
Mitford does not seem to have given many interviews or cultivated
the limelight, since otherwise the basic details of his career in the
Eastern Daily Press, noting in 1896 the recent publication of *The Sign
of the Spider*, would in all likelihood already have been too familiar
to repeat:

Mr. Bertram Mitford, the author of "The Sign of the Spider," is
a quick writer. He says that he "can turn out a 320 page novel in two
months, if in the vein." He works best in the morning, all day long
in winter, but never at night. A firm believer in outdoor exercise, he
is a great walker. Twenty-three years ago he went to South Africa,
and during his long stay there became personally acquainted with
Cetewayo and all the prominent Zulu chiefs and leading men who
engineered the Kaffir war of 1877, on the Cape border. Most of
them figure in his South African novels. Mr. Mitford, before he
turned his attention to fiction, had a very varied experience. He
was at one time engaged in stock-farming, and he has held several
Government posts. He is the third son of Mr. Osbaldeston Mitford,
of Mitford Castle, Northumberland. (Issue 7687, pg. 8)

Dante Gabriel Rossetti's painting *Lady Lilith* **(1867) and sonnets.**
The Neo-Platonic interpretations of physical and spiritual love in
the poetry and paintings of D. G. Rossetti were a clear influence
on Mitford. Two of Rossetti's paintings, *Lady Lilith* and *Sibylla
Palmifera,* are paired with two "sonnets for pictures" in Rossetti's
The House of Life: "Body's Beauty" and "Soul's Beauty":

LILITH
(For a Picture)

Of Adam's first wife, Lilith, it is told
   (The witch he loved before the gift of Eve,)
   That, ere the snake's, her sweet tongue could deceive,
And her enchanted hair was the first gold.

And still she sits, young while the earth is old,
   And, subtly of herself contemplative,
   Draws men to watch the bright web she can weave,
Till heart and body and life are in its hold.

The rose and poppy are her flowers; for where
   Is he not found, O Lilith, whom shed scent
And soft-shed kisses and soft sleep shall snare?
   Lo! as that youth's eyes burned at thine, so went
   Thy spell through him, and left his straight neck bent
And round his heart one strangling golden hair.

SIBYLLA PALMIFERA
(For a Picture)

Under the arch of Life, where love and death,
   Terror and mystery, guard her shrine, I saw
   Beauty enthroned; and though her gaze struck awe,
I drew it in as simply as my breath.
Hers are the eyes which, over and beneath,
   The sky and sea bend on thee,—which can draw,
   By sea or sky or woman, to one law,
The allotted bondman of her palm and wreath.

This is that Lady Beauty, in whose praise
   Thy voice and hand shake still,—long known to thee
   By flying hair and fluttering hem,—the beat
   Following her daily of thy heart and feet,
How passionately and irretrievably,
In what fond flight, how many ways and days!

Henry Callaway, *Izinganekwane, Nensumansumane, Nezindaba Zabantu* [*Tales, Traditions, and Histories of the Zulus*] (Natal: John Blair; London: Trübner, 1866). Mitford's shocking subjects of slavery and cannibalism were not mere melodrama and fantasy for an African novel set in 1890-94; other writers such as William Charles Scully in *Kafir Stories* (1895), "Ghamba," also had dealt with such recent events. Of Cannibalism among the Zulus, Callaway says: "It is worth noting that the Zulu-Kafir considers it as unnatural, and that those who practise it have ceased to be men." Callaway transcribes this account of Ulutuli Dhladhla (Usetemba) in both Zulu and English in parallel columns:

All I know is, that it is said that the Amazimu deserted other men and went to live in the mountains. For at first the Amazimu were men. The country was desolate; there was a great famine; and they wished to eat men because of the severity of the famine. When the famine was great, and men were in want and there was no place where they could obtain food, they began to lay hold of men, and to eat them. And so they were called Amazimu; for the word Amazimu when interpreted means to gormandise,—to be gluttonous. So they rebelled against men; they forsook them, and liked to eat them; and men drove them away. They went everywhere seeking men for food, and so they were regarded as a distinct nation, for with them men became game. They no longer cultivated the soil; they no longer had cattle or houses or sheep, nor any of those things which they had had whilst they were men. They went and lived in dens. When they found a cave, it became their dwelling place whilst they went to hunt men . . . .

If they saw a man going alone, they went to him; they decoyed him, and made themselves out merciful people; they treated him kindly, and spoke gently with him; and appeared incapable of doing any evil. When the man was thus beguiled and entirely unsuspicious, regarding them as pleasant people only, they would then lay hold of him: if he was a powerful man, he might fight with them, and perhaps drive them off; or they might overcome him, and carry him away to eat him. . . .

Again the Amazimu hunt and fall in with other men: when they fall in with them, perhaps they see that they are Amazimu, and run away, and the Amazimu pursue them, until they overtake them; when they overtake them they lay hold of them. Others hide themselves, and they do not see them. If they have caught sight of a man who has not hid himself, he must run a great distance, they pursuing him till he is tired. For if a man does not hide himself, but contends with them by running only, they pursue him till they overtake him, for they do not readily tire. Then they carry him away with them, seeking a place concealed from men in the wilderness; when they come to such a place, they boil and eat him. (155-157)

R. F. Burton, *Two Trips to Gorilla Land and the Cataracts of the Congo* (1876). The "Mr. Layland" to whom Burton refers was a pseudonym used by Mitford's second cousin, Col. James Bowker:

I made careful inquiry about anthropophagy amongst the Fán, and my account must differ greatly from that of M. Du Chaillu. The reader, however, will remember that the Mayyán is held by a comparatively civilized race, who have probably learned to conceal a custom so distasteful to all their neighbours, white and black; in the remoter districts cannibalism may yet assume far more hideous proportions. Since the Fán have encouraged traders to settle amongst them, the interest as well as the terrors of the Coast tribes, who would deter foreigners from direct dealings, has added new horrors to the tale; and yet nothing can exceed the reports of older travellers. . . .

As will appear from the Fán's bill of fare, anthropophagy can hardly be caused by necessity, and the way in which it is conducted shows that it is a quasi-religious rite practised upon foes slain in battle, evidently an equivalent of human sacrifice. If the whole body cannot be carried off, a limb or two is removed for the purpose of a roast. The corpse is carried to a hut built expressly on the outskirts of the settlement; it is eaten secretly by the warriors, women and children not being allowed to be present, or even to look upon man's flesh; and the cooking pots used for the banquet must all be broken. A joint of "black brother" is never seen in the villages: "smoked human flesh" does not hang from the rafters. . . .

Anthropophagy without apparent cause was not unknown in Southern Africa. Mr. Layland found a tribe of "cave cannibals" amongst the mountains beyond Thaba Bosigo in the Trans-Gariep Country. . . . Anthropophagy, either as a necessity, a sentiment, or a superstition, is known to sundry, though by no means to all, the tribes dwelling between the Nun (Niger) and the Congo rivers; how much farther south it extends I cannot at present say. On the Lower Niger, and its branch the Brass River, the people hardly take the trouble to conceal it. On the Bonny and New Calabar, perhaps the most advanced of the so-called Oil Rivers, cannibalism, based upon a desire of revenge, and perhaps, its sentimental side, the object of imbibing the valour of an enemy slain in battle, has caused many scandals of late years. The practice, on the other hand, is execrated by the Efiks of Old Calabar, who punish any attempts of the kind with extreme severity. During 1862 the slaves of Creek-town attempted it, and were killed. At Duke-town an Ibo woman also cut up a man, sun-dried the flesh, and sold it for monkey's meat—she took sanctuary at the mission house. Yet it is in full vigour amongst their Ibo neighbours to the north-west, and the Duallas of the Camarones River also number it amongst their "country customs." The Mpongwe, as has been said, will not eat a chimpanzee; the Fán devour their dead enemies. (I: 210-217).

The Congo Report of **Roger Casement** (1903). The 1890-94 activities in Mitford's tale are amply supported as occurring in the twentieth century in rubber exporting areas by this official consular report of 1903. "Cannibalism had gone hand in hand with slave raiding," Roger Casement observed, reporting that it was still widely practiced in the far interior:

The New York Times, December 6, 1903.
SLAVERY IN THE CONGO
British Consul Finds It Exists in Revolting Form.
Speedy Intervention Will Be Recommended — Worst Reports
of Outrages Confirmed.

London, Dec. 5—Roger Casement, British Consul in the Congo State, has just completed a tour of investigation undertaken under the orders of the British Government, and he fully confirms the worst reports of outrages perpetrated on natives of that part of Africa. Mr. Casement's tour was to have lasted six months, but after the scenes he witnessed and the information he obtained in the first two months, the Consul decided that further evidence was unnecessary.

The report which Mr. Casement is now preparing for the Foreign Office will show that the most horrible outrages are still being perpetrated under the "rubber regime," and that slavery and barbarism in their most revolting forms still exist. The Casement party traveled over 1,000 miles from the coast, along the Congo and its tributaries, visiting the Abir and Lulonga rubber zones. Pending the delivery of the report to the Foreign Office the investigators refuse to furnish any details, but a member of the mission summed up the situation by saying: "The most terrible slavery exists, the administration is atrocious, and if there is not speedy intervention it will be too late."

From Casement's Report to the Foreign Office, *The Black Diaries*, ed. P. Singleton-Gates and Maurice Girodias (New York: Grove, 1959, 138; and Paris: Olympia, 1957):

Lake Mantumba is a fine sheet of water about 25 or 30 miles long and some 12 or 15 miles broad at the broadest part, surrounded by a dense forest. The inhabitants of the district are of the Ntomba tribe and are still rude savages, using very fine bows and arrows and ill-made spears as their weapons. There are also in the forest country many families or clans of a dwarf race called Batwas, who are of much more savage and untameable disposition than the Ntombas, who form the bulk of the population. Both Batwas and Ntombas are still cannibals and cannibalism, although repressed and not so openly indulged in as formerly, is still prevalent in the district. . . .

The towns around the lower Lulongo River raided the interior tribes, whose prolific humanity provided not only servitors, but human meat for those stronger than themselves. Cannibalism had gone hand in hand with slave raiding, and it was no uncommon spectacle to see gangs of human beings being conveyed for exposure and sale in the local markets. I had in the past, when travelling on the Lulongo River, more than once viewed such a scene. On one occasion a woman was killed in the village I was passing through, and her head and other portions of her were brought and offered for sale to some of the crew of the steamer I was on.

Evelyn Waugh, *Black Mischief* **(1932).** Evelyn Waugh's morbidly comic satire in *Black Mischief* on the decadence and incompetence of British colonial administration is evidence of its political legacy as late as 1932. In the penultimate chapter, the dependents at the Azania Legation, including Basil Seal's fiancée Prudence, have been evacuated by aircraft; but when her plane is reported missing, Basil goes cross-country in search of her, only to be stunned by Africa's intrinsic savagery:

The company split up into groups, each round a cook pot. Basil and Joab sat with the chiefs. They ate flat bread and meat, stewed to pulp among peppers and aromatic roots. . . . The hand drums throbbed and pulsed; the flames leapt and showered the night with sparks.

The headman of Moshu sat where they had dined, nursing the bowl of toddy. He nodded down to the lip of the bowl and drank. Then . . . he nodded again and drew something from his bosom and put it on his head. "Look," he said. "Pretty."

It was a beret of pillar-box red. Through the stupor that was slowly mounting and encompassing his mind Basil recognised it. Prudence had worn it jauntily on the side of her head, running across the Legation lawn with the *Panorama of Life* under her arm. He shook the old fellow roughly by the shoulder.

"Where did you get that?"

"Pretty."

"Where did you get it?"

"Pretty hat. It came in the great bird. The white woman wore it. On her head like this." He giggled weakly and pulled it askew over his glistening pate.

"But the white woman. Where is she?"

But the headman was lapsing into coma. He said "Pretty" again and turned up sightless eyes.

Basil shook him violently. "Speak, you old fool. Where is the white woman?"

The headman grunted and stirred; then a flicker of consciousness revived in him. He raised his head. "The white woman? Why, here," he patted his distended paunch. "You and I and the big chiefs—we have just eaten her."

Then he fell forward into a sound sleep.

LaVergne, TN USA
12 December 2010
208450LV00003B/9/P